I'M GONNA CUT YOUR EARS OFF

I0615000

Ronald K. Myers

I'M GONNA CUT YOUR EARS OFF

DOUBLE DRAGON

Chapter 1

Flying sprays of orange sparks from the back of the dilapidated shed in One-Finger-Burke's back yard intrigued Breed. Although One Finger-Burke was a crooked cop and it was dangerous to trespass onto his property that looked like a radioactive waste land, Breed had to see what was making those sparks.

Running his fingers through his long black hair and acting as if he were not concerned about the danger, he walked closer. The sound of grinding met his ears. He peeked around the corner of the shed. Flashing a fiendish rotten-tooth smile, the crooked cop's son, Burkie, held a long pointed knife on a rotating emery wheel attached to the back of the shed. He removed the knife from the wheel. The sparks quit. He picked up a piece of newspaper and ran the blade of the knife down it. The ease at which the knife sliced through the paper signaled to Breed that the knife was razor sharp.

When Breed placed his hand on the side of the shed, a splintered board creaked.

Surprised, Burkie jerked his long, sickly pale face back and slapped his hand over his rotten-tooth mouth. Before Breed could do or say anything, Burkie lifted the knife. "My dad's a cop." A menacing look filled his face. "I can do anything I want." Towering over Breed, he lifted the knife to slice. "I'm gonna cut your ears off."

Not sure if Burkie was serious, Breed grinned.

"You think that's funny?" Burkie swung the knife down.

Breed jerked out of the way. The knife swished right next to his face. He thought the knife had missed, but a sharp pain came from his ear. He reached up and felt his ear. It was warm and wet.

Watching Breed, Burkie lifted the knife and held it high.

In defense, Breed held his hand in front of his face. When he did, his palm was splotched with blood from his ear.

Smiling, Burkie jerked the knife. "Let me cut the other ear clean off."

Breed dropped his bloody hand and took off running. Swishing the knife and viciously cutting the air, Burkie ran right behind him.

Breed felt the air from the knife swish past his back. He ran faster. The knife scraped down the back of his arm. It was only a scratch, but Burkie was much bigger and faster than Breed. The next time the knife swished down it would cut deep. Breed took a sharp right into a garbage-can-lined alley. Burkie couldn't make the turn as quickly as Breed had. Breed had room to maneuver. He grabbed a garbage can, threw it behind him. Burkie's knees hit the can. He fell. The knife stabbed deep into the foot-hammered, dark ground.

Breed escaped to safety, this time; but he needed to get out of Traptown, and he hoped he knew a way to do it.

A while later, after his pounding heart had settled down from being scared, and his ear had stopped bleeding, Breed walked along Rat River. Cloaked in the spooky movement of the steel mill's swarming smoke shadows, he searched the shores for a drifting boat that could deliver him from the

6

knife threats and the stench of Traptown. He didn't find a boat, but high on the riverbank, somewhere close to the Pennsylvania Railroad tracks, puppies yelped. He hoped it wasn't what he thought it was. Faster than a kid on a shelving board flying in a tornado, he raced along the railroad tracks until he cut into the tall weeds where he crouched down and listened.

Whap! A sickening sound of wood smacking something filled the humid air. He cringed but stayed down. Hunched over, he cautiously walked closer. When he lifted his head for a look, tall, green weeds stuck against his sweating forehead. He couldn't see who was making that hostile noise. Holding his breath, he lifted his hand and carefully parted the weeds.

Older kids, he had never seen before, were tossing puppies around like they were baseballs. Breed gasp. They were the puppies a stray dog had hidden in a hole next to the railroad tracks.

When one of the kids caught a puppy, the puppy yelped. When one of them missed a puppy: Thump! It hit the hard ground and let out a painful yelp.

A pimple-faced kid, with a barrel chest, waggled a bat over a flat rock and yelled, "Pitch it right over here."

The pitcher set his bottle of beer on a flat rock and picked up a puppy. Breed didn't believe the pitcher would throw a little puppy over the plate. The mills and alcohol may have replaced God, but Breed didn't believe anyone would be that cruel. But he watched anyway.

The pitcher wound up and let the puppy go. It

sailed toward home plate. The pimple-faced batter swung the bat. Whap! He slammed the puppy. It yelped once and slammed onto the ground. The kid on third base ran to the puppy and stopped.

The pitcher held out his hand. "Don't just stand there, Flat Top. It belongs to the flats gang. Make sure it's dead?"

Flat Top rubbed the top of his flattop haircut and kicked at the puppy with the toe of his shiny shoe. The puppy didn't move. Flat Top lifted his arrogant face and smiled. "It's dead."

The pimple-faced batter walked back from first base. "Foul ball," he yelled. "That's another one Rat Boy and his buddies will get blamed for." Laughing in short grunts, he picked up his bottle of beer and tilted it to his thick lips.

Breed stood up for a better look. A lone puppy lay at the picture's feet. On the makeshift field, the bodies of six other puppies lay motionless. Breed wanted to dash out, grab that last puppy, and run. but he wasn't sure he could do it.

Long dirty-blond hair covered half of the batter's purple pimpled face. Shirtless, his muscular body rippled under greenish skin. He looked drunk enough to swing the bat in Breed's direction. It would be dangerous, but Breed decided to take the chance.

He stood up and took one step out of the weeds. The pitcher picked up the last puppy. Without warning, he threw it at the batter. While the puppy was in the air, the catcher snorted a big hollow nosed laugh and yelled, "Here it comes, Purple."

With one hand holding his beer bottle and the other hand on the bat, Purple swung. Sling! The bat hit the puppy with a grazing blow. It flew high into the air.

Breed ran onto the makeshift baseball field. Like an outfielder, he ran under the airborne pup. The sun blocked his view of the falling puppy. Holding out both hands, he prayed he would catch it. With a soft thud, it landed in his hands.

With beer spewing out of his mouth, Purple yelled, "Get that black-headed rat boy."

Trying to earn a little money, Breed had tried to trap muskrats on Rat River. But poison sludge that had choked the current and killed most of the fish had been absorbed into the soil and had killed most of the river plants the muskrats needed to survive. He had only managed to catch river rats. He was going to try upriver, but the older kids took his traps, told him he was stupid, and called him Rat Boy.

Purple threw his beer bottle onto the ground. "We'll kick Rat Boy's ass up to his shoulders so bad that he'll have to take his shirt off to shit."

With the nightmarish baseball players right behind him, Breed took off running.

Along the river, at the bend in the path, he turned; and even though they would be able to see him, he slipped behind a stand of head-high itch weed stocks and stopped.

Huffing and puffing, the players ran up the path and slowed to a jog.

They were about to jog past the itch weed.

Breed yelled, "Hey, you big dummies."

They continued to jog, but in unison, they jerked their heads in Breed's direction. Usually, when they came after Breed, they would plow through or over just about anything in their paths. This time was no exception. They crashed right through the tall canes of itch weed.

Holding the puppy, Breed sprinted away. Behind him, in a whining almost crying voice, Purple cried, "It's itch weed."

Slowing to a walk, Breed looked back over his shoulder. Being in unfamiliar territory, Flat Top and the pitcher had stopped too late. They were in the middle of the six foot high canes of itch weed. The prickly nettle on the plants caused skin irritation on contact. They would have to slowly weave their bodies around the canes. After that they would be itching for the rest of the day.

Standing in a tangle of itch weed and with its spiny-toothed leaves stinging his knees, Flat Top jerked his fist at Breed. "When we get out of here, your little rat ass is ours."

***

Breed carried the puppy home. It was still alive, but its one back leg had swollen.

There was never enough food at his house. A puppy was the last thing he would be allowed to bring home, so he hid the puppy under the floor of the wooden back porch. The little food he could sneak from the table caused him to be hungry for weeks, but he had fed the puppy.

The puppy matured and its leg healed, but it constantly wandered out from under the porch. It followed Breed wherever he went. He loved the dog he had saved. He hoped it had grown enough to run away from those baseball players, but there were other threats: Burkie had been seen hiding in the bushes with his long knife, and bullies from the

10

flats gang had been hanging around, too. If Breed could find a boat drifting downriver, he could go upriver with his pals. He could go to Shell Island. He could take the dog, too. Burkie would never find him there, and there would be no bullies on Shell Island.

***

In the night, an immature growl woke Breed. He prayed it wasn't his dog. To be sure it wasn't, he sat up, let his feet drop over the edge of the bed, and listened. Outside his open bedroom window, painful howls echoed into the black night. His mind jerked to a state of immediacy. It *was* his dog. It was his best friend. His sleepy body jolted into a state of alarm. Now he was wide awake.

It would take too long to run down the stairs, rush through the kitchen, open the door, go under the porch, and see what was wrong with his best friend.

He stepped out the bedroom window and crawled onto the front porch roof. When he bent over and grabbed the edge of the roof to swing down to the ground, his hands slipped off the slippery slate. Although it was dark, a dull thud told him he had landed on the grassless ground.

A short yelp came from between two houses. His dog wasn't under the porch and it sounded like it was in pain. Breed ran toward the sound.

In the dark, he tripped over an empty beer bottle, stumbled, but caught his balance. When he ran past alcoholic Toney's dilapidated shack, as if he were under a spell, Toney yelled out the only window that hadn't been boarded up "Hey, where you goin'? Back that way again. Hey!" And his voice reverberated off the rusty tin roof of his shack.

When Toney drank too much, his frayed baseball cap would be turned to the side. Sitting in a stupor, he would nod off, jerk his head up, and say, "Hey!" open his eyes, droop his head and say, "Back that way again," over and over. Breed didn't have time for his drunken ranting. He kept on running.

He ran out of Toney's yard, across the road, stopped at the edge of a wooded lot, and searched the darkness. Beneath the leaf-laden trees, it was deep dark. His dog wasn't yelping, and he couldn't see it. He rubbed his eyes to try and make them adjust to the dark. When the moon slipped out from behind a purple cloud, his eyes focused on one thing: A rope thrown over the branch of a tree. On its end, his dog hung by its neck.

Breed ran up to it, wrapped his arms around his little friend, and slipped the rope from around its neck. Kneeling down on one knee, he lowered his dog to the ground. It wasn't moving. Dim light from the moon revealed the dog's eyes were glassy. Breed placed his ear to the dog's side and listened. No heartbeat. His dog was dead.

Behind him, out on the road, the doors of a car bammed shut. He jerked his head around. A kid stuck his head out the window of a 1940 Ford and yelled, "Hey, Rat Boy, how do you like us now?"

Breed couldn't believe they had hung his dog. He put his ear to the dog's side again. He thought he heard a faint heartbeat. Maybe there was still a chance. He placed the dog on the ground, tried to make it stand. It fell over. He stood up and looked

12

down at its lifeless form. All hope faded.

As the motor of the Ford roared into the night, and drunken laughter faded down the street, Breed held the rope in his hands. He wanted to take it and wrap it around those flats gang kids' necks. If he were bigger and stronger, he would send them where they belonged, and it wouldn't be dog heaven.

He dropped to his knees, picked up his dog, hugged it; and with tears forming in his eyes, he rocked back and forth. He couldn't understand why those older kids did what they did. They had no reason to kill his dog. It was friendly. It never bit anyone. Now, what Purple hadn't done with a baseball bat, these flats gang kids had managed to do with a rope.

Flats gang kids had stolen things and beat him up so many times that he expected it. But they had never done anything like this. He had to get away from them. He had to get away from the ignorance of Traptown.

He would keep searching the river for a drifting boat, but now he had a new plan. He was going to build a motorbike. Then, anytime he wanted, he could ride out of Traptown.

Before he could finish the motorbike, he needed more parts. But he didn't have any money.

The next day, with tears in his eyes, he dug a deep hole, laid his dog in, and shoveled the dirt over it. He said the prayers and asked God why he had let his dog die. No answers came. Feeling like a filthy rag before the holiness of God, he hung his shoulders in defeat. Then he cussed at himself for being a crybaby. He straightened his shoulders, and the fury raged inside him. He knew what he had to do.

Going in alone would be dangerous, but now that his dog was dead, he didn't care if wild dogs charged out of the heaps of filth that stretched across the horizon. He was too mad to be scared. What ever happened in there couldn't be any worse than what had already happened.

He slipped past the wild dogs and snuck into the arena of sacred stink. He snuck into the Traptown dump.

Slogging between two mountains of garbage, he tripped over an old washing machine. He held out his hands to break his fall and just missed having the palm of his hand slit open with a broken piece of green canning-jar glass. Something tumbled down the pile of garbage. It could be a rat or a wild dog. He stiffened and looked up. A broken gasoline motor rolled next to his head. He stood up, brushed himself off, and picked up the motor. Now, he had an important part. But he would need more.

While he searched, clouds ran away from the sun and let its hot rays beam down on the dump. The sleeping stench of the garbage awoke. Like an enormous whoopee cushion with a real smell, the stench suffocated all the good air; and freshly hatched flies buzzed happily in the sickening air.

When Breed used a splintered board to separate heaps of rotting garbage, the lung-menacing malodor of the rotting garbage intensified. He wanted to quit. He wanted to get away from that rancid smell. He needed to suck in at least one breath of good air. But he needed one more part for his motorbike.

He covered his face with the front of his T-shirt and dug out an old bicycle frame. Now he had everything he needed.

He threw the frame onto his shoulder; and with the greasy motor in the crook of his arm, he lugged the parts back to his slum neighborhood.

***

Every day he worked in his secret workplace under the porch floor. In a few weeks he had pieced together a motorbike. In his neighborhood this was something that only a rich kid could have. He wasn't rich, but he had a motorbike. If it started, he would be the richest fourteen-year-old kid in the world.

He knelt next to the motorbike, tightened the last bolt, and checked the gas tank. It was almost empty. As usual, he didn't have money to buy more gas, but he wasn't worried about that. He had enough for a test run.

The flats gang usually prowled the neighborhood looking for something to smash or steal. Breed crouched and duck-walked out from under the porch. Outside, he stood up and looked around. He didn't see Burkie's rotten-tooth face, his long knife, or any of the flats bullies.

He crawled back under the porch, put his hands on the crossbar of his motorbike, and dragged it out into the bright sunshine. As he pushed it across the street and into the tall grass of drunken Toney's backyard, the front wheel smashed down the tall grass and made a path. Out the other side of Toney's yard, skinny, scrappy weeds stuck up out of the dead ground and struggled to live.

15

He jumped on the seat, coasted past a small mountain of topsoil, stopped, and looked across the spatter of dusty-yellow land his friends called the vacant lot. If his motorbike would start, he could ride to his favorite place. He could ride to Shell Island.

The motorbike didn't have a kick-starter. It didn't have a clutch. But it didn't matter. He could push it with the engine engaged. But would it start? He gripped the handlebars and muscled the heavy motorbike around in a big oval. Looking down over his right shoulder, he watched the engine turn. Gas vapor puffed out the exhaust pipe, but the engine did not start. No spark.

He stopped pushing, took the broken-handled screwdriver from his back pocket, bent over, and turned the points, just a tad. Then he jammed the screwdriver into his back pocket and pushed the motorbike. Running alongside, he tilted his head and listened to the little motor for signs of life. His legs tired, but he kept on pushing. Deep inside the motor, stubborn steel teamed up with the strong compression strokes. It resisted his every movement. His breath came in short gasps. He pushed more. When he felt his blood pounding in his ears, he stopped.

His buddy, Screwball, rode up on a pedal bike and stopped at the edge of the lot. He jerked his head and flipped his long blond hair out of his eyes. Breed looked beyond him. A 1940 Ford cruised down the street and stopped. A skinny arm hooked out of the passenger side window and a flung a beer bottle in Screwball's direction.

From inside the Ford, someone yelled, "Hey,

Rat Boy, catch."

The beer bottle sailed straight for the back of Screwball's head. "Watch out!" Breed yelled and pushed Screwball to the side.

The flying beer bottle swished past Screwball's ear, smashed on the frame of his bike, and scattered onto the ground.

Screwball looked toward the Ford. Breed expected him to yell back at the kid. Instead, using a carton voice, Screwball talked out the side of his mouth. "Ha-ha, you didn't get me."

The driver in the Ford revved the engine of the car and popped the clutch. The back tire on the driver's side gripped the hot pavement. Skeek! Echoed above a stutter of drunken laughter, and the carload of beer-bottle-sucking bullies thundered away.

If the kids in the Ford knew something agitated someone they would do it every chance they could. Screwball acted as if the skeeks didn't bother him, and Breed didn't want to admit that they bothered him either. But they did.

He suppressed his feelings, pushed his motorbike next to Screwball, and looked at the shards of glass. "I don't need a flat tire." With one hand holding up the bike, he bent over to pick up the glass.

Screwball held up his hand like a traffic cop. "I'll get it."

Breed straightened up. With the side of his tennis-shoed foot, Screwball scraped the spikes of broken glass away from the tire of the motorbike.

With both hands on the handlebars of the bike, Breed looked down the road. The '40 Ford was gone. "Rotten bastards." He took a deep breath, dug his toes in the yellow dirt, and pushed. Ratchet-ahh! Ratchet-ahh! Ratchet-ahh! Thrashed deep in the engine. Mists of blue smoke huffed out the exhaust. He pushed and pushed. The little engine sounded like it wanted to start, but did not.

Breed stopped and gasped for breath. His body told him to quit, push the bike back under the porch, work on it some more. His mind said, "One more time."

He took a deep breath, squared his shoulders, forced his last reserve of strength into his legs, and strong-armed the bike around the lot, again. The engine sniffled and cracked like an angry firecracker.

In his mind, Breed pictured what was happening inside the little engine. It was getting enough gas. It was getting enough spark. There was no reason it should not start.

He kept on pushing. Finally, the little piston sputtered and bucked with uneven bursts of energy. It was running.

As its revolutions increased, strong spurts of power jerked the back wheel around and around. The bike moved forward on its own power and caused the handlebars to pull from the palms of Breed's hands. He re-gripped and hung on. The bike jerked erratically and picked up speed. He loped alongside. Yellow-blue flames licked out the exhaust. The little motor stuttered and thumped.

Blue-black smoke rolled out the exhaust pipe. The engine beat into a triumphant rhythm. Exhaust smoke smoothed to a steady white color. Like the heart of a running tiger, the engine purred with positive power.

"Yeah, man!" Breed yelled over the Thump! Thump! of the engine. He hopped on the seat and pulled the white cotton string that was tied to the throttle on the leaking carburetor. The worn belt rotated around the back wheel and put power to the ground. With the wheels churning over the dirt, Breed raced around the vacant lot. The motorbike worked. He had a way to get out of Traptown. He was going to ride to Shell Island. He was happy.

Up ahead, an empty beer can sat in the wheels path. "Nothing can stop me now!" Crunch!

Screwball pointed at the can and laughed. "It's flat now," he said over the beat of the engine.

Looking over his shoulder, Breed held the string to the carburetor and motored around the lot. His long black hair waved in the wind. Behind him, a tail of dust wagged in the summer air and drifted toward Screwball.

With an offhand flip of his hand Screwball waved the fine dirt-filled air from the front of his face and yelled, "It works."

Breed wanted Screwball to know the thrill of riding the motorbike. He let the string to the carburetor go slack. The engine slowed, he motioned to Screwball. "Come on, Screwball, take it before it stalls."

Screwball ran next to Breed and yelled over the sound of the engine. "This thing don't slow down for nothin'."

Breed dismounted and loped alongside his motorbike. He motioned with his head. "Come on. Hop on."

Screwball grabbed the handlebars and the pass

was completed. He jumped on and pulled the string. It looped around the sharp edge on the chrome headlight and broke. The engine stuttered and stopped.

An unexpected silence surrounded the lot.

Screwball lowered his head and looked at the bike. "Ahh, man."

Breed came alongside. "Nice try, but it's probably out of gas."

The sound of a truck motor grew loud. Then, Bang! . . . Thump! Thump!

Breed snapped his head in the direction of the sound. Screwball's pedal bike lay in the middle of the road.

Screwball jumped off Breed's motorbike and looked toward the road. "He ran over my bike!"

Breed grabbed his motorbike and looked down the street. A dull-black panel truck was driving away. The truck's manual transmission whined like it needed oil. The truck slowed.

Breed pushed his motorbike a few steps toward the road. "Maybe he's going to stop."

The truck's transmission gears ground into second gear. The clutch clunked on the floorboard and the driver stepped on the gas. Blue smoke poured out the rusted tailpipe. The truck sped off; and like a bad joke, the smell of burnt oil filled the air.

Breed gave Screwball a bleak smile. "That was on purpose."

Screwball stormed across the lot, jumped over the sewage ditch, and looked down at his bike. Cussing, he shook his fist at the disappearing truck.

Breed pushed the motorbike next to him and

stopped.

Screwball's voice quivered as if he were about to cry. "Rotten no good, Lard Man!"

Breed felt a line of tension form on his mouth. "That fat ass is always doing something to us. I wish we knew where he hides that truck."

Like a kicked dog, Screwball's eyes misted over. He turned his head away and wiped his eyes. "I'd like to fix that truck for good. That bike was the only thing I ever had that wasn't junk."

Staring at the bike, Breed nodded. "Your bike was almost new."

"It ain't now."

Running his fingers through his shiny crow-like hair, Breed studied Screwball's run-over bike. "The frame's bent," he said low and then suddenly talked upbeat. "But you still might be able to ride it."

"It figures," Screwball said. "I finally get something decent and some elephant-ass has to run over it."

"It's a good thing you weren't on it." Breed forced a smile.

Screwball didn't smile back.

Breed held onto the handlebars of his red motorbike and looked down. The sun gleamed on the chrome drainpipe he had rigged up as an exhaust, and reflected like a bright curved mirror. He raised his head. "Maybe we can scrounge some more parts at the dump and fix it."

"I'm tired of working with stinkin' junk." Screwball bent over, grabbed his bike, pulled it upright, and ran his hand over the frame where it was bent. "We'll never find anything like this." He wiped the beads of sweat from his forehead. "In this heat that dump stinks really bad."

"I don't mind working with junk," Breed said. "But I hate it when a bunch of jerk-offs ruin everything we make."

"Maybe I can straighten it out." Screwball placed his foot on the frame of his bike, grabbed it with his hand, and pulled. It didn't bend. It didn't budge. He gave up. "Anyway, I don't think we could hold our breath long enough in that dump to find enough parts."

As if he were in the dump, Breed breathed in shallow breaths. "I can smell the place just thinking about it." As if he were trying to force the smell of the dump out of his lungs, he shuddered and shook his head.

Screwball put his hand on his own rear end. As if he had just been bitten, he rubbed it. "Those dogs ain't too friendly, either."

"They say those wild dogs get rabies in the summer. It'll be tough to get past them and find parts like the ones we found when we made these bikes."

"That dump smells like someone died." Screwball made a face. "Dead bodies give me the creeps."

Breed let out a nervous laugh. "Maybe someone did die, and they threw the bike parts away."

"I guess it's better than not having any parts at all," Screwball said, and his voice gained a businesslike edge. "It doesn't really matter where they came from."

Breed patted the gas tank on his motorbike. "We still got a motorbike."

"Yeah, all we got to do is keep it away from the flats gang and One-Finger-Burke."

Chapter 2

Breed stood at the side of the road and stared at Screwball's bent bike. It reminded him of how his dog's neck had been bent after the bullies had hung it. He hadn't told anyone that it had been hung. He wanted to believe it was still under the porch, waiting for him. A tear formed in the corner of his eye. Not wanting Screwball to see him cry, he sucked in a deep breath and exhaled slowly. Turning his head, he wiped the tear on the sleeve of his shirt. "Your bike looks like Lard Man sat on it."

Screwball flipped the kickstand down, balanced his bent bike, and sat on the ripped seat. He took his hands off the handlebars and blinked back the tears forming in his eyes. "Look, it still holds me."

Like Screwball, Breed had never owned anything first-rate. All his worldly possessions had always been worn out hand-me-downs, or something from the dump. He knew Screwball felt like crying, but he would never tell him. No one wanted to be called a crybaby. All his buddies suppressed their emotions. He did, too.

Thanks to someone in a black panel truck, Screwball didn't even have a decent pedal bike, but Breed still had a nice motorbike. Before he could stop himself, he blurted out, "Wanna trade bikes?"

A grin of approval formed on Screwball's face. "Not really. But when you get it running, you can tie a rope around my handlebars and tow me to Shell Island."

Breed jerked a finger toward Screwball. "I can do that. Lard man will never find us there."

Screwball lifted his foot. With the end of his

worn tennis shore, he tapped the frame of his bike. "It's bent but it ain't broke. Maybe I can still ride it."

The faint rumble of a car motor snuck into the summer air. Breed glanced down the road. In the distance, a flash of black and white appeared. He jerked his head toward Screwball. "See if you can ride your bike. The cops are coming up the hill."

Screwball grabbed the handlebars of his bike, flipped up the kickstand with his foot, and leaned forward. "Let's go, Breed. Burkie's old man's on duty."

Breed hated to move when any cop was coming. It made him feel like he wasn't living in a free country. He turned his head and listened. The sound of the threatening cruiser grew louder.

Screwball impatiently motioned with is arm. "Come on, Breed. Let's go."

"Why should we move? We ain't doin' nothin'."

Screwball pointed to the back fender on Breed's motorbike. "It doesn't matter. You ain't got no license on that bike. If we don't get out of here, One-Finger-Burke will use it as an excuse to take it. Then he'll say it belongs to little Burkie." He tried to put his feet on the pedals without looking, but because of the bent frame the pedals rotated in an unfamiliar circle. His feet touched nothing but air. Looking down, he placed his feet on the bent pedals and pumped toward the alley.

Breed pushed his motorbike a few feet. The motor turned over and caught on the compression stroke. The back wheel locked up. The skidding tire drew a long dark line in the gravel. He stopped

25

and wrestled the fan belt off the pulley of the motor. The back drive wheel turned free. Following Screwball, he pushed his motorbike and looked ahead. The way the back wheel on Screwball's bent bike wobbled reminded him of the way he had seen dogs run when they were scared. They ran so fast that that their rear ends looked like they were trying to pass their heads.

They steered their bikes around a bushy pine tree and hid.

The cop car cruised past.

With his hands resting on the handlebars, as if he were laughing, Screwball leaned forward and shook his shoulders. "Looks like Burke ain't gettin' a motorbike today."

Like a dog protecting a bone, Breed hunched over and held the handle grips on his motorbike. "He'll never get this bike."

A loud whistle pierced the air. Breed snapped his head in the direction of the sound. "That's Flick. Maybe he found a boat." He whistled back.

Along the alley, a small gust of wind swept across the tall green hedges. The tops bent up and down like sleepy sentinels nodding their heads. Breed watched the center of the hedges. Little dark-green leaves quivered. Branches parted, and like a red-headed magic trick, Flick popped out of the hedges.

Before Flick could speak, Breed asked, "Did you find a boat?"

"Not yet." With an inquisitive smile on his freckled face, Flick stared at Screwball's bike. "Hey, Screwball, what happened to your almost new bike?"

"I left it by the road so I could ride Breed's motorbike, and a black panel trunk ran over it."

"It's bent so bad you can go around curves without turning the wheel." Flick ran his hand along the bent crossbar of the bike. "You ain't even had this bike a day. Now it's junk."

Breed proudly held his hand toward his bike. "Mine ain't junk."

Screwball gave him a sour look.

Breed regretted he had said it.

Flick looked at the chrome exhaust pipe. "This is a nice motorbike. You guys sure you didn't steal it?"

Screwball's sour look faded. "We got parts from the dump. If that's stealing, then we stole it."

"You're gettin' pretty good at fixin' stuff up, Breed," Flick said admiring the bike, "but everybody's gonna say you stole it."

Breed pointed to the motor wedged into the red frame. "You were there last year, when I picked up half of this motor."

"I remember when you found it. It had so much grease and dirt on it, I thought it would never run."

"Cleaned up nice." With his toe, Breed pointed to lettering on the motor. "You can read the name, Whizzer."

"You know," Flick said and shook his head. "Nobody in Traptown cares how you got it or what name's on it."

"That don't matter," Breed said with hope. "When I get some gas, I'll ride out of this dump town."

"It ain't gonna matter what you say or do."

27

Screwball sighed. "If Burkie's old man wants your motorbike, he'll say you stole it."

"That's true," Flick said with a look of discomfort. "Just because he was out after dark, Burkie's old man threw Blo in reform school."

Just the thought of Burkie's dishonest father irritated Breed. "Burkie's old man should be in jail. Anytime he wants something, he gets that three-fingered hand on it, and takes it."

Screwball held up his hand and held one finger down like it was missing. An expression of wonder filled his eyes. "His short finger looks weird."

Flick lifted his hand to his face and looked at his fingers. "Better count your fingers when he's around. He'll steal one."

Breed glanced at his own fingers. "There's nothing One-Finger-Burke wouldn't steal."

Holding his finger in front of his nose, Screwball stared at it until his eyes crossed. "How'd he lose it?" He uncrossed his eyes and dropped his finger.

Flick curled his lip like a gangster's smile. "They say he lost it in the war."

"If he did," Breed said, "he must have been on the other side. He don't act like no American."

"If he's anything like his rotten son," Screwball said, "he got his finger chopped off trying to steal something."

Sitting on the seat, wishing and listening for gas to swish around in the tank, Breed wiggled his motorbike. Nothing.

"One-Finger-Burke must want something Blo has," he said. "He didn't do anything to get sent to reform school."

28

Flick turned his palm up and shrugged. "They took him anyway."

Frowning, Breed nodded. "They told him it was just a visit."

"They like to do that kind of crap," Screwball said. "They're just trying to scare him."

As if he were talking about a gangster who had gotten out of jail, Flick talked out the side of his mouth. "He came back different, hasn't been the same since."

Pretending to finger the keys on an invisible trumpet, Screwball wiggled his fingers in front of his face. "He used to play 'Taps' almost every night."

"He doesn't anymore," Breed said. "But he never lets that trumpet out of his sight." He unscrewed the small gas cap on the motorbike. Hoping that somehow gas would be in there, he looked into the tank. "It's empty." He shifted his weight. He lost his balance. The motorbike, with him on it, began to tilt to the ground. He jerked his foot to the ground, held onto the bike, regained his balance, and didn't fall.

"Sit on bikes much?" Screwball jeered and Flick laughed.

Breed regained his balancing confidence and smiled. He was glad Screwball was getting his stupid sense of humor back. He looked toward Flick. "I ain't used to sitting on anything that ain't junk."

"Yeah, I know what you mean. If we were rich we would have it made."

Hooking his thumbs into the sides of his T-shirt, Screwball stuck out his chest. "If we were rich, we could buy some gas and ride to Shell Island."

"If everybody would just leave us alone," Breed said, "we wouldn't have to ride to Shell Island."

Screwball smiled; and even though his spaced teeth looked like a picket fence, his sarcasm came through. "What are you, a crybaby? Don't you like it when cops chase us for something we didn't do?" He spread his arms wide. "And isn't it great when those flats gang kids beat us up?"

"Sure, I like it." Breed smiled a sarcastic smile. "But don't you really love it when some elephant ass runs over your bike."

Screwball's smile faded.

Flick's eyes opened with surprise. "Elephant Ass? Did you see who did it?"

"Didn't have to," Screwball said. "We know it was Lard Man."

Over the years, Breed had been blamed for things he had never done, and he didn't like the way it felt. He didn't want to blame someone for something if he wasn't absolutely sure they had done it.

"It could be Lard Man," he said. "It could be anybody in this stinkin' town."

Flick bent over, picked out a little jagged stone from the flapping sole of his clodhopper work shoe and held it as if he were a man examining a rock for a diamond. It was just a stone. He threw it into the sewage ditch. "We can find out if it was the Lard Man . . . tonight."

***

Warily watching for Burkie and the knife,

Breed pushed his motorbike home. When he hid it under the porch, he looked for his dog. The dog's empty tin feeding pan sat in the corner. Dust and dirt covered the once licked-clean surface. He picked up the pan. With the knee of his pants, he wiped the dust off. He looked at the shinning pan for a moment, and intense empty feeling invaded his chest. For a moment, he couldn't breathe. He dropped the pan into the dirt.

When he went into the kitchen and looked for something to eat, no one was home. He made dough from flour and water, rolled it into a pancake, scooped some white lard into a big black skillet, and fried the dough until it was brown. He didn't like the fried dough, but the awful taste didn't matter. He was hungry. He ate it all except for one small piece. Out of habit, he put it in his shirt pocket for his dog.

He climbed the worn wooden stairs that led to his bedroom. Even though it was afternoon, he stepped to his bed. It was going to be a big night, even bigger if he went to Shell Island. He laid himself down on the ragged blanket to rest. With his eyes closed, he arranged the thoughts in his mind. His buddy, Hog, always scrounged just about anything he wanted. Tonight, he would probably show up with a can of gas. They could go to Shell Island; but with that carburetor leaking the gas all over the road, they'd run out of gas before they got there.

He jumped out of bed, ran down the stairs, and went back under the porch. Out of habit and a wish that somehow his dog would come back, he dropped the piece of bread into the shinning pan and worked on the motorbike's carburetor. At dusk, the carburetor was fixed, but the piece of bread was still in the pan. He dragged the motorbike out from under the porch and headed for the gang.

Pushing the motorbike along the streets, he passed in and out of patches of the semi-dark neighborhood. When he pushed his shining red motorbike to where the gang stood, he stopped. Above their heads, the lone naked streetlight flickered and burned bright.

Flick greeted him with a big smile. "Hey, rich man with the new bike, did you get some gas?"

"Not yet," Breed said and looked to Hog. Black curly hair filled the top of Hog's head and long hours in the summer sun had turned his face bronze. Being his usual agitating self, Hog snarled. "What are you lookin' at me for?"

"You always scrounge things," Breed said with hope. "I was sure you'd find a little bit of gas."

Hog raised an eyebrow. "What would I do with gas?"

Breed patted the gas tank on his motorbike. "Put it in the tank. Then we could go to Shell Island."

"What are you gonna do there?"

"Build a fire. Fish all night. Might even catch Big Mike."

Hog put his hand on the light on the fender of the motorbike. "That big muskie would pull you and your dinky motorbike to the bottom of the river." He looked at the light on the motorbike. It wasn't shining. "And anyway, how are you going to go in the dark?"

"The light only works when the motor's

32

running."

"So what, you can only take one guy. How would the rest of us get there?"

"I'll tie a rope on Screwball's bike and tow you guys. I'll have to make a couple of trips, but there's nothing to it when you're riding."

"That sounds like a plan," Flick said and looked around. "When we get back from Lard Man's house, the cops will be out. We won't be able to get any gas tonight."

Breed had counted on going to Shell Island tonight, but he knew it would be ignorant to siphon gas from somewhere with the cops hanging around. Like a kid who had just been told he wasn't getting anything for Christmas, he hung his head and looked at his motorbike. Under the streetlight, the flawless red spray-painted fenders glistened and shined like new. It didn't seem real. He felt as if he were in a parade riding on the back seat of a Cadillac convertible, but he was dressed in the shame of ragged clothes, hoping no one would notice.

"Hey, Breed," Screwball said. "Watch a black panel truck don't run over your bike."

Screwball's attempted humor made Breed feel weak and helpless. He didn't think Screwball's remark was funny, and he felt the blood fill his face. "Yeah, I heard," he said and pretended not to be agitated.

"Don't let your face turn the same color as your motorbike," Hog said. "When Burkie's old man takes it off you, he'll think you're part of it."

What's the matter with me? Breed thought. I'm not a crybaby. He flexed his jaw and regained

33

the tough edge that was expected of everyone in the gang. The embarrassment flew from his mind, and he put on his tough face. "One-Finger-Burke ain't gettin' this bike."

"Even if he don't," Screwball said, "the flats gang's gonna take it."

Hog tilted his head to one side, reached across his chest, and scratched his arm. "Don't kid yourself. One way or another, Burke's gonna take it. We can't have nothin'."

Screwball placed his hands on the handlebars of the motorbike, leaned on them, and crossed his legs. "What are you worried about, Breed? You got it for free."

"Yeah," Hog said, "you wanna be like little Burkie and get things free just cause your old man's a crooked cop?"

Breed whirled around and faced Hog. "It wasn't free. I had to find the right parts and put it together. If I had to be like little butt-sucking Burkie, I wouldn't want anything for free."

Car lights flashed in the distance and lit the soft night. Flick swept his arm across his chest and pointed to the weeds at the side of the road. Everyone but Breed leaped in and dropped out of sight. Breed weaved his motorbike into the weeds, laid it on the ground, and ducked down. The car and its lights passed.

"It ain't the cops," Screwball said and they all stood up.

Flick pointed to a spot where the weeds were tall and concealing. "Hey, Breed. Hide your bike there. We don't have any gas, and you can't ride it where we're going."

34

Car headlights blazed on Breed's back. His buddies jerked further back into the weeds, but Breed had waited too long. If he moved backwards, his movement would be seen. He dropped on the ground. Red lines of light slashed over his head and chopped into the black night. The cops were searching for something.

Breed lay on his side and pulled his motorbike a few more feet into the tall weeds. The front wheel cocked. The bike would not move.

Flick whispered out from the weeds, "Get out of there, Breed."

Breed turned his head and looked back at Flick. "They can see my bike from the road. I have to move it." A giant white scythe of light sliced the air over his head.

Flick stretched out his arm and jerked on the leg of Breed's pants. "Don't let that spotlight hit you."

Waiting for the police to drive past, Breed lay beside his motorbike. The strong light nipped the toe of his ragged tennis shoe. As if his foot had been shocked, he jerked it away. The horror of One-Finger-Burke spotting his motorbike and taking it caused his heart to jump with fright. He took one last look at his motorbike. Trying to create a diversion, he jumped up, and took off running.

Everyone else did, too.

Down the alley they flew, running like their legs were going to fall off, laughing and moving like the electric in the telephone pole wires above. They stumbled and struggled, but kept their balance. In the darkness, they zipped behind houses and zigzagged around the hazards of the neighborhood's miniature backyard burning dumps.

Breed's feet sailed across the grass. He ran smooth and strong. Without effort, his feet pounded the ground. Like the extra-unexpected step at the bottom of a dark stairs, his one foot plunked down. His ankle jolted. A shock wave flew up his right side. His body tipped sideways. Pain raced up his spine. He stumbled. To break his fall, he threw his hands out in front of himself. In the dark, he hadn't seen the unexpected miniature drop-off in the ground. Now he was falling. One hand hit the grass. He regained his balance, pushed off the ground, and shot upright. He was running again.

It had happened so fast he didn't have time to feel pain. Now his ankle hurt. He ignored it. He wasn't a crybaby.

Up ahead, a huge pile of smoldering garbage blocked the gang's path. They plowed through. Their flying worn-shoed-feet slammed into rusting cans and burnt-black bottles and banged against tin cans and dirty glass canning jars, causing them to rattle and break. The noise and a cloud of gray, stinking garbage dust told the world of the Traptown neighborhood where they had been. Now they couldn't stop. They ran on.

On a street corner, a bright-unbroken streetlight threatened their escape. The outer glow touched their faces. They jerked to the right and leaped through a tall blue-gray row of hedges.

On the other side, they sailed through the dark and touched down in Lard Man's backyard.

A complete lack of motion would hide them. In the dark shadow of the hedges, they collapsed flat onto the ground and lay still. Like a secret

36

cloak, the blue silent night wrapped around them. They were invisible. Light from a kitchen window escaped into the dark. It burned an uncomfortable amber stripe into Breed's face. He jerked his head away from the light, rolled, and blurred into the shadow.

The stripe of light blinked. Lard Man appeared in the doorway. In the semi-darkness, he waddled onto his little green paint-peeled porch. The dim light from the fifteen-watt porch light bulb shined on his bald head. He lifted a quart bottle of beer to his brown-bearded, monkey-butt face and stopped.

The sight of Lard Man's monkey-butt face caused Breed to bury his face in the grass and hold his hand over his mouth, but he let out a muffled giggle.

Lard Man opened his mouth, lifted the bottle, and took a long pull. He wiped his butt face on his sleeve and squinted in Breed's direction. Trying to peer through the black night, his fat enclosed goggly eyes blinked, and his forehead wrinkled with loose rolls of skin.

Screwball turned toward Breed. "He can't see us."

"Quiet," Flick whispered and pointed to the porch. "Let's see what monkey-butt does."

Lard Man lifted his hand to his chest. Breed hoped he wasn't reaching for a gun. He got ready to run.

With his short stubby fingers, Lard Man pulled out a pack of cigarettes, took one out, and lit it. The glow of the match flame lit up his face, amplifying and accenting its fat features. He guided the cigarette to his mean skinny lips. Dragging hard, he created a long orange ash that glowed brighter than his cheap porch light. He coughed, shook his clinched fists, and hacked at the night. "I hear you out there," he called out and breathed deep. "Puff—, Puff—, just keep it up . . . puff—, you goddamn reliefers won't be sponging off of society much longer. You'll all be in reform school."

Breed and the others didn't move.

They watched.

They waited.

Lard Man sucked out one last drag on his cigarette and flicked it into the wet grass. As he took a deep breath, his stomach swelled, and his shirt spread tight across his balloon belly. "Just keep it up." He puffed. As if it were a big chore, he sucked in three big gulps of air and hacked out a loud guttural cough. Then he turned, took in another deep breath; and as if he were in pain, he forced out a nicotine-throat-clearing roar.

The pressure on his fat encased sausage intestines must have been too great. It seemed that his beer brain had no control. Fermented beer-joint food and built up gas, escaped violently and fluttered the seat of his pants. He grabbed his overrun rear end and cussed under his breath. "Goddamn little assholes. You made me crap my pants . . . Damn! . . . Damn all you indigent bastards! I'll run over every bike you have . . . And I hope you're on the goddamn things."

Holding his quart of beer securely in his chubby hand, he pinched his accident-spattered ass together. Using little pigeon steps, he slipped into his brown house. Inside, he slammed the door behind him.

Outside, Breed and the others watched the house. The light from the bathroom brighten the window, and the sound of the toilet flushing couldn't drown the sound of Lard Man's cussing.

Flick rubbed the back of his neck and sighed. "I'm glad I don't have to wipe that big ass."

Screwball chuckled. "If anyone wants to wipe that fat ass, they'll have to set him on the ground, spread his legs, and tie ropes around his ankles."

Confused, Breed stared at Screwball. "Then what?"

"Then, they'll hook the ropes to a bulldozer, drag his fat ass over the grass, and wipe it clean."

The gang stood up. Red spinning police lights blinked in their direction.

"It's the cops," Flick said and they raced away.

Breed tried to keep up with swift-footed Screwball, but he wasn't fast enough. Screwball ran out of sight. Now, Breed led the remaining pack. Directly in front of him, like a nightmare, a mongrel dog barked wildly and charged out of the chain-worn opening of its wooden doghouse. It jerked on the end of its chain and snapped its vicious fangs in Breed's direction.

Breed tried to slow down and turn away from the dangerous dog, but he was running too fast. The dog was in already in front of him. Awakened from its lethargic state, it charged. Breed felt the wind from its whirring teeth graze his leg. He jerked away, leaped over the dog's snapping mouth, and sailed toward the roof of the doghouse.

Clunk! He landed on the roof. The dog charged back on its chain and stood on its hind legs. Breed tensed to jump and kept his wide opened eyes on the dog. When its clawing paws dug at the edge of the doghouse roof, hanging globs of ugly hairballs shook on the dog's body like loose cancerous growths. Its scraping teeth slashed the ends of the shingles into little pieces and flung them into the fierce air.

As if someone were shooting at his feet, Breed danced on top of the doghouse. When he moved, the dog opened its mouth. With teeth like deadly shards of glass, it lunged for Breed's feet, but missed. The dog's mouth continually opened and slammed shut, but this nightmare was too close for Breed to jump free. He was trapped.

Vicious ear-banging barks clogged the air with confusion. Sharp snarls stung the edges of Breed's sanity. The wolf–like dog jumped higher and closer. Those shingles whirred into the air. The dog's hot barking breath blasted Breed's feet and those razor fangs snipped closer.

Behind him, Flick and the others ran toward the dog, but stopped just at the end of the dog's paw-beaten circle path. Flick jerked his hands into the air and encouraged Breed. "Jump, Breed, jump!"

The dog's ears perked up. It rotated on its back legs. Then it rushed toward Flick and the others. As if they were on the end of a snapping chain, everyone but Flick jumped back. Like a matador teasing a bull, Flick swerved from the charging dog's path of pursuit. It just missed him, but the miss just made it meaner. Now the dog wanted Flick. It ran and charged to the end of its chain. The sudden stop jerked the dog's neck. As if an invisible hand had swept the dog's body sideways, it went flying into the air. For a brief second it was

in a horizontal suspended state. Then it landed —
Thud! — on the hard paw-hammered ground. It
yelped in pain. Breed danced sideways, sprang off
the roof, and hit the ground running.

Breed and his friends were off again. A frantic
run and a gigantic leap over a fence brought them to
a plowed, tree-lined field.

Blinking like Morse code, headlights of the
police cruiser flickered through the tree leaves.

Breed and the others wilted to the ground and
became dormant. The cruiser stopped. A long
white cylinder of light from the chrome spotlight of
the police car beamed over them. They stretched
flat and stuck to the ground.

The searching beam burned over Ballpeen's
head.

"Hey, Ballpeen," Screwball said. "Those cops
are stupid. They can't tell your clump of garbage
body from a mound of dirt."

Ballpeen started to say something. Flick
looked back over his shoulder and motioned with
his fist. "Shut up!"

No one did. In hushed tones, they talked at
random.

"You ain't the boss."

"We'll do what we want."

"Here it comes again."

"Get your big, stupid head down."

"Let him talk. The cops won't pick him up.
They're not collecting garbage today."

"Perch and rotate!"

"You agitating bastard."

"Hant!"

"What the hell is Hant?"

41

No one answered.

As the spotlight randomly passed overhead, Breed lay in the freshly plowed furrow of the field and watched the sky. Heavy darkness surrounded a yellow moon and molded it into a deformed pear.

Expecting to suck in the clean night air of the summer, Breed breathed in deep. The sour sewer smell and slow curling smoke from smoldering garbage flowed down his throat. As he tried to fan the sickening stench from the front of his face, wind fanned the open sewers that ran into long ditches along the front yards of the neighborhood and enhanced the aroma. He blew out a disgusted breath of air; and as if he were back in the Traptown dump, he breathed in shallow breaths.

From where he was, Breed could not see the neighborhood, but he knew what would happen. He had seen the same thing over and over. Lights would be turned off, people would roll over, the nightmarish dogs would crawl back into their doghouses, and the police radio would scratch an, "All Clear!"

The cruiser would pull away. Lard Man would flush his toilet and another load of black stinking raw sewage would flow underground to the sewer ditch in front of his house. It would continue on down the steep street and run under rickety wooden foot bridges and ooze through old, rusty, open-ended hot water tanks that were used to guide the widening black filth water under driveways. Then it would gush on down the valley and into the river, where it would be sucked into the water treatment plant and be pumped back up hill and start the process all over again.

Lard Man would juggle the handle and the water would run to refill the toilet tank. He would cough, open his back door, stagger down the creaking steps, throw his last empty beer bottle into the garbage can, and bang the lid shut.

Then, a lady in light-green hair rollers would give herself one last nervous look out the lighted window and tuck herself in for the night. The crickets would begin their soft soothing sleeping music. The neighborhood would drift into that limbo state ready to go over the restful sleeping edge. The police would return from time to time and try to keep it that way. It would be the same. It always was.

Breed didn't like things being the same. Shell Island was never the same. He was going to go there.

Chapter 3

Breed and his friends lay in the plowed furrows of the field and watched. The lights from the police cruiser quit flickering through the trees and went away. Flick stood up. They all stood up, brushed the dirt from their ragged clothes, and eased away from the security of the field.

Like fleeting apparitions, they snuck through a few backyards, filed across the road, swished through the hedges, and walked into Lard Man's backyard. Flick held up his hand and signaled to stop. Everyone froze. Quiet hovered in the night. Crickets began their nightly symphony.

Standing next to the dark hedges, Flick looked back at Breed and shot him a crooked grin. "Lard Man said he would run over all our bikes," he whispered. "Now we know who ran over Screwball's bike."

Grumbling under his breath, Screwball stepped next to a garbage can and jiggled it. A tinny rattle filled the night. The crickets stopped. Screwball lifted the lid off the garbage can and jerked his head toward the roof of Lard Man's garage. "Let's fix his fat ass."

Flick nodded in approval and waited. The crickets continued their music. Flick crawled on top of Lard Man's tar-papered garage roof. Breed climbed up behind him. On the ground below, Screwball and Hog hoisted one of Lard Man's garbage cans over their heads. Flick grabbed the can and dragged it up onto the peak of the roof. Screwball and Hog lifted another can. It was filled to the brim, with beer bottles and trash. Breed reached down and grabbed it. The heavy can slipped from his grip.

Before it fell, Hog caught it. "Hey, Breed, don't drop it yet."

Breed re-gripped the can and pulled it up onto the peak of the roof. Balancing the two cans on the tipsy top of the roof, Breed and Flick waited.

Screwball and Hog climbed up on the roof, shuffled up to the peak, and grabbed the bottoms of the cans. Standing on the tippy top of the roof, Breed, Hog, and Screwball tilted the cans to a ready position and looked to Flick.

Like a Halloween cat silhouetted against the black sky, Flick's patched figure arched. He held his signal hand high.

As if they knew, the crickets ceased their music.

The hand came down.

The bottoms of the garbage cans were flipped up. Fermenting beer bottles tinkled. Dirty bean cans rattled. Blood-soaked meat paper gushed. The sickening sounds avalanched down the steep roof and snarled at the quiet night.

Holding the cans, Flick and Breed waited until the sounds quit. Then, they freed the empty tin garbage cans. Like the final symbol clashes of a misguided orchestra, the cans rolled hollow and rumbled off the roof. And the startling sounds reechoed, sending more unwanted noise into the summer night.

Nodding his head with satisfaction, Screwball stood on the peak of the garage roof and admired the mess. "That'll teach that monkey-ass-face to run over my bike!"

Porch lights of the surrounding houses sporadically blinked on. Flick pointed to the ground. They leaped off the roof and landed on the dew-covered grass. The faint sound of a truck engine filtered in and out of the night. Lard Man's bathroom light didn't snap on. Flick took one step to run, but slipped on the wet grass. He regained his balance. In an instant, they were off, running.

Right on cue, the choir of smiling-faced dogs ran to the ends of their chains, stood on their circles of paw beaten paths, and barked at the sight of churning legs and escaping rear ends. A rapid succession of yellow porch lights blinked on. Inside houses, heads appeared in orange-lighted windows; and eyes searched into the dark.

Slowing to a walk, Breed and the others trooped out of the revealing light and plowed through the garbage-strewn alley. After kicking rotting lettuce off their worn shoes, they ran through the tall grass of alcoholic Toney's yard and sprinted toward his broken-down shack. Breed tripped over a beer bottle and landed next to a cracked car windshield that leaned against a stack of dirty cement blocks. He lay on the ground facing the mirror-like window. He was going to jump up, but motion on the window amazed him. Like little lighted windmills, reflections of his friend's legs ran in midair.

The amusing reflections disappeared but were replaced with a reflection of horror: Burkie's rotten-tooth face. Burkie was so close, Breed could smell his rotten tooth breath.

Burkie lifted the long sharp knife. "I'm gonna cut your ears off."

It had happened so fast and unexpectedly that Breed wasn't sure what he was seeing was real. But he wasn't taking any chances. He jerked to his hands and knees; and on all fours, he ran around the stack of cement blocks. Then he jumped up, grabbed the side of the stack of cement blocks, and pulled them over. As he raced after his friends, he looked back over his shoulder. Burkie tripped over the blocks and tumbled to the ground.

When Breed caught up with his friends, they zoomed through small alleyways, ran smack out of the darkness, passed little lines of rusty wire fences, and cut around streetlights that sparkled into the shadows.

Slowing, they cut into the tall weeds and trotted toward the edge of the road where Breed had hidden his motorbike. Breed wanted to take it home and put it under his porch, but something was wrong. He hoped Burkie wasn't hiding in the grass, waiting with his sharp knife.

Flick looked toward the road. He huffed once and whispered, "It's the cops." He held up his hand like a cavalry officer halting his troops. They all stopped and crouched down into the cover of the tall weeds.

Breed and the others watched. The police shined their spotlight on Breed's motorbike. The frame was bent into a banana shape, worse than Screwball's bike had been bent. The headlight had been smashed, and the broken spokes lay like pick-up-sticks. The motor, he had worked so hard on, was split wide open. Thick black oil oozed from the crankcase like an open wound. The spotlight from the police car went out.

47

"Hey, Hank," One-Finger-Burke said. "Something hit this motorbike."

"You won't want this," Hank said. "It's just junk."

One-Finger-Burke bent over, picked up the motorbike, and held it against his black and red flannel-shirted chest. "Let's throw it in the trunk so that little black-headed half-breed doesn't get it.

Breed gasp. They were going to take his motorbike. Cops or no cops he wasn't going to let them take it. He stood up. Flick grabbed him by the shoulder and pulled him down. Breed felt his jaw tighten. With his breath coming in quick breaths, he helplessly watched.

Hank waved his hand toward the ground. "Just leave it here. Rat Boy doesn't have any money to buy parts."

One-Finger-Burke shook his head. "We can't let his kind have anything this nice." He jerked his hand with the missing finger into the air. "That little bastard is good with his hands."

Looking at the motorbike, Hank smirked. "He'll still need parts."

Holding the bike, One-Finger-Burke paused then grunted. "They don't call him Rat Boy for nothin'. He'll snoop around like a rat. He'll dig out parts. He'll fix it again."

Hank's lips curled into a smile that looked like a snake's mouth. "So what? Let him fix it. He doesn't have a license for the bike. We'll just take it from him."

As if he were going to throw the bike on the ground, One-Finger-Burke loosened his grip.

Breed breathed easier, but Burke hesitated, then

he re-gripped the bike. A demented look formed on his face. "We can't. If he fixes it, it'll go to his head, make him screwy."

A sick, rotten feeling crawled from Breed's stomach and went into his chest. "What the—"

Flick waved his hand in front of Breed's face and whispered, "Quiet!"

Breed checked his speech and watched.

Hank opened the trunk. "Throw it in."

One-Finger-Burke threw Breed's motorbike into the trunk and jumped into the cruiser. The doors slammed shut. With the trunk lid flapping against the motorbike's chrome exhaust pipe, the car sped away.

Breed stood up. "What the hell does that one finger asshole mean? It'll make me screwy." He looked on the dark ground for something to throw.

Hog tossed a rock into the air and caught it. "You lookin' for this?"

Breed snatched the rock from Hog's hand. "Thanks."

Flick looked down the road. The red taillights on Burke's police car blinked to black. "It won't do any good to throw it now."

"That's right," Screwball said and shot Breed a crooked grin. "One-Finger-Burke and his pet monkey are gone."

Breed felt his red-brown face turn hard. He reared back and threw the rock toward where Burke's police cruiser had been. The rock sailed into the dark and landed on the empty road and let out a faint clunk. "Police officers my ass," Breed whined. "They're the ones screwy in the head." He realized he was about to cry. He turned away from his friends and shut his mouth. Sorrow replaced anger.

Experience has shown Breed that when something happen to other people, it was always different. If anybody else's dog had been hung, honest police would have arrested the murderer. If anybody else's motorbike had been run over, the police would have put it in the back of the police car and taken it back to the owner. But that hadn't happened with his motorbike. Trying to clear the thoughts from his head, he squeezed his eyes closed, but another thought plowed through. Any cop who would out-and-out steal a kid's motorbike didn't care about the people he was supposed to protect, and that meant the flats gang bullies were free to hang another dog. It also meant that Purple and Flat Top could use puppies for baseballs anytime they wanted. But what Breed feared most was that Burkie could cut his ears off and nothing would be done about it.

Now he knew how Screwball had felt when his bike had been run over. He told himself that rotten things had happened so many times that he should be used to it. But he wasn't.

By stealing Breed's bike, One-Finger-Burke had made off with Breed's ride to Shell Island. His way out of Traptown was gone.

Breed's anger subsided, but tears welled up in his eyes. He held his hand to his forehead. He couldn't cry now. Everybody would think he was a crybaby. He lowered his hand. With his thumb and forefinger, he secretly wiped the tears from his eyes.

Screwball cupped his hands to his mouth and pretended he was talking into a police car microphone. "What happened, Breed? Did you go screwy in the head?"

Breed wanted to tell him to blow it out his ass, but now that they both had had their bikes run over, he felt a sort of brotherhood. He kicked the ground and forced a smile. "Yeah, this damn Traptown makes everybody screwy in the head."

"That ain't no lie," Flick said. "But we're gonna find a way to get out of this shit hole."

Breed looked toward the weeds where his motorbike had been. "Maybe if I would have hidden it better, they wouldn't have taken it."

Flick placed a hand on Breed's shoulder. "Don't be stupid, Breed. Somebody drug it out of the weeds and deliberately ran it over."

Screwball pointed to the skid marks in the gravel at the side of the road. "You can see where they dragged it."

"Maybe it was Lard Man," Hog said. "He might have seen us in his yard and snuck out while we were there."

"That's right," Breed said. "He could have snuck out and just threw it in front of his car, ran over it, and drove back to his house."

Flick nodded in thought. "Come to think of it, I did hear a motor running when we were there."

"The way the bike was smashed," Hog said, "it looked like he ran over it a couple of times."

A swishing sound breezed into the night. All eyes turned toward the sound. A voice came from the tall grass in front of Toney's shack. "Did you get the number of that truck?"

A kid in a gray beret with a brass trumpet tucked in his belt walked out.

51

"Hey," Flick said and smiled. "It's Blo." He stepped toward Blo; and putting his arm around his shoulder, he intentionally shifted Blo's beret. "How long were you in there?"

Blo tilted his head away and shrugged Flick's arm off his shoulder. "Long enough to watch that black panel truck run over Breed's motorbike." He adjusted the gray beret on his head, making it tilt to one side and droop down over his right ear.

Being careful not to bump Blo's beret, Breed hunched his shoulders and leaned toward him. "Did you see who it was?"

Blo put his hand on his chin. His brows pulled down in concentration. "Probably Lard Man." He paused. "Didn't see who was driving though." He dropped his hand from his chin. Excited, his eyes opened wide. "Want me to roust him out?"

"That's okay, Blo," Flick said with a weary tone to his voice. "We're hangin' it up for the night."

Blo pulled the trumpet from his belt, put it to his lips, and belted out a low blast.

Signaling Blo to stop, Flick waved his hand downward. "Don't get the cops back here."

"Ahh, come on," Blo said. "Let's get Lard Man one more time."

As if he were holding an invisible bag, Hog held up his hand. "Another possum in the bag trick?"

Blo smiled a mischievous smile. "Nothin' will ever be as good as that. But let's get him anyway."

As if he were going to change his mind, Flick paused, but shook his head. "It's late. Maybe tomorrow."

"Hey, Blo," Breed said. "Put everybody to sleep. Play 'Taps' like you used to."

Blo's chin sunk deep into his chest. "I can't."

Screwball jerked his head toward Blo. "Why Not?"

Blo didn't answer. As if he were in pain, he slowly turned and walked toward Toney's shack. As the tall grass swished against his legs and whispered to silence, the gathering darkness swallowed him.

The gang didn't say good-by or goodnight. As Screwball would say, "What for? When I'm gone, you'll know I have left."

The gang split up and slipped away.

The dogs quit barking and crawled through the chain-worn entrances of their wooden dog boxes. "To save money on electric bills," the lights of the neighborhood were turned off.

All was quiet, again.

Breed liked it when Blo played "Taps". Hoping he might play them tonight, he hid in the shadows and waited.

Blo swished out of the tall grass, stepped into the street, and held the dented trumpet to his lips. He was going to finally play "Taps", again.

Holding the trumpet high; and with the gray beret tilted on his head like an emblem granting him the right to play his trumpet anytime or anywhere he wanted, Blo proudly marched from streetlight to streetlight, wailing, loud, sour, painful notes. He wasn't playing "Taps," but he was blasting all the quiet from the night.

Between the blasts, an excited housewife yelled to her husband. "Get up! Someone's out there. Go out and see who it is. Get up!"

Her husband woke up bitching. "There's idiots out there on them roofs. Ther' out there, runin' around in that goddamn moonlight. I'll bet my whole damn paycheck one of those little smart-mouth kids found a way to turn it on just so they can pull their nightly horseshit."

A light flicked on and shined out the opened bedroom window. Breed slunk under the white shaft of light and ran into a wooden clothesline prop. It fell. The steel clothesline sprang back. Thong! It bounced against his throat. He pulled the line from his neck, but jumped into the light.

"There goes one now," her husband yelled. "Get me my shotgun. I'll blow his long-haired head off."

Breed broke into a run.

"Son-of-a-bitch!" Blasted from the window.

"Honey, did you hit your toe?"

"Ahh! The hell with it! I have to go to work in the morning. Turn off the light and go to sleep!"

Breed made it home without getting a butt full of rock salt, but it was late. If he got caught coming in late, he would get beat with the belt. He climbed up the porch pole, pulled himself up on the roof, and snuck into his bedroom window.

Sleep didn't come easy. After he forced the thought of his dead dog out of his mind, he remembered the nights he had dreamed about riding to Shell Island on his motorbike. He remembered the days of hack sawing wobbly garbage-scummed steel. He remembered the weeks of throwing out parts and digging them back out of the garbage. He remembered the endless days of trial and error.

Under the covers, he felt the scars on his hands. Maybe he should have never tried to build anything. Then, he wouldn't have cut his fingers. Then he wouldn't have pinched the palms of his hands and turned them blue and red. Then he wouldn't have scraped his knuckles trying to work with tools that had been used beyond their lifetime limit.

Everything on his motorbike had been rigged. All his friends had told him, "It was impossible to build." But he had built it anyway, made it out of junk. And even though it was gone, he was still glad he had built it.

Now, he wondered if it would have been better if he never had figured out how to make things out of junk. Then things would be like they were when he didn't have anything, and he didn't have anything to lose.

He began to drift off to sleep. A vision of Purple's dirty pimple-face coming at him with a rope jerked him wide-awake. With his eyes wide with fright, he realized that even if he had nothing, those flats gang bullies would still beat him up, and Burkie would still be hiding someplace, waiting to cut his ears off.

He closed his eyes again. Pretty soon he wouldn't have to be afraid anything. He had sent for the Joe Lewis boxing book. But until that came, he still had his BB gun.

Chapter 4

Tick! Something hit the weathered clapboards on the side of Breed's house. He stirred under his thin covers and opened one eye. The hole in the wall where the plaster lath showed through was still there. A crumbling black wire hung down from the water-stained ceiling. A lone light bulb hung on its end. It had burned out so long ago that it had a thick layer of gray dust on it. The cracked, lopsided door was still closed, and the worn brown linoleum on the floor showed no signs of footprints. Nothing was different or out of place. With morning light streaming through the window, he closed his eye and drifted back to sleep.

Tick! There it was again. This time Breed opened both eyes. A shrill whistle filled the air. Alarmed, he jerked himself fully awake, sat up, and stuck his head out the open bedroom window.

As if he were aiming a rifle, Flick stood in the middle of the road, held his arms up, and pointed his elbow out to the side. He wanted Breed to get his BB gun and come down for target practice. Breed whistled down and gestured with his middle finger. As an exaggerated sneer spread across his face, Flick wrinkled his nose and curled his upper lip. He knew Breed would be down.

Breed sprang out of bed, jumped into his cloths, and ran down the worn wooden stairs. He stopped in the yellow-brown kitchen and opened the cupboard. Except for an empty tipped over box of oatmeal, it was empty. He looked at the stove. As if they were waiting for a big event, a black iron skillet and a blue can of lard sat there. He turned.

A half a loaf of stale bread lay on the table. It was Saturday. The stale bread would be dinner. If this day turned out to be a typical day with Flick, Breed wouldn't be home to eat that bread fried with lard. He wouldn't be home when his mother and father would fight and fill the kitchen with chaos. He was sick of eating lard bread. To him it was just pig lard for a kid trapped in Traptown.

He walked toward the screen door. The blue-gray cat brushed up against his leg and meowed for something to eat. Breed put his hand on the handle of the screen door, but he didn't open it. The faded words scrawled on an old sign he had seen in the dump flashed in his mind: 'IF YOU AIN'T GOT NO MONEY, YOU ALREADY ATE'.

Breed didn't have any money. The steel mill was still on strike, and his father would be down on the strike line drinking homemade wine and eating turtle soup or something another striker killed and brought in. There would be no food brought into the house today.

Breed turned and looked at the bread. "Ahh, man," he said out loud. "No use going around lightheaded. Any food is better than no food."

He stuffed a piece of the dry bread into his mouth, and the cat purred and clawed at his leg. He tore off a piece of bread and dropped it in front of the cat. The cat chomped down on the bread, held it in its mouth, and growled.

Breed stepped to the iron-stained, porcelain sink and turned the calcium-crusted brass faucet. Below his feet, somewhere in the dark cellar, pipes groaned and rattled. The cat stopped eating. With the bread in its mouth, it looked up and drew its ears back. Then it dropped the bread from its mouth and hissed. Keeping his eye on the cat, Breed bent over the yellowed sink, sucked in a stream of water, and shut the green oxidized valve off. The pipes complained one more time and stopped.

The cat mouthed the bread. In a blue-gray blur, it ran under the table. Breed chewed the disgusting bread, forced it down his throat, and shuddered. He shook his head and waltzed across the linoleum floor that had been worn past the pressed layers of rosin-powered cork and pigments clean down to the dirty-black burlap backing. He pushed on the side of the fly-covered screen door. The rusty spring stretched and screeched. As if they had been shocked, flies danced away. He opened the door, scooted out, and let the dark green wood of the screen door slap behind him.

Outside, with the birds signaling occasional peeps, he walked across the cracked stone sidewalk and around the corner of the front porch. With the warm sun reflecting off the huge brass safety pin on the front of his brown-leather World War II pilot hat, Flick stood at the side of the road.

Breed had always hated hats. Hats were for the rich kids. Hats were for the well-washed peanut gallery type kids who had televisions to watch and watched hours of it. Hats were for kids who had nothing better to do than to stare out from under their curved baseball caps and wine to their mothers, "What's there to do?" Hats were for crybabies.

Flick wasn't a crybaby. His hat was different. The frayed flapping earmuffs that he turned away from his ears, made his hat look like something a

58

hero would wear. It accented his red hair, but it didn't match his typical slum neighborhood clothes. He was a wiry kid. If you didn't cross him, he was easy to get along with. The pilot hat didn't change that.

Flick leaped over the sewage ditch in front of the house. "Where's the BB gun, Breed?"

Breed smiled big. "You're right on top of it." He watched Flick to see if he could find it.

Now that his motorbike was gone, Breed loved his BB gun more than before. He felt his gun was like a last piece of gold in a raided treasure chest. It was against the law for a kid his age to have a BB gun, but he had found a way to hide it.

When the small wooden footbridge in front of his house had broken, he had fallen into the sewage ditch and landed knee deep into black stinking sewage. He got mad and dragged an old hot water tank all the way from Toney's junk pile. Then he banged a heavy sledgehammer on a dull cold chisel until he had cut off the ends of that thick steel tank. With a pointed shovel, he dug the stinking sewage out of the ditch and rolled the open-ended tank into the hole. Off to the side of the tank, he stacked stones and a few bricks and built a small tunnel, just big enough to hide the gun. He covered the tank and the secret hiding place with dirt and purple ashes from the coal furnace.

Flick stood on top of the driveway and looked at the ash-covered tank. Just a tiny speck of the stock of the BB gun stuck out the end of the secret tunnel. A bright spark of energy shone in his green eyes. "I see it."

He held on to the mailbox post, bent over,

reached into the hiding place, put his finger around the trigger, and pulled out the gun. He examined it from end to end and glanced at the sewer ditch. "You sure picked a good place to hide it."

Breed smiled with satisfaction. "I knew no one would go snooping around right next to that sinkin' sewage."

Flick inspected the gun for signs of black sewage. "It'll stink for a while." He waved it back and forth. "But there ain't any on it."

Breed glanced toward the mailbox. "Did the mailman come?"

"There ain't no mail," Flick said. "He already went, didn't even stop."

Breed was disappointed, but he didn't want Flick to know it. He felt himself start to shrug with disappointment. To hide his revealing gesture, he straightened up.

Flick raised the gun and aimed across the road at an empty beer can. "That's too easy." He lowered the gun. "Were you expecting something in the mail?"

"No," Breed lied. "I was just wondering."

But he was expecting something: A boxing book written by Heavyweight Champion, Joe Louis. Once the book came, he was going to secretly learn how to box. He wouldn't be learning the everyday boxing techniques that just about anyone could learn. He would be learning how to box like a world champion. He didn't want anyone to know about it, but in a short while, he wouldn't have taken crap from anybody. A few years back, he had studied and gotten an 'A' on his report card. When Flick and his friends had seen it, they pointed and laughed, called him, "Teacher's suck ass". If they knew he was reading books, not only would they call him a teacher's suck ass, they would call him an *A student*, treat him like he was a candy ass. It would save him a lot of trouble if he kept the book a secret.

He walked across the road, placed dirty chunks of gravel on the empty beer can, and looked back at Flick. "Try and shoot those off."

Flick gave the gun a quick shake. A few BB's swished up and down in the chamber. "Got any more BB's?"

Breed felt his usual pang of poverty. He sloughed it off. "Nope! Ain't got no money."

"Don't sweat it," Flick said with triumph in his voice. "We'll be rich some day . . . honest Injun'." He cocked his pilot hat back on his head, turned his cheek to the wooden stock of the rifle, and took aim.

Breed placed his hand on Flick's shoulder and tugged. "Wait, a car's coming."

Flick dropped the barrel of the rifle. Down the street a 1956 pink Ford with expensive glass-packed mufflers purred at cruising speed.

Impatiently tapping his foot and looking up, Flick stood at the side of the road. "Come on, go past."

The engine of the car growled under the hood. Its purring mufflers exploded into a raging roar. The speed of the car increased, raced right at them. Inside, a lone driver hunched over the steering wheel and held his middle finger next to the windshield.

Flick stood shock-still.

Breed yelled, "He's trying to hit us."

As if he had just come out of a temporary trance, Flick jerked to action. Amid the deafening roar of the engine and the roaring mufflers, Breed and Flick jumped over the sewage ditch. The car sped past, shot a gust of wind onto their backs. Breed turned and watched the fleeing Ford. As the rumbling mufflers faded in the distance, contempt replaced his fear.

He jumped over the ditch and back onto the road. "You think he would've hit us?"

"I don't know," Flick said. "If he comes back, stand in the road and see." Giggling, he jumped over the ditch, raised the BB gun, and shot at the gravel on the can.

"Wait," Breed said. "Another car's coming."

Flick lowered the gun. "Ah, man. What is this, Grand Central Station?"

A 1956 yellow Buick cruised up the hill and stopped in front of the beer can.

Flick and Breed sat on the edge of the sewage ditch. Flick took a deep breath and exhaled a disgusted sigh. "The shooting range is shut down."

Breed knew who was in the Buick, and he didn't even want to look at him. He lowered his head and waited for the Buick to move.

It didn't.

Lard Man sat inside the idling Buick. The front of his unbuttoned clean white suit coat revealed the steering wheel burrowed deep into his Jell-O belly.

As if the Buick were a bothersome fly, Flick waved his hand in a shooing gesture. "Come on, Lard Man." He moaned. "Get out of the way."

Exhaust fumes stung Breed's eyes. He turned

his head from the fumes and blew air from his mouth. "He ain't gonna move until he starts something."

Lard Mad stayed behind the steering wheel. Staring forward, he reached out his chubby hand; and with his thumb and forefinger, he held the ignition key for a half a minute before he twisted it and turned the motor off. Noisily clearing his throat, he adjusted the gearshift lever and jammed the shifting linkage into reverse. Then, he applied the emergency brake; and to make sure the Buick would not move, he rocked his heavy body back and forth in the seat.

Breed figured Lard Man was finally going to get out of the Buick but he didn't. As if he were going through some mandatory check list, he checked the mirrors, made sure the radio was turned off, pushed the headlight switch, looked in the rear view mirror, straightened his suit coat, cleared his throat, opened the door, turned, placed his fat shiny-shoed foot on the road, grunted from the strain, and stepped out.

Flick cupped his hand in front of his face and whispered to Breed. "He did everything else. When's he gonna start the dog and pony show?"

As if he were trying to cast an image of importance, Lard Man stood tall and tried to put on a stone face, but a devious grin broke through his monkey butt face. He tightened his jaw. The grin vanished. Looking down at Breed and Flick, he talked with authority. "What the hell do you kids think you're doing?"

Breed and Flick didn't show him the courteously of standing up. They sat on the ground and looked away.

Lard Man cleared his throat and raised his voice. "I'm talking to you!" He raised his hand and jerked his finger at them. "You little bastards."

Breed shook his head in an it-figures manner and Flick glared at Lard Man. But they didn't answer.

Lard Man grunted with irritation and shouted, "Did you hear me?" His bearded, blubbery face quivered with the effort.

They didn't answer.

Lard Man tucked his billowing shirt into his pants. Flab around his enormous waist oozed over his tight belt and hung downward like thick sludge. "What do you kids think you are doing?"

Flick snickered at Lard Man's hanging fat. "Target practice."

Lard man shook his puffy-pink finger at Flick. "Wipe that smirk off your face! You know it's against the law to be shooting across a public road?" With his face simmering and his stomach expanding and contracting with labored breathing, he waddled around his Buick.

"Well don't get excited and have a heart attack," Flick advised the sweating lard man.

The act of Lard Man running over Screwball's bike and the possibility that he had run over his motorbike, burned in Breed's mind. He jutted his chin out and sneered. "Since when do you care about the law?"

Lard Man pointed to his own face with his thumb. "Don't tell me about the law." He puffed up his sunken chest. "I belong to the Policeman's Association."

As if he were going to fight, Flick handed the BB gun to Breed, stood up, and waved his hand at Lard Man. "Didn't your association tell you it's against the law to run over our bikes?"

Lard Man cast a defiant stare at Flick's waving hand. "I didn't run over your junk motorbike."

Now Breed knew Lard Man had ran over his motorbike. He jumped to his feet. "If you didn't run over it, then how do you know it was a motorbike?"

Flick jerked his finger toward Lard Man. "Yeah. How do you know?"

Lard Man shook his stubby finger in Flick's face. "I know what I said. You're not going to make a circus out of this."

Flick smiled an exaggerated smile. "If a circus is too big for you, how about if we make a little carnival out of it?"

Lard Man shook his finger, faster. "Don't start your smart mouth with me! You goddamn kids need your asses kicked from here to China, puff—, puff—. If you were my age, I would be just the man to do it!"

Flick backed away from Lard Man's aiming finger. "Why don't you get your monkey-ass face away from us, before you trip over your balloon belly and your round body rolls down the hill?"

As Breed nonchalantly waved the BB gun from side to side, in his mind, he could see the round lard man rolling down the street. Like a peek-a-boo game, his monkey-ass mouth was yelling, and his puffed-up red face flashed with each revolution. Breed tried to hold back the laughter. He couldn't. A laugh, ha-ha'ed out.

Lard Man's face contorted. His fat-framed eyes glared in Breed's direction. "And you . . . you little half-breed, what the hell are you doing with that gun? You're not even allowed to have a gun at your age."

"It's only a BB gun," Flick snapped back, paused, and grinned. "We're not big game hunting."

Lard Man looked as if he had been slapped. He held his palm out toward Breed. "Be a good boy. Hand over the gun."

With comforting realization that Lard Man was too fat to run with threatening speed, Breed stood next to the Buick, held out the gun, and waved it in front of him. "Well come here and take it off me, Humpty Dumpty!"

Lard Man grabbed for the gun.

Breed jerked it back.

Lard Man missed. He clinched his fist into a fat ball and shook it at Breed. "Let me catch you. I'll Humpty Dumpty your ass."

Breed shuffled to the back of the Buick, nonchalantly leaned on the trunk, crossed his legs, and waited.

Lard Man leaned against the door of the Buick. Then he looked away from Breed and appeared to calm down. But Breed knew he would try to weasel close. He looked left. Lard Man panted for breath and inched his stubby feet toward Breed. Breed continued leaning on the trunk, crossed his arms, and let the BB gun lay across them. He looked off to his right, but he could see Lard Man inching closer. He didn't move. Acting as if he didn't see him coming, he talked into the air. "Just roll down the hill, round man."

Lard Man slithered closer. When he was close enough to grab the gun, he telegraphed his great move: He lunged. Breed took one step and slipped away. Lard Man's slow reaching hand only grabbed air. He lost his balance and fell against the side of the Buick. To keep his wobbly balance, he grabbed the fender. Huffing, he looked up at Breed. "Come here you little black-headed bastard!"

Breed shook the BB gun. "Come and get me."

Lard Man straightened up and waddled after him. Using the Buick as a shield, Breed moved back and forth. He allowed Lard Man to toddle just close enough to make him think he could catch him and dashed away. And it kept Lard Man trying.

After a few more failed attempts, Lard Man stopped trying to catch him. Breed stood next to the right front tire. Lard Man stood next to the left front tie. Lard man reached across the hood of the Buick; and like an animated cartoon, he turned his palm up, jerked it in a begging gesture, and pleaded. "Give me that gun!"

Shaking his head, Breed smiled directly into his face.

Lard Man lunged and lost his balance. His hand thumped on the hood of his Buick, and the bottom of his suit jacket rode up the past the top of his wide ass.

Breed ran to the Lard Man's side of the Buick, stopped, looked right in Lard Man's pink puffing face, and said clear and distinct, "You ain't getin' it."

Lard Man looked down the front of his suit coat and straightened it. With the veins on the side of his forehead bulging, he looked up and yelled, "Don't tell me, I ain't getting it. Give me that goddamn gun!"

Breed smiled a mocking smile in his direction, held it, and softly said, "No."

Lard Man assumed a posture of superiority. "They might as well throw you in jail right now, save the trouble later. You'll just grow up to be a drunk like your old man."

Breed knew Lard Man was trying to get him angry by bringing his father into the scene. His father drank too much sometimes, but all the mill workers did. Whisky was the only thing that cut the cancer-causing mill dust that had collected in their throats. To show that his verbal dig hadn't work, Breed didn't turn away or lower his head in shame. He kept his smile directed right into Lard Man's Face. "Well, Mister Dumpty, I'd rather be a drunk than a puffed-up lard-ass trying to impersonate a human being."

Apparently Lard Mad didn't catch on that Breed was still calling him Humpty Dumpty by using Dumpty as Humpty Dumpty's last name. A shadow of confusion shone on Lard Man's face. "You're just a waste of life," he said. "You'll land in jail."

Breed pointed to his own ear and twirled his finger around in a circle. "You're crazy. You ain't no authority of the future."

"I don't have to be an authority on anything," Lard Man bellowed. "I see your kind every day.

Breed felt his forehead wrinkle with confusion.

"That's right," Lard Man said and smiled. "You're in the newspaper, right on the front page."

Flick leaned against the opposite side of the Buick. "Hey, Lard Man. You're the one who should be on the front page for being the world's fattest man."

"Sorry Lard Man," Breed said, and pointed to Lard Man's stomach. "You'll never make the front page. They put the funnies in the back."

Flick laughed and Breed giggled.

"You might laugh now," Lard Man said, "but you won't be laughing later." He stared at Breed. As Breed watched the hate grow in Lard Man's fixed gray eyes, Lard Man continued. "The good people of this town won't think it's a joke when they have to waste their hard-earned tax money to keep your black ass in jail."

"Why don't you go back to the fat farm?" Flick said, and Lard Man made another sluggish attempt to catch Breed.

Breed slipped away. "Sorry, Mister Dumpty, not even close."

Lard Man must have realized Dumpty was Humpty Dumpty's last name. His face tensed with a spasm of irritation.

With his knees bent and his feet pointed outward, Flick stuck out his stomach and walked around the Buick. Then he bent his arms at the elbows, puffed up his cheeks, and pointed at his stuck out stomach.

Breed laughed at Flick's imitation of Lard Man.

Lard Man opened his mouth to say something, but relaxed his face. He opened the car door, stood there and shook his chubby finger. "I'll make sure your kind never have anything. I'm going home. I'm calling One-Finger-Burke."

69

"Go ahead," Flick said and waved his hand into the air. "Tell that crooked cop anything you want to. We don't care."

Lard man's face cramped with mean lines of hostility. "You're probably the two creeps that rape little girls and cut their ears off." His mouth curled into a vehement sneer. "If One-Finger-Burke can't take care of you little smart-mouthed bastards, I'll find someone who will." As if he didn't want anyone to hear what he was saying, he shifted his eyes uneasily and talked low. "And you're not going to like it."

Breed wondered if Burkie was the one cutting little girl's ears off, but he didn't want One-Finger-Burke coming around. When he did, he always ruined the whole day.

"We ain't doin' nothin'," Breed said in a nice tone of voice.

Lard Man didn't see Flick cup his hand and raise it to his mouth, but Breed did. *Don't do it.*

The over excited sweating Lard Man turned his back to get into the Buick and Flick did what he was named for. He 'flicked' a slimy, green hawker, underhanded, off the little finger side of his flicking hand. The hawker flew through the air and found its mark. It silently landed on the back of Lard Man's tailor-made white suit.

Lard Man plopped heavily into the seat. With the steering wheel burrowed into his overblown stomach, he slammed the door. Wiggling the jammed shifting linkage, he jerked the transmission into neutral and stepped on the gas. But the Buick didn't move. He pushed in the clutch and raced the engine. Blue smoke rushed out the tailpipe. He forced the shifting lever into low gear and let out the clutch. As the engine moaned, pissed off and perspiring in his freshly hawkered attire, Lard Man drove away

And the emergency brake was still on!

Flick smiled at Breed and imitated a little kid tattling to his mother. "Maw! He's flickin' hawkers on me!"

Shooting at the gravel on the beer can, their laughter sporadically continued, but the BB's dwindled. They sifted dirt through their fingers and searched for already shot BB's.

Breed scooped up a handful of dirt. "I feel like a bum diggin' out cheap BB's that we should be able to buy."

Flick wiped his dirty hands on his pants. "We got to find—" he started to say but stopped. Tires screeched. "Now what?"

Breed turned his head toward the sound. "It's that pink Ford."

The Ford had returned. It slid to a halt at the shoulder of the road. Breed looked inside. Looking like a painted prostitute, a girl sat next to the driver. The driver whispered something in her ear. She laughed and exposed her crooked teeth. Her face flushed for a moment; and as if she were embarrassed about her crooked teeth, she held her hand in front of her mouth. The doors of the Ford swung open. Not moving or leaning forward, the driver and the girl stayed in the front seat.

An older kid, who looked like a squalid undertaker from a horror movie, squeezed through the small space behind the front seat and the door jam and stumbled out. He straightened up, tensed his face; and as if he owned it, he surveyed the area.

Flick held the BB gun like a soldier about to engage in combat and turned his head toward Breed. "There was only one kid in that Ford when it went past."

A wave of dread crept into Breed's chest. "Yeah, I know. He must've gone to get help."

Flick tensed his body. "They're looking for an easy fight, but there's only two of them. Get ready."

The driver, a blond kid with greenish skin and a purple-pimple face stepped out of the Ford. Breed knew there would be trouble. It was Purple, the kid who had batted the puppies. The front seat on the driver's side of the Ford flipped down. Like a snake, Flat Top, who had been hiding in the back seat, slithered out.

The girl slid over to the driver's side and turned toward Breed. Then she let her legs hang over rocker panel and watched.

Purple tore off his five-and-ten-cents-store shirt, held it in his hand, and stepped toward Flick. "What the hell did you shoot at my car for?"

Flick cocked the BB gun with a threatening snap of his wrist. "We didn't shoot anything at your car!"

With Flat Top hovering behind him, Purple turned and threw his cheap shirt at the girl. "Hold this, honey."

She caught the shirt and held it in front of her crooked-toothed smile.

Purple turned toward Flick and repeated, "What the hell did you shoot at my car for?"

Flick repeated, "We didn't shoot anything at

your car!"

Breathing in deep, Purple expanded his chest. His size small T-shirt molded to his skin. "You calling me a liar?"

Flick waved the barrel of the gun from side to side. "I ain't callin' you nothin'."

Purple's greenish skin and purple pimples seemed to fit his sickening aura of dislike. His very presence gave Breed the creeps.

"It isn't our fault that you look like you've just been dug up out of a grave," Breed said, and then he knew another reason why he didn't like Purple. Not only was Purple the creep who had batted those puppies down by the railroad tracks, he was the creep in his nightmares. He was the one who had hung his dog. Purple was evil.

Through blood-shot eyes, Purple fiercely stared at Breed. "Dug up out of a grave?" he questioned. "What are you trying to do, Rat Boy?" He let out an icy growl. "Be some kind of a smart ass?" He clinched his fist.

Breed forced a thin smile. "I didn't mean it."

"I suppose you didn't mean to shot at my car."

Flick put his finger on the trigger of the BB gun. "Like I said, we didn't shoot nothin' at your goddamn car!"

Breed studied the other two kids. A hawk nose stood out on the narrow face kid who looked like an undertaker, and Flat Top's haircut and brown freckles, reminded Breed that Flat Top had been the third baseman at the puppy-killing baseball game.

These kids were just too big to fight. Worse than that, they weren't right in the head. Anyone who played baseball with puppies would be

73

mentally mean. They wouldn't fight fair. Breed needed something to even the odds. He glanced at a broken brick at the edge of the driveway. With his fingers tingling with adrenaline, he slunk toward the brick.

With the steel cleats on the heels of his shoes clicking on the pavement, Flat Top walked toward Flick.

Breed bent over and reached for the brick.

Flat Top bolted away from Flick.

Before Breed could grab the brick, Flat Top tromped down on his hand and turned his foot. The hard leather and steel cleats on the bottom of Flat Top's shoe dug into the back of Breed's hand and caused dirt and gravel to cut into his palm.

Flat Top lifted his foot and grabbed Breed's arm. Breed jerked to get free, but he couldn't break the grip. Flat Top yanked on Breed's arm and wrapped it around his back. Each time Breed moved, Flat Top lifted the arm up against the joint. Breed winced with pain and fought to escape. Flat Top lifted the arm higher, and kicked at Breed's legs. The steel cleats on his shoes stuck glancing blows to the bones of Breed's shins. Pain shot up his legs and burned into his brain. Blood flowed down his legs. He quit squirming and turned away. Flat Top quit kicking and punched Breed in the kidney. Pain like he had never felt before, radiated to his back, traveled to his lungs, and sucked out the air. He gasped for breath. Flat Top lowered him to the ground and held him by the back of the neck.

Hovering over Flick, Purple stood with his legs apart, bouncing, and his fists shaking with nervous anticipation. He stopped bouncing and smiled at

Flat Top. "This is gonna be easy."

Flick turned to run. Undertaker circled behind. Flick was trapped. Like a sleazy landlord about to raise the rent, Purple smiled.

Flick took two steps back and stopped. He needed an escape opening. His panic-filled eyes darted in all directions. There was none. He would have to fight. He re-cocked the BB gun. It snapped with authority.

Purple moved closer.

Flick lifted the gun and pointed the barrel right on Purple's eye. "Touch me. I'll shoot!"

"Go ahead, big man! See what happens."

Flick dropped the gun barrel and slowly backed off. The gun was empty. He turned and stepped away from Purple.

Undertaker shoved him back.

Purple smiled.

"What are you smiling for?" Flick asked.

"Who wants to know?"

Flick shrugged. "I was just wondering," he said and paused. "Cause you look like a smiling shit salesman with samples in your mouth."

That was the wrong thing to say. But maybe Flick knew what he was doing. Maybe he was trying to distract Purple so he could run.

Flat Top's grip loosened on Breed's neck. Breed jerked and tried to jump to freedom. Flat Top lifted him off his feet and shouted, "Quit moving, you black-headed Rat Boy!" His beer and cigarette breath blasted into Breed's face.

Trying to distract Purple, Breed yelled back, "Hey, turd breath. Blow it out your ass."

Flat Top's face filled with irritation. With no

warning, he drove his fist into Breed's ribs. Air escaped from his lungs and was replaced with pain. Those kicks started again.

With his fist hung low and ready to strike upward, Purple waded toward Flick. Flick tossed the BB gun to the right. It swished into a little stand of tall grass. For a brief second, Purple looked toward the gun. Flick jumped to the left. Breed thought his diversion had worked, but Flick bounced off Undertaker who had snuck up behind him. Flick dug his feet into the dirt at the side of the road and stood, ready to fight.

A whirl of punches filled the air. Purple's fists battered Flick's body. Blood flew. Flick floundered backwards. Just before he would have fallen, his feet hit the pavement. He regained his stance. Purple wound up for a bone crushing strike. Flick ducked and bobbed his head. Purple's headhunting fist plowed the air. Flick stepped aside, swung from the ground up. His fist sunk deep into soft flesh and plowed up under Purple's unprotected floating rib. In pain, Purple bent over sideways. Flick stepped to strike again. Before he could deliver the powerful blow, Undertaker reached out and grabbed his fist. Flick turned his back to Undertaker. Behind his back, Purple wound up and swung down. Thump! A low base sound from the sneaky fist slamming into Flick's back pounded in Breed's chest.

Air rushed from Flick's lungs. Gasping for air, he bent over.

Purple stood over him and puffed up his chest. "That'll teach your smart ass."

Somewhere in the distance, a siren wailed.

Flat Top threw Breed to the ground. Breed reached out to cushion his fall with his hands. But when he hit, sharp gravel dug into his palms. With his hands bleeding, he picked up the brick and staggered to his feet.

The three bullies ran for the Ford. Flick reached into the tall stand of grass, snapped up the BB gun, and bolted toward the escaping Purple. The girl had released the brake and put the transmission in neutral. She was steering the coasting Ford. With the doors open, it slowly rolled down the street. As Flat top and Undertaker dove into the back, the girl scooted over but kept steering. She turned he head toward Purple and shouted, "Come on, honey, jump in before the police come."

Purple caught up and jumped in the driver's side. Trying to steer the Ford, he stretched his arm out to close the door. Breed lifted the brick over his head. He wanted to throw it, but Flick was in the way. He waited for an opening. For savage striking power, Flick grabbed the BB gun by the end of the barrel and lifted it high. It flew down. A glancing blow from the tip of the stock dented the Ford's roof. Then it smashed down on Purple's shoulder. The wooden stock snapped off and clunked on the road.

A sharp pain pinged in Breed's chest. He didn't have a BB gun anymore. As if it had been knocked from his hand, the brick dropped to the ground.

Purple yelled, "Stop the car. They dented the roof."

"The cops are coming," Flat Top said. "But it don't matter. He gave us enough money to fix it

77

and drink all night."

The doors on the Ford slammed shut. Its engine started. In a rush to speed away, Purple didn't shift the transmission out of neutral. He raced the motor. The glass-packs roared. The Ford continued to slowly roll. Flick held the barrel of the broken gun and stood beside Breed. As if it were another humiliating gesture, the pink Ford's exhaust fumes blasted into their faces. Letting the engine slow, Purple sifted into low gear, then revved the engine again and let out the clutch. Whitewall tires caught on the dry pavement and burned briefly. Skeek! Echoed into the air, and the Ford sped away.

Breed hated those stupid skeeks. Every time he got beat up, those bullies from the flats gang always skeeked those stupid tires. When the Joe Louis boxing book came in the mail he would learn how to box like a world champion. Then those creeps wouldn't be coming around beating him up. They wouldn't be celebrating by skeeking those tires. They would be picking their teeth out of the gutter. For a moment he was satisfied with the thought of how he could get revenge, but then he realized that the flats gang kids never started anything unless there were three or more of them. Boxing was one on one, a fair way to fight, but the Flats gang never fought fair.

Flick reared back and flung the broken gun into the sewer. Then he jumped over the ditch, sat on the ground, and leaned his head against the dirty-white picket fence. With blood dripping from his nose and onto his unbuttoned shirt, his unruly red hair spilled over his brow; and his chin set in a sullen pucker. He was on the verge of tears, but he took a deep breath, shuddered, and shook it off.

Breed knew it wasn't the beating that hurt. It was the feeling of not being able to fight back that stuck in Flick's chest and kept boiling up in his throat. And what was coming up the hill made it worse. It was a police car. Before it got to Breed and Flick, it slowed to a crawl. The driver was Burke, the crooked cop. Loud enough for Breed and Flick to hear, Burke talked to his partner. "Look, Hank!" He pointed to Flick and Breed. "There's two hoodlums sittin' on their asses waitin' to go to jail."

Both cops laughed.

Burke increased speed and drove on.

At first, it seemed as if Burke's cutting remark didn't bother Flick, but a snarl of agony spread across his face. He held up his middle finger and jerked it in the direction of the fleeing police car.

In an effort to disguise his wounded feelings, Breed shrugged. "Hey!" he said with sudden realization. "Did you hear that flat top kid say, 'He gave us enough money to fix it and drink all night?'"

Nodding, Flick leaned forward in a helpless heap. "Lard Man must've paid them to beat us up."

Flick nursed his lips with the sleeve of his torn shirt and looked to Breed. "If we wanna get an even break, we gotta go someplace where nobody knows us. We gotta get a boat and go to Shell Island."

"We would've been out of here if Burke hadn't stolen my motorbike," Breed said and felt tears well up. He held them in; and to avoid eye contact, he looked at the World War II pilot hat that Flick wore on his head. The huge safety pin on it was open.

Flick lifted his clodhopper shoe and stomped it onto the dirt. "I'll pound that smart ass someday."

"Yeah, they're not so hot. You should've stuck that pin up his ass."

Flick kicked the splintered stock of Breed's gun into the sewer. "Just a bunch of smart-aleck kids showin' off for that crooked-toothed girl."

Breed watched his gunstock float in the black sewer water. He might be able to fix it, but right now he felt it would be useless. He just didn't care. "If I ever see that faggot Ford, those tires are gonna be flat."

Chapter 5

Crouching at the side of the road, Flick hung his head and tried to hide his tears. Breed walked across the road and crouched next to him, but before he could speak the guttural roar of a V-8 engine filled the air. Breed snapped his head to see what kind of car it was. Kicking up gravel and dirt, the '56 pink Ford thundered along the side of the road. It was rushing right at them.

In a fraction of a second, the Ford's chrome grill was in front of them and coming fast. Flick leaped up out of his crouch and stepped out of the way. Breed scrambled to get out of the way, but before he was fully erect the Ford's bumper was a foot away. Like a jack-in-the-box on a spring, he sprang from his crouching position and dove out of the path of the car. He avoided being hit, but the front bumper grazed the side of his pants. He hit the ground and rolled. Spinning tires shot a staccato of gravel towards his eyes. He threw his hands in front of his face. The gravel stung the backs of his hands and then stopped. Lying on his side, he watched through a cloud of dirt-filled dust.

Purple's sick laughter and the Ford sped away.

Breed crawled through the weeds, breathed in a lung full of dust, and grabbed Flick's shoulder. "You okay?" The fine dirt between his teeth ground like tiny abrasive stones.

Flick waved the dust away from his face. "I'm okay. Those guys don't play fair."

Trying to get the dirt from in between his teeth, Breed spit on the road. "There's something wrong with those kids."

Flick gave Breed a sidelong glance. "Anybody that tries to run somebody over has to have brain damage."

Breed felt the delayed nervous reaction, which comes after being scared, rise in his throat. His eyes teared up, but he didn't want Flick to see them. As if he were swishing dirt from his eyelids, he ran his finger over his eyes and secretly wiped away the tears. Swallowing, he forced the nervous feeling out of his throat. "If Screwball was here," he said and forced a smile, "he'd say they have drain damage."

Flick sprang up off the ground, brushed himself off, and straightened the huge safety pin on his hat. "Well, there goes the BB gun tournament. Let's go up to the corner. Screwball said he'd meet us there. He wants to go down the river and look for a boat."

Breed stood up. "I'm tired of getting beat up. Maybe those kids in that Ford will come back."

"So what?" Flick said. "Old Lady Vanko might have a pitchfork waiting for them."

Breed looked down the road. The Ford wasn't coming back, yet. "We should be safe for a little while. Those guys won't come near Vanko."

Flick shot Breed a crooked grin. "I don't see why not."

"Maybe because everybody knows her husband was a faggot."

"I never heard that," Flick said. "I heard that she poisoned him and her kid, too. Buried them in her back yard."

Breed shook his long hair. Fine dirt and dust filled the air around his face. He waved it away. "That could be true. When we stand there, Lard

Man doesn't even stop and mouth off."

Walking as if they had springs on their feet, they bounced up the long semi-steep road. Off to the right, little Jummy stood in his green lawn that had been cut with something Breed and Flick wished they had: A gasoline powered lawnmower.

As Jummy's shoes shimmered in the sun. Compared to Breed's and Flick's worn and tattered attire, his white shirt seemed out of place; and his hands and face didn't have a hint of dirt on them. And he had something Breed had never had: A fresh barbershop haircut.

Jummy excitedly waved at Breed.

Flick jerked his thumb toward Jummy. "How come that little kid always waves at you?"

Breed smiled in Jummy's direction. "I don't know." He paused. "He has a weird name, but he's okay."

"Too bad his parents won't let him out of the yard."

Jummy smiled.

Breed waved at him. "Yeah, it's like his yard's a jail."

Flick stopped bounce-walking and looked down at little Jummy. "How you doin'?"

"Okay," Jummy said back. "Where are you guys going?"

Flick pointed ahead. "Up the hill, wanna come?"

"Yeah, but I'll have to ask my mom first."

"Okay," Flick said, but walked away. He talked back over his shoulder. "We'll wait for you."

Jummy turned; and with his little shiny shoes blinking back the sun's rays, he ran into his house.

Flick and Breed didn't wait. They already knew Jummy's mother's answer. She looked out the window and deliberately bitched loud enough for Breed and Flick to hear. "You'll go nowhere with those hoodlums. They'll only get you into trouble. They won't even get a haircut."

"But Mummy!" Jummy pleaded.

"Shut up! You're not going anywhere with that long-haired half-breed."

The further away Breed and Flick walked, the louder Jummy's mother bitched.

They walked faster.

Breed turned and walked backwards. He looked at the window on the side of Jummy's house. Jummy's mother stuck her head out and bitched until her face turned whitish-blue.

Just to agitate, Breed put his hands over his ears and yelled, "What? I didn't hear you."

As if she had got caught doing something she was ashamed of, her face reddened; and she disappeared from the window.

Breed turned toward Flick. "I got my legs kicked in and lost my BB gun. "You got a bloody mouth, and now we gotta hear Jummy's old lady bitch at us."

Flick reached up and rubbed his ear. "With all that bitching, it's a wonder Jummy ain't deaf."

As if she had only stopped bitching long enough to catch her breath, Jummy's mother came back to the window and filled the empty air with more insults. Breed yelled once more, "What? I didn't hear you."

They put their hands over their ears and continued up the hill.

The area around the old wooden telephone pole on the corner of Vanko's land was a meeting place. Here, at the Ohio and Pennsylvania State line, the paved road formed a T and stopped. On the Ohio side, bushes and trees lined a yellow dirt road. Off to the right, a ways from the road, Vanko's garden grew in front of a broken-down chicken coup.

Breed and Flick stopped and threw their pocketknives at a mark on the telephone pole.

They didn't talk. Breed didn't feel like smiling, and not a single flicker of expression touched Flick's face. They threw their knives harder and harder. Clunk! Clunk! The knives stuck into the pole. They walked to the pole, pulled the knives out, and threw again. The knives rocketed to the mark and sunk deep into the golden-brown wood.

The rotten feelings of being beaten churned in Breed's stomach and traveled to his chest. He tried to ignore the feelings, but as if they were planning to set up a tent, build a fire, and camp overnight, the unwanted feelings stayed there. Each toss of his knife helped those pains decide to break camp and go back where they had come from.

The knife clunks softened and the pain went away. Breed's mind cleared. Other thoughts entered and stimulated his imagination. He relaxed, and without concentrating, he threw his knife. It took an unexpected flip, went whirling through the air, tumbled past the pole, skidded on the pavement, and slid under a bush next to the road.

When Breed walked to the side of the road and bent over to pick up the knife, a whiff of garlic and old age puffed past his face. He peered into the thick bush. A dirty-yellowed dress hung over chicken-shit-spattered shoes. A sharp glint of metal sent a sensation of impending death over his entire being.

Vanko was hiding there — right in that bush. She was standing right next to his lowered head. He didn't pick up his knife. He jumped up. He was face to face with Vanko.

Old garlic breath huffed into his face. He jumped back away from the smell. Vanko raised a rusty pitchfork over her head and held it as if it were a spear.

The garlic odor hovered around Breed's face. He shook his head to make it go away. It didn't. The wooden handle of the sharp forks sailed from her arthritic fingers. A quick flash of the incoming three-pronged flying fork flashed in his eyes. He had no time to step away. He had no time to wait for his mind to think what to do. His body drew from the well of ancestral instinct. It wasn't fight. It was flight.

He dove to the ground. The metal prongs zinged past his head. Like sharp skinny fingers of death, they hit the pavement and twanged. The wooden handle rattled on the road.

Breed shuddered. "Damn! My soul almost went to another place."

Vanko gushed out of the cover of the bushes and snatched the fork off the road.

Breed's heart thumped as if it were going to pound through his chest. Adrenaline surged through his body. He screamed at Flick. "Vanko's got the fork!"

Vanko held the fork high and pumped her arm. The fork poked the air. She aimed and yelled,

"Greek! You steal from my garden. Dirty Greek! Get away!"

Flick darted from side to side and flashed smiles in Breed's direction. "Who let the old lady out of the bag?"

"She almost got me." Breed stepped out of range. Now that she was in sight they could toy with her until the police came.

Breed's heart slowed.

Like wild dogs tormenting a deer, they danced and taunted her, dared her to throw the deadly fork.

Breed looked down the road. A few houses away, a semi-retarded kid called Pud snuck out of his yard and walked toward the dodging exhibition. As a joke, Screwball had told him a flood was coming and that if he didn't want to get the bottoms of his pants wet, he should cut them off. Pud had cut one leg of his pants off so short that they hung just below his knee. He had cut the other leg off so that it hung to the center of his calf. His shirt was buttoned, but the buttons were misaligned. The side of his short-haired head had a dent that looked like it had been hit with a baseball bat.

Walking along the road and whistling a mindless tune, Pud looked back over his shoulder every few steps to make sure his father wasn't watching. He arrived on the scene eating a worm-eaten winter turnip he had apparently stolen from Vanko's garden.

With disbelief, Breed looked at Pud's cut off pants.

Flick glanced at them and smiled. "How you doin', high-water?"

Pud didn't make the connection. He didn't

answer.

With renewed vengeance, Vanko's mouth started again. "Greek! Get out. Dirty Greek! You be takin' my chickens, get out!"

Breed had no idea why she was yelling Greek. He glanced at Flick for a clue. Flick shrugged. He didn't know either. Now they both didn't care.

Flick placed his hands on his hips and leaned his elbows back. "We didn't steal nothin' from your goddamn garden."

Breed stepped next to Flick and pointed to Vanko's chicken coup. "And we didn't take your shit-eatin' chickens."

Breed turned toward Pud. Pud dipped his skinny neck and swallowed the last of the turnip. Vanko threw the fork at him. Zinging past, it just missed his knee. But the danger must not have registered in Pud's limited mind.

He bent over, picked up the fork and politely offered it back to Vanko. "Here, Mrs. Vanko," he said in an exaggerated show of respect. "Here's your fork back."

She reached out and placed her hand on the fork's handle.

Pud continued. "These are bad boys," he said as if he were the gentle savior of the situation.

Like some kind of mythological stone God, Vanko cocked her head sideways. Her powerful eyes opened wide. Like a slot machine that had found its payoff, they rotated and fixed on Pud. She ripped the fork from his hands and threw it at him, again. It pierced the cuff of his high-water pants and skidded on the pavement.

Pud jerked fretfully. His eyes bulged wide and

revealed his strange pupils. Yellow spatters against a brown and green iris made them look like little squares. He blinked and jumped back. "Hey, she's throwing that pitchfork at me."

Warily keeping an eye on Vanko, Breed shook his head. "Glad you figured that out, Pud."

Pud stared at her. "She's crazy," he cried and stepped away from the fork.

Flick smiled at Pud's ignorance. "If you don't want that pitchfork stuck up your ass, you better get out of here." He looked toward Pud's house. "Your old man's callin' you."

Pud looked toward home. His father wasn't calling him, but just the thought of getting his ass beat was enough to send him running back to the safety of his yard.

Vanko threw the fork with renewed vigor. Breed's and Flick's agile cat-like antics made it impossible for the fork to hit its targets. The exertion and excessive excitement tired Vanko. She calmed down.

Flick hopped and skipped in a circle and sang, "If Vanko wouldn't have grabbed that dick lying there on the ground, she just might have starved to death instead of the other way around." He stopped hopping and dancing, and looked straight into Vanko's face. "Ain't that right?"

Flick's spontaneous tomfoolery was out of place. Vanko stood motionless and silent. With her trusty pitchfork in hand, she blinked her eyes.

The unmistakable red flashing bubblegum-machine shaped light on top of a black and white police cruiser blinked up the hill.

"Time to go, Breed," Flick said. "Lard Man

must have greased the doorframe to his house, squeezed his fat ass in, and called the police."

Breed glanced at the approaching cruiser. "Let's split up so they don't know who to chase."

Flick talked out the side of his mouth in his gangster voice. "We'll meet up in Ballpeen's yard." His mouth widened into a playful smile. "If he ain't makin' another airplane to fly in a tornado, maybe we could help him make a boat."

Breed wondered why he hadn't thought of building a boat before. Ballpeen was always building something. Building a boat would give them a new way to get to Shell Island. He cut across the road, jumped through a stand of low hedges, and got his foot snagged on a wire fence hidden in a patch of dead weeds. To keep from falling, he stepped through a stand of wild grass, tramped down filth-loving weeds, and sloshed into the black sewage oozing from a sewer tile. Cussing, he kicked the clinging filth from his foot and raced through the high grass in Toney's yard.

When he got to the apple tree in Ballpeen's back yard he stopped and waited for Flick.

Chapter 6

Breed waited under the apple tree at the edge of Ballpeen's yard and watched his usual slipshod workmanship. Trying to nail a board in place, Ballpeen held a nail on the board and pounded. Thwack! Thwack! He missed the nail. The board slipped out of place. He repositioned it and tried to hit the nail again. Before he could swing, the board fell and bounced off the head of his shiny ball-peen hammer. He reared back and viciously pounded the stubborn board, and the sound of his maniacal pounding echoed through the stillness of the neighborhood.

Flick jumped over a sewage ditch and stopped at the apple tree. Watching Ballpeen, he reached up, placed his hand on a branch, and leaned on one foot. "Ballpeen really makes those boards flap."

Leaning against the trunk of the tree, Breed jerked his head toward Ballpeen. "He pounds on everything."

"It looks like he's trying to make a boat." Flick stepped away from the tree. "Let's go see."

In Ballpeen's yard, they walked past a big pile of scrap wood.

Ballpeen cocked his head to one side. A strand of his blond hair hung down; and like a windshield wiper, it flapped across his forehead. Holding a board in place with his knee and with rusty nails sticking out of his mouth, he lifted his hammer and whacked at the board.

"Hey Ballpeen," Breed said with muffled mischief. "There ain't no tornado coming?"

Ballpeen kept the nails in his mouth and

mumbled something in response, but Breed couldn't understand what he had said.

"What are you making?" Flick asked. "I hope it isn't another plane."

Ballpeen stopped pounding and set his hammer down. Even though his cheeks grew tight with fury, he kept the nails in his mouth and muttered, "That plane would have worked."

Breed shook his head in wonderment. "That tornado would have blown you away."

Wiping his rust-covered hands on his yellow-striped pullover shirt, Ballpeen leaned forward. Excitement danced in his eyes. "That's what I was counting on." He lifted his hammer toward the sky. "A tornado ain't nothin' but wind. You can't get hurt if you have a plane to fly in it."

Squinting one eye, Breed studied Ballpeen. "Are you sure about that?" He pointed upward. "What were you going to do when you fell out of the sky and hit the ground?"

Ballpeen took the nails from his mouth. "You don't fall. Just like any other plane, you land." Imitating an airplane, he held out his arms and tilted from side to side. "Too bad that tornado passed over. I would've flown."

Breed pointed to a broken board. "When your old man found out you busted the ends off his brand new shelving boards to make wings, you did fly."

"Yeah," Flick said. "If you wanna call getting kicked in the ass and flying down the cellar steps, flying, then you flew."

Ballpeen made no effort to hide his wounded feelings. "Come on you guys, "he pleaded, "don't jinx this thing like Hog always does."

"Jinx?" Breed questioned. "How can Hog jinx anything?"

Ballpeen stuck his jaw out and agitation filled his face. "Easy," he said and grunted. "Every time I try to build something he comes around, points at whatever I'm makin', and says the same thing, 'Hey, Ballpeen! Who shit in your yard?' And then whatever I'm makin' gets jinxed."

Flick put his hand over his mouth to conceal a smile. "Come on, Ballpeen, tell us what you're makin'. We won't jinx it."

Ballpeen cast an eye of suspicion toward Flick but answered anyway. "I'm trying to make a boat to go to Shell Island, but I ain't got enough stuff."

Breed's heart jumped with a sudden jolt of excitement. A boat could get him out of Traptown, but Ballpeen's building skills were limited. Breed wasn't sure Ballpeen could build a boat that would float. He didn't want to say anything to discourage him. He waited for Flick to talk first.

Flick examined the skeleton of the boat. "We might be able to scrounge what you need from the dump."

Ballpeen's face filled with delight. "We could do that?"

Breed knew the dump might have what Ballpeen needed. Although Shell Island was a long way off, it just seemed to have gotten closer. A sunny feeling welled up in his chest.

"When me and Screwball found the parts to build our bikes," he said and ran his hand down a smooth board sticking out the side of the boat. "I saw some old boards, but they had a lot of rusty nails sticking out."

As if it were an only child, Ballpeen caressed the hammer in his hands and looked at it. "I can pound those out."

Breed felt the hot sun on his face. "We can go into the dump, but with this heat it stinks real bad."

Ballpeen took a deep breath and puffed his cheeks out. "I don't care." He exhaled. "I can hold my breath."

Walking out of the yard, Flick looked back over his shoulder. "Let's quit talkin' about it and just do it."

Ballpeen held up his hand. "Wait!" He tried to tuck the handle of his hammer between his belt and his hip, but the hammer fell to the ground.

Tapping his foot, Flick waited at the edge of the road.

When other kids were young they sucked their thumbs or carried blankets around for security. Ballpeen's father had said. "Ballpeen has slept with his hammer since he was a baby. He even cut his teeth on the handle."

Ballpeen's ball-peen hammer had the rounded end like all ball-peen hammers have, but his hammer was different. His father had complained, "Ballpeen ripped the teeth out of a hundred hacksaw blades just to cut a little slot in the steel head so he could use it to pull out nails."

The slot wouldn't fit under a nail as close as a claw hammer or a crowbar, so Ballpeen had to pound nails almost all the way out of boards to get the head of the nail in the slot, but it worked. And he always kept that ball-peen in his belt or nearby.

He picked up his ball-peen hammer; and while he adjusted his baggy pants, he slid the hammer to one side. With his hand clutching the hammer, he happily ran after Flick and Breed.

They were off for the dump.

Along the side of the road, Flick walked at a peppy pace. The open wounds of Breed's kicked shins hurt, and the dried blood rubbed against his pants. He struggled to keep up, but he wasn't going to complain. He liked the idea of building a boat. He didn't like the idea of smelling and breathing the hot putrid air at the dump; but for a chance to go to Shell Island, he would suffer through it one more time.

A few houses down the street, the trunk of an old dead tree on a broken sidewalk, blocked their way. They stopped and turned to walk around it.

Ho-o-o-o-nk! The loud sour note of a brass trumpet blasted into their faces. A frightening figure with a gray beret pulled down over its eyes sprang out. Ballpeen jumped in fright. Breed's ears rang from the unexpected powerful noise. It was Blo.

"Cocksucker!" Ballpeen yelled at Blo.

Blo laughed and pointed at Ballpeen. "You don't have to get pissed off just 'cause you got scared."

Swishing his hand, Flick grabbed for the trumpet.

Blo jerked it away, fast.

Flick missed.

"If I get that thing," Flick said, "I'll make you blow it out your ass."

Blo held the trumpet behind his back. With his tongue, he turned his two false teeth over and pushed them out. Making a buzzing sound, he talked through his nose, "Eeeeuuu, huck eeuuu!"

Smiling at Blo's antics, Flick said, "Hey, Blo. You wanna go to the dump?"

Blo didn't answer yes or no. He put his teeth back in place and laughed.

Lifting his hand, Breed made a follow-me gesture. "Come on, Blo, we're going to get some wood to build a boat."

Blo tightened his lips and talked through a thin slit. "Nope, I ain't goin'."

"We can go to Shell Island," Breed said with encouragement. "We'll get away from the flats gang."

Blo held the trumpet behind his back with one hand, and with the other hand he pinched his nose closed. "No way, man," he said with a nasal sound. "This hot weather makes it stink in there."

"All we have to do is pull the front of our shirts over our mouths," Flick said. "Come on, Blo. We need all the help we can get."

Blo took his fingers from his nose. "Tough shit! I ain't goin'."

"Why not?"

"That wood gets way too heavy. And if the rats don't get you, the wild dogs will." He shuddered as if something were crawling up his back. "The last time I went in there, those wild dogs packed up on my ass."

Ballpeen swung his hammer. "I can hit them with my hammer."

"We don't have to get that close." Flick lifted his arm. "We can throw something at 'em. They'll run away."

Blo's eyes opened wide and round. "Like hell

96

they will. The only way I got out of there was when I grabbed onto the back of a garbage truck." He pointed to his foot. "Damn dog grabbed my shoe, ripped it right off my foot."

"What's the matter?" Flick asked. "You scared of a little dog?"

"Scared, my ass. I just ain't stupid. Those dogs ain't little."

Breed had carried wood before. The fewer pieces a person had to carry, the easier it was. It was a long way from the dump to Ballpeen's yard. The further they had to carry the wood the heavier it would get. He wanted Blo to help. He downplayed the danger. "The last time I saw one of those dogs it looked like a little puppy."

Blo winced. "Those puppies grow up."

"Yeah," Breed said. "But they never get very close."

Blo let out a nervous laugh. "You're lucky the other ones didn't come around. They'll pack up and surround you, bite your little scared ass right out of your scared, shit-in pants."

"Maybe," Breed said, "but besides getting a couple pieces of wood, we might find something really good."

"So what. If you build a boat or make a motorbike." Blo smiled and looked directly at Breed. "The flats gang will beat your ass and take it, or Lard Man's just gonna run over it." Watching Flick, he took the trumpet from behind his back, placed it to his lips, and blew right in Breed's face. Bl-a-a-a-t-t-t!

Breed jerked back.

Laughing, Blo put the trumpet under his arm

97

and walked away.

Breed held up his middle finger. "Hey, Blo!"

Blo looked back.

Jerking his finger, Breed smiled. "Run over this!"

Shaking his head, Blo placed the trumpet on his lips and buzzed away.

Breed, Flick, and Ballpeen walked up a long gravel road, cut across the dusty dirt road, and stopped at the edge of the tall trees that lined the outskirts of the Traptown dump. No signs were needed to tell them they were almost there. The unmistakable aroma of dog shit and firecrackers surrounded the place.

The Traptown dump was not a daily earth-covered sanitary landfill project. Trucks dumped the garbage, and it stayed naked and exposed until more garbage covered it. Hidden deep in the recess of the dark dampness of old, abandoned, underground coalmine shafts that would open up and swallow a person alive, the dump was not a safe place to visit.

At the outer fringes of the dump property 'No Trespassing' signs hung on thin metal spans of wire. Flick tugged on one of the wires. It twanged. The signs dropped to the ground.

"This wire ain't strong enough to land a sunfish," he said and they marched over the wire.

The wild dogs that usually patrolled the perimeter of the dump, constantly sniffed the air, and searched for food. Today, there were no signs of them.

Ballpeen waved his hand in front of his face. "This place stinks already, and we ain't even there yet."

Flick took in a deep breath and slowly let it out. "Once you get used to the smell, it ain't that bad."

Breed turned, walked backwards, and searched the area where they had just been. "Just keep an eye out for a garbage truck." He turned and walked forward. "On one of those garbage trucks, there's a crazy guy called Joe."

Flick pointed to his own eye. "I've seen him before. He's got a screwy eye. He likes to sneak up and grab you by the throat."

Listening for the threatening groan of a heavy garbage truck, Breed and the others walked down the one-lane road. In the past, yellow sticky mud and clay had clung to their feet. Now, black foundry sand from the local casting factories made their walk easy. Brush lined the road edges; and broken and bent branches that the tall garbage trucks had hit, created a haphazard canopy.

When they were close to the main gate, Flick stopped. "You guys wanna walk around or go through the gate?"

"I tried going around before," Breed said. "There's poison ivy all around that gate. We'd have to take the long way around it."

With a look of terror, Ballpeen whirled around and looked at Flick. "If there's a dog at the gate, we'll have to go around anyway."

Flick lifted one finger and assumed a superior air. "That's *if* there's a dog there."

They continued down the road.

At the main gate to the dump, a dirty-gray watchdog slept next to a flat-roofed, corrugated metal shed that resembled an outhouse, but didn't have a door, the seats, or the crescent moon.

Ballpeen walked up to the dog and stopped. It didn't bark. It didn't move. "That dog's old. It won't even wake up."

"Look at him," Breed said amazed. "He's so old he's got dust on his fur and rust on his collar."

Flick lifted the latch on the gate and looked back at the dog. "Some day those wild dogs will kill that dog and eat him."

Breed shuddered at the thought, and Flick held the gate open.

As Ballpeen and Breed slipped through, motors of overloaded garbage trucks labored and groaned in the distance.

They were coming down the road.

Ballpeen ran into a dark regiment of trees and hid. Breed and Flick looked down the long road. When the white roof of the first truck appeared, they walked to Ballpeen and crouched down. Going slower than Breed could walk, two dump trucks, with mountains of garbage in their beds, crawled passed. It seemed as if the truck drivers were in no hurry to drive into the putrid place ahead.

Breed waited and listened. The grumble of the truck's motors held steady until they slowed to an idle. Then, after a short pause, the engines revved up. The steady whine of dump truck beds being tilted traveled into the humid air. Levers banged. Heavy lumps of wet garbage thumped on the ground. Bass booms transmitted down the road and vibrated under his feet. He looked at Flick. "The smell must be really bad. It sounds like those guys are in a hurry."

As if he already smelled the outrageous odors

100

that lived in the heart of the dump, Flick shook his head. "That sun makes this garbage stink real fast."

Clunk! A heavy door slammed shut. From the direction of the dump, someone yelled, "Okay, Joe, let's go!"

Breed didn't want Joe sneaking up and grabbing him by the throat. He still hadn't gotten over Burkie trying to cut his ears off. He was glad Joe was in a hurry.

As the emptied trucks pulled out of the dump and onto the black sand road, Breed hunched down and watched. The trucks roared past. Their massive chrome exhaust stacks shot diesel fumes high into the air that gathered into a light-blue cloud that hovered over the black sand road. As the trucks drove out of sight, the cloud floated down and gently nudged tree branches where it split into fluffy corkscrews. Then, like pieces of a torn fleecy blanket, they curled around Breed and the others.

Flick held his hand in front of his face and fanned the fumes. "Those guys really move those trucks."

A burning sensation crept into Breed's eyes. "Yeah." He turned his face away from the curling fumes. "They want to get away from this stinkin' air as fast as they can."

In the distance, the trucks roared down the black road. When the rumble of their motors faded, Breed and Flick came out of hiding; but Ballpeen stayed crouched behind a big tree. Flick looked back and motioned with his arm. "Come on, Ballpeen, you ain't gonna get any wood hiding back there."

Ballpeen stood up and pointed behind himself.

A dirty-white fender peeked between two dark green bushes.

Flick turned and looked. "It's only a junk truck." He gestured with a jerk of his head. "Come on, Ballpeen, let's get some wood before those trucks come back."

"Hey, wait a minute." Breed walked through the thick brush toward the truck. "Let's see if there's any gas in that tank."

Flick and Ballpeen followed and stopped next to the gas tank of the truck.

Breed unscrewed the gas cap and looked into the tank. "I don't see anything."

"Get a stick," Flick said. "Stick it into the hole."

Breed snapped a twig off a tree, ripped the leaves off with his hand, and cut the small branches off with his penknife. Then he stuck the stick into the tank opening, moved it around, and listened. "Something's splashing."

Flick stepped closer. "Take it out and smell it."

Breed withdrew the stick. The end was wet and smelled like gas. "Oh just great!" He slapped his forehead. "Now I have a giant tank of gas, but I don't have a motorbike."

"Oh well." Flick shrugged. "Maybe you'll get it back."

Ballpeen turned toward the road. "If we find enough wood, you won't need that motorbike. We'll be going to Shell Island in style. We'll be riding in a boat."

Breed put the gas cap back on the tank, and they walked down the black road.

At end of the road, they entered into the

incredible kingdom where dead rotting smells saturated the air, coated their skin, and crawled into their lungs. In this rancid land of the unwanted, running rats and buzzing flies never went hungry. They bred and easily multiplied. It was a strange paradise.

Breed put his hands on his hips and surveyed the vast hoard of garbage. Standing out in an ocean of scattered papers, boxes, cans, bottles, twisted and rusting metal, and splintered wood, an occasional broken toy sat like a ship adrift on a sea of filth. He shrugged and threw his hands up. "At least it's free."

As if he were trying to keep the smell out of his mouth, a tight grin formed on Flick's face. "This stuff really ain't free. We have to work to breath in all this stinkin' air, find what we need, and dig it out."

"That ain't no lie!" Ballpeen said; and to keep the sticky smell out of his lungs, he breathed in shallow breaths. He looked toward Breed. "Hey, Breed. Where's those boards you were talking about?"

Breed picked up a skinny stick of wood and got on top of a big heap of garbage. "Ladies and gentleman welcome to the Traptown dump." He pointed with the stick. "You will find your boat materials right over there."

"It figures," Flick said and looked at the garbage-buried boards. "They just had to be a thousand miles deep in filth."

Breed turned toward the dump. "They're still free." He looked over the tall heaps of truck-dumped garbage. As if he were a symphony conductor in front of a sea of people, he waved the stick. "Let me point out that rich people's garbage is the same as everybody else's." He pointed to a pile of garbage. Clothes he would never have thrown away, half-full cans of peaches, and other food that he wouldn't have wasted, meshed into an affluent heap. "It doesn't matter how rich you are, your garbage stinks and rots just like everybody else's."

Looking for wood, Ballpeen's eyes darted from side to side and stopped on Breed. "So what's that got to do with finding wood?"

"Nothing," Breed said. "But after people die" – he waved the stick gesturing to the vast expanse of garbage – "they'll all be just like this."

A board stuck out of a stack of cans and glass. Flick grabbed it and pulled. It didn't move. He looked to Breed. "Get off that shit pile and help."

"In a moment, gentleman," Breed said in a low voice. "Let me continue." He cleared his throat. "You will notice over here." He pointed to a rat carcass crawling with maggots. "None are preserved or cherished because they are rich rats."

Ballpeen stopped digging in the garbage, spun around, and faced Breed. "The only thing preserved here is stink."

The sun grew strong. Flies buzzed in front of his Breed's face. Then the fragrance of the terrible humid odor covered him like a stench-scented blanket. Trying to get the smell out of his lungs, he let out a long breath of air. "This place is really bad."

Flick waved a hoard of flies away from his mouth. "You ain't kiddin'. You can't breathe without gettin' a fly in your mouth."

Ballpeen pounded a nail out of a board and giggled. "You guys know Hog wouldn't be so great in this place."

Flick glanced at him sideways. "Why not?"

"If he cut one of his famous farts no one would notice."

Breed felt the stench of the dump sink into his very soul. "I'm glad he ain't blasting his flatulent vapors here. It smells bad enough already."

"This ain't no sermon on the mount," Flick said with authority. "Quit usein' those twenty-nine cent words. Get your high flatulent ass down off that pile and help me pull out this board."

Breed climbed down off the pile and grabbed the board. Together, they pulled. The board broke free and slipped out.

While Breed and Flick held their breaths and took turns wading into the piles of freshly dumped garbage, like a little kid waiting for a new toy, Ballpeen stood with his hand on the handle of his ball-peen hammer.

When an occasional rat jumped out, Breed and Flick jerked back momentarily and Ballpeen laughed. Cussing the putridity of the air and swatting at the flying flies, they continued searching for boards.

After they had dug out a few boards, they threw them out onto a small, cleared area for Ballpeen to inspect.

Most of the boards had nails or screws sticking straight out. Breed stopped and stared at them. The threatening position of the nails reminded him of the time he had stepped on a nail. Just the sight of the nails made him feel the pain of the nail sinking deep into his foot bone all over again. He shuddered and stood still.

Flick threw a board onto the pile and turned toward Breed. "What are you stopping for?"

Breed exhaled a deep breath. "Those boards look like they are just waiting for somebody to step on them."

"Don't step on a rusty nail," Ballpeen said and shook his finger. "You'll get lockjaw."

Breed lifted the end of his stick. As if it were a BB gun, he pointed. A crow as big as a chicken flew down, grabbed a dead rat, and held it in its black beak. A foot away, another rat jumped up and hopped across a trail of glass. The crow dropped the dead rat and flew off into the trees.

Between batting buzzing flies and kicking at running rats, Breed and Flick rummaged through the garbage and dug out boards. Ballpeen discarded a lot of them because they just stunk too bad, or some sort of garbage was embedded in the wood. When he finally had a pile of wood good enough to work with, the stench overwhelmed him. He pulled the front of his pullover shirt over his mouth. Then he pounded and pulled nails out of the salvageable wood and jammed them into his pockets.

Flick picked up a board and looked down its edge. It was rotten and useless. He tossed it over the dead rat. "Hey, Breed, where did you and Screwball find those bikes?"

Breed threw the stick. It speared into the tree leaves, stopped for a moment, and rustled to the ground. "Right through there."

Flick walked toward the stick.

"You ain't gonna find another bike," Breed said, walked across the cleared area, stopped at a brand new white clothesline rope that was strung across a no dumping area, and cut the rope.

Making a coil, he wrapped the rope around his thumb and elbow. "This will make a good anchor rope." As he slipped the neat circle of rope onto his shoulder, like black sparks, flies danced around his head. He took the rope from his shoulder and swatted at them. They scattered, but off to his right – There!

A renegade wild dog loomed up huge. Its matted fur gave it an unmistakable predatory look. Breed snapped erect. His heart thudded. The dog ran across the road and stopped. Then it sniffed the air, turned its head, and growled. It had found them. More would be coming. Breed slapped the coiled rope onto the ground. "Git!"

The dog didn't move. The hackles on its back stood up in an offensive posture. Breed stomped his foot. The dog let out a low threatening growl. Breed held the coil of rope high, ready to whip down on the dog. It hunched down and crept toward him. Thud! Breed stomped his foot on the hard ground. The dog didn't move. Swish! He swiped the rope at the dog. "Git!"

The dog didn't move.

Whack! Whack! Ballpeen whacked at the nails in a board. The dog turned and ran toward him.

"Watch out!" Breed cried. "Wild dog!"

Ballpeen looked up from his pounding. The dog came straight at him. The front of his pullover shirt fell from his face. Fear and panic flashed in

107

his eyes. He turned to run.

Breed waved the rope around in the air. "Don't turn your back on him. He'll rip your throat out!"

If he were going to help Ballpeen fight off the dog, Breed needed something better than a soft rope. He dropped it and began searching in the pile of garbage. He looked for a stick. He looked for a board with nails. He looked for anything to use on the dangerous dog. Right next to Ballpeen, a pile of nail-filled boards waited. The dog was in front of them. Breed had to do something — fast.

His mind screamed, "Grab something! But what? Think! Think! I gotta get that dog off Ballpeen before it rips his throat out — and right now."

He looked across the garbage heap. The lifesaving board he needed sat on top of a stack of maggot-covered cans. A thick jumble of broken bottles, unbroken bottles, dirty jars, broken jars, half empty bottles, half full bottles, brown glass, green glass, rusty cans, bean cans, old wood, rotting lettuce, decaying cabbage, filthy rags, dead rats, old newspapers, and a grease-covered broken sled blocked his way. But the board was there.

Yes! Yes! flashed in his mind. That will work. Get it.

It was out of reach.

He stopped for a moment and looked back.

The dog growled and crept closer to Ballpeen.

Breed wanted to avoid rats and maggots. He wanted to pick his way toward the board, but there was no time. "Ah, man!"

He forgot about the rats and maggots, leaped into the heap and sunk up to his knees. A dirty-gray, pink-toothed rat jumped out at him. He kicked the filthy threat away and jumped on top of the broken sled. Then he swung his hand down and grabbed for the board. Ballpeen cried, "Watch out!"

Breed jerked his head in Ballpeen's direction and missed the board. Instantly irritated at the interruption of his lifesaving efforts, he yelled back, "What?"

Then his foot slipped on the greasy sled. Wind milling his arms, he fell into the stinking heap.

With garbage up to his neck, he snapped his head around and checked on Ballpeen. Ballpeen waved his hammer above his head and smiled. "He's gone."

Breed looked around. "Where'd he go?"

With the handle of his hammer, Ballpeen pointed to a shield of trees. "He ran in there. Two rats ran up and scared him."

Breed lay in the garbage and let his heart slow. The smell and a greasy feeling sunk through his clothes and crawled onto his skin. He didn't want to reach into the heap and push himself up. His hands would get covered with more greasy garbage. He looked for something to grab and pull himself up.

Whack! Whack! Ballpeen pounded on a board.

Out of the corner of Breed's eye, he watched a dirty-gray streak speed across the garbage. Again, the dog raced toward Ballpeen.

Ballpeen reached for a board. The dog stopped and snapped at his hand. Ballpeen cried out, "Get him, Breed."

Like a warning siren, the dog's barking brought Breed's heart back to a full race. He jumped up. With bits of garbage avalanching off his body, he swooshed his hand down and snagged the lifesaving board. He leaped out of the heap. With the board in his hands, he plowed through knee-deep rubbish and rushed toward Ballpeen and the dog.

Ballpeen raised his hammer and shouted, "Git!"

The dog stopped a few feet in front of him, growled and threatened. Ballpeen shielded his neck with one hand; and swishing his hammer with his other hand, he looked toward Breed and cried, "He's gonna rip my throat out!"

The dog avoided Ballpeen's swiping hammer, but it crept closer. Trying to get behind Ballpeen, it circled. Ballpeen quit swishing the hammer and flexed to run.

"Don't run," Breed yelled and stepped on a round slippery bottle. He lost his balance, but checked his fall with the board. He screamed at Ballpeen, "You'll never outrun him."

Ballpeen took one step and stopped. The dog lowered its head and charged Ballpeen's leg. It grumbled from deep in its throat and snapped its sharp, yellow-toothed mouth. Ballpeen jerked his leg away and swung the hammer. It missed. The dog's rabid mouth bit nothing but air. It retreated a few inches, growled, bared its teeth, and puffed up its fur.

Still knee-deep in rubbish, Breed looked toward the edge of the dump. Walking over a bed of broken green glass, Flick yelled, "I ain't got nothin' to throw. Hit him, Breed!"

Breed finally plowed out of the garbage and

rushed across the clearing. With that long, nail-loaded board, he was ready to whack the dog and sink those nails into its skinny worm-riddled ribs. The dog turned and ran away from Ballpeen, but it rushed toward Breed. It came up fast. Now the board, Breed had struggled to get, was too long. The dog was snapping too close for him to execute a decent swing. He kicked at the dog. It nipped the tip of his tennis shoe and ripped the rubber. He backed up to make room to swing. He couldn't. The dog jumped right in front of him. With white foam drooling down its jaws, it growled long and threatening. It flexed to jump. Looking for weakness, Breed stared into the dog's red eyes. It didn't move.

Thump! Thump! He stomped his foot on the ground. The dog didn't move. Flick threw a quart-canning jar, full of mold-covered peaches. It landed on the dog's right. It jerked sideways and backed up a foot. Then it hunched low, and bared its teeth. Breed covered his throat with one hand; and with his other hand, he held the board high. "Git!" Thump! He stomped his foot. "Git!" Thump! He stomped his foot again. Again, the dog didn't back off.

Breed yelled at Ballpeen. "I'll keep him busy. Sneak up behind him. Hit him with that hammer!"

Realizing he had a chance to swing his hammer, Ballpeen didn't hesitate. He quietly trotted behind the dog and wound up. Whomp! He slammed the rounded hammerhead into the growling dog's backbone. The dog jerked its head back toward Ballpeen. Ballpeen lifted the hammer for another blow. Before he could strike, Breed lifted the board high and let it fly. Whap! It smacked into the dog's side. It let out a painful yelp. Ballpeen lowered the hammer. The dog put its tail between its legs and whimpered into the cover of the trees.

Flick picked up an unbroken green Coke bottle and threw it toward the dog. The bottle landed in the trees, ten feet away.

"That was just one dog," Flick said in haste. "Let's get out of here before the whole pack comes."

They gathered all the decent wood they could carry and trudged off down the black sand road.

When they stopped to take a rest, Ballpeen sat by the side of the road and waved his hand in front of his face. "Why does everything still stink like the dump?"

As if he were afraid, Flick hunched over and shifted his eyes about uneasily. "It's the ghost of invisible floating shit."

"I don't care what it is," Breed said. "It doesn't have to follow us."

As they kept looking back for the dog, the awful odor of the dump followed them all the way home.

After Breed went into the house, he doctored his kicked shins with dark iodine. It stung and he pretended it didn't bother him. He wasn't a candy ass, but when he thought about his motorbike, it brought tears to his eyes. There was no butter to spread on the stale bread, only oleo, which was actually lard that had been colored with yellow food coloring. He managed to wolf down a lard sandwich. It tasted like the dump. It made

Saturday feel like just another day in Traptown. Tomorrow he would be back on his old junk bike. Maybe he could find a piece of tape to tape his dog-bitten tennis shoe together, and maybe there would be something different to eat.

But no matter what happened, tomorrow he was going to help Ballpeen build that boat. He was going to get out of Traptown.

Chapter 7

In his dream Breed sat on his motorbike. The wind whistled through his hair. He was riding to Shell Island. One-Finger-Burke, Burkie and his sharp knife; Purple, and the flats gang; and the sickos who played baseball with puppies, had been left under a pall of Traptown smoke.

When he was on the hill just above the island, the sound of Blo's trumpet wafted into his open bedroom window. Shell Island vanished. Breed woke up. It was still dark, but a wonderful thought occurred to him. If he had been dreaming about riding to Shell Island, maybe he had dreamt that his bike was gone. Better yet, his dog could still be alive.

He jumped up out of bed, ran down the stairs, went outside, and looked under the porch. It was too dark to see. He reached up under the rafters, took down his candle and lit it. The warm glow of the yellow flame traveled under the porch and brightened the dark ground.

It hadn't been a dream. Where his motorbike had been, dark oil that had dripped from the motor was spattered onto the ground. Skinny wheel furrows marked the gray ground where he had dragged his motorbike out for the last time.

He stooped over and walked under the porch. The candlelight beamed on his little workbench. Like injured orphans waiting for medical attention, two broken motorbike motors sat on a splintered board. Below the motors, the front of an old dresser drawer, with brass handles, the color of gold, peeked out from under a smooth sheet of aluminum

114

that covered the brown drawer.

He dropped to one knee and lifted the sheet of aluminum. Neatly laid out on the wooden bottom of the drawer, his tools stood out like old friends.

He loved his hammer with the mushroomed metal end, his half-handled screwdriver with the bent shaft; and he really liked the Model-A Ford wrench that looked like a piece of a jigsaw puzzle and would fit almost any bolt. He loved his dull files, his hand brace and bit, and the white and flesh-colored tin Band Aid box full of broken drill bits.

His hand-cranked emery wheel had been thumb-screwed into the floor joist next to the stone foundation of the house. The handle lobes where the emery wheel attached to the shaft had been used so much that they were egg shaped and could only be rotated in one direction, but that one direction was good enough. With this emery wheel, he had ground broken drill bits into sharp forty-five degree angles and used them to drill through metal. When he had found his hacksaw it didn't have a solid, easy-to-hold handle. He had gone into the woods, chopped a piece of wood from a hickory tree, carried it home, and carved a new handle. He fastened it to the steel hacksaw with nails, peened the sharp ends over, and filed them until they were smooth. Then he sanded the wood until it fit the grip of his hand. The hacksaw blades always had missing teeth, but it didn't matter. Using short cutting strokes, he sawed with the good ends of the blades and made them cut beyond their normal life expectancy.

He had adopted these broken unwanted tools

and had given them a home in his dresser drawer toolbox. Even though he didn't have money to buy what other kids had, with his tools, he could make something out of junk.

After he had made his motorbike, he thought his days of riding his old junk pedal bike were over. He had pushed it way back under porch into the dark. He had felt rich on his motorbike. The shiny chrome light actually worked. Rust had not eaten away the red spray-painted fenders, and the silver wheels ran straight and true. It had been all new to him.

He dropped to both knees, walked forward until he held the candle over his old pedal bike. It looked like it had come from the dump. It did. It had missing spokes, a chipped coat of thick house paint, and a bent frame with matching bent wheel rims. The back tire had blown out weeks ago. He had patched the tube and wrapped layers of black electricians tape around the tire. The tape kept the tube in the tire, but the resulting bump thumped each time it rolled over the pavement. He didn't want to, but in the morning he would crawl into the dark and dig his old pedal bike out.

He slowly pushed the candle toward his dog's tin feeding pan. The piece of bread he had left in it was gone. For a moment there was hope: His dog was still alive. But he knew better. Ants had carried the bread away.

The next day he crawled under the porch to get his bike and ride to Ballpeen's house, but when he took one step toward the bike, his toe popped out of his wild-dog-bitten tennis shoe. He reached into the corner of his tool drawer and found the small roll of black friction tape. He folded the torn rubber over his toes and ran the tape around the tip of the shoe. When he flexed the toe of the shoe, it didn't look good; but the tape kept his toes from popping out.

In a squatting position, he dragged his pedal bike out from under the porch. Outside, he wiped the spider webs off the bike, jumped on; and standing up, he pedaled to the edge of the road. He forgot about the broken flipped up seat and sat down on the semi-sharp seat clamp.

"Damn!" he cried and sprang off the bike. He stood up, let the bike fall on the road, and rubbed his butt. Compared to his motorbike, this bike was just junk. He wanted to just leave it there; just leave it in the middle of the road and let somebody run over it; then throw it into the ditch at the side of the road and let it rust away. He took one step away from the bike and stopped. The bike was junk, but it was better than no bike. He picked it up, flipped the seat back over, and peddled up the hill.

At Vanko's corner, Screwball was sitting on his bent bike. Breed whistled at him. Screwball smiled and waved his middle finger at Breed. Then he pushed his straight blond hair back from his forehead and rode in a tight circle.

Breed didn't hear Ballpeen hammering. He figured he was still asleep. To kill time, he pumped the pedals on his bike and fell in behind Screwball. Screwball jerked his head and flipped his hair out of his eyes.

Screwball's hair hadn't been in his eyes, and Breed was going to tease him about his habit of jerking his head for no reason, but Screwball spoke first. "Hey, Breed, I found your motorbike."

117

Motorbike, flashed in Breed's brain. "What?" He stopped his bike.

Screwball stopped and put his feet down. "I know where your motorbike's at."

Breed felt like he had found an old lost friend, and better yet, he wouldn't have to put up with Ballpeen's ignorant building skills. "Way to go, Screwball. Let's go get it. Maybe we can fix it and ride to Shell Island."

Screwball stared off into space. "We can't."

"What do you mean, we can't? I found a place where we can get all the gas we need."

As if he were listening for the telltale motions of Vanko sneaking through the bushes, Screwball cocked his head. "It doesn't matter." He looked to Breed. "I hid in the weeds and watched One-Finger-Burke drop your motorbike off at Henry's old man's gas station."

To keep his balance, Breed shifted his weight; and the seat clamp ripped through the covering and rubbed the rusty steel. It screeched like an injured bird. Breed ignored the broken seat. He had something more important on his mind.

Henry was much bigger than Breed, but Breed didn't care. He wanted his motorbike. "I'll just go down there and take it back."

A sour expression formed on Screwball's face. "The last time Henry and Burkie caught Blo in the station they rubbed his face in dog shit."

Breed's stomach churned at the thought. Sometimes a light-colored dog hung around Henry and Burkie. It was said that it would crap on command. Thinking about how the dog would stink up a place, Breed reached up and waved his hand in front of his face. "It's my motorbike. Maybe we could just sneak in and take it back."

"I doubt it," Screwball said. "They said they were going to fix it up, give it to One-Finger-Burke's kid or something."

Breed readjusted the seat on his bike. "What would Burkie want with another bike? He has two already."

"Maybe he's tired of screwing little girls and needs something else to play with."

"That's not right," Breed said. "Lard Man runs over your bike, I finally build something half decent, and then One-Finger-Burke steals it."

Breed waited for Screwball to say, "Oh yeah, go call a cop." But he didn't. He placed his feet on the pedal of his bike and shrugged. "Anything's right if your old man's a crooked cop!" He continued to ride in that tight circle.

Breed wished Screwball would tell him one of his off-the-wall jokes. It would make him feel better. It always did. And Screwball did it all the time. It was just plain ignorance.

Someone could be doing some serious talking, or be trying to do something important. Then, just like a pesky salesman who had snuck in the back door, Screwball would come waltzing in, throw the monkey wrench in the works, intentionally make the person's mind work, ambush it, throw it off track, question authority, ask why, be flippant, and manage to say the wrong thing at the exact right time, or as Screwball would say: "The right thing at the wrong time, or the wrong thing at the wrong time, and back that way again, hey!"

He could get away with his tomfoolery because

119

he was a fast runner, but when he ran, his right foot flicked sideways and resembled someone trying to kick dog crap off their foot. Sometimes Flick called him shit foot.

Screwball steered his bike into a figure eight and rode in the opposite direction. Following the figure eight direction, Breed pedaled behind him. "Hey, Screwball, I wonder how Neal would get my bike back."

"I don't know, but he's pretty friendly for an older kid."

Breed shot Screwball a knowing wink. "Every time he gives me a ride, he says he owes me."

"Maybe he means he owes you a punch in the mouth."

"He's strong but I don't think he'd ever do that. All I did was adjust the points a little. His old Hudson started right up."

"Did he pay you anything?"

Breed stopped his bike and put his feet down. "No, he patted me on the back and we jumped in the car. Then he banged his big fists on that steering wheel and made me feel like he was talking about me."

Screwball stopped peddling and slowed to a stop. "If Neal wanted to get your bike back, he'd just go right up to Henry and take it. If Henry tried to rub Neal's face in dog shit, Neal would reach out with his meaty paws, rip his head off, and shove it right up his ass."

Breed burst into a laugh. "I think that's physically impossible."

Screwball lifted one finger. "You're right. Henry's head's already there."

120

Breed laughed again, paused, and stared at the pavement.

Screwball jiggled the handlebars of Breed's bike. "What are you thinking about?"

Breed looked up. "Neal told me that when poor people get something, the rich people always come out like sharks and try to take it."

Screwball rubbed the back of his neck and looked at the telephone pole. "If they're so rich, why don't they just buy their own stuff?"

"Neal said that rich people don't want poor people to have anything different."

"Why?"

Trying to remember what Neal had said, Breed closed his eyes for a moment. "Oh, yeah." He opened his eyes. "When poor people change they can't be controlled anymore. Rich people want them to keep doing the same things."

Screwball pushed off with his foot. His bike glided to the telephone pole and stopped. He put his hand out, leaned against the pole, and looked at Breed. "What same things?"

Moving his hands, Breed talked. "Things like living in the same kinds of houses, driving the same kinds of cars, and everyone dressing the same."

Screwball lowered his eyes and looked at his patched pants and worn tennis shoes. "We don't dress like anybody else."

"Maybe we don't count," Breed said. "Neal said when we get older we'll be like everybody else in Traptown. We'll be too stupid to know we're getting caught a trap that keeps us from being rich."

Screwball jerked the hair out of his eyes and grinned. "The only thing that keeps me from being

121

rich is no money."

"Neal said we could be rich if we use our heads, but the rich people make rules to protect their money."

Screwball squinted one eye. "What kind of rules?"

"That's what I asked him. He talked in a low voice. Said, 'Rich people make foolish rules because they know foolish people will follow them.'" Then he put that big hand of his on my shoulder, looked me right in the eye, and said, 'Hold yourself accountable, kid. You don't have to do the same things everybody else does. There's always a way to get what you need. Sometimes people don't even know they're helping you to get it.'"

Screwball put the kickstand down, and sat on the seat with the stand holding him and the bike up. He didn't say anything. A look of deep thought dawned on his face. "That's weird." He paused. "I'm gonna have to think about that one."

"Me too."

"Where did Flick go?"

As if he had just woken up, Breed jerked his head. "He's probably over Ballpeen's waitin' for him to wake up."

Screwball grinned. "He'll be waiting a long time. I saw Ballpeen and his father jump into his uncle's car. He'll be gone all day."

Breed's hopes of helping Ballpeen build the boat that would take him to Shell Island sank. As if it didn't bother him, he shrugged and looked to Screwball. "You know some big kids jumped out of a pink Ford and gave Flick a bloody nose?"

"Oh, yeah. What happened?"

Breed rattled off a detailed account of the Ford incident and scanned the bushes for Vanko and that fork. Screwball digested the story and ticked a finger at Breed. "He'll get even some day."

"He'd have chance if it was one-on-one, but they always gang up on us."

Like a bad dream that wouldn't go away, the vision of his dog hanging flashed in Breed's mind. To hide a tear forming, he closed his eyes for a moment. Then he looked up. "Anybody that uses puppies for baseballs shouldn't be a member of the human race."

Screwball lifted both hands. "Maybe they ain't."

"If I had my motorbike we could leave them in the dust."

"I do that already. They can't catch me."

"Yeah, but we can't run all the way to Shell Island."

"We could if we got a ride and got dropped off real close."

Breed grinned at Screwball's attempted humor and thought about telling him about the Joe Louis Boxing book he had sent for. Maybe they could read it together, but Screwball might make some kind of joke about it. He decided not to tell him. "Do you think the flats gang would follow us to Shell Island?"

"They'll never go there," Screwball said. "They can't swim." He broke into a cheery grin. "And they're probably afraid of the dark."

123

Chapter 8

At Vanko's corner, Breed and Screwball waited for Ballpeen to come back and work on the boat. He didn't. They gave up and bicycled away.

When Screwball's bike tires raced onto the loose gravel at the side of the road he slammed his brakes on. His back tire skidded sideways until he stopped in a cloud of gray dust.

Being wary of flats gang bullies or Burkie who might be hiding in the weeds, Breed slowed to a stop. "Now what?"

Screwball pointed to the weeds along the side of the sewer ditch. Scattered next to the black sewer filth, empty pop bottles lay in the grass. Screwball laid his bike down and straddled the ditch. "They're pretty clean." He picked up the bottles and handed them to Breed.

Breed stuffed as many bottles as he could in the front of his shirt and set the others on the side of the road. Screwball jumped out of the ditch, picked up the remaining bottles, and stuffed them into his shirt. They jumped on their bikes and rode to the little corner store where they collected the bottle's deposits and bought two ice cream Fudge-Sickles.

With Fudge-Sickles in hand, they pushed their bikes up the long hill.

When they got to Flick's house, they stopped at the driveway. Music flowed from the radio in Flick's father's 1953 green Buick. Flick's two feet stuck out from underneath the back bumper. Breed and Screwball rode up to the Buick and stopped.

Trying to loosen a rusted nut, Flick lay on his back and banged on it. To get some traction, he scratched his feet in the black dirt of the driveway, repositioned his body, and banged on the tailpipe. Struggling for breath, because of the cramped position his body was in, he stopped banging and hollered out from under the car. "Hey, Breed. Reach in the car and turn that radio off. I don't wanna run the battery down."

Breed got off his bike, opened the door, and reached in the car. He put his thumb and finger on the knob and hesitated. The disc jockey on the radio was announcing a contest.

Breed motioned with his hand toward the radio. "Hey, Screwball, listen."

"Yes, friends out there in radio land, this is the chance of a lifetime. All you have to do is find the secret key, and you'll win all the cash."

"Hey!" Flick yelled. "Turn that thing off. "I gotta get this tailpipe on before my old man comes home from work. If that battery goes dead, I'll be diggin' his work shoe out of my ass."

Breed sat on the edge of the seat and leaned over. He stretched his arm and turned the chrome knob until the radio was off. "Maybe we could find that key and get some money."

Continuing to work, Flick said, "Don't be stupid, Breed. Those things are rigged."

"Hey, Flick!" Screwball said with immediacy in his voice.

Flick quit working and barked out an agitated, "What?"

Screwball's shoulders shook as if he were holding in a laugh. "When you get done—" he said and stopped.

Flick waited for Screwball to finish the

sentence. He didn't. Screwball flashed Breed a conniving grin.

Thump! Flick slammed the sledgehammer against the ground. "Damn it, Screwball, don't stop talking in the middle of a sentence. "I ain't got time to wait for you to think of something stupid to say."

Screwball bent over and looked under the car. "How much do you think you're old man will pay you?"

Flick looked out from under the car and narrowed one eye. "Are you out of your mind? There ain't no pay."

"Yeah, Screwball," Breed said, "you think we're rich."

"That would be just fine," Screwball said. "If we were rich, we'd get a weekly allowance. We'd get paid for doing nothing."

"That ain't no bull," Flick said and clanked on the tailpipe. "The only pay I get" — Clank! Clank! – "is not getting my ass kicked. My old man says it's simple and efficient" - Clank! - "Damn rounded bolt."

The wrench slipped and Flick's knuckles tore open on the sharp end of the pipe. He put them to his mouth and cussed.

Screwball smiled and noisily slurped on his Fudge-Sickle.

Flick looked up at the stubborn bolt and whacked it with the sledgehammer. A burst of rust, dust, and all that kind of under-car-crap blasted into his eyes. "Hey, Shit Foot, don't suck that slop around here. Can't you see I'm having a hard enough time already?"

"Okay," Screwball said, but his upturned mouth

hinted at his devilish wit. He slurped the Fudge-Sickle — louder.

Flick stopped banging. "Damn you, Shit Foot! I ain't got the right tools and you gotta be standin' there suckin' that goddamn sickle."

Screwball's grin widened and his shoulders shook with suppressed laughter. "Finish the car tomorrow. Slurp! Slurp!"

"Tomorrow my ass! You know I hate those sickles. I don't need you hanging around pullin' your stupid shit." He pounded on the pipe and then stopped. "And you better not hide one of those goddamn wrenches like you did the last time you were here."

Screwball slopped the Fudge-Sickle around in his mouth and made irritating, piggish sounds.

As if it didn't bother him, Flick continued to work. But it did bother him. He quit pounding — yelled out, "I'm not gonna tell you again."

Screwball quit.

Flick clanked the wrench and pounded on the tailpipe.

Breed watched Screwball's receding chin form a playful smile. His Fudge-Sickle melting quickly, he had to lick — "lap, lap" — and suck — "slurp, slurp" — faster, faster — to keep it from dripping.

Flick stopped working and threatened — again. "I know you're out there, Shit Foot! If you don't stop slopping like a sucking pig, I'm comin' out from under here."

"Slurp!" Screwball sucked on the sickle. "Then what?"

Flick raised his voice to the point of screaming. "I'm gonna sink this hammer right in your pig-suckin' head!"

Screwball put his hands on the handlebars of his bike and got ready to pedal away. "What?" He paused. "I didn't hear you!"

Flick stopped hammering. Screwball waited for him to come out from under the car. He didn't. Screwball relaxed and sat on his bike next to the car. Then he slurped away, but his feet were on the ground — in range.

Flick secretly spit a hawker into his flicking hand, took aim, and fired. The unexpected flying hawker shot toward Screwball's tennis-shoed foot. His lightning quick foot jerked out of the line of fire, but the hawker landed on the other foot.

"You hawker flicking pig!" Screwball yelled with the stark realization that he has not been fast enough to avoid the marksman accuracy of the hawker-flicking Flick.

Flick mockingly laughed and put a C-clamp around the pipe. "What?" He paused. "I didn't hear you, Hawker Shit Foot!"

With a quick shake, Screwball flicked the hawker off his foot and went back slurping on the Fudge-Sickle. Flick continued to tink away. Screwball's agitating was getting to Flick, but Breed knew Flick didn't want to take the time to crawl out from underneath the car and do something about it.

Screwball kept right on slurping and didn't miss a slurp. When Flick looked away, Screwball bent over, took the nine-sixteenth wrench, and placed it on the trunk of the car. Breed pushed his bike backward to a safe distance.

Flick squinted out of his dirt-covered eyes and

stretched his greasy arm out from under the car. He felt around the toolbox and searched for the nine-sixteenth. He couldn't feel it. He lifted his head to look into the toolbox. More under-car-crap fell into his eye. He turned his head and looked with his good eye. "Why you little shit-footed bastard! I know you got that wrench. It's gonna be your ass!"

"Ha! Ha!" Screwball yelled, jumped on the pedals of his bike, and rode out of reach.

Flick jerked up before he was completely out from under the car. Clunk! His head bashed into the rocker panel. "Goddamn, hog-ass-suckin' shit!" He flung every tool he could grab at the fleeing, laughing, shit-footed Screwball.

Chapter 9

At Vanko's corner, Breed leaned his bike against the telephone pole, sat on the seat, and watched old lady Vanko digging in her garden. Screwball and Hog rode up the hill and stopped next to him.

Hog jerked his head toward Vanko. "What's she doing?"

Breed leaned on the handlebars of his bike. "Just pullin' weeds."

Screwball smiled a sly smile. "Maybe she's trying to dig up her husband."

Breed swatted at a stray mosquito. "The way she keeps that dirt dug up, she could bury someone there and no one would know."

"Don't try and make something out of nothing," Hog said. "She's only weeding her garden." He waved his hand down. "Wanna ride downtown? We can check the garbage cans behind the stores."

Screwball flashed an exaggerated smile in Hog's direction. "Why, are you looking for something to eat?"

"Go suck on your shit foot," Hog said back. "I don't dig in that stinkin' garbage. I just kick the can over. One time I found a lady's purse."

"I remember that," Screwball said with amusement in his voice. "Too bad when you opened it, it was full of shit."

A flash of embarrassment crossed Hog's face. "So what? It could've had money in it."

Screwball leaned forward and smiled in Hog's face. "Yeah, but it didn't."

Hog waved Screwball's attempted agitation aside.

Screwball let his mouth go slack, and an empty look appeared in his eyes. Looking looked like an idiot, he stared at Hog. "And you looked in it twice."

Hog laughed at Screwball's antics. "You damn half-wit. You looked in it, too."

Screwball kept up his antics, and Breed wondered if he should go to town with Hog. Hog always got things riled up. Flick's father had said: "If they locked Hog in a room with nothing in it, no windows, no doors, in twenty minutes, he would be in trouble." But then again, Hog could find a diamond in a manure pile and not get any on him.

There was a good chance Ballpeen would never finish building the boat. If Breed went downtown he might be able to get a job. Then he could make some money for motorbike parts. He looked at Screwball's contorted face. "If you guys are going, let's go. I could use some extra money."

"Extra money?" Screwball questioned. "I could use any money."

Hog moved his arms as if he were moving an invisible broom. "Maybe we could sweep the front of a couple of stores, make enough money to go to the show."

Breed wanted to go to the show, but he wanted to go to Shell Island more. Any money he made would go into building another motorbike. He shook his head. "I ain't gonna waste any money on a show."

"We know that," Screwball said. "If we get enough for one guy, he can hold the side door open

131

and we can sneak in."

Keeping his foot on the bike pedal, Hog cocked his leg. "We ain't makin' no money here." He pushed on the pedal of his bike and took off.

Screwball spun his back tire in a fine patch of gravel at the side of the road and followed. Breed tried to do the same thing. He rode into the fine gravel and slowed to almost a stop. He pushed the pedals with strong pumps. The bent rim rubbed on the frame. The bald tire did not spin. It grabbed the pavement. The bike wobbled. "Damn junk." He teetered away.

Halfway there, the sun hammered heat into their shirts. They took them off and stuffed them into the crossbars of their bikes.

In town, they stopped in front of the Dinner Bell Restaurant and parked their bikes on the sidewalk. They walked under the blue, neon liberty bell sign and went inside.

A man with a bald head and a pot belly, re-tied the strings in the back of his dirty-white apron and looked up. Puffed up with self-importance, he stood in front of the cash register and held up his hand. "You kids can't come in here. You don't have shirts." His eyes narrowed with disgust. "This is a respectable place. Get out."

"But, sir," Hog objected, "we're looking for a job."

Breed stepped forward. "We can wash dishes or anything."

A waitress, wearing a little blue and white paper hat on her frizzy blond hair, came up to the counter. "Why don't you let these kids clean up the kitchen?" She gestured to the back of the

132

restaurant. "There's a big mess back there."

As if to say, shut your mouth, the bald man glared at her and tapped his fingers on top of the cash register.

She started to open her mouth. The bald man held up his hand. "I'll say who works here."

The waitress turned and headed toward the kitchen.

The bald man put his hands on his hips, stood with his legs apart, and looked down at Breed. "Burke told me all about you. You ain't workin' here, boy."

Confused and angry at being called boy because of his dark Indian skin, Breed stood in momentary silence. "Just forget it."

They all walked out.

After they jumped on their bikes, they deliberately pedaled through a red traffic light, rode across the sidewalks, and stopped on the Traptown Bridge catwalk where they leaned over the railing and looked at the river.

A gigantic dead bloated carp drifted on top of the bluish-gray feted water. It stopped under a maroon sewer tile that jutted out of the foundation of the bank building. As if the tile were the sickening round mouth of some kind of ceramic monster, it vomited a gush of sewage onto the carp. The carp disappeared in a swirl of raw sewage, and a long ribbon of blue filth drifted under the bridge.

Breed and his friends turned their heads away from the sickening sight, leaned their bike wheels against the green steel catwalk railing, and sat on the seats of their bikes.

Hog pointed over the railing and down toward

133

the river. As if it had a nervous disorder, a dirty-yellow carp quivered on top of the water. "Think anybody would eat that?"

"No way." Breed shuddered. "Flies are landing on it, and it ain't even dead yet."

"If they drain a couple more sewers into the river," Screwball said with a sly grin, "the water will be so thick, you'll be able to walk on top of it."

Breed tilted his head and shrugged in a helpless gesture. "They say it's all for the progress of mankind."

"If there was a kind man he would give us a job," Screwball said. "You guys sure you ain't got any money?"

"Money? What's that?" Breed asked.

Breed looked across the river. The marquee on the tumbled-down Gable Theater read: 'CREATE YOUR HAPPY HOURS WITH THE BEST IN SOUND AND PICTURES'.

He turned toward Hog. "If we had money we'd be in that rat house."

Hog jerked his thumb toward the marquee. "Those rats in that dump have happy hours."

Screwball spun the handlebars of his bike around in a circle. "They should be happy. They get in free."

"They just about control the place," Breed said. "If you have something to eat in your hand, they'll run up your leg."

Hog tilted his head toward Breed. "What are you? Some kind of an idiot. That's why they call it The Rat House."

Breed knew Hog was just trying to agitate. He didn't answer.

Screwball jerked his head. His hair flipped out of his eyes. "Hey, Breed. Do you see those people walking by?"

"They're right in front of me," Breed said and joked, "No, I can't see them."

Screwball ignored Breed's attempted humor. "Don't they look like two giant fingers reached down from the sky and squashed their shoulders down to their asses?"

Breed had never thought of people that way, but Screwball's description fit. "Yeah," he said with sudden realization. "They look like big pears with arms and legs made out of skinny sticks."

Screwball went into his arrogant teacher act and changed his voice to a low tone of authority. "You kids will also notice that the people with the best clothes have the smallest shoulders and the biggest asses."

Hog spit over the railing. "They just don't have big asses, they're total assholes."

An overstuffed man in a three-piece suit walked onto the bridge at a brisk waddle. His small upper body projected through the padded shoulders of his expensive suit jacket, and his patent leather shoes flashed richly with each step that caused his expensive pants to flap around his skinny legs.

The man stopped in front of Breed. "Why don't you foul-mouthed long-hairs quit sitting around." With each word he spoke, his stomach jiggled and tugged at the buttons on his vest. Then, as the jiggling traveled to his face, he said, "Why don't you get a job like normal people?"

No one answered.

As the man turned to go, his lustrous watch

135

chain buried into a flap of fat around his bloated stomach. When he walked across the bridge, his big rear end stuck out like a shelf and caused the back of his silk-lined pants to wrinkle and hang down like window curtains.

Screwball pointed at the executive's swishing blubbery behind. "Look, a curtain ass!"

"In this town," Screwball said, "that's an average person."

Breed placed his foot on the pedal of his bike. Then he put his elbow on his knee and placed his fist under his chin. "What's average?"

As if he were adding numbers on a machine, Hog pointed his finger and wiggled it. "Not all people have two legs. If we average it out, the average person has one and a fraction of legs."

"I get it now." Screwball's mouth curved into a devilish grin. "The reason we can't get a job is because we have two legs."

"Ahh, who gives a shit?" Hog waved his hand down. "We don't need—"

Screwball interrupted and pointed. "Look across the bridge."

Breed couldn't see what Screwball was pointing at. "Where?"

"Up by the Rat House. That guy's putting something on the back of that stop sign."

Breed jerked his head to look, but at the end of the catwalk, a uniformed police officer waltzed toward them and stopped. "Are you the kids that were digging in the garbage behind the Army Store?"

Hog's body stiffened. "We wasn't diggin' in no garbage."

136

The officer waved the back of his hand in a shooing motion. "I don't want you kids hanging around where respectable people have to walk. Get those bikes off the sidewalk." He made a fist and brought the fleshy bottom of it down onto the railing. "And get off this bridge!"

Breed slowly pushed his bike until he had inched his way off the bridge and onto the edge of the street. He turned and glared at the officer. The officer's eyes turned cold. "If you're going to move that slow, maybe you can show me your bicycle licenses?"

Breed did not want to go through the usual ordeal of trying to explain something he had no money to do anything about. "What license, officer?"

The officer held a keep-your-mouth-shut look, placed his hand on his gun, lifted his other hand, and shook his finger at Breed. "The bicycle licenses you boys are supposed to have to ride in this town."

Breed figured it was time to try the old stupid act. He lowered his head and shamefacedly stared the sidewalk. "We didn't know."

"That's no excuse," the officer said and his icy voice began to melt.

"Yeah but—" Screwball whined and spoiled his act with a grin.

The officer picked up on the grin. His face froze back to ice. "Yeah, nothing," he said with authority and pulled a black book from his back pocket. "What's your name?"

Screwball hunched his shoulders and cringed. "Ted Deffen," he lied.

The officer held the tip of a stubby yellow pencil on a white, blue-lined page in the book but didn't write anything. "Deffen? Isn't your father the J.P.?"

"Pardon, sir?" Screwball said and lowered his head.

"Deffen," the officer repeated. "Isn't your father, the Justice of the Peace?"

"No," Screwball said, lifted his head, and lied again, "That's my uncle."

The officer snapped his black book shut and shook his finger in Screwball's face. "I'm going to give Ted a call and see if we can't get you boys licenses for those bicycles." The officer looked at the bikes and then studied Screwball's clothes. His pants were ripped out at the knees, and brown mud stains covered the canvas of his worn tennis shoes.

The officer shook his head and rubbed his chin. "You know it's not respectable to dress like that in public. If Ted knew you were downtown dressed like that he'd tan your hide."

Like a mistreated dog about to be hit, Screwball bent over.

The officer grabbed his shoulder and yanked him upright. "Don't slouch over, straighten up." He reached across, took Screwball's shirt out from between the crossbars, and pushed it into Screwball's chest. "Here! Get your shirt on."

Screwball and the others pulled their shirts on and the officer walked away.

Hog bounced his middle finger behind the officer's back. A few steps away, as if the officer could feel Hog's gesture, he stopped and turned toward Hog. Hog opened his hand and turned it over like he had just finished a friendly wave.

The officer didn't see the obscene gesture, but said, "And keep those bikes off the sidewalk!"

Like a cautious dog Breed, raised his lowered head. "Okay, thank you, Officer."

"Yes, thank you," Screwball said and did his best to hold back a snicker.

They played nice boys, mounted their bikes, and pedaled to the stop sign next to the Rat House.

Screwball looked up at the sign. What is it?"

Hog put his foot on the crossbars of his bike, balanced on one leg, and reached up. "Give me a chance to get it down." He lost his balance, plopped down on the seat.

"That's it," Screwball said. "Break your ass."

Hog laughed, and playfully looked at Screwball. "Go screw yourself."

With his mouth agape, Screwball nodded like a simpleton. "Okay, I'll do that."

"Come on, you guys cut the crap," Breed said and held onto Hog's bike frame. "It's too high. I'll hold your bike. Stand on the seat and get it."

Hog stood on the seat, grabbed the taped object, and pulled it off the back of the stop sign.

Screwball reached over and shook the bike, but Hog jumped down before he lost his balance. He ticked a finger at Screwball. "Nice try, Shit Foot, but you're not fast enough."

Ignoring Hog, Screwball's eyes focused on what was in Hog's hand. "It's a brass key."

Breed horned in close. "It has the name of the radio station on it."

The key was passed around. Everyone inspected it, and Breed handed it back to Hog. Hog put it in his pocket, sat on his bike, placed his feet on the pavement, and folded his arms across his chest. "I think we found that key that guy from the radio was talkin' about."

"That can't be it," Breed said. "They ain't even given out any clues yet."

Hog ran his fingers through his semi-curly black hair. His arm flexed and showed an arm that matched his stocky build that broadcasted his cocky demeanor. "Screw that!" he snapped back. "We found it."

Screwball's eyes lit up. "Maybe we won that cash prize."

Hog looked at the entrance to the Gable Theater. "Yeah, maybe enough to go to the Rat House and get two bags of popcorn."

Screwball held up two fingers. "Why two?"

"One for the rats and one for myself."

"That's no lie," Breed said. "You buy one bag, those rats will smell it and crawl right up your leg. You gotta throw one bag on the floor to keep them off your lap."

Screwball hunched over and jerked his shoulders like he was riding a horse. "Let's go to the radio station and get the money before we spend it all."

Hog pulled the key from his pocket and looked at it again.

Anticipation surged through Breed's veins. "Maybe we won enough money to go to Shell Island in style."

"Hell," Hog said and shook with a muffled spasm of amusement. "We'll go in a Taxi." He put the key back in his pocket.

They rode away from the mill town, and its tall false front buildings faded behind them.

Chapter 10

When Hog opened the door of the yellow-brick radio station, a huge mustached man, with his shirtsleeves rolled up past his elbows, flexed the muscles in his huge arms, and stood with his hands on his hips. Like some kind of a legendary God, he blocked the doorway and looked down at Breed and the others. "Where do you filthy kids think you're going?"

Hog reached into his back pocket, took out the key, he had taken from the back of the stop sign, and held it up in front of the man's face. "We found the key. Where do we go to get that prize money?"

As if he had just smelled the Traptown dump, a scrunched-up sour look deformed the man's face.

With expectations of winning enough money to take a lavish trip to Shell Island, Hog excitedly waved the key in a tight circle. "We won."

The man's forehead wrinkled, and his face smoothed to almost normal. "I guess you kids have a reason to be here." He stepped aside and pointed down the hallway. "Go down there and turn right. Pinky's in his office."

The promise of winning enough money to end all their troubles seemed to invade Breed's and his pal's senses. They all tried to get through the doorway at once. Breed squeezed through and quickly walked down the hallway ahead of Hog. Hog rushed up behind and elbowed alongside. Passing Breed, he looked over his shoulder. "I ain't no fly-back-fart catcher. I ain't walkin' behind nobody."

They stopped outside Pinky's office and looked

through the glass window in the oak-framed door. Mirrored sunglasses covered Pinky's eyes. His bright Hawaiian shirt seemed to be hanging on a coat hanger, but it was supported by the small shoulders of his frail body. When he reached up to adjust his glasses, his pointer finger flashed a weird pinkish color.

Hog didn't knock. He turned the doorknob and swung the door open. They all walked in. Pinky tilted his head up and peered through the one-way reflecting lenses of his glasses. "What can I do for you, boys?"

Hog walked around the desk and held the key in front of Pinky's face. "Here's the key. Give us our prize." Clink! He dropped the key in the metal ashtray on Pinky's paper-cluttered desk.

"Now boys, you know you shouldn't be in here." A defiant smirk covered Pinky's face. "It's not polite not to knock before you enter a room?"

"Oh." Hog turned and walked out the door. "Come on, you guys."

The others followed Hog into the hall. He slammed the door. With the back of their fists, they all pounded on the door so hard it sounded like thunder. The glass rattled and just before it was about to break, the door swung open.

Hog strolled in and stopped in front of Pinky's desk. "How's that?"

The others walked in and Breed stepped next to Hog. "Did you hear us knock?"

Hog held out his opened hand. "Just give us our prize money, and we'll be out of here."

Tilting his head down and waving his hands in a halting motion, Pinky stood up. "Now, boys." He

143

shook his pinkish finger at them. "You know the contest hasn't officially started yet."

Hog plucked the key out of the ashtray and shook it in Pinky's face. "Ain't this the key?"

Pinky rocked his head from side to side. "Tisk, tisk!" he said through his yellowed teeth, turned his back to them, and looked out the window. "It's the key all right, but the contest hasn't started."

Screwball stuck out his lower jaw and hunched toward Pinky's back. "Didn't you say over the radio that the finder of the key would be awarded a cash prize?"

Pinky turned around and faced him. "Well, yes."

Screwball waved his hand in the air. "When were you planning to end the contest?"

"When somebody found the key."

Screwball held up his hand. "Wait!" He pointed at Pinky. "You just said the contest hasn't been started. Ain't that right?"

Pinky nodded. "That's right."

"But if you started the contest, you'd give us the money, right?"

Pinky kept right on nodding. "That's right."

"That means that when we found the key the contest ended."

Pinky's shoulders jerked in sync with the movement of his nodding head. "Oh yes, the contest is over."

Screwball held out his hand. "Give us the money."

Puzzled, Pinky looked down at Screwball's outstretched hand. "What?"

"You can't end something that ain't been

144

started?"

"That's right," Hog said. "You ended the contest, so it was started. He held out his hand. "Give us the money."

Pinky's face grimaced with confusion. When he turned his back to them, the tail of his Hawaiian shirt rode up and revealed a rear end that looked like a camel's hump with a flowered tablecloth over it.

He talked at the window. "But that's not the way it works."

"What are you trying to pull?" Breed asked. "We heard the contest over the radio, and we found the key."

"That's right," Screwball said and mockingly pointed to the hump.

Pinky kept his back turned. "I hear ya."

Screwball tilted his head, put his finger below his eye, and pulled the skin down until his eye bulged. "Oh really? Why don't you turn your hump ass around? Then you'll be able to see us, too."

Like a man whose wig had shifted and revealed a bald head, Pinky pulled his shirttail down and concealed his humped ass. Then as if he hadn't heard Screwball's cutting remark, he wheeled around. His mirrored sunglasses flashed like ugly fly eyes. "I don't care what you found." He stepped away from his desk.

Hog cupped his hand, put it to his mouth, and let a big hawker slide onto the tips of his fingers.

Screwball lifted his finger from his eye and whispered to Hog, "Do it."

Pinky glared at Screwball. "I heard that."

145

"Oh yeah?" Screwball questioned and smiled. "What do you think this is? A hearing test?"

Pinky didn't laugh. Breed jerked his thumb at him. "What are you trying to do, cheat us out of the money?"

Hog dropped his hawker-loaded hand. "Yeah, Pinky, what are you doin', running a rigged contest?"

As if he were trying to puff up his sunken chest, Pinky took in a deep breath. His chest didn't expand, but he peered down at them. "Look, boys, we didn't even give out any clues."

"We don't care about the clues. "Screwball held out his hand. "Give us the money."

As if he were in pain, Pinky shook his head. "We can't give you kids any money. You're underage. You know how it works."

Hog put his un-hawkered-filled hand on a stack of papers on Pinky's desk and gripped them into a wrinkled ball. "In other words, we ain't gettin' nothin'." He dragged the ball of papers off the desk and let them fall to the floor.

Pinky glanced at the papers and then directed his attention toward Hog. "Just get out of this office." He waved the back of his hand as if he were shooing flies. "Come on . . . Out! Git out! I have work to do." He turned his back to them.

Hog reared back and flicked the hawker off the ends of his cupped fingers. It shot toward Pinky's brightly colored floral-print shirt, but Pinky turned. The hawker zinged past his face. Splat! It landed on the wall.

Pinky jerked his head toward the splat. "What the hell's the matter with you?" He pointed to the hawker. "Are you some kind of pig? I told you, you weren't getting any money. What did you spit on my—"

"Wait!" Hog held up his hand. "Your radio said that you would give a cash prize for the key. I found your goddamn key." He snatched the key out of the ashtray and shook it in front of Pinky's face. "So give us the cash prize like your station advertised."

"What?" Pinky thundered. "You come in here, call me names, throw my important papers on the floor, and then like some filthy mouthed hog, you spit on my wall." He stepped forward and unintentionally tramped on the papers. He looked down at the papers and then at Hog. "Now you want a prize?"

"Pardon me!" Hog said slow and calm. "Sir, do you mean we are not going to receive your wonderful prize?"

Pinky reached for the phone. "I don't have to repeat myself. I'm calling the police."

Hog didn't put his hand to his mouth this time. He spit a hawker. It landed on the phone. "Oh excuse me, Mister Pinky. We didn't give out any clues. You shouldn't have a prize on your phone."

Pinky drew his hand away from the hawkered phone. "You're just a goddamn hog!" he screamed, and the veins in his neck popped out.

"Pardon me, sir," Hog said and arrogantly lifted his chin. "Could you repeat that?"

Pinky reached into his pocket, pulled out a white handkerchief, and patted his forehead. He checked his shirt pocket for a pack of cigarettes. He pulled out a flat white pack with a red circle on it

147

and fingered it for a cigarette. It was empty. "Damn it." He crumpled the empty package into his fist.

"What's the matter?" Screwball asked. "Can't you find a weenie to suck on?"

"You damn kids — Whooee!" Pinky reached to his empty shirt pocket for a cigarette pack that wasn't there and patted his forehead — again.

Hog shook the key at Pinky. "Give us that prize money, you cheap gyp."

Pinky looked at the hawkered phone and shook his head with disgust. Then he threw the empty crumpled cigarette pack at Hog. Hog reached up and nonchalantly snatched it out of the air.

Pinky screamed, "I said, you ain't getting no money. You goddamn hog! Did you hear me?"

"Thank you!" Hog politely replied. He grabbed the crotch of his pants and shook it at Pinky. "Open your phony shit-eatin' mouth and hog up on this!"

Pinky balled up his fist. "You dirty little hog-ass bastard! Get your filthy mouth out of this station!"

"Station?" Hog questioned. "This ain't no radio station. It's just a big shithouse and you're the shit!" He threw the key at the ashtray. It hit with a loud clink, bounced up, skidded across the desk, and fell to the floor. "And you can shove that key up your ass."

"He can't," Screwball said. "His face looks just like his ass. He's so stupid, he won't know which ass to shove it into."

Hog nodded in approval. "He'll know. All he has to do is put it where his head is."

Pinky reached for the hawkered phone, but he

148

drew his hand back. Then he violently shook his head. Hate radiated from his eyes. "You goddamn kids, can just get the hell away from me."

Breed edged toward the door.

With his arms crossed across his chest, Hog stood in front of Pinky. "Make us."

Pinky held out his hands and pushed Hog toward the door. Hog defiantly straightened his legs and resisted the forced exit.

"Hey, you trained monkey," Hog said. "Get your gyp-ass hands off me."

Pinky stopped pushing and yelled, "Hey, Dave! Help me get this troublemaker out of the station."

Breed and the others stepped into the hallway, walked backwards, and watched. The huge mustached man came running down the hall.

With his big hands, the mustached man reached for Hog, but Hog jumped through the doorway.

"There!" Pinky slammed the door and locked it.

Hog yelled through the glass. "You ain't hurtin' my feelings. I've been thrown out of better places than this."

"Just don't come back," Pinky yelled back through the glass and then muttered, "You goddamn hog."

Flexing the muscles in his arm and smiling a wide toothless smile, the huge mustached man stood like a stone statue and pointed down the hallway and the exit.

Breed and his friends left the building. Outside, they jumped on their bikes, pedaled away from the radio station, and took a shortcut through the flats.

When they rode close to the red brick food warehouse, a stack of empty cardboard boxes blocked the big truck entrance doorway

They stopped.

Breed grinned to himself. "If I had my motorbike, I could crash right through those boxes." He pedaled his bike to an opening in the cardboard, stopped, and looked in. Far into the warehouse, something that could be a red motorbike frame stuck out between stacks of skids.

Hog pedaled next to him and stopped. "Hey, there's only one line of boxes here. Let's crash right through them with our bikes."

Breed continued looking at the red object. "We could, but my motorbike might be in there."

Leaning forward, Hog peered inside the building. "That ain't your bike. If one of those fat guys sat on a bike, the tires would blow out."

Ignoring Hog's observation, Breed's heart raced. If that was his motorbike, he could ride to Shell Island faster than waiting for Ballpeen to build a boat that might not float. "Maybe they're fixin' it up for One-Finger-Burke. Let's go see."

Hog reached down and felt his pocket where the radio contest key had been. "We got screwed out of that prize money, and your bike probably ain't there. But if you wanna go in, we might be able to get some paint for Ballpeen's boat."

"That's a pretty big place," Breed said. "Where you gonna look for it?"

Hog grinned. His voice was reassuring. "They keep the paint locked up in that big steel locker."

Breed didn't want to get caught stealing.

Gnawing apprehension filled his mind. Getting his motorbike back wasn't stealing, but taking paint was. He wanted to discourage Hog from stealing the paint. "We could, but Ballpeen isn't going to finish that boat."

"If he does." Screwball chuckled. "He'll need the paint to hold it together."

Breed smiled. "That's true, but that's a big lock on that locker." He turned toward Hog. "You'll never break it."

As if he were turning a key, Hog placed his thumb and forefinger together and twisted his hand. "The bigger the lock, the easier it is to pick."

Breed still didn't want him taking the paint. "That fat guy they call Pie Man always sits in front of that locker and eats pie. You'll never get past his fat ass."

Hog face took on a look of suspicion. "What-a-ya keep making excuses for? You afraid to go in?"

Breed placed his foot on the pedal of his bike as if he were ready to go. "I ain't afraid of nothin'. You're the one that has to get past Pie Man."

Hog's face beamed with satisfaction. "You guys get him to chase you. If there's any paint in that locker, I'll get it."

Breed still didn't like the idea of stealing the paint. He could ride past the warehouse and go home, but if he did, Flick and everybody would call him, chicken-crybaby, forever. He might be able to live with it, but he couldn't live without knowing if that red frame was his motorbike. Taking a measly can of paint to get his motorbike back was worth taking the chance. He jerked his head toward the pile of cardboard boxes that were blocking the entrance to the warehouse. "Let's get their attention first."

They got a big run, pedaled hard and fast and crashed into the boxes. The boxes parted, thumped, and spun out of the way. Expecting the noise to cause a diversion, Breed and his friends rode through the opened truck entrance doorway. Inside, noisy forklift motors roared, but no warehouse workers noticed them. When they pedaled behind a short stocky man driving a forklift, just as the man looked to the left, Hog veered to the right, sped down an aisle, and stopped at the paint locker.

Pie Man wasn't there.

Hog jumped off his bike and picked the lock. He yanked on the door. It flew open. He looked inside. A row of bright-yellow gallon cans of paint sat on the shelf. He grabbed a full can and slipped it on the handlebars of his bike. He jumped on and pedaled once. The wire handle on the paint can popped off. The can fell onto the hard cement floor. The lid sprang open. Yellow paint gushed out and brightened the floor. Hog stopped to pick up what was left in the can. It was empty.

"Damn!" He looked to the locker for another can.

Like a jack-in-the-box, Pie Man sprang out. With cruel and insulting delight on his fat–fluffed up face, he reached for the handlebars of Hog's bike. "Your thievin' ass is mine."

Hog jerked the bike away from Pie Man's chubby hands. "Hant! You didn't get me." He jumped on his bike and zipped out the warehouse door.

Enraged, Pie Man waddled after Hog, but after

a few yards, he grunted, wheezed, and gave up.

Back in the warehouse, Screwball pedaled in front of Breed — slow. He made faces and pointed at the stocky man driving the forklift. Breed pedaled behind him and scanned the warehouse for his motorbike. The piece of red frame he was after, stuck out from a pile of wooden skids. He stopped, hooked one foot over the crossbar of his bike, and put the other foot on the floor. Then he reached over and picked up the red frame. It was not a part of his motorbike. He jumped back on the seat of his bike. Staying behind the forklift, he pedaled halfway through the warehouse until the stocky man on the forklift wrenched the wheel to the right, tromped on the brake, and stopped. He jerked his head in Breed's direction.

With his finger pointing at Breed, he cranked up his siren mouth and triumphantly yelled, "It's those smart-ass kids again. Get those laughing bastards."

He took his heavy foot off the brake, gunned the engine, and turned the forklift in front of Breed. Breed was blocked. Screwball wheeled around the open side. The stocky man jumped off the forklift and ran after Breed. Panic grabbed Breed's mind. He threw his bike over a wooden skid of dented cans. The stocky man jumped in his path and blocked that escape route. "I got you now! You goddamn white nigger!"

The stocky man's grabbing hand was a foot away, primed to snatch Breed right off the floor. Breed made an Olympic winning — Jim Thorpe — jump over the seat of the forklift and landed next to his bike. He picked it up and pushed on the

153

handlebars. The front wheel cocked sideways. It wouldn't roll. He forced the bike forward. The roll-less front tire burned a black slid mark on top of the hard cement and stopped. The stocky man was right behind him. Breed pushed forward — faster, faster. The wheel would not go. He stopped and kicked it. It un-cocked and turned free. He straddled the bike. When his feet hit the pedals, he strained and pumped power to the back wheel. The stocky man's hand swished over the back of his shirt. Air rushed down his back. The stocky man grabbed again — missed. Breed pumped harder. His bike lunged forward. He looked back over his shoulder. Dirty fingernails scraped down the back of his arm.

Breed looked toward the only exit. Quick shit-footed Screwball skinned out to the street. Right behind him, more fat guys than Breed could count, formed a wall. They blocked his escape. He was alone. He was outnumbered. The heavy hand of the stocky man grabbed and beat threatening gusts of wind against his back, and a quivering jelly mountain of fat was right in front of him.

For a split second his mind flashed a vision of tomorrow's paper. His picture was on the front page, just like Lard Man had said it would be. Big black print read, 'BOY CAUGHT TRYING TO ROB WAREHOUSE'.

He didn't need that. His mind cried for a way out. There was only one chance. If he could get going fast enough, he might be able to crash through that wall of fat. The barrel-bellied guy, with a thick splotch of mustard on his unshaven face, yelled and spit food through his tobacco

154

stained teeth. "We got you now. Punk!"

Out of nowhere, Pie Man's hand plowed air close to side of Breed's face. Breed forced his leg muscles to pedal faster.

Go! Go! Go! He told himself. My body is a machine and I have the control switch jammed on wide open. I'm not stopping for anything. I'm smashing right on through that line of lard.

He sucked in needed air, pedaled harder, gained speed.

As if they didn't know if he were going to stop, the ballooned-bellied men of the lard line stutter-stepped, but stood fast. It was a game of chicken, bike against man, machine against fat, but the big blubber line of men didn't move. With arms stretched out, waiting to rip Breed's body from his moving bike, the lard line gelled solid.

Breed realized he wasn't going fast enough to scare them. He mentally prepared for a crash. With his eyes closed tight, he made one last powerful push on the pedal and tensed to plunge into the line of lard.

At the last instant, a nervous mouth blared, "He's not going to stop!"

Breed opened his eyes.

Tumbling over themselves, the lard linemen jumped out of the way.

Breed slipped through.

"You slippery little bastard!" Pie Man yelled; and as fast as his chubby feet could carry him, he quickly waddled after him.

Breed steered his bike out the exit. His back tire bit into the gravel parking lot. With stones and dirt spinning off his back tire, he escaped onto the road.

Shaking his fist and wheezing for breath, Pie Man stood in a little puff of dust.

Down the road, next to the river, a huge pile of coal loomed up like a lifesaving shield of safety. Breed slipped behind it and watched. Pie Man and a member of the lard line squeezed into a pickup truck and raced up the road. They rode past the coal pile a few times, gave up, and went back to the warehouse.

Before Breed could breathe a sigh of relief, the faint whisper of someone talking met his ears. "If you tell, I'll cut your ears off."

A little girl, about seven-years old, rushed out of the weeds and stopped in front of Breed. Tears flowed down her red face. Her thin plaid dress had been ripped from her shoulder to her knees, and blood flowed from little cuts on the side of her ears.

Concerned, Breed bent over and looked into her red face. "Are you okay?"

Stuttering like children do when they are in-between crying, the girl took one look at Breed and burst out with a big "Waaa! He's gonna cut my ears off." She ran down the road.

Wanting to make sure she was all right, Breed turned his bike around to go after her, but a blond bony dog came around the coal pile and stopped in front of him.

"Do your business," rang in Breed's ears. On command, the dog squatted and crapped. Then it dug its feet in the loose coal and took off running.

"Hey, asshole!" filled the air.

Breed turned. Henry, the dirty magazine freak from the gas station, and One-Finger-Burke's son,

Burkie, came out from around the coal pile.

Although Burkie suggestively tilted his long, sickly pale face in the direction of Breed's crotch, Breed was thankful Burkie didn't have his long knife. As if he didn't want Burkie to look at Breed's crotch, Henry stepped in front of Burkie and blocked his view. Henry's tight pants and a tight-fitting polo shirt showed off his weightlifter's muscles, but his body didn't fit his elf-like face.

Henry glanced at the dog crap and smiled a sickening smile. "We're writing down names and shoving faces in dog shit."

With his hands in his pants pockets, Burkie chuckled. "And we ain't got no paper." He opened his mouth to laugh, and revealed a cavern of bluish gums and rotten, broken teeth. Breed knew Burkie's father had the money to send him to a dentist, but he figured Burkie was afraid to go.

Breed shook the thought from his mind. He had just dodged a line of lard men, now he would have to get away or have his face rubbed in dog shit. Or worse yet: If Burkie had his knife, he would cut his ears off. Sickening fear flooded his heart. He froze.

When he finally fought off the fear, he stepped on the pedal of his bike to pedal away, but Burkie grabbed the bike seat and held on. Breed couldn't move.

Henry came up and grabbed Breed by the front of his shirt. "Where do you think you're going?"

"I'm going to see what happen to that little girl. "You better not have done anything to her."

Henry snarled. "So what if we did?" Just as Lard Man's face had done, Henry's face cramped

157

into mean lines of hostility. "What are you going to do about it?"

Breed reached up, grabbed Henry's wrist, and pulled. It didn't come off. Breed silently cussed at himself for not trying to ride away sooner.

"What are you going to do about it?" Burkie said. "You can't prove nothin'. And even if you could, my dad's a cop. He'll put you in jail for lying."

Burkie pulled his hands from his pockets. As he did, one of his hands dragged out a small piece of plaid cloth that matched the little girl's torn dress. It fell to ground. Burkie didn't see it. But it proved that Henry and he had done something to the little girl. Before Breed could say anything, Henry let loose of Breed's wrist, pushed him, and pulled the bike out from under him. Breed tumbled to the ground.

Henry grinned with scornful satisfaction. "Thanks for the bike, Rat Boy."

Breed never knew just how rotten these two were. Anyone who would rape a little girl would have no problem cutting his ears off or killing another person. Lying on the ground, he held up his hand in a helpless gesture. "Your old man already stole my motorbike. What do you want with this bike?"

Henry folded his arms across his chest, lifted his head in a posture of superiority, and looked down at Breed's bike. "I ain't never saw such a piece of shit."

Burkie lifted his skinny arm and pointed to the dog crap. "Let's rub his face in it. It'll match his shitty bike."

Henry grabbed Breed's wrist. Breed bucked to his feet and tried to pull away from Henry's grip. He couldn't.

Burkie grabbed Breed's other wrist and held tight. Breed wiggled, kicked, and tried to punch free, but he was no match for the combined muscles of Burkie and Henry. They pulled him toward the dog crap, but he dragged his feet in the loose coal on the ground.

When his skid marks stopped in front of the dog crap, Burkie laughed a high-pitched girlish laugh. "Let's make him eat it."

Henry smiled. "We couldn't do that," he said as if he meant it.

Breed relaxed for a moment.

Henry laughed. "I lied."

He reached up, grabbed the hair on the back of Breed's head, and yanked his face down toward the dog crap. Breed jerked his head away from the awful threat. Like a stone shot out of a slingshot, his right arm broke free, but the uncontrollable force caused his hand to land right in the dog crap. He reached up with his crap-covered hand to grab Henry's hand. As if Breed's hand were a stick of dynamite about to explode, Henry jumped back. Burkie jumped back, too. Breed realized he had a weapon on his hand. He reached out for Henry. Henry turned and ran toward the river. Breed reached for Burkie. Burkie shrieked like a schoolgirl afraid of a mouse and scampered after Henry.

After he was sure they were gone, Breed rubbed his hand in the loose coal dust on the ground. The dog crap came off, but the smell stuck like invisible glue.

He jumped on his bike and pedaled down the road as fast as he could.

When he caught up with Screwball and Hog, Hog asked, "Did they catch you?"

Panting for breath, Breed blurted out, "No," and sucked in much needed air.

Screwball looked at Breed and grinned. "If Pie Man had both hands in his back pockets, he wouldn't be fast enough to catch his own ass."

Breed continued to catch his breath and huffed, "Yeah . . . he's so slow, huff — huff — he has to speed up to stop."

Screwball sat on his bike and moved his arms as if he were running. "Run, run, as fast as you can, you can't catch me, I'm the Fudge Sickle man."

Hog stared at Screwball with his mouth half open. Then he shook his head. "Goddamn nut." He pedaled away.

Before Breed could tell Screwball about the little girl and what Henry and Burkie had done to him, he pedaled away, too.

Breed pedaled after them, but his legs burned with pain. It felt as if the forklift driver's hand was still grabbing at his back, and the dog crap was still an inch away from his face. He shuddered, shook off the eerie feeling, and continued down the road.

When he caught up with Hog and Screwball, the chain on his bike fell off. Screwball and Hog kept riding. He stopped, bent over, re-threaded the chain as far as he could, and kicked it back onto the sprocket.

Screwball and Hog turned around and came back.

"You think you'll make it home sometime before tomorrow?" Hog said and laughed.

The dog crap odor was still on Breed's hand. He it away from his face. "I would've been all right if Burkie and Henry didn't try and rub dog shit in my face."

Screwball's eyes widened. "What?"

While his relief turned to anger, Breed told them what had happened.

Then Hog pointed to a healthy green clump of grass a few yards away from the road. "Rub your hands in that grass. It'll take the smell right out." He paused. "They should have never done that to that girl."

Usually flippant, Screwball made no effort to disguise his feelings. "Burkie's crooked cop father's just as bad for letting him do it." He hesitated. "We gotta find a way to make them pay for that."

Breed walked to the grass, bent over and rubbed his hands with it. When he looked up, two new bikes were lying in the tall weeds. He looked back over his shoulder. "Hey, you guys, look what we have here!"

Screwball jumped off his bike, ran toward Breed, and stopped. "Holy cow! "There has to be a God." He looked around, searching.

Hog sat on his bike and scanned the area. "I don't see anybody."

Screwball looked at the bikes. "When Burkie and Henry weren't screwing some little girl, they stole these bikes."

Keeping a wary eye out for Burkie and Henry, Hog glanced at the bikes. "They're probably

161

fishing."

"They ain't fishing," Screwball said. "They're taking turns playing with each other's worms."

An immediate flash of excitement filled Hog's face. "Let's take these bikes and strip 'em for parts."

Even though Henry and Burkie deserved to have the bikes stolen, Breed thought about Burkie and his long sharp knife. He was afraid to steal the bikes. "Burkie's old man will try to arrest us," he said. "The parts on these bikes probably won't fit our bikes. They're too new."

Screwball looked down at the bikes. "They'll fit, but ass-kissing Burkie will know we took them."

"This is true." Hog lifted one finger. "If One-Finger-Burke catches us with the bikes or the parts, he'll get us for having stolen property."

Breed placed his foot on the frame on one of the bikes. "So what do you wanna do, just leave the bikes here?"

Hog grinned fiendishly. "No way! We'll never get a chance like this again."

Breed lifted his foot and pushed on the frame of one of the bikes. "If we don't take them, Burkie and his old man will think they got away with stealing my motorbike."

Screwball moved his fingers as if he were adding up columns on an adding machine. "Wait a minute!" An idiotic grin spread across his face.

Breed recognized that grin. "You just thought of something, didn't you?"

Like a pecking chicken, Screwball nodded with little, short snappy jerks. "Yup! Yup! If you kids are good, I'll give you a treat."

Breed turned his palm up and jerked it with encouragement. "Come on, Screwball, what's your great plan?"

Hog moved his bike a few feet down the road and pointed to Screwball's jerking head. "Quit actin' like a chicken peckin' air, and get over here so they can't see us."

Screwball and Breed pushed their bikes next to Hog.

"Okay, you kids," Screwball said. "It's simple. We ride across the bridge, hide our bikes in the weeds, and come back here."

"If we hide our bikes there," Hog said, "those kids from the flats gang will take them."

"No they won't," Screwball said. "You can stay there and watch them."

"Yeah right." Hog's eyes filled glared with disapproval. "Like I'm gonna fight off three or four flats gang guys all by myself."

"Breed let out an exasperated sigh. "You won't have to. If you see them coming just call them names and ride away. They'll chase you and never think about looking for the bikes."

Hog looked scared but killed the look with a grin. "After what they did to that little girl, I could do that."

A Ford station wagon with fake wooded sides and rusted rocker panels rattled down the road. With his head out the window, the driver honked indignantly, and yelled, "Get the hell off the road."

Hog nonchalantly held up his middle finger. The driver quit honking and looked straight into the windshield. With his mouth flapping and cuss words filling the car's air, he went on by.

As if the station wagon had never come and gone, Screwball continued talking. "Me and Breed will walk back here and take these bikes. But before we ride away, we'll make Burkie and Henry chase us."

Hog smiled with approval. "They'll never catch you guys on foot."

Breed looked past Hog's shoulder and to the bikes. "Let's do it. Those little-girl-screwin', dog shit lovers deserve everything they get."

They pedaled down the road, crossed over the Rat Street Bridge, and hid their bikes in the weeds.

"If that flats gang comes," Hog said, "I'll be ready, but I'll need something to slow them down."

Screwball shrugged. "You'll be on your bike. They'll be on foot. They'll never catch you." He turned to go.

Breed held up his hand. "Wait a minute."

Screwball turned back. "What?"

"Let's dig a hole in this path for those little-girl-screwin' thieves to step in when they're chasing us."

"That's a good idea," Screwball said with expectant delight, but frowned. "But we ain't got no shovel."

Breed looked toward the river. "We don't need one. I'll get a flat rock. We can use it to dig with."

"Just don't get that rock the cow pissed on."

"What?"

"You know, that rock when they say, 'It's rainin' like a cow pissin' on a flat rock.'"

Breed ran down the cinder path to the riverbank. A flat rock sat in the water. He didn't pick it up. He picked up a rock that wasn't wet and carried it back to the bikes.

They dug a deep hole in the path, scattered the fresh dirt across the field so it wouldn't be seen, and covered the hole with long stiff grass.

Hog brushed his hands together and leaned back. "That should do it."

"Wait," Breed said, "lets dig another one. We'll space it a step from this one. That way, when they step in one hole and try to catch themselves from falling, with their other foot, they'll step in the second hole and fall."

In approval, Screwball jerked his thumb upward. "Nothin' like a double whammy."

After they had dug another miniature pit and covered it with grass, Breed and Screwball jogged back to where the stolen bikes were hidden.

Standing next to the bikes, Breed and Screwball watched the path that led along the river. In the distance, now clad in shorts, Burkie and Henry walked along the riverbank.

Breed pointed to them. "Only faggots and sissies wear shorts."

"Not only that," Screwball said. "They look like the kind of kids that when you first meet them, you don't like them. Then, after you get to know them, you hate them."

Burkie and Henry waded through the tall weeds and walked toward the bikes.

Screwball shouted, "Hey, Burkie! I did you a favor the other day."

Burkie looked up. "What are you talking about, asshole?" He kept walking.

With Henry so close behind him that his nose was in Burkie's butt, Burkie started climbing up the steep riverbank.

Screwball yelled down to him, "I saved your life the other day." He lifted one of the bikes into an upright position. "I killed a shit eatin' dog."

Breed tilted the other bike up and stood next to it.

Walking closer, Burkie sneered at him. "Hey, Indian dog shit, get away from those bikes."

Henry pulled his nose away from Burkie's butt and yelled out, "Why don't you go back where you came from?"

He can't," Screwball said. "He don't have a reservation."

Breed ignored the remarks and pushed the bike onto the road. He looked back over his shoulder and yelled, "We're takin' your stolen bikes."

Henry caught up to Burkie, and they both ran toward Breed and Screwball. Before they could get close, Breed and Screwball mounted the bikes and rode away. Burkie and Henry chased them for a few yards, began gasping for breath, and stopped.

A ways down the road, Breed and Screwball stopped and waited for Burkie and Henry to catch their breaths and run after them, again.

Breathing heavily, Burkie stood in the middle of the road with his hands on his knees. "Come back here!" he huffed. "I'll tell my dad. He'll put you in jail."

With his feet flat on the pavement, Screwball sat on the bike. "You, and your crooked old man, can eat shit and bark at the moon!"

Henry shook his fist at Screwball. "You can't talk to us like that."

"We're sorry," Breed said. "Your old man

doesn't have to bark at the moon."

Deciding to give up on running, Burkie and Henry walked toward Breed and Screwball.

When they got close, Screwball held out his hand and motioned to them with his little finger. "Come on, you little babies, call your daddies. Maybe they'll catch us for you."

Breed held his arm straight out and motioned with his middle finger. "Come on, Burkie. See if you can steal this."

Burkie clenched teeth and made a face. "When I get you, you're going to jail." He ran after Breed, came within a few feet, and slashed out. But his swishing hand only caught air.

"Ha! Ha!" Breed taunted and sprinted away.

Burkie and Henry chased Screwball and Breed a few yards and stopped.

Breed and Screwball stopped, too.

"What's the matter, Burkie," Screwball jeered. "Is the little baby tired from screwing a little girl?"

Henry looked at Burkie and let out a rasping snort. "She told?"

"I guess so." Burkie's face filled with renewed rage. "I'll cut her goddamn ears off."

Even though they were exhausted, the chase continued. Burkie and Henry kept trying to catch Screwball and Breed. But they leapfrogged down the road and kept just ahead of them. When they ran, Breed and Screwball pedaled faster. When they stopped, Breed and Screwball stopped. And all the time, they taunted and called them names, just daring Burkie and Henry to catch them; and it took more and more time for Burkie and Henry to catch their breaths.

When the Rat Street Bridge was in sight, Breed and Screwball leisurely pedaled the twice-stolen bikes to the center of the span, stopped, and waited. Hog peeked out from the weeds and yelled, "They're coming on the bridge."

Breed and Screwball turned to look. Screwball pointed to the bike he was standing beside and yelled across the water from the bridge, "Hey Burkie! Tell your old man to jump in and steal this. You ass kissing thief!" He picked up the bike, held it, and turned his head towards them.

"Don't do it," Henry pleaded.

With his head bobbing with sadistic laughter, Screwball threw the bike into the river.

Breed dismounted, held the other bike over the water, and yelled directly at Burkie. "Steal these bikes now, you flat-kneed, round-mouth faggot!"

The bike started to slip before Breed wanted to drop it. He felt a sudden delayed fatigue from the warehouse escape. His arms and legs screamed in pain.

Burkie yelled across the bridge at Breed. "Go ahead, drop it, Rat Boy! I'll cut your ears off."

"What's the matter?" Breed said. "Can't your puny mind think of anything else to say."

"You even think about throwing that bike in, I'll kick your nigger ass!"

This instantly infuriated Breed. All pain went away. "Stick your baby-fucking pointed head in the ground," he yelled back with vehemence. "Spin your dumb ass around and drill yourself to hell!"

Breed held the bike and waited for Burkie to get closer. The awkward outstretched position he used to hold the bike over the railing caused his

168

arms to shake uncontrollably.

When Burkie and Henry were only a few feet away, Breed let the bike fall from his quivering grasp. While he dashed across the bridge, the bike splashed into the water and disappeared beneath the surface. Air in the tires caused the bike to pop up and float for a few seconds. Then the current took it downriver and gracefully sucked it under the green water.

Breed and Screwball ran down the path, hopped over the miniature pits, walked into the field, and stood next to Hog and their bikes.

Breed tensed. "When they get close, we'll jump on our bikes and lure them into the pits."

"They look really pissed now," Hog said, and they stood and waited.

The blond, bony dog came out of the tall weeds and stopped on the other side of the pits.

Hog pointed to it. "Do your business."

Breed brushed his hair from his forehead. "He won't do anything. He already crapped."

The dog squatted and crapped in the path.

Screwball shook his head in amazement. "That dog's like Henry and Burkie. He's always full of shit."

Henry and Burkie walked a few steps toward the end of the bridge and stopped. While Henry leaned on the catwalk railing, Burkie weakly warned, "Let's see you ride from us now!"

Breed pointed at Burkie, arched his arm, and swung it into a come-here gesture. "Come on and get us."

As their breaths came in labored gasps, Burkie and Henry didn't take a single step.

Hog sat on his bike and looked toward Screwball and Breed. "You guys are gonna have to get them mad. They're too tired to run anymore."

Screwball cupped his hands to his mouth and yelled, "Screw you and your queer!"

Burkie and Henry continued the chase with a renewed vengeance. Breed, Screwball, and Hog waited until they got close. Burkie and Henry raced up the path right for the miniature pits. But they didn't step in them. They luckily leaped over the tripping holes and rushed right at Breed. Hog and Screwball jumped on their bikes and rode away. Breed jumped on his bike and pushed on the pedal once. The chain fell off, jammed between the tire and the frame. The back wheel locked up. Burkie was twenty feet away — coming fast.

But Breed's luck changed.

Burkie's foot slammed down on the slippery dog crap.

Falling forward, his foot flew back and flung the crap into the air. As usual, Henry was right behind him with his nose next to Burkie's butt. Splat! A piece of flying crap hit Henry in the face. He reached up, grabbed his face and fell on Burkie.

Breed put his chain back on his bike, jumped on, and pedaled down the path. A few yards away, he looked back. Burkie and Henry lay in a jumbled heap, gasping for breath.

Trying to wipe the crap off themselves, they got up, walked back onto the bridge, stopped in the center, and leaned against the railing. It seemed as if they couldn't figure out what had happened. And like opened-mouthed trolls lurking under little bridges of grass, the pits waited to gobble up someone's feet.

After he left the field, Breed pedaled up the long hill toward home. Screwball and Hog were coming down the hill.

Screwball dismounted and walked alongside his bike. "We were coming back to see what took you so long."

"I never thought they would miss both pits."

Hog jumped off his bike. "We thought they caught you."

"They almost did, but that dog saved my life."

Hog's eyes widened. "What?"

"Burkie slipped in that dog shit. His foot flew up and flicked shit right into Henry's face."

Laughing, Hog hunched his shoulders and pushed on the handlebars of his bike. "I wonder if Burkie's old man's gonna fix Henry's shit face. He fixes everything else."

Screwball cast a thoughtful look in Hog's direction. "Maybe he'll steal him a new face."

"He probably will," Breed said matter-of-factly. "I still don't have my motorbike back, and the cops won't do anything about it."

"Whatta-ya expect?" Screwball said. "You live in Traptown."

Breed forced a pang of sadness from his heart. "Yeah, but Ball-peen's building a boat."

Chapter 11

That night, porch lights twinkled on galvanized garbage cans, and the wind pushed on. Like mischievous pranksters, little whirlwinds danced down dark alleys and spun in one place long enough to flip up the lids off galvanized garbage cans, spin them around, and let them fall to the ground where they banged once, winked a dull silver; and in the dust of the fleeing whirlwinds, they blinked to black.

Behind the cans, tall bushes cast rumpled cylinders of swaying shadows onto the ground. The wind eventually died down, but the smiling-faced dogs barked all night.

In the morning, a bright new sun came out of a brilliant blue sky. As its rays swept the cool night away, its shafts of warmth smiled down on the steel beams of the Rat Street Bridge; and Rat River flowed below, smooth and cool.

Days like this were made for swimming.

Flick claimed the weekly ritual of going to church and catechism was just a waste of time, and Screwball said it gave him a glorious pain in the ass.

They didn't go.

Breed had no intention of going on a day like this. He stood by the porch and looked at the empty place his motorbike used to be. He walked to the ditch in front of his house and looked at the remains of his broken BB gun. When he had found it in the dump, it had been a happy day. The only thing wrong with it was that it had a bolt missing. He had put a nail in the hole, peened it over, and the gun worked perfect. What had given him pleasure had caused him to get beat up. His shins still hurt, and the pain in his side came and went. In a way, the BB gun was responsible for his pain. Something in his mind was stopping him from taking the gun under the porch and trying to fix it.

He wondered why Blo didn't play "Taps" anymore. Maybe something bad had happened to him. Maybe he had gotten beat up, too. If he did, maybe that was the reason he couldn't play "Taps" anymore. Shuddering, Breed fought off the bad feelings.

He picked up a long stick, hooked it into the BB gun's trigger, and pulled the gun up into the weeds. If it dried out and didn't stink too bad, he would try to fix it. Then he thought about shooting Purple's eye out. He stared at the gun. If he shot Purple's eye out, the act would be just as rotten as playing baseball with puppies. It wouldn't be right. But after the Joe Louis boxing book came, he would beat Purple to a pulp; and he wanted Purple to see who was doing it. If he shot his eye out, Purple might not be able to see who was beating him up. Breed decided not to shoot Purple's eye out.

Mail wasn't delivered on Sunday, but Breed jumped across the sewage ditch in front of his house and checked the mailbox anyway. The Joe Louis boxing book didn't come.

Breed thought about skipping Sunday school and going swimming. It wouldn't get his gun fixed or his motorbike back, but that nun in Sunday school had said that evil destroys itself. Those kids that played baseball with puppies were evil. Maybe she knew something he didn't.

***

173

Breed joined up with Hog and Ballpeen and walked to the church. Once inside, they tried to be like the rest of the minnow-like kids. They tried to be respectable. They tried to obey every word. They sat out of sight, in the back of the church, in the loser's pew.

In front of them — for all to see — fresh washed kids sat with matching parents, dressed in expensive suits and white shirts with stiff tie-choked collars that chafed their white sun-screened necks.

They were surely on their way to heaven.

Up front, the priest talked in Latin until it was time to ask for money. When he announced that the church was taking up a collection for the poor, Hog whispered, "I'm poor," put a slug in the collection basket, and took out a quarter.

After church, Breed went to the cork bulletin board at the front entrance. He ran his finger down the list of contributors and stopped at his name. Zeroes followed.

A man in wearing a dark-blue suit and a brown tie lifted his head and looked down at Breed. As if Breed had a contagious disease, the man backed away.

Loud enough for Breed to hear, the man whispered to the makeup-painted lady standing next to him. "Those kids should go to a church for their own kind."

As if she were announcing it to the world, the wide-butt lady asked, "How much did he give?"

The man turned; and like a man who needed to boost his own self-importance by mocking someone less fortunate, for all to hear, he raised his voice. "He didn't give anything."

174

Breed turned his head, and like a kicked dog, he skulked away. He pretended he didn't hear the better-than-thou church-goer's snide remarks. But he did hear.

He figured the man hated him because he didn't have any money. The more money the man gave to the church, the more he could brag to the phony lady about how holy he was. It didn't matter if Breed helped a million old ladies across the street or saved somebody's life. Everybody was created equal until their name came up on the weekly bulletin board. If their name had zeros in the column next to their name, they were no hero.

Breed stopped in front of Hog. He didn't want him to see the hurt in his eyes. He looked away. Hog patted him on the shoulder. "I got zero's, too. Looks like we ain't getting into heaven until we come up with the admission fee."

"Don't worry about it," Ballpeen said. "I hate those rich assholes and their kids, too."

In unison, they walked down the cracked sidewalk.

Breed kicked at a stone and sent it into the open storm drain at the side of the street. "I don't really hate those kids. They only live that way because their mommies and daddies train them to live like that."

Hog picked up a rock and flung it down the street. "I guess it's not their fault their parents sent them obedience school." He flapped his arms at his sides "Hell, they're probable related to that dog that's been trained to shit on command."

"Yeah, they do whatever they're told," Breed said, "but we don't."

Close to the sidewalk, a big black Cadillac drove alongside of them. Its highly polished surface glimmered in the clean sunlight. The driver acted as if his expensive ride were a float in a parade. Although the man's mouth remained shut, Breed swore he could hear him announcing, "Hey, everybody, look! Look at me." And the kids inside sat affluently and looked out with their noses tilted upward.

There they go," Ballpeen said. "They're on their way to some fancy restaurant for Sunday dinner."

Hog tilted his head back and looked down his nose. "The way they hold up their noses you'd think they have boogers up there and they want everybody to see how big they are."

"Yeah," Ballpeen agreed. "They'll do anything to make you believe they're better than anybody else."

"Rich showoffs," Breed said with a hint of resentment. "Sometimes when I see those kinds of people, it makes me think money makes them stupid."

Ballpeen adjusted the hammer he had hid in his belt. "They don't even know how to use a hammer."

As if he couldn't decide what to do, Hog pondered in silence for a few seconds. "I ain't going to Sunday school today." He felt his pocket. "I didn't bring any more slugs. And anyway, it's just another chance for those rich kids to show off."

Ballpeen turned away from the church. "Let's get out of here."

They walked a few steps away from the church

and Breed stopped. "I'm going to go. Maybe one of those nuns can tell me how to get my motorbike back."

"Don't be stupid, Breed," Hog said and flicked his wrist. "All she'll do is smack your hand with that steel-bladed ruler."

"Yeah," Ballpeen said, "it's all fixed, like everything else. I'm going home. If I don't make too much noise, I can work on the boat."

Work on the boat, Breed thought. Ballpeen doesn't like anyone helping him. If he could help, they could build a boat good enough to go to Shell Island. But there was a whole tank of gas in the truck at the dump. If the nun could tell him how to get his motorbike back, he could ride there, and it would be easier and faster.

"I don't want to get caught not going again," he lied. "I'll catch you guys later."

Hog and Ballpeen slipped around the corner of the church and were gone. Breed turned and walked into the brown brick Sunday school.

Walking down the dim-lit hallway, Breed's tattered clothes made him stand out. He didn't care. He wanted to ask the nun about his motorbike and how it could be right for the cops to take it. He wanted to ask her why someone would hang his dog. And he wanted to know why Burkie and Henry were allowed to rape little girls. Wasn't there another greater law? God's law.

Breed had it all arranged in his head. He knew just what he would ask, and he knew how he would answer any question. He just couldn't believe that everything was fixed. Before the day was over he would have some answers.

He walked into the Sunday school room, sat in the little wooden desk, and waited. He knew he would have to show respect, and once the nun started talking he could not interrupt her. He would pick the right moment and raise his hand.

As if he weren't there, well-dressed kids walked past. He slouched down in the desk, made himself smaller, sat still, and studied the other kids in the class. The boys puffed up their chests and tried to impress each other. They talked about the bulletin board; and even though it had been their parent's money, they bragged about how much money they had given to the church.

The girls, usually prudish and proper, sat and giggled. Then they pointed at the boys, whispered loud enough for them to hear, and commented on how nice they looked; but when they pointed to Breed, their eyes turned from him. They didn't giggle. They glared sideways, put their cupped hands to their mouths, and whispered words in each other's ears that Breed couldn't hear.

To ease his poverty-riddled mind, Breed told himself that he felt sorry for the other kids. They were forced to wear hot tight fitting suit coats that rubbed under their arms and forced them to sit like they had something stuck up their butts. It hurt them to move naturally, so they had to sit up straight. Their actions were strict, precise, trained, and correct. Their studious and obedient behavior not only hid their phony intelligence, it broadcasted ignorance.

The bragging and pointing stopped. Breed looked to the front of the room. The black and white terrifying figure of a nun breezed into the room. It was like God had walked in.

All was quiet.

The nun took the long hardwood stick from the corner of the room and stood in front of the class. Her black and white presence stood out bold against the old brown walls and created an aura of respect and power. She pointed to a kid with a fresh haircut. "Who murdered Adam's son?"

The hair cut kid said, "Able."

"No!" she slammed back. "Say three Hail Mary's to refresh your memory."

She swung the long stick around and pointed it right under Breed's nose. "Who murdered Adam's son?"

"Cain," Breed answered.

"Who did Cain murder?"

Breed thought this was easy because of the mark of Cain. A correct answer would make it easier when he asked about his motorbike. He smiled and sat up straight. "Cain murdered Abel out of jealousy when God refused Cain's sacrifices."

The nun hissed and yelled, "Wrong! Say ten Our Father's and five Hail Mary's." She turned her lordly head and gently pointed the stick at a rich kid. "Do you know the answer?"

The kid hesitated but blurted out, "Cain murdered Abel?"

"Correct!"

"Breed raised his hand. He didn't wait for her to call on him. "That's what I said."

She waived the stick in Breed's face. "If you would come to Sunday school once in a while, maybe you could give a correct answer."

179

Breed's throat constricted. When he talked, his voice strained and the words came out like he was crying. "That *was* the right answer." He swallowed. "Cain murdered Abel and God gave him the mark of Cain."

The nun raised the stick and threatened Breed's face. "Don't answer unless you're called upon. You should show some respect and dress properly. I hope you didn't go into the church dressed like that."

Breed slouched back down in the desk. He didn't ask about the right or wrong about his motorbike or the laws of God.

The nun asked him another question. He didn't even bother to listen to what it was.

"I don't know," he said, and to shield himself from further ridicule, he slouched further down into the seat.

The nun smiled and brushed imaginary dust off her sleeve.

Ballpeen was right. The Sunday school crap was rigged. The whole goddamn world was rigged.

From somewhere in the back of Breed's mind a voice spoke out. "Somewhere in this world there is a straitjacket waitin' for that man."

Breed bolted and sat up straight in his chair. He figured she was trying to make him think he was crazy. He wondered why he ever thought she could help him get his motorbike back. She was the one acting like she had the mark of Cain and her brain was wondering around in a distant land.

Almost shouting out loud, he replied to the voice in his mind. "There ain't no straitjacket waitin' for me. I ain't screwy in the head."

He didn't wait for the class to be dismissed. He stood up so fast the desk tipped over and fell to the floor.

With fiery disdain, the nun slapped the stick across the desk. Whap! She gave Breed a stern look and smugly snapped, "Pick up that desk and sit down!"

Breed stepped away from the desk. "This is all a joke." He jerked his finger at the nun. "I don't need people like you. I ain't got no money, but I ain't no goddamn stinkin' lousy liar."

As if the word, "goddamn", would somehow creep past their lips and into their bodies, the girls clasped their hands over their mouths.

Like idiots with emaciated chests, the boys wilted into their seats.

As if afraid the hand of God would come down and strike, the num's eyes opened wide with alarm. "You can't talk like that in here."

Breed couldn't understand it. The nun had just lied to him, and now she was worried about one cuss word.

In tortured amazement, the nun stepped toward Breed. She whacked the palm of her hand with the big end of the stick and yelled hysterically, "Get out!" She raised the stick to strike.

Breed clinched his fists and glared back at her. Pent-up hate beamed out of his wet eyes.

Staring at his fists, she lowered the stick and backed off.

Holding up his hands in defense, Breed walked backwards to the door and stopped. He stuck out his emancipated chest. "All you goddamn, stinkin', lousy sons-a-bitches, can go where you belong.

181

You can go to hell." He walked out.

When he paced to the front steps of the church, the man in the dark-blue suit stood with one hand in his pocket jingling change. He waved his other arm in the air and talked to a tight-ass lady with a powered face and red dyed hair. "Oh my, yes!" the man said. "My three children go every Sunday. They are very smart for their age."

Breed walked a few steps toward the lady. A horrifying aroma of sweet sickening sweat crept into his lungs. It was the lady's cheap perfume trying to cover up her body odor. He huffed the foul air from his lungs and stopped. He had not kept quiet in the presence of the nun. Still feeling emancipated, he wasn't going to keep quiet in front of these filth-loving idiots.

"Yeah, buddy!" he said loud and clear. "And if you jump up in the air, spin around three times and land on the truth. You'll find out it's only a show."

As if Breed were the cause of the bad odor, the man grimaced and waved his hand down at him. Then, with a smirk, he turned his back to Breed and faced the stinking paint-and-powdered lady. "Don't mind him."

Breed stepped in front of the man. "For their age, your dumb-ass kids don't know a damn thing."

Flicking the back of his fingers at Breed, the man arrogantly said, "Just keep walking, boy. We don't need your kind here."

And Breed realized he didn't need to be there. He had other more important things to do.

Chapter 12

Taking a short cut through the flats, Breed walked past the warehouse, across the railroad tracks, and down the road next to the river. When he came to the coal pile he wondered if Burkie or Henry had stolen more bicycles and his them in the weeds. He stopped and listened for Burkie's or Henry's voices. He didn't hear anything but the faint cry of a lone hawk.

He cautiously walked around the coal pile, stopped at the path that led to the river, and searched the tall weeds.

He was just about to give up, when a strong odor of something dead hit him right in the face. He tramped the tall weeds down and the odor became worse. He turned from the smell, and when he did, the sight of a small baby met his eyes. At first he thought it may be a mannequin from a clothing store. But the dried blood, the buzzing flies, and crawling maggots told him this was a real baby. Part of the head had been ripped or bitten off. The baby's legs were spread. The umbilical cord curled down the waist and curved across the stomach and then turned and covered the place between its legs. Breed couldn't tell if the body was a boy or girl. The arms and legs looked healthy and showed no bruises or cut marks. One side of the head lay off to the side. It seemed intact but the ear had been sliced off. Breed's first thought was to call the police, but figured that if a nun didn't treat him right, no one else in authority would either. And to make it worse, with One-Finger-Burke on the job, Breed would get blamed for whatever had happened to the baby. Then he thought about telling Flick and the others, but if he did and they let it slip, he could go to jail. He turned and walked away, but stopped at the coal pile. He couldn't just walk away. He had to tell someone.

Searching his mind for a way to alert someone, his eyes fixed on a piece of dusty plywood setting against a steel post. He took a piece of coal. And as big as the plywood would allow, he printed black letters on it that read. 'LOOK HERE' and drew an arrow pointing to where the body lay.

At the side of the road, he leaned the sign against a tree and walked home.

His encounter with the body and his failed quest for the truth in catechism class didn't help his anger. When he walked into the dingy nicotine-yellowed kitchen of his house, he knew his father had stood in line for hours and begged like a reliefer at the surplus-food truck. Powdered milk, orange cheese, a big square of butter, and flour in a brown sack, sat on the table. He wouldn't have to eat grease bread today. He was hungry, but that nun and that rich guy bothered him. He only ate a little bit of the best meal he had had in weeks.

He riffled through last week's Sunday comics. Today, nothing was funny. He went outside and climbed the big maple tree in the front yard. When he was high enough, he defied the height and stepped around the top of the tree from limb to limb. One misstep or slip and he would be rewarded with broken bones or death.

If he fell, he thought it wouldn't matter much. Death might be better than living with the people of Traptown. If he were dead he might be with his dog again. Without holding onto other branches, he walked out on the highest limb and looked down. He could easily dive off headfirst. Then it would all be over.

"What's the matter with you?" he asked himself and grabbed onto a branch for support. "Are dumb enough to jump off because that stupid nun tried to make you feel worthless? She ain't God. Those rich Sunday school kids never had to go hungry or do any work in their entire babied lives. They never saved a dog just to have flats kids hang it. I could beat every one of their weak asses. And that guy in front of the church is just another Traptown phony."

Breed stepped to a lower limb. His dog was dead and his motorbike was gone, but he wasn't stupid. He cussed his suicidal foolishness and then laughed inside. After all, Ballpeen might finish the boat. He felt his bathing suit he wore under his pants, and decided that he couldn't die today. The river would fix everything. It always did.

Like a hawk waiting for prey, he sat in the tree. From his perch on the roller-coaster-hill-shaped limb, he peered through the green Maple leaves and searched up and down the street.

With ragged towels clamped under their arms, Ballpeen and Flick ambled down the road.

Breed jumped out of the tree, ran to the clothesline, grabbed an old worn towel, and yanked it off the line. He rolled it into a cylinder, tucked it under his arm, and scrambled to meet Ballpeen and Flick. He was going swimming, too.

Out of nowhere, Hog ran out ahead of Breed. "Wait for me, turd breath." He joined the migration.

Ballpeen's hammer dropped onto the road. He immediately reached down and scooped it up. The thought of the boat and Shell Island jumped into Breed's mind. "Hey, Ballpeen, how come you ain't workin' on the boat?"

Ballpeen snarled. "It's Sunday, a day of rest. I ain't allowed to work."

"How about if I come over tomorrow and help?"

Clutching his hammer, Ballpeen shook his head. "Naw, if One-Finger-Burke sees you in my yard he might say the boat's his and take it."

It was a flimsy excuse, but Breed didn't push it. He kept on walking.

Down the hill, Screwball leaned on a shaky mailbox, his feet crossed, waiting, but his hands were empty. He wasn't allowed to take a towel to "that filthy river." Flick and Ballpeen didn't stop. They didn't have to.

"Just look at that," a lady spumed from her front porch. "They're just like magnets. They draw out all the hoodlums."

Breed caught up and fell in step. Screwball leaned on the mailbox, waited until they were directly across from him, uncrossed his legs, and joined the troop.

On down the road, little Jummy stood in his manicured lawn.

"Hi, Jummy." Breed gave him a friendly wave. "Want to go swimming?"

"I'll have to ask," he said with excitement in his voice and rushed into his perfect white house.

Breed stopped walking. They all stopped. As if he were directing a movie, Screwball pointed to

186

Jummy's house. "Action!"

He dropped his hand.

Right on cue, Jummy's mother began yelling. Almost screaming, she gave Jummy the same old answer, "No! You're not going swimming in that dirty river. What's the matter with you? You'll fall into one of those deep drop-offs and drown!"

Jummy moped out of his house and its perfect white color seemed to turn to a sad brown. With his shoes shining in the sun, he walked to the edge of his yard and sullenly stood at the edge of the road. His hair was cut and combed, and he was well dressed. He looked like a little jewel.

Breed lifted his hands in a helpless gesture. "I wonder if his warden mother has visiting hours."

They continued walking down the street. With a dejected frown on his sad little face, Jummy waved and watched.

A glimmer of hurt shown in Flick's eyes. "He does look like he's in jail."

Breed knew Jummy would never be allowed to go swimming. None of the rich kids would ever go to the river. They might get their expensive clothes dirty. Why, they couldn't even jump off the Rat Street Bridge.

With a haphazard weave, Breed and his pals lollygagged down the street and migrated toward the friendly river of liquid understanding.

As heat from the melting tar-and-chip pavement of the street radiated into Breed's feet, he quickened his pace. The others caught up, faded left, and filed in front of Henry's father's gas station. Breed walked around the back of the station and scanned the junk behind a pile of used

187

tires. The end of a bright-red bike frame stuck out from under a dirty canvas tarp. He walked to the pile of tires and bent over to lift the tarp.

"Hey!" someone yelled.

Breed jerked back and looked. Henry's father placed his hands on his hips, hooked his thumbs into his belt, and rocked back and forth. On his head, a dirty-yellow paper garrison hat with a winged, red horse insignia, tilted to the side. Grease stains covered most of his brown work pants, but his short-sleeve shirt that covered his muscular mechanic's body was spotless.

He flexed the muscles in his arm and pointed to the road. "Get the hell out of here. Don't be comin' around here tryin' to steal things." He adjusted the paper garrison hat on his head and lowered his voice. "You goddamn half-breed."

Breed lowered his head and walked toward the road, but when he was out of Henry's father's sight, he turned and stopped in front of the station. Blo was there, tearing the red and white paper wrapper off a Power House candy bar.

Breed hoped Blo would snap the bar and offer him half. "Hey Blo," he said in a cheerful voice. "What are you doin'?"

Blo jammed the whole candy bar in his mouth and mumbled between chews, "Eating a candy bar to make my life interesting."

Temporally perplexed, Breed watched. Blo gobbled the candy and swallowed hard.

Breed didn't know if he had wolfed the candy down because he didn't want to share it, or he was just trying to make him laugh.

After he swallowed the last of the candy bar,

Blo sneered through his two chocolate covered false teeth. "Did you want some?" He turned his head.

Breed started to grin but then he saw it. The side of Blo's face was back and blue.

"What happened to your face?"

"Some tall skinny kid hit me with a beer bottle cause I walked in front of him."

"Why didn't you duck?"

Blo reached up and touched the side of his face. "I didn't see him. I was trying to remember something really important."

Breed sighed. It was already bad enough when bigger kids beat them up, now they were going to be blindsided with no chance to run or defend themselves. "Rotten Traptown bastard." He jerked his head to the side. "Maybe the river water will take the pain away."

Blo smiled, but it turned into a resentful sneer. "If I stick a possum up that kid's ass, that'll make the pain go away."

Blo had a way with possums. Even though they looked like gigantic rats, and hissed through yellowed teeth, Blo could pick them up and do just about anything he wanted with them. Breed figured Blo would do something with a possum, and whatever it was the kid that had hit him wasn't going to like it. Breed jerked his head toward the river and started walking. Blo followed. The others walked away from the gas station and joined them. They made a sharp left and paraded down Rat Street until the bridge was before them.

Breed stopped and stood in front of the mighty steel structure. On the slanted I beam of the bridge, between the strong rows of humped rivets, and on top of the chalky coat of flat brown paint, a cracked cast iron plaque honored the once thriving muskrat trapping area and the date the old steel bridge was built: 'RAT STREET BRIDGE 1883'.

"We're here!" Screwball yahooed.

Flick glared at him. "No kiddin', Shit Foot. I'll bet it took you three days and five nights to figure that out."

"Almost," Screwball said with a self-satisfied smile. "It was just as complicated as a one-piece jigsaw puzzle."

A pipe plant worker, with a silver lunch bucket tucked under his arm, walked across the steel catwalk grating of the bridge. Breed and the others moved to one side and made room for him to pass.

The worker stopped. His mill-filth-coated clothes reeked of zinc, oil, and the unmistakable sharp smell of acid; and they were stained dark from his own sweat. The sickening odor saturated the air like metallic bad breath. His rough face looked like something matches could be struck on. When he smiled, rows of acid-eaten, black teeth lined his mouth.

He spoke. "How do you boys like this new steel catwalk?"

"Pretty good." Screwball turned his eyes away from the worker's teeth. "Now when we stretch out under the grating, we'll get a checkered suntan."

"It's sure better than those old wooden planks," the worker said and continued on his way. And like a flowing ribbon of evil air, the acid fumes trailed behind him.

Flick turned toward the river for some good air and didn't see Screwball pretending he had a

Fudge-Sickle. Breed shook his head at Screwball and signaled him not to agitate.

Screwball slurped the imaginary Fudge-Sickle one more time, and then followed Breed and the others down the cinder path that spiraled around the bridge base and led to the river.

At the end of the path, a skinny snake sunned itself on a flat rock. Hog plowed the toe of his shoe into the path and flung cinders at it. "Get out of here you sneaky tong-waggin' son-of-a-bitch."

The snake crawled into a crack of one of the huge, waved gray-black blocks of stone that supported the spanned ends of the bridge.

Across the river, the pipe plant released its toxic waste. A rainbow of carcinogenic future health problems rushed through the big maroon tile pipe and gushed into the water. Brightly colored, menacing, mutations of tomorrow, swirled psychedelic; and stagnated on top of the dismal shallow water before they blended with the current and traveled downstream where they joined slime and sludge that ran along the edge of the river and was sucked into the water treatment plant.

As Breed stood on the riverbank and watched, the tail end of the oil and acid mix drained into the water and formed a sluggish swirl. Slowly it flowed and ran black and blue. Then it picked up speed and blended to a metallic-green with purple edges. Further out into the river, it changed to blue-red and spun into a silver oval frame.

Flick tapped Breed on the shoulder. "I'm glad that stinkin' stuff don't come out on our side of the river."

As if he were trying to prevent the water from

191

going into his mouth, Breed tighten his lips. "It's hard to believe that stuff goes downriver and the water plant sucks it in so we can drink it."

Flick shuddered. "I never thought about that."

Directly beneath the bridge, Breed walked out onto the ramshackle wooden dock that jutted out into the water. He placed his foot on one of the solid anchor posts they had cut from the trees upriver, and a rat swam under the black and blue water near the shore.

Screwball pointed to it. "A muskrat."

"No way," Flick said, "those things got poisoned out years ago."

Even though muskrats had died in the dirty water, the river gave Breed a feeling of survival. It was a refreshing relief from the horrors of his Traptown neighborhood. The river gave him hope. "Yeah," he said. "But those river rats didn't die. They can live in anything."

Bending over, Hog picked up a nice round rock. "If that rat gets close, he ain't gonna live after I bounce this off his cheese-eatin' head."

The rat swam into a little dark grove of cattails. Its long skinny diamond-marked tail snaked around a black tree root and was gone.

Breed and the others ignored the rat and the hazard across the river. They began taking off their clothes and revealing the faded swimming suits they had worn underneath.

Flick's pants were so tight he had to peel them off. Hog watched him and asked, "Can't you get pants that fit any tighter? Those are kind of baggy."

Flick pulled his foot free. "These are special made banana pants. See how you peel them off just

192

like a banana." He hopped on one foot. "And besides, I don't have to worry about a snake crawlin' up my pants leg."

Ballpeen rolled his clothes into a ball, threw them onto the sand, and ran toward the river. "Last one in hides the clothes."

Blo ran down a parade of crocked water-logged slabs of uneven driftwood that was the floor of the dock and dove into the water. While Breed struggled with one of the many knots in his shoestrings, the others jumped in. Being last, Breed would have to gather up the scattered clothes and hide them.

One of the big stone blocks in the bridge support stuck out like a small shelf. Breed rolled the clothes into a tight ball and held them in one hand. He placed his barefoot on the shelf, reached up with his free hand, and grabbed a round metal brace that ran under the bridge. Then he balanced on his toe, reached up, and hid the clothes on top of the wide I beam.

Brushing the powdery oxide from the old lead paint from his hands, he jumped down and watched Flick check the deep diving area under the bridge.

It was a long drop from the bridge. Before anyone dove off the tall bridge, they needed to know what was in the dark water below. After a person hit the water they always traveled fast and hard. If someone dove in, rammed their head into a solid log; smacked into a big boulder; got their eye poked out with a bicycle frame; got caught up in a sunken tree branch; or got their feet snared in a burlap bags full of rocks and dead cats, it could be the end of life as they knew it.

As Flick checked the bottom of the river, the kid who had jumped off the bridge and never came up was always in the back of Breed's mind. Police and volunteers had thrown big treble-hooks over the sides of boats and dragged for his body. Weeks later, they snagged on to a hidden branch. When they pulled it to shore, the kid's blue-white swollen body was tangled in the black branches. After that, it was a long time before anyone jumped off the Rat Street Bridge. Breed was always glad when Flick checked the bottom of the river.

"Screwball dives today!" Flick announced and pointed to Screwball. "And you ain't fudge-sucking out of it!"

Breed figured it was Screwball's day to dive. The unwritten rule of the bridge had always been, "Dive or get thrown off."

Screwball was scared and actually needed more time to work up the courage to dive, but when he agitated Flick with the Fudge-Sickle, his deadline had automatically been moved up.

There was a lot of air space between the bottom of the bridge and the top of the water, and that air space didn't slow a person down. The dead kid had jumped feet first and died. No one could ever be sure they were going off that high bridge without getting hurt or killed; and today, Screwball would have to dive headfirst.

Halfway across the river, Screwball treaded water.

Flick pointed to the bridge above his head.

Screwball ignored his gesture.

Flick swam behind him and pushed him toward the dock. "Get your Fudge Sickle ass up on that

194

bridge and dive!"

Screwball swam to the dock and stopped. He pulled himself halfway up onto the dock and looked straight ahead. That skinny snake Hog had kicked gravel at was staring him right in the face. "Snake!" he yelled in surprised fright and dropped back down into the water.

Flick reared back. With both hands, he sent a huge wave of water in his Screwball's direction. "Don't start something to keep from diving! Get up there and dive. And don't be diving off that baby-ass pier either!"

Hog dove to the bottom of the river and picked up a flat rock. He eased his head out of the water and snuck behind the snake. With one swift blow, he smashed the snake's head into the wooden dock. The snake wiggled into a tight knot, fought for life, and tried to escape right into the rock that had ended its life.

Hog picked up the snake and held it in front of Screwball's face. It twisted and curled. "There you go, Screwball." He swung his arm to the side and ushered Screwball toward the cinder path. "You may dive."

Screwball scrambled up onto the bridge, and Hog set the dead snake on the rock shelf at the base of the bridge. The end of its tail vacillated as if it were still alive. Breed had heard that a dead snake's tail would move until sundown. If they stayed long enough, today, he might find out if that were true. He made a mental note of it and followed Flick, who walked up onto the bridge.

Flick stood on the top of the bridge catwalk railing. He flexed his legs, hopped off, and executed a slow jackknife dive. His graceful flight speared him into the water; and when his feet slurped under the surface, a white splash winked on top of the green water.

Screwball stood on the bottom rung of the catwalk railing. This would be his first diving presentation. To get closer to the water, he held onto the railing with one hand and leaned over.

Breed held his breath, waited, and then said, "It looks like he's going to dive."

Flick yelled encouragement from the water below. "Dive! Shit Foot, dive."

Screwball looked to the center support of the bridge and pointed. "How about if I go off the pier?"

"Stay off that cement pier," Flick said. "That's for babies."

Screwball's face crumpled like a little kid's face about to cry.

Hog stood on the top of the skinny steel railing. "Nothin' to it, Screwball." His bare feet departed the rail. His body flew into the air, swished down headfirst, and effortlessly slipped into the water below.

Blo and Breed jumped from the top rail and did Tarzan yells — "Ahh-e-e-ah-e-e-ah-e-e-ahh!" — all the way down. Their ingress into the water created lofty lifting waves that caused Flick and Hog to bob gracefully up and down in the water until those waves traveled across the river and beat against the muddy shore.

Screwball sat up on the bridge, alone. Breed knew he wanted to be included as a diving participant; and he did start to dive; but at the last

196

second, he jumped. He hit the water. It foamed up like the mushroom of an atomic bomb.

Flick bobbed in the resulting waves and screamed at Screwball. "Dive! Not Jump! You chicken shit!"

"I was starting to slip," Screwball defensively lied.

"You don't dive this time, your ass gets thrown in! You can do it. Don't be a candy ass."

Breed knew what had happened. "Hey, Screwball," he said. "Don't stand there and think about it. If you give yourself too much time to think, you'll chicken out every time. Don't wait. Just do it!"

Screwball nodded and they ran up the cinder path. Everyone but Screwball dove off the bridge. They surfaced, treaded water and looked up at Screwball. They waited for him to dive. Again, he froze on the railing.

"You don't have to dive today Screwball," Flick said with a reckless grin. "We won't throw you in."

Breed knew what was next. Everyone ran up onto the bridge and watched Screwball try to get up enough nerve to dive off.

"Come on, Screwball, dive!" Ballpeen pleaded. "There's nothing to it."

"Let me take a rest first," Screwball begged and lifted his foot to climb off the railing.

Flick stopped him. "You had your chance. Dive! Or your ass gets thrown in."

Screwball continued to climb off the railing. If he got his lightning fast feet on the catwalk, he would run. No one would catch him.

Ballpeen and Flick would have none of it. They grabbed him by the shoulders and the rear of his bathing suit and flung him off the bridge. His physical being was propelled into space.

Flick dipped his knees and opened his arms wide. "Introduction to diving, Rat River style."

Screwball flew into the air and landed, face first — belly smacker supreme — on top of the water. He went under, bobbed up and floated motionless.

Breed remembered how he had blacked out the day he had been thrown off. He was worried that Screwball had blacked out, too. He looked at Flick. "Maybe we'll have to go in after him."

Ballpeen leaned over the railing for a closer look. Screwball's arms quivered like a dying carp. "Maybe he's dead.

Flick stepped up on the railing. "Damn! I gotta save him."

Screwball's foot fluttered. His arm stroked the water. He lifted his head and turned toward them.

Flick stepped down from the rail.

Screwball treaded water, gave them the finger, and piped off, "Screw you turd face bastards. I would've dived off."

Hog laughed. "So what? You dove."

Flick smiled a big know-it-all smile. "Diving school's over. You passed. I told you, you could do it."

Screwball swam to shore and came back up onto the bridge. His chest and face were beet-red from the hard smack when he had hit the water.

Flick glanced at the redness. "Are you going to dive now, or do we throw your ass off again?"

Screwball stepped up on the top railing, flashed

198

Flick the finger, and gracefully dove into the water below.

Breed was glad Screwball wasn't afraid to soar off the tall bridge. Only one spot under the bridge was safe to dive into. Breed and the others knew where it was. They all yelled Tarzan yells and dove in behind Screwball.

Hog swam to shore, ran to the base of the bridge where the snake was hidden, and pretended to be peeing on the weeds. Ballpeen started up the cinder path to go past him. Hog grabbed the dead tail-waggling snake and threw it on top of Ballpeen's head.

"Get it off! Ballpeen shrieked. "Get it off!" He tried to throw the moving snake from his shaking body. His hands fluttered around in midair. The snake slid down his back and onto the path. And that tail continued its hypnotic death motion.

"Hahh! Hahh! Hahh!" Ballpeen huffed out of his scared lungs. He ran in place. His feet beat on the ground.

Hog opened his mouth to laugh, but was struck speechless. He pointed at Ballpeen.

Ballpeen fidgeted as if he were trying to disguise his feelings, but the expressions on his face changed from angry to hysterical. Then, too confused to be scared, the odd combination took his breath away. He breathed in stuttering breaths. When he exhaled, a loud "HANT!" came from deep in his scared restricted throat and flew out of his mouth.

All eyes turned toward the strange sound.

Flick pulled himself up onto the dock and smiled. "What did he say?"

"Hant!" Breed said. "I think somebody said it before."

"What the hell is Hant?" Blo wanted to know.

"Hant on Ballpeen!" Screwball said to poke fun at him.

"Yeah, Hant on you, Hammer-ass!" Hog added.

***

And "HANT!" was born. It was now the proper mock, ridicule, tee-hee, or jest. The weird word evolved into a peculiar way of looking at things that went bad. It was a different way of reacting to things Breed and his friends could not control.

Hant became an attitude, a tool that enabled them to shake off useless conditioned responses the general public expected from everybody. It showed them how to laugh at themselves and others in a new way. Mostly because it never mattered how angry, scared or excited someone became, it would do little or nothing to change the situation.

Most of the time, expected responses made things much worse than they actually were. Like the man who works for weeks on his old car: He finally gets it running, drives up the road, and the engine blows up. The man could stay mad the rest of his entire life, but his anger would not repair the car engine. This conditioned response of getting angry would not have stopped the engine from blowing up. It had already happened. Only a time machine could change that. "Hant!"

Or, when fishing, someone thinks they have hooked into a monster of a fish. They fight it to shore and anticipate a huge trophy winning catch. The person's expectations are extinguished when he pulls in a big, ugly, tiny-footed brown water dog. "HANT!" would be the proper mock, ridicule, tee-hee, or jest. Hant became a way to mentally step back from any situation, not let it bother them long enough to cloud their judgement, and pause to see what they could do to fix it. Now when Breed and the others did something stupid or something happened they could not control, instead of getting angry or telling themselves, "You dumb ass. You should have known better," a simple, "HANT!" did the job.

Chapter 13

Breed, Screwball, Flick, Hog, and Blo ran up the cinder path, and scattered along the catwalk. Then they leaned their backs against the wide slanted beams of the bridge and lay back. From these comfortable positions they enjoyed the pleasant warmth of the friendly summer sun.

A Traptown road-maintenance truck pulled onto the bridge and stopped. Breed and his friends pulled away from the beams and watched. Two men stepped out of the truck and dragged a big metal sign off the bed of the truck. They placed the sign across the bridge. One man jumped back in the truck, put it in gear, and let it slowly putter to the other end of the bridge. The other man followed on foot. The truck stopped. The men took another sign off the truck, placed it in front of the bridge, and drove away.

Breed read the sign aloud, "BRIDGE CLOSED."

Flick jumped up. "What?"

Hog walked to the sign and shook it. "There ain't nothin' wrong with this bridge."

"Must be temporary." Breed leaned back against the bridge beam. "They only set those signs against the beams. They didn't bolt them in place."

"The way they run this town," Flick said, "they probably put them on the wrong bridge."

Breed laced his hands behind his head. "Ahh, what the heck, it'll give us some peace and quiet"

"Yeah." Hog leaned against the beam. "Those flats gang kids won't be able to drive across and throw things at us."

They lay back on the bridge beams and eased into a restful state of relaxation. Ballpeen stood next to the beam; and with his ball-peen hammer, he whacked at the rivets on the steel bridge. The ear-hurting metallic twanging rang across the water and bounced around the bridge.

Rubbing his ear, Flick jumped up and shouted at Ballpeen, "Cut that out!"

"Yeah," Hog added, "If you wanna pound something, go pound sand up your ass."

Ballpeen ignored the request. He continued pounding and let out a loud, "Hant!"

Standing next to Ballpeen, with each beat of the hammer, Flick's head nodded; and his face winced with pain. "Give me that hammer you little pounding fool." He reached over and snatched the hammer out of Ballpeen's hand.

"Stick it up his ass!" Hog blurted out.

"Give me that back!" Ballpeen whined. "I need that."

Flick held in his outstretched hand and offered it to him. "Here take it."

Ballpeen made a quick grab for it. Flick dropped it. The hammer clanked on the steel grating, bounced off the bridge, and thunked onto the wooden dock below. It spun around and teetered on the edge, just above the dark water, but didn't drop in.

For a moment Ballpeen's face grimaced with pain. He blinked it away, turned; and to get the hammer before it fell into the water, he rushed down the cinder path.

Hog yelled behind him, "Watch out for that snake!"

A yellow car, with rusted out rocker panels, pulled next to the bridge closed sign and stopped. The driver looked at the sign, bitched, and turned around.

"Hey," Blo said, "we can't make any money with the bridge closed."

Screwball placed his hands on the back of his head and leaned back. "Well, take the signs down."

"I can do that." Hog jumped up and kicked one of the metal signs over. It banged on the steel grating and lay flat. He walked to the other end of the bridge and kicked that sign over, too. "There," he said with an exaggerated smile. "The bridge is open." He lay back down on the bridge beam.

"Ahh man," Breed said. "If cars run over those signs, we won't be able to use them if we want to close the bridge."

"Flick got up and walked to the sign. "Come on, Breed, let's drag them into the weeds. We can make this bridge our own private swimming place anytime we want."

Breed shook his head in agreement, and they dragged the big signs off the bridge and hid them in the tall weeds.

Once again, cars hummed across the steel mesh of the bridge.

Blo yelled, "Three dives for a dime."

But the cars didn't stop. When the people in the cars drove past, they kept their heads directed straight ahead and held their necks perfectly stiff.

A car slowed and a lady wearing a new hat that nearly covered her eyes, talked loud enough for Breed and the others to hear. "I don't want to see those filthy kids swimming in that filthy river." She pulled the hat down — more.

Blo flashed the lady the appropriate obscene gesture. "Nobody's gonna stop." He stepped off the railing. Just then, an old three-hole Buick, with a sun-faded green paint job, rattled onto the bridge.

Blo waved his hands at the car and shouted, "Three dives for a dime."

The car drove past, but one brake light flashed from a cloudy-red lens. Smoke puffed out the tailpipe. The car backed up and stopped directly across from Blo.

From within the darkness of the raggedy interior of the car, a raspy voice strained, but eked out, "What did you say?"

Flick looked up with a start. "Three dives for a dime."

"What?"

Flick raised his voice. "You can watch us dive off this bridge for a dime."

A toothless, unshaven, skeletal-face poked its head out of a mold-scented window. Breed and the others watched in disbelief. The bright sun reflected on the face and burned in a florescent glow of horror. It radiated a sick bluish color and darkened where the skin stretched tight over the bloodless protruding bones that seem to strain in an attempt to break through the face.

The face spoke, "I'll give you a dime."

"Blo leaned over and extended his hand. "Okay!"

The head's hand slithered over the seat and out the window. Between the only two fingers on the hand, a dime dangled, blinking and waiting. Scabs, some hanging and some not quite a scab, spotted the arm. Up the arm and on a wrinkled biceps, yellowish, infected, open sores took on the appearance of ghoulish eyes set in an arm of rotten Swiss cheese.

Blo filched his hand back and gasped. "I'll dive first!"

Flick turned to take the dime but shuddered at the sight. "We'll all dive at once." He squirmed uncomfortably and turned toward his right. "Get the dime, Hog."

But Hog had already left the rail and bombed into the water.

"Take it. Here take it!" the vermin head pleaded.

"Naw, that's all right," Breed muttered and jumped into the river.

Flick took one last look at the hand and dove off.

Treading water, they waited for the Buick to clang off the bridge. The man's hacking from inside the Buick echoed off the bridge. The door opened. A rush of vile blood and vomit cascaded down through the steel grating and sprinkled into the water. As the current took the puke particles down toward the water works, Breed and the others swam to the dock and the Buick rattled off the bridge.

At the dock, repulsion spread across his Flick's freckled face. "Did anybody get the dime?"

"Are you kiddin'," Blo said and wagged his head from side to side. "We wouldn't be able to spend it anyway.

Breed shivered and shook off the eerie feeling. "It would probably burn a hole right through your hand."

As if he were sick, Flick made a face. "That guy's got cancer."

Breed had seen mill workers with cancer, but none as bad as that one. "Yeah," he said, "that's what you get when you go work in the stinkin' mill. He probably got his fingers chopped off there, too."

Like a fortune-teller looking into a crystal ball, Flick stared into space. "That guy smelled like acid. Maybe that cancer's eating him alive." He paused, and it seemed like a dark cloud had cast a shadow over his face. "If we work in a mill, we'll get cancer, too."

After a moment of silence, Breed riffled the water. Screwball mimicked the rotten head. Blo dove off the bridge a few more times, then they all basked in the sun, climbed to the top of the bridge, and watched people drive beneath them.

As the uplifted skirts, in the cars below, inched higher, the sun slid to soft orange. The great artist in the sky blended blue with a glow of red. A gentle breeze swept across the bridge and a warm-purple sunset waltzed across the horizon.

Breed dove off the bridge one more time, and looked under the bridge for the snake to see if its tail was still moving, but he couldn't find it. He gave up looking, and a curtain of darkness closed the show in the purple sky.

They all donned their clothes; and in the dark, they walked away from the bridge.

Breed wanted to sneak behind the gas station, pick up that tarp, and see if his motorbike was under it. The others had agreed to watch while he checked it out.

Walking to the gas station, a motor hummed behind them. Breed turned back and looked. A cop car, with its lights out, cruised across the bridge.

"There's the cops again," Hog said. "I wonder what those dummies want now."

Flick glanced at the approaching car. "Ahh man! Henry's old man probably called them. Probably told them we're taking fenders off cars with can openers."

Looking to where Flick and he had dragged the bridge closed signs, Breed said, "They probably want to know where those signs went."

Blo sneered through his false teeth, "Eeww! Dat's right. Let's run."

"I ain't stickin' around for that half-ass cop crap!" Flick stepped off the side of the road.

Everyone, except Screwball, trotted like trained dogs and swished into the weeds at the side of the road. When they were out of the cop's line of sight, they stopped, crouched close to the ground, and watched. The lights on the cruiser came on and bathed Screwball in their brightness.

"I ain't afraid of those bastards," Screwball said in a snit. "It ain't One-Finger-Burke, and I didn't do nothin'."

He stood by the road.

The cops drove the cruiser close. They pulled their usual trick: They tramped on the bright headlights to blind him. On the car's black roof, the red flasher revolved and flicked red lines of light into the darkness. Screwball began trotting along the side of the road, but only fast enough to get out of the light flickers.

Breed and the others rose up out of the weeds

and joined him at the slow pace. The cruiser pulled closer. Breed motioned with his arm for the cops to drive around. He just knew the cops weren't after them. They hadn't done anything.

With the red and white light at their backs, they trotted and laughed. One of the cops shouted, "Halt! Or I'll shoot!"

They slowed a little, but kept trotting.

"They won't shoot," Blo said. "They only say that in the movies."

"Maybe he got a new comic book and learned some new words," Hog added.

"They're just trying to scare us," Flick said and slowed to a walk.

The familiar sound of a shotgun's trigger being cocked, clicked. A voice in the dark said, "An ass full of rock salt will straighten Rat Boy and his hoodlum friends right up."

Breed recognized the voice. It was One-Finger Burke!

Before he could say or do anything, Breed felt something like a bee sting on the end of his ear.

BOOM! The shotgun went off.

Gasp! — Air rushed into Breed's lungs. He thought Burkie was trying to slice off his ear. He slapped his stinging ear.

Hearts jump-started and legs jerked to a sprint. Flying more than running, and with their toes scarcely touching the ground, they sped away.

When they were out of sight and hidden in a bunch of weeds, thorns, blackberry bushes, and skinny trees, they flattened out and hugged the ground.

Breed lay breathless and tried to control his

noisy panting. There was something wet on his ear. He reached up and felt with his fingers to see what it was. It wasn't a slice, but right next to the place where Burkie had cut his ear, a piece of rock salt continued to sting and burn. As he picked the rock salt out of his ear, next to him, leaves rustled and crunched under high stepping feet. He forgot about his ear and looked up. Behind the outline of a maze of black skinny trees, a profile marched. Someone was trying to run, but they weren't going anywhere.

A choking voice strained, "Where you guys at?"

It was Ballpeen.

"Right here," Breed whispered. "Drop down!"

Ballpeen didn't answer.

Breed looked up. The outline of Ballpeen's body silhouetted against the sky. A half-fallen tree was right in front of him. The Y of a branch forked under Ballpeen's chin. Like a dark phantom hand, it was choking him.

Breed figured Ballpeen was so scared that he was running in place and couldn't feel the branch. He was trying to run through it.

"Hey, you dumb ass," Breed whispered. "There's a branch on your throat. Drop down."

Ballpeen stopped marching and dropped to the ground.

"Dumb, Shit!" Breed whispered, and the spotlight passed over them. The police had motored around the other side and surrounded them. Breed figured that someone had robbed a bank or something and the cops thought they had done it. Those newspaper pictures flashed in his mind again, bold print, right on the front page. He would be in jail — like Lard Man had said — maybe they'd strap him in the electric chair, and he didn't even do anything. "Ahh man! Not again," he said out loud.

"Shut up!" Flick whispered. "They'll hear us."

Like it had come straight out of a western movie, someone threw a rock. The spotlight flooded the place where it landed. If the cops kept the spotlight there long enough they wouldn't see anyone flee in the darkness.

Flick ran out first. The others bolted from their hiding places and shot across the road. One jump, and they were on a carpet of low, ground-hugging, foot tangling, trip your ankles, dew berry bushes. The light searched directly behind them. They knew what to do: They ran into those jaggers; and after each stride, they kicked the heels of their feet up behind themselves. It worked. They didn't trip.

When they ran on a fresh plowed field, their feet clipped the tops of dark deep furrows. When they tripped, their hands sank into the soft earth, but they didn't stop. They pushed themselves up off the ground, popped back up, and kept running. If that searching light beamed on them, they would be targets for that smoking gun. They ran faster, sometimes on their hands and feet, but they kept going.

When they finally managed to hobble out of the plowed field, a flat piece of grass-covered ground appeared under their feet and gave them traction and balance. They rocketed to a barbwire fence and stopped. Freedom was right on the other side in that enclosed cow-patty-littered field.

Flick grabbed onto a wooden fence post for support and huffed. "Let's take a rest."

Breed placed his hands on his knees, bent over, and breathed in gasps. "We should" — gasp — "be okay here."

The spotlight skimmed across the area where they had just been.

Screwball let out a loud, "Hant!"

The little rest was over before it had started.

They dropped to the ground, crawled under the sharp rusty barbs of wire and breathed easier on the other side.

Breed knew they wouldn't get caught now, but to be absolutely safe, they zigzagged around the cow-patties, ran across the meadow, and escaped into the real cover of the big overpowering woods.

If One-Finger-Burke and his buddies went in after them now, they would be up against unfamiliar surroundings — in the dark. They would not come in. They never did. One-finger Burke and the cops in the cruisers flipped down their law-lights, gave up, and drove away.

On the other side of the wire, the summer air changed. It was like the cloudy days of November, with the threatening gusts of wind and the nostalgic smells of winter. In the semi-darkness of the moon, a nighthawk circled above and the air changed again — back to the surroundings of the bright days of warm summer. Now, graceful tropical air hugged their tired bodies.

When it was safe, they came out from behind the wire and weaseled through the neighborhood. As they jerked against their restraining chains, the barking dog's savage attempts to snap free were fueled with the promise of a reward: The long overdue, sought after, chance of a dog's lifetime: A chance to bite the ass out of Breed's and his pal's pants.

Just to get even for the police chasing them for no reason, Breed and his defiant friends knocked over garbage cans like they were lines of dominos. Tired mill workers jerked from drunken slumbers and flipped on switches. Lights flashed systematically and a sequence of angry bitching erupted.

Breed managed to sneak into bed and not get beat, but his hands stunk from the garbage cans and had traces of dried blood on them. He couldn't wash them. Those rattling water pipes would make too much noise — wake up his father; then he would get his ass beat. He put his hands under the thin blanket to cover the smell and thought about how knocking over all those cans didn't change a thing. Tomorrow, those people would still point and put him down. Little Jummy would still stand in his jail-like yard, watching Breed and his friends walk to the river; and Burkie would still use his sharp knife to cut the ears off of little girls he had raped.

When school started, it will be the same. Breed would be embarrassed because he wouldn't have money to buy lunch. He wouldn't even have a little brown bag to carry one. But there was a ray of hope: If he ever got that Joe Louis book in the mail, he would be able to box those wise guys — maybe even catch One-Finger-Burke off duty and knock him out. Then he could shove that shotgun right up his ass.

He rolled over and placed his arm under the pillow. He hated the craziness of Traptown. People were as phony as see-through plastic. They were plastic people. When they lied, they were polite and well mannered. When they rubbed the crap of their so-called high-class upbringing in other people's faces, they smiled.

Although the houses in Traptown were a different color and had different yards, they were all the same. Sometimes the backyards even had the same clothes hanging outside on the same dirty-gray clotheslines. Inside, the people dressed the same. And those same people had the same thin, mean, suspicious faces. They all told the same lies and half lies; and every time they lied, they smiled those same phony smiles. Breed wanted to know why there was so much sameness in Traptown.

When he had been younger, he knew he was different. And because he had been different, he had been afraid to look at those people that all acted the same. They had made him feel ashamed; and when he had walked away from them, he had cried. Back then, he had wanted to be the same as they were. Now he didn't want to be the same as they were. He didn't want to cry anymore. He was tired of getting crapped on, and he was tired of the way the same people sat back and laughed about how they had done it.

Traptown no longer made sense to him. He wondered why so many people went to work in the mills and got trapped in artificial jobs. He had watched when they went on strike and battled each other for money. It was the uneducated leading the unwilling to do the unnecessary, so they could do the same job, day after day, and end up in a life of sameness until they died and were buried beneath a

214

maze of look-alike tombstones in a typical Traptown cemetery.

He didn't want that for his future. He needed to find a way out. For some kids, sports were a way to gain some respect. Not for him. The weak sports programs catered to the rich and to kids that got good grades. Jummy, the happy jail yard kid, had parents that would make sure their son could swim in the air above the football field. He would have the money to go and eat big steaks at school banquets. He would get his letter. Breed never would. He didn't fit into the typical athlete mold.

When he tried out for a sport, the other kids got sore or tired, he never did. He knew his participation was a joke. It was fixed, too. All Traptown kids were cut. But no one could cut him from the river. That river could take him to a better place.

Chapter 14

At the edge of Ballpeen's yard, Breed and Flick sat with their backs against the apple tree and watched. Ballpeen fitted, bent, and broke boards into unwilling curves and tried to build a boat that would gracefully cut through the water.

Breed knew he could build a better boat than Ballpeen could, but Ballpeen's pride was still hurt because his plane didn't fly in the tornado. To prove he could build the boat by himself, out there in his back yard, he banged and sawed alone.

Flick laced his fingers together and put them behind his head. "Hey, Breed, if that boat doesn't work, do you think you could build another motorbike?"

"I already tried," Breed said, "but it might be years before I can scrounge enough parts." An uneasy feeling crawled into his chest. "And, the last time we went in the dump, those dogs almost got us."

"We shouldn't have to worry about wild dogs. We should just go to the gas station and take your bike back."

Breed thought about it for a moment. "I might, but I don't feel like getting dog crap rubbed in my face." He shuddered. "And I don't want to get off guard and give Burkie a chance to cut my ears off."

Flick nodded. "If Ballpeen's boat works, we won't have to worry about any of that. We can get out of this place."

"That's right. The Flat's gang don't even know where Shell Island is. They can't steal the boat if they can't find it."

Chewing on the end of a long piece of green grass, Flick leaned back against the tree. "Without them sneaking around, Shell Island will be like heaven."

Breed lay on the ground, stuck out his elbow, and placed his hand on his chin. "And we won't have to watch out for flying beer bottles." He looked over his shoulder. "Or Burkie sneaking around with his knife."

When Ballpeen's hammer lay silent and the sniffing sound of sawing no longer filled the air, Breed jerked his head around. As if he were looking into a window to the future, he stared at the boat. Ballpeen walked around it and admired his work. Two yellow pine-boards curved along the old brown wooden sides and stood out bright and bold. Twinkling in the sun, a myriad of shiny nail heads held the boards in place.

Breed pulled his back away from the apple tree and sat up. "Do you hear that?"

Flick poked his head from behind the tree, listened for a second, and then leaned back and closed his eyes. "I don't hear anything."

Breed jumped to his feet. "That's what I mean."

"Ahh-ha!" Flick opened his eyes. "The boat must be done." He sprang to his feet.

Breed shifted restlessly from foot to foot. "If he would have let us help, it would have been done days ago."

Together they stepped across the ditch, walked to the boat, and stopped next to Ballpeen.

They didn't speak. The very presence of such a craft mesmerized them. Breed's mind began to work. Would it float? What else could it do? If it sank, it would be no big loss. But if it could actually float, the trip to Shell Island would be next. The turds and turmoil of Traptown would be left behind.

Breed looked back toward the apple tree. As if he were an actor entering the stage, right on cue, Hog appeared and placed one hand against the apple tree. With his other hand, he tilted a bottle of homemade root beer to his lips and swilled it down.

Flick made a face and shuddered. "I don't know how he swiddles that stuff down. They put too much yeast in it."

Hog pulled a hard-boiled egg out of his pocket and popped it into his mouth. Then, he reared back and threw the empty bottle. It sailed into Toney's yard. Hog smiled; and as if he owned it, he strolled into Ballpeen's yard. Swallowing the last of the hard-boiled egg, he stopped at the boat.

"Hey, Ballpeen," he said with merriment. "How'd you make this piece of shit without getting any on you?"

Ballpeen squinched his lips together and didn't answer.

"Hey, Hog," Breed said. "Did you enter that new most kissable lips contest that radio station has going?"

Hog threw a rock up in the air, caught it, and threw it up again. "Yeah, I did."

Flick flashed a look of discomfort. "You guys didn't get nothin' the last time you found that key. What makes you think you'll win something this time?"

Hog tilted his head back and grinned. "It

218

doesn't matter."

As if he were putting on lipstick, Breed moved his hand in front of his lips. "You mean you put lipstick on your lips and kissed a piece of paper and sent it in?"

With a look of amusement, Hog shook his head. "Nope."

Flick puckered his lips and sucked them toward Hog. "Whose lips did you use?"

"Nobody's. I got a big piece of wallpaper, covered my ass with lipstick, and sat on it."

"Postage for something that big would be a lot of money." Breed said. "How'd you send it in?"

"I rode up to the station and stuck it in the mailbox. Pinky can kiss my most kissable lips." He smiled and banged on the boat with the rock. "This thing's pretty flimsy for a transatlantic steamer."

Ballpeen ignored Hog, walked around the boat, and looked for one last thing to pound.

"What's the matter, Ballpeen?" Hog asked. "Did you nail your mouth shut?"

Like a diplomat trying to use skill and tact to smooth out his adversary, Ballpeen smiled a cautious tiptoe smile. "Hi, Hog, how you doin'?"

Hog looked sideways at him. "What do you want? Hammer-ass!"

Flick laughed. "We need some paint for this boat."

As if he were holding an invisible paint brush Ballpeen waved his hand back and forth. "Yeah, yellow paint would cover these old boards and make them look new."

Hog threw the rock up and caught it. "So?"

"If you can get some paint, we'll let you go to Shell Island with us."

Hog stopped tossing the rock and held it in his hand. "What do you mean *you'll* let me go? If I want to go, I'll go! I go wherever I want!" He walked to the back of the boat and shook the side. A nail popped. A long line of curved boards twanged loose. "What makes you think you can go in this piece of junk?"

"It ain't done yet," Ballpeen said as if he were forcing himself to be nice.

Hog tilted his head back and smiled at the boat. "With you working on it, it never will be done. It's fallen apart already." He looked to Breed. "Hey, Breed, show him how to curve those boards."

"Ahh, come on, Hog," Ballpeen said, "I'll fix it. Are you going to get the paint or not?"

Hog didn't answer right away. He stood there as if he weren't going to.

"Well?" Ballpeen said, waiting.

Hog looked up into the sky.

Ballpeen stared at him.

Hog looked back down.

"Come on, Hog." Flick waved his hand with encouragement. "Quit foolin' around."

Hog took a deep breath and exhaled. "Maybe, but I'll need someone to go with me."

Ballpeen stepped forward and stuck out his chest. "I'll go."

Hog laughed. "You'll shit and fall in it!"

"I'll stay here." Breed voluntcered. "Me and Ballpeen can curve those boards with hot water."

Hog looked at Ballpeen. "You can do that while we're gone. We might need Breed for a

220

distraction."

Flick got up from the pile of wood he was sitting on, and Hog threw the rock across the alleyway. It sailed toward the tin roof shack where Tony was sleeping. Thwack! It hit the rusted roof and clacked down into the rickety spouting.

Breed looked over the tall grass and through the torn screen window. Alcoholic Toney rose from his dirty cot, staggered around the room, and started his usual drunken babble. "Hey! . . . I wanna tell you! Hey! . . . And back that way again. Hey!" he barked loud and clear. He emphasized each, "Hey!" And barked on, "Hey! . . . And back that way again. Hey!" Over and over and over.

Between a, "Hey!" and a "Back that way again," Toney stood up and noticed what was on the table in front of him. Grinning a toothless grin, he took a drink from a fly-covered bottle of beer. "Hey!" he said in a festive tone and lay back down.

"Come on, you guys," Ballpeen begged. "Don't get Toney mad. He'll tell my old man. I'll get my ass beat."

Hog laughed and imitated Ballpeen's father's favorite warning. "I'll kick your keister right up to your mouth. Then you'll have to talk out your ass!"

Flick walked out of the yard. "Come on, Hog, let's get movin'."

Ballpeen looked at a rock on the ground and then at Hog. "Come on, Hog, don't throw it."

"Okay, Ballpeen, I won't throw anymore," Hog promised, turned, and picked up the rock. He grinned at Ballpeen and flung it at Toney's shack. Thwack! It hit the tin roof. Clap! Bang! Clap! It tumbled and rolled until the metallic racket trailed off.

Ballpeen placed his hands on his hips and stared to Hog. "I thought you just said you wouldn't throw anymore."

"That's right. I didn't throw anymore. I threw a rock. Dumb shit!"

A dumbfounded look came over Ballpeen's face, and Toney stood up again. "Hey!" he barked out, loud and mean.

Ballpeen ran into the house.

Hog and Flick left the yard

Breed ran to catch up.

A melody of Toney's muffled sounds, "Hey! I wanna tell you, and back that way again," and, "Hey!" were heard over and over until the trio were out of listening range and well on their way to the Traptown Warehouse store.

Chapter 15

Hog, Flick, and Breed eased through the red-bricked entrance and walked to the back of the Traptown Warehouse store where a new employee was working.

In front of the gray-cement block wall, tall stacks of light-brown, cardboard, empty boxes were lined up. When closing time came, the towering boxes would be crumpled and burned. The blue smoke would fill the night air and sting anyone's throat who happen to pass by and breathe it in. Breed had asked for empty boxes before. The owner had always turned him down.

Hog had said that the only reason the owner wouldn't give them the boxes was because he wanted to let everybody know he was an asshole. After all, if he gave them the boxes, it would save him the trouble of burning them.

Hog reached over, grabbed an expensive gallon of green marine paint and snatched it off the shelf. Holding the paint, he tapped the new employee on the shoulder. "Sir, can we have some empty cardboard boxes for our cabin?"

"Why sure boys," the employee said in a cherry voice. "Help yourself."

"Thank you, sir," Hog said, and they picked up more boxes than they could carry.

With the paint in one hand and three cardboard boxes in the other hand, Hog walked down the rear isle of the store. Flick followed. With each step, he kicked the boxes. Irritating low bass sounds boomed across the store. Breed pulled a huge box down off the pile and dragged it across the cement

223

floor.

Not to be outdone, Hog let his boxes drop to the floor. Like a disgusting drum, they banged and thumped. A customer peeked around the aisle, made a face, and walked away.

One of the smaller boxes Flick was carrying slipped out of his hand and fell to the floor. He intentionally tripped over it, rumbled onto the other boxes, and fell to the floor.

Breed scraped his box around the corner and looked down at Flick. "Walk much?"

"Not with these boxes under my feet." Flick stood up. "You guys sure we need these boxes?"

Hog picked his boxes up off the floor. "Just for a little bit. Make as much noise as you can." He turned and thumped toward the checkout counter at the front of the store.

Every three feet, Breed and Flick dropped the boxes and banged them extra hard. Every time a customer looked at what they were doing, the customer turned and walked away.

Close to the counter and next to the restroom door, Breed scraped up with his big box and caused a cardboard train wreck.

The grouchy owner came out of the restroom with his fly open and his belt unbuckled.

"Just what is going on?" He pulled his brown dress pants up and tightened his belt.

Hog dropped the boxes and banged on them. Thump! Thump!

Breed scraped closer with his huge box.

Using short nervous bites, the owner chewed on the end of his cigar. He glared at Flick. "Why are you kids banging those boxes in my store?"

No one answered. Flick dropped his boxes and pretended to be trying to pick them up. He kicked them with his feet, bumped them with his knees, and punched them with his fists. Bang! Thump! Boom!

The owner's eyes turned to narrow pools of ice water. He raised his voice over the drum-like thumps. "What the hell do you kids think you're doing?"

Flick looked at him with sad pleading eyes. "We're getting these empty boxes for our cabin, sir."

The owner's voice became low-pitched and controlled, but each word snapped like a slap in the face. "I didn't say you could have those boxes. What are you filthy kids trying to do, steal them?"

Hog stopped and stood straight, extra erect. "No, sir," he respectfully said in a most pleasing tone of voice. "We have gotten permission to take these boxes, kind sir."

The owner was not accustomed to manners such as this, especially from an across the tracks kid like Hog. He stopped chewing on his cigar and glared down at Hog. Even though the owner was looking at Hog, Breed could feel the blatant arrogance of authority coming from his cold eyes.

Hog was the object of the owner's complete attention. Hog turned and looked up at him. "Sir, do you know that I am famous? If you do, it would be quite an honor for you to let us have these boxes."

Flick poked Breed in the back with the end of a box. He wanted Breed to continue the agitation. Grinning and snickering, Breed walked in a circle and scraped his big box — loud.

Like a hedonistic deity on a throne, the owner turned toward Breed. Hog thumped his box. The owner turned back, lowered one eyebrow, and squinted at Hog. "I don't care what you are." He jerked his finger toward Hog. "You can't have those boxes. They're mine."

"Oh yeah." Hog flashed him a superior grin. "If you want the boxes so bad, you can have this, too." He flippantly lifted his leg, grunted, and forced out a very respectable, loud, low base, groaning fart.

With arms full of merchandise, an assumed rich, fat lady held her breath and shimmied past Breed. Perspiring into her tight blue dress, she stopped for a moment, and panted through her double chinned face. Then she toddled toward the checkout counter.

Flick laughed at Hog's ignorance of farting and kicked his boxes in front of the fat lady's little pigeon-toed feet. Her heavy leg hit the side of a box. It caved in. She looked down over her big belly and stopped.

Hog's obnoxious fart odor permeated the area. The lady wiggled her pig nose like a puffy-faced rabbit. The smell wafted into the owner's nostrils. He bit down hard on his dark-brown cigar and grabbed Hog by the neck. "You filthy pig!" He breathed in and gasped like a man breathing tear gas. He released Hog from his grip and stepped away from the offending odor. "You're blocking paying customers." He tried not to breathe. "Pick up those boxes and get out!"

As if he were praying, Hog held his hands

together. "We would be most happy to grant your wish, O kind and gracious, sir." He grinned. "However, *you* said we couldn't have them."

Before the owner could answer, the lady's nostrils on her pale, twitching nose opened wide. She drew in a great agitated sniff of air. One small whiff of the nauseating fragrance was too much for anyone to stomach, and the owner's prize customer had sucked in a big dose. Her forehead wrinkled in disbelief. Her lips curled with disgust, and her flabby arms shuddered as if she had breathed in an incurable disease. She dropped her purchases. They fell and scattered onto the counter. She lifted her gracious nose in the air. "I despise you." She walked out in a smelly huff.

This was not your everyday run-of-the-mill, circus-tamed fart. Instead of dissipating and allowing a little good air to sneak into one's nose, this obstinate wild cloud of concealed, floating shit intensified.

The horrible vapor caused the owner's nose to run and his eyes to flow with tears. It just did not dissipate. It hung in the air. It engulfed the entire store. Everyone squinted with vapor vision.

Two well-dressed customers started through the front entrance and squinted. "What's that smell, honey?" the lady asked the well-groomed man on her arm.

The man's jaw muscles bunched into quivering knots. He held his breath and didn't answer. He dropped her arm.

Huffing for air, the lady waved her hand in front of her face. "I didn't know anything could smell that bad."

227

Turning their eyes from the burning haze, they left in haste.

Now, the owner wanted Hog's vulgar, gaseous ass out of his store, and – Don't breathe — "Right Now!"

Hog purposely held the gallon of paint in front of the owner's cigar-biting, puffing red face.

The owner shouted blindly into the dangling can of unpaid-for-paint, "Get out! Get out! You goddamn pig!"

The overpowering immediate need to rid his store of this farting, white-hoodlum trash controlled his entire mind, and he wasn't feeling the hawkers Flick was silently flicking on the back of his white shirt.

Breed scraped the big box. The owner's ears perked up. He jerked his head in Breed's direction. As if he were some kind of moron, Breed let his lax mouth drop open, spun around in a circle, and let out a goofy giggle.

Befuddled, the owner gaped at him.

Like a toothache that wouldn't go away, Hog spoke up. "Sir," he said loud and clear. "It's not pig."

Red-faced with anger, the owner snapped his head toward Hog. "What?"

"It's Hog!" Hog calmly corrected to purposely inject more agitation into the exhibition.

Cash paying customers were literally fumigated right off the premises. The unhappy owner pushed Hog and his thumping boxes past the check-out counter and right on out of the store; and during the process he never noticed the can of paint Hog swung in front of his face.

Flick was at the counter holding the boxes. The owner started after him. "Didn't I tell you kids to get out?"

Flick dropped the boxes and blocked the counter lane, again. As if he had all the time in the world, he stretched sluggishly. "What? I didn't hear you."

The owner stuck his arm out straight and pointed to the door. "Get out!"

Breed scraped the big box. The owner turned toward him.

Flick picked a shiny gallon of tar off a stack at the counter. "If that's the way you want to be," he said with a flick of his wrist, "you can have your goddamn boxes!" He waved his hand in front of his face and blew. "They smell like shit anyway!"

The owner forcefully pushed Flick and the shiny can of tar out of the stinking store.

Breed scraped the box one more time. The owner shook his piercing finger of rebuke in Breed's Face. "You too!

Breed ran out the door, and tripped into the boxes Hog had left in front of the store. He got up and ran after Flick and Hog.

On the way back to Ballpeen and the boat, the obnoxious odor lingered in Breed's lungs. He looked to Hog. "What the hell did you eat?"

Hog laughed. "You like that? If you say, 'Please!' I'll make you another."

"No way, man," Breed said and thought about the smell and how bad it was. It must have lingered and floated around the store a long time before it finally made its way outside and rose up, higher and higher, until it was high enough to eat away at the

229

earth's precious ozone layer.

Flick looked at Hog and forced a long breath of air out of his lungs. With tears in his eyes, he said. "If farting was an Olympic sport, you'd have won a gold medal."

***

Breed heard the pounding coming from Ballpeen's house before he could see the boat. When they arrived, they presented the paint and tar to Ballpeen. He studied the label on the can of paint and looked up. "Hey, I wanted yellow paint. This is green."

"It was yellow when we picked it up. " Flick made a face. "But Hog cut one of the greatest farts in the world and turned the paint and everything else in the store green."

"That's right!" Hog held out his arms and turned his palms up. "If you hurry you can run down to the store and smell it. You want me to show you the way?"

Ballpeen shook his head in numb astonishment.

Breed ran his hand along the bow of the boat and felt uneven bulges in the bent boards. "You should have cut a couple of shallow lines on these boards. They would have curved into place nice and even."

"The hot water worked," Ballpeen said. The green paint will cover those humps, but I still wish it was yellow."

"Quit complaining," Hog said. "You're lucky you got any paint at all."

"The color don't matter," Flick said. "But green will be harder to find when those flats kids come looking for the boat."

230

"I guess you guys are right." Ballpeen opened the can of paint, picked up an old wisp broom, and dipped it into the paint. On the first stroke, loose straw bristles came out of the makeshift paintbrush and were randomly ingrained into the freshly painted surface.

When he was done, the rough paint job embellished the craft. Although it wasn't a tremendous improvement, it looked like a boat, of some kind.

Ballpeen looked at his paint-spattered shirt, ignored it, and looked to Hog. "Let's take it to the river now."

"Why?" Hog laughed with mischievous merriment. "Can't you wait to see it sink?"

Ballpeen ignored Hog's laughter and turned toward Flick. "Can't we carry it to the river today?"

"Don't be stupid." Flick pointed to the boat. "That's good marine paint. It won't be dry for at least a couple of days." He touched the wet paint and wiped the green from his finger on Ballpeen's paint-spattered shirt.

"Hey, cut that out!" Ballpeen said as if one more spot of green would be noticed.

Flick continued, "And, anyway, if we carry it in the daylight everybody will know we have it."

"Yeah," Breed agreed, "those flats gang kids will take it off us before we even have a chance to start for Shell Island."

Flick put one hand in his pocket and talked moving his other hand. "We'll carry it at night, throw her in the water, and head upriver before that flats gang even knows we have a boat."

Hog looked toward Ballpeen and smiled.

"Yeah, if it doesn't fall apart before you get it to the river." He stuck out his elbow and nudged Ballpeen. "Right, Ballpeen?"

Now that Ballpeen had used Hog to get the paint, he didn't have to be nice anymore. He looked at Hog with contempt. "Just blow it out your ass . . . Hog!"

"I did, sir." Hog hooked his thumbs in the sides of his shirt. "That's how we got the paint."

Flick placed the end of a short board on the side of the boat and pushed. The side moved, but the board didn't pop out. "Maybe we should test this thing. Then we could make any last minute adjustments before we start for Shell Island."

Hog put his hand to his chin. "Actually, we should." He deliberately looked at Ballpeen. "If we don't test this junk, and it sinks, the trip to Shell Island sinks with it."

"That's right, "Flick said. "We could pretend to be swimming, test the boat, and look for a place to hide it."

Breed shook his head in disagreement. "The flats gang's gonna find it no matter where we hide it."

Touching the green paint, Ballpeen shook with excited enthusiasm. "It's almost dry. Let's take the boat to the river and try it out now."

Tapping his head as if he had secret insight, Hog said, "If you want to get paint all over yourself, that's a good idea."

"I'm tellin' you," Breed said, "they'll find it, and even if we find a place to hide it, we'll still have to carry it at night."

Ballpeen looked at the boat and dropped his

hands to his sides. "We'll just have to wait. Now that it's painted, it's a nice boat, ain't it?

Hog stepped back and tilted his head to one side. "Yeah, if you want to call it a boat."

I am not gonna stand around all day and watch paint dry," Flick said and took a step toward the apple tree. "I'm going to get my towel and swimming suit."

"Whistle for whoever else wants to go," Breed said. "If Henry and little Burkie ain't hangin' around the gas station, I'm going to see if my motorbike's under that tarp."

Hog tilted his head in a questioning slant. "I don't mean to put a damper on your plans, but ain't you afraid they'll rub dog shit in your face and cut your ears off?"

"I would be if you guys weren't coming with me," Breed said. "They always gang up on us. Let's gang up on them for a change."

With the prospect of agitating, Hog's eyes lit up. "I'll swing around and get Blo. Maybe he'll bring a possum."

Flick smiled. "Good idea. I'll meet you guys at the gas station." He tramped out of the yard.

Chapter 16

The gas station-grocery store on the corner of Rat Street and River Road boasted two red, brush-painted gas pumps, a gravity fed kerosene tank, a hydraulic car lift, and a free air hose with a hand crank to present tire pressure.

Inside, on the grocery store side of the gas station, long, tall wooden shelves displayed cellophane covered chocolate cupcakes; wax paper bags filled with little round fruit pies in tin foil pans; orange, green, white, red wrapped candy bars; paper packs of cigarettes; loose cigars with gold foil bands; dog-eared paperback books — no one bought — glossy magazines; and little blue and clear bags filled to the top with greasy Wise potato chips. Off to the side, among bright orange, red, green, and purple bottles of pop, dark bottles of carbonated colas, sat in a big red cooler.

The store also carried various emergency items like light bulbs, fuses for electric fuse boxes, and cough medicine.

Breed and his friends stood in front of the building and looked through the wide plate glass window. Inside, Henry jiggled the crank on the gumball machine next to the candy counter.

"What's Henry doing?" Blo asked.

Breed pointed to the gumball machine. "See that big pile of yellow prize-balls with the green stripes?"

"The ones inside the round glass?" Ballpeen asked.

Jerking his head like a pecking chicken, Screwball said, "No, the ones floating in midair."

Ballpeen ignored Screwball's antics and looked at Breed. "So what about them?"

"If you got enough pennies, you can turn the crank and win one of those green-striped yellow prize-balls from the machine."

Hog flashed Ballpeen a secret wink. "One of those balls is good for a lucky rabbit's foot on a gold chain."

"Yeah," Breed said and leaned against the red brick station wall. "Henry's old man says it really works, because if you get one of those winning yellow, green-striped balls, your luck has already changed."

"Your luck could be changed forever." Flick placed his foot on the brick window ledge below the plate-glass window. "All you got to do is rub the foot three times and your wish comes true."

"Only a dumb ass would believe that." Hog leaned against the side of the window. "That's just a trumped up story to get a dumb kid's pennies."

Henry's job was to watch the station while his father was gone. With his hand on the gumball machine, he turned and looked at Breed and the others standing outside. He quit shaking the machine and walked to the rack with the girlie magazines. He pulled a glossy magazine from the rack; and as if he had a disease and were looking for the cure, he quickly opened it. He stared out the window, held up one finger, and wiggled it in a come-here-motion.

"He wants one of us to go in," Flick said.

"He's just a filth freak. " Hog jerked his head and shuddered. "He's just trying to get someone to suck his dick."

235

"I ain't goin' in." Breed covered his mouth with his hand and talked through his fingers. "His mind's messed up. I don't even like to breathe the same air he does."

Blo adjusted his trumpet under his arm. "Yeah, that asshole offered me twenty bucks from the register last week to jack him off."

Hog bent over and let out a long theatrical moan. "That's sick." He looked up at Blo. "Did he pay you, yet?"

Without missing a beat, Blo inverted his front teeth and sneered. "Eeeuuuu! Blow it out your ass!"

Breed glanced toward the back of the station and that tarp. He could not see his red motorbike frame.

"Hey, you guys," he said. "I got to check under that tarp."

Flipping his hand into the air, Hog said, "Be my guest."

Breed started for the tarp, but stopped and came back to the window. "You guys keep Henry busy while I look."

"That bastard ain't gittin' away with screwin' that little girl." Ballpeen placed his hand on the hammer in his belt. "I wonder what that would sound like."

Flick turned his head in a quizzical tilt. "What are you talkin' about?"

Ballpeen gave Flick a secret wink. "Wait here. I'll be right back!" He opened the door to the gas station store and stepped in.

Inside, he turned and swaggered toward the magazine rack.

"He's walkin' like a faggot," Hog said. "Maybe he's turnin' into one."

Flick's forehead wrinkled. "I don't know, he was pretty mad about Henry and Burkie screwin' that little girl. When he has a chance to hit something with that hammer he gets brave. Let's watch through the glass."

While they watched, Breed walked over to the tarp and lifted it. And there it was: His bent motorbike frame, no wheels and no motor. The gas tank was dented, but he could fix that. He looked around. Henry's old man was nowhere to be seen. Breed pulled his frame out from under the tarp, picked it up, ran down the road, and threw it. It swished into the tall weeds and grass but could still be seen. He looked around, jumped in the ditch, pulled grass out by the roots, and covered his bike frame. When it was hid, he ran back to the station window and acted like nothing had happened.

Inside, Ballpeen stepped to the magazine rack. Henry nuzzled next to him and flipped open magazines until he came to the centerfolds. "Hey!" he excitedly said. "Ballpeen, look at these!"

Ballpeen pretended not to be interested. "I don't have time."

"You have time for this." Henry held the center fold in front of Ballpeen's face. "Ain't these really hot babes?"

Ballpeen nodded as if he were interested.

Henry got excited, dropped the girlie magazines, went to the cash register, opened it, and took out a bill. "I'll give you five dollars if you suck my dick."

A look of repulsion flashed on Ballpeen's face.

237

"No way!"

Henry took out another bill. "Ten?"

"No!"

"Fifteen?"

"No!"

Henry held up a twenty-dollar bill. "Last chance. Twenty bucks?"

The look of repulsion eased from Ballpeen's face. "Okay, but let's go in the back."

Henry waved the bill at Ballpeen. "You'll get this after you're done." He smiled, put the twenty-dollar bill back into the register, and they walked into the back room.

Outside, on the other side of the window, Blo's mouth gaped open. "Ballpeen's going to do it!"

Shaking with anticipation, Henry stumbled to the back of the room.

I'm not stayin' out here." Hog said, "While they're back there, I'm gonna get one of those rabbit's feet to hang on Ballpeen's junk boat, maybe it'll make it float." He stepped through the door, reached up on the shelf and grabbed a little peach pie. Then he reached in the little wax paper bag and pulled the pie out of the tin. He took three quick bites, shoved the half-eaten pie back in the little pan, and put it back on the shelf. Wiping his mouth on his wrist, he turned around, waltzed to the gumball machine, and put a round paper bingo marker in the slot. Swallowing the pie, he turned the crank. The marker stuck and the one turn crank became freewheeling. He spun the handle. The gumballs avalanched into his cupped hand.

Outside, Screwball tiptoed to the air hose and turned the hand crank tire pressure gauge down to

238

five pounds. He put the nozzle of the hose on the pointed corner of the hose hanger and pushed in the air release valve. The air rushed out and the bell dinged loud and fast — Ding! Ding! Ding! — over and over.

Screwball tapped his foot to the rhythm of the dings, and Breed and the others ambled into the store. They spread out and positioned themselves at various locations where they could see into the back room. Breed sat on a round metal stool and peered into the side door of the oil rack. The broken motor from his motorbike sat next to the trash can. He started to cuss.

Flick motioned with his hand. "Wait! Henry's standing by the pop cooler with his dick hanging out."

Screwball quit dinging the air hose and watched.

"Go ahead, do it, twenty bucks." Henry waited for Ballpeen.

Ballpeen looked back over his shoulder, made eye contact with Breed, winked, and looked back to Henry. "Okay, shut your eyes."

Henry shut his eyes.

Ballpeen took the hammer from his belt, and grabbed Henry's dick. With one skillful motion, he swished the hammer high into the air and swung it down. Wham!

Henry had to feel that pain, but he didn't scream. Nodding profusely with his eyes wide, he stumbled backward. Then, as if it were a delayed reaction he cried, "A-h-h-h-h!"

A big smile spread across Ballpeen's face. He looked into Henry's face and roared, "H-a-a-a-nt!"

A painful look of confusion radiated from Henry's entire body. "You rotten little bastard!"

Roaring with laughter, Ballpeen ran out of the back room and zipped past Breed.

Bent over and holding his broken, hammered dick, Henry ran after Ballpeen.

Outside, Screwball held the air hose wide open. Ding! Ding! Ding! Its irritating bell rang — loud.

Henry started through the doorway. Blo lifted the trumpet to Henry's ear. Baalllaaatttt!!!

Henry jumped back, held his dick with one hand, grabbed his ear with the other hand, and stopped. He was muscular but would not fight unless his opponents were outnumbered. With a face filled with pain, he zipped up his fly, put his hands in his pockets, and as if nothing had happened, he tried to smile.

Breed sat on the metal stool and rotated the seat back and forth. He looked at his motorbike motor and placed his feet on the bottom of the counter. Pushing hard, he tried to break the stool. It squeaked loud.

Henry stepped forward and pointed at Breed. "Stop that or I'll rub your face in dog shit."

Hog stopped spinning the gumball machine crank and stood with his back to it. The machine was dam near empty. He had no prize ball. They were all still in the machine. He put his hands in his bulging pockets and concealed the gumballs. "How did you like that blow job, Henry?"

Breed turned. The stool squeaked and metal shavings fell beneath it. "Yeah, how'd you like it? You baby fucking thief."

Henry lifted his hand to strike and stepped

toward Breed. Flick cleared his throat. Henry lowered his hand and turned around. He was outnumbered.

Taking on a look of innocence, Henry turned toward Breed. "It's not your motor."

Outside, Ding! Ding! Ding! continued.

Flick triumphantly smiled.

Pain showed in Henry's contorted face. As if he were trying to make Flick feel sorry for him, he bent over and moaned in a high-pitched voice. "You think that's funny?"

Flick smiled bigger.

Henry stood upright and repeated, "You think that's funny?" In renewed pain, he grabbed his dick, and bent over again.

Hog leaned close and yelled directly in Henry's ear, "Pardon me! Sir!"

"You heard me," Henry groaned, still holding his dick.

Squeak! Squeak! Squeak! Came from the turning seat.

"You're goddamn right, sir!" Hog said. "We think it's funny, you dim-witted freak."

As if he had something foul on his hands, Flick wiped his them on the back of his pants. "Let's get out of here. I feel like I'm gonna catch some kind of a disease."

As if he wished he hadn't eaten it, Hog looked at the half-eaten pie.

Breed rocked the seat again. Squeak! Squeak! He jumped off the stool and stood in front of Henry. "That motor's mine. He walked over and picked it up.

Henry blocked him from going out the door.

"You take my motor, I'll tell One-Finger-Burke. He'll put you in jail."

"It's not your motor." Breed directed a look of hate straight into Henry's eyes and lifted the motor high ready to bring it down on Henry's head. "If you want a broken skull" — he lifted his leg to kick — "and broken balls to match your broken dick just stand there."

Henry backed off.

Breed carried *his* motor through the door.

The Ding! Ding! Ding! intensified. Screwball held the red air hose in one hand, danced, and waved his other hand in the air. Ding! Ding! Ding!"

Hog jerked the door. Three brass entrance-warning bells rang loud. He kept it up. R-i-i-i-n-n-n-g-g-g!

Over the dings and rings, Hog looked over his shoulder. "Hey, Henry, if you ever need another blow job just let us know. You won't have to screw babies."

As Henry straightened up, a submissive look filled his face. "It was Burkie's idea to screw that little girl." He held his hands in front of his face, his voice pleading for relief. "It's all his fault. If I tell, he'll cut my ears off."

"We don't care whose fault it was," Flick said. "You still did it. He should cut your broken dick off, too."

Ding! Ding! Ding!

Henry placed his hands over his ears. "If you don't stop, I'm telling my dad."

Hog continued jerking the door. Jerk! Ring! Jerk! Ring! Jerk! Ring!

242

Blo sneered at Henry through his false teeth. "What are you going to tell him? Ding-a-ling! You took money from the register for a blow job? Eeuuu, dumb freak!"

With the brass bells ringing, Henry gripped the doorknob and tried to keep Hog from jerking it. Screwball danced in place, held the red rubber air hose on the pointed edge of the gauge, and dinged the air gauge bell. Air rushed out of the hose — faster, faster. The air compressor kicked on — Hut! Hut! Hut! It sped up. H-u-u-t-t-t-t-t! It pulsated and echoed to a loud throb. The gauge dinged faster. Hog jerked the door, faster. Above, the three bells rang intermittently, and chronic chimes sang in the air. Brang! Brang! Brang!

Henry tried to push the door shut. Flick held his foot at the bottom like a doorstop.

Henry couldn't close it.

Blo stuck the end of his trumpet in the door opening. Blat! Blat! Blat! blasted into Henry's ear.

Henry turned away, put his hands over his ears, and yelled hysterically, "Quit ringing that air gauge." He waved his hand at the trumpet. "Get that trumpet away from me."

Blat! Blat! Blo blew louder.

As if in intolerable pain, Henry bent over and whined, "Leave me alone."

"Don't worry, Henry," Flick said with malicious glee. "You are alone, unless you got a turd in your pocket."

For a moment, Henry's arms dropped helplessly with exhaustion, and he stood like an idiot.

243

"Jolly good show, old man. "Hog lifted his chin and talked down to Henry. "In spite of your falling out with your acquaintances, I'm glad to see you're still enjoying the local tourist sites in comfort."

With his mouth agape, Henry stood motionless in one spot.

Savoring Henry's situation, Blo pointed at him. "Look, everybody, look at the moron."

Enraged, Henry bucked up against the door and pushed with all his might. Flick pulled his foot away. Brang! The bells rang once. The door banged shut — right in Henry's face.

As if he had just finished a dirty job, Flick brushed his hands together. "That should put an end to that queer crap!"

Henry locked the door, ran to the throbbing compressor, and pulled the plug. The dinging slowed and stopped. Blo pointed the trumpet toward Henry and wailed a parting sour blast. Screwball ran behind the station and picked up Breed's motorbike wheels. Breed carried his broken motor and walked down Rat Street. The others followed and headed for Rat River.

Screwball came up behind Breed with the wheels of the motorbike in his hands. "Hey, Breed, you think you'll need these."

Breed turned and smiled happily. "Thanks, Screwball. I ain't goin' swimming now. I'm takin' my bike parts home."

"You can if you want," Flick said. "But if Henry's old man or One-Finger-Burke and his buddies see you, they'll say you stole them."

"Better wait for night," Hog said and they

tramped into the weeds and hid the parts.

Chapter 17

Ballpeen had never stopped running until he reached the river where he immediately washed his hands and hammer at the flowing water line. He was still laughing when Breed and the others arrived at the dock.

Many dives later, Breed and his friends sat on the bridge, chewing stolen gumballs and letting the sun broil their bodies a reddish-brown.

Cars buzzed over the steel grating of the bridge, and Hog occasionally threw a gumball at whomever he pleased.

A sewer rat swam across the river, scampered in the dirty water flowing toward the water treatment plant, and disappeared into the darkness of an exposed sewer tile.

"Boy!" Ballpeen said, "I can't wait until that boat is dry so we can try it out."

Hog heightened one eyebrow in a questioning tilt. "If you want to kill time, go up and suck on Henry's dick!"

Ballpeen immediately snapped back, "You're just jealous cause you didn't think of it first."

Hog laughed and wiggled his wet rear end on the railing. "Ballpeen, I'll have to admit, that was pretty good."

"Yeah, hant! on Henry," Ballpeen added.

Hog tapped his barefoot on the railing. "They should make a new song about you," he said and sang. "Step on a rock, . . . 'tap, tap, tap, tap' . . . I'll suck your cock!"

"Hey!" Ballpeen flecked back. "Blow it out your ass, Hog." He paused. "You can't get serious about anything."

Hog put his hand on Ballpeen's shoulder. "Okay, Ballpeen, I'll get serious. I'll write a book."

Ballpeen shrugged Hog's hand off his shoulder. "Yeah, Hog, kiss my ass and make it a love story."

"Hell, Ballpeen. Suck my dick and make it a novel."

"Hant!" Screwball chimed in.

"Oh, real funny." Ballpeen looked away. "That was so damn funny I almost broke out in assholes and shit to death."

Flick raised his arm, stretched it straight and pointed upriver. "Hey look! There's a boat drifting down river."

"Let's get it." Hog turned to dive. "Ballpeen's boat will never float."

Before Ballpeen could reply, everyone but him dove off the bridge. Ballpeen looked around the bridge, stepped up on the railing and dove in, too. As they all swam to the boat, the current sucked on the bow of the boat and turned it sideways. Flick and Breed swam up and grabbed it. The others caught up and turned it out of the strong current.

They crawled in, held on to the sides; and as if they were miniature oars, they dipped their arms into the water. Using long strong powerful strokes, they propelled the boat; and it plowed water all the way to the dock.

Screwball bent over the side of the boat, lifted two oars from the bottom, and held them for all to see. "You guys think we'll need these?"

For a moment, Flick tilted his head in despair, then looked to Screwball. "Blow it out your ass."

Screwball smiled big. "H-a-a-a-nt!"

Hog jumped up onto the dock, grabbed the rope that was attached to the port side of the boat and tied it to a support. "Looks like we ain't gonna have to use Ballpeen's junk boat."

"That's what you think." Ballpeen pointed to the bridge catwalk above their heads.

Screwball's face sagged into a hangdog hopeless look. "Talk about shit and look what comes waltzing in."

Five flats gang bullies, with their arms crossed across their chests, stood — waiting.

"Doesn't this shit ever end?" In exasperation, Breed held his hand to his head. "We just got the damn thing, and now they're gonna take it."

To stall for time Flick and Hog ran up the cinder path.

It was the big bad kids from the flats gang. The ones the good people of Traptown hid up their asses and then walked as if they weren't there; the kids with the turned up collars on their dime-store sport shirts; the zit faces, who lived on a diet of pretzels and beer; the kids who waited to beat up Breed and his friends — "Just for kicks!" — and then combed their greasy hair into DA's and repeated, "Like man!" over and over; and stood, with their skin tight blue-jeaned legs apart, flicking their black-handled, gravity-operated stilettos, constantly building their plastic wall to show that they were the one and only, "Mister Cool!" bad asses of the narrow-minded world of Traptown.

The leader unrolled a pack of Camels from the sleeve of his dirty white T-shirt, tapped one from the bundle, and lit up. He inhaled. The strong smoke crawled into his lungs, where it seemed to deceive his limited mind and signal his body to pull strength and authority from the nicotine. The other gang members straightened their shirt collars and smiled arrogantly. They were bigger and stronger than Breed and his friends. They could kick their asses at will.

As Flick and Hog approached the gang, Hog held out his hand in friendship. "Good afternoon, gentleman."

The leader batted Hog's hand down. "Thanks for getting us another boat."

Under the bridge, while Screwball gently stepped into the boat, Breed and Blo eased into the water. Breed untied the boat and looked up. Flick was watching through the holes in the steel grating.

Blo and Breed braced their backs against the back of boat, cocked their legs on the dock, and pushed. As they hung on, the boat glided toward the center of the river.

Up on the bridge, the gang leader looked toward the boat, but Flick stepped in front of him and blocked his view. "What do you mean, another boat?"

In a vain attempt to show his masculinity, the leader deliberately bent his elbow and flexed his little biceps. He put the non-filtered cigarette in the side of his liver lipped mouth and talked through his teeth. "Like I said, 'another boat!'" He squinted his eyes from the smoke that curled from his cigarette. "We always take anything we want." He shifted his feet into a fighting stance and clinched his fists. "What makes you think we're going to stop now? Punk!"

Hog put on his nice act, tried to reason with the

kid. "Why do you guys always have to take our stuff?"

As if he were looking for an answer, the leader looked up into the sky. "Why?"

"Yeah." Flick glanced at the escaping boat. "Why do you guys always take everything we get?"

The leader smiled and looked to his companions for approval. "Reason? We don't need a reason. That's our reason." He cocked his head to one side and smiled an exaggerated smile.

"Yeah," the gangling, gawky kid tee-heed. "We don't need a reason. That's our reason."

His companions giggled and bobbed their heads as if they had weak springs on their necks.

Under the bridge, as Breed held onto the side of the boat, his black and blue ribs and shins still hurt from the last kicks he had gotten from Flat Top. He didn't want more. But he didn't want the flats gang to take another boat. He pushed the boat further out into the water, but it wasn't far enough.

At the top of the cinder path, the leader shifted his weight from one foot to another. He was getting impatient. Breed hoped Hog and Flick could stall him until they slipped the boat out of sight. He kept pushing.

When the leader moved, Flick moved in front of him. When he moved again, Hog moved next to Flick and blocked his view. The other members watched Flick and Hog, and didn't look toward the escaping boat.

Flick pointed at the leader. "Hey, man, that's a really cool shirt you have on."

The leader looked uncomfortable and puzzled. A compliment was completely off-the-wall. It did not fit into his narrow thought process. He cast a suspicious glare at Flick.

Hog took Flick's lead and continued, "Yeah, that's a really nice shirt. Too bad somebody shit in it!"

The leader's face scorched to anger. He stared hard at Hog.

Hog lowered his chin, opened his eyes wide, and smiled a big ear-to-ear mocking smile. "What would you do with a brain if you had one?"

Under the bridge, Breed and Blo placed their hands on the back of the boat; and kicking their legs under the water, they quietly guided the boat into the current. Screwball slipped the oars in the holders and pulled. The boat glided out of the current and toward the cement bridge support.

Up on the bridge, the leader reached for Hog. "What did you say about my shirt?"

Splash! Skip! Splash! Screwball dragged the oars across the top of the water. The sound sprinkled through the holes in the steel grating. The leader dropped his hand away from Hog and turned his head down toward the dock.

The gangling, gawky kid looked at the boat in the middle of the river. His phony bad-man shield dropped. "T-t-hey g-got," he stuttered and caught himself. He regained his phony front and blurted out, "Like man. They got the boat! Let's get these punks!"

The sickening scowl on the leader's face vanished behind his big flapping mouth. "Get that boat right back where we can take it," he yelled and grabbed for Hog.

Hog jerked away from the grasping hand.

The leader only grabbed air.

He balled his hand into a fist and drew back. "I'll kick your ass." He swung.

Hog ducked under the swishing fist, turned, and sprinted behind Flick, who was running down the cinder path. The leader hesitated for a second and then ran after them.

Hog stopped at the base of the bridge, grabbed the dead snake from where he had hidden it on the stone shelf, and leaned back — out of sight.

The leader stumbled down the cinder path.

Flick stood on the end of the dock waving his hand in a come-here gesture.

The leader was in such a hurry to get at Flick that he didn't see Hog and rushed toward the dock. Hog flung the snake. It wrapped around the charging leader's neck.

"Hant!" Hog jeered and pointed at the snake.

The leader grabbed the snake to pull it from his neck.

"Don't touch it," Hog said with immediacy. "It's poisonous. You'll get bit and die."

The leader jerked his hand away. The snake slithered from his neck, unrolled and clung in the center of his back. "Ah-h-e-e-e!" he wailed, wiggled, and begged, "Get it off! Get it off!"

The gangling, gawky kid loped down the cinder path with his fist clinched. At the bottom, he looked at the snake, unclenched his fists, and leaped back.

Hog ran off the end of the dock and dove into the water.

Panic blazed in the leader's face. He ripped a handful of long grass from the bank and stepped

252

backwards. Using the grass, he tried to sweep the limp snake off the center of his back. He couldn't reach it.

"It won't come off," he cried, stamped his feet, and reached up to rip his shirt off.

Hog yelled, "Don't take off your shirt. That water moccasin's gonna bite you in the back."

The leader yanked his hand down. As if it were glued there, the snake stayed on his back. He whined and whacked. The snake stayed there. His arms waved like paddle wheels. "Get it off before it bites me!" he boo-hooed and slung himself off balance. His feet flew up. His butt hit the steep muddy riverbank. He spun around and slid down the bank, sitting and backwards. Like a shovel, the waist of his pants scooped up mud and packed up his ass. He came to a stop in the shallow water. When he stood up, his legs struggled with the weight of the mud and the suck of the filth below him. He felt for the snake. His voice filled with fear and immediacy. "Where is it?"

"It crawled up your ass," Hog said from the safety of the water.

The leader felt for the snake in his mud-packed ass. He didn't find it. He looked toward the bank for help. The gangling, gawky kid held up his hands and backed away. "I ain't touchin' no poison snake." He turned and looked toward Flick. "Don't just stand there, help him."

"We put the snake on him." Flick crossed his arms across his chest and chuckled. "What more do you want us to do?"

The leader shuddered. The snake fell off. A look of relief filled his face. He breathed easier,

253

pointed at the snake on the ground, and talked in a humble voice. "It's dead."

Blo tauntingly yelled across the water, "Ha-a-a-nt!"

Flick defiantly stood at the edge of the dock smiling.

The leader shook his fist at him. "Just keep standing on that dock, I'm coming over there." He started making his way up the slippery riverbank.

Shaking his fist and stomping on the ground, the gangling, gawky kid sputtered a few unintelligible threats. When he lifted his foot to stomp, he slipped and fell. He pushed himself up, took two steps, and skidded on the slimy riverbank. In an effort to catch is balance, he grabbed onto the leader's arm. The leader swung around, and they both fell to their backs. As mud packed into the back of their pants, they skidded down the muddy bank until they stopped in ankle-deep water. Splashing, they struggled to their feet. While the gangling, gawky kid squatted in the water, the leader unbuckled his pants and dumped the mud out. With his pants down around his knees, he stood there and scooped mud out of his underwear.

Flick laughed so hard he slipped; but before he fell, he dove into the water.

"Ha-a-a-nt!" Screwball jeered from the center of the boat.

"You think that's real funny?" the leader said through his mud-covered face.

Treading water, Hog laughed. "Yes, yes, sir! I think it's very funny." He laughed again. "I told you that shirt had shit in it. Now your pants have shit in them, too."

As mean lines of hostility filled his face, the leader puffed up his chest and screamed, "I'm coming in after your ass!" He took one step and his pants dropped around his ankles. He spun his arms, slipped and fell, again.

"Hant!" Screwball yelled, again.

Out in the river, near the safety of the strong current, Breed and his friends laughed at the leader's clumsiness and pushed the boat toward the tree branch in the water.

Hog could always be counted on to flirt with danger and agitate when the person couldn't do anything about it. He swam close to the dock and screamed across the water, "Your mother eats shit!"

The leader whipped his head around and shouted at Hog, "What did you say about my mother?"

"Your mother?" Hog replied in a most dignified tone of voice. "I talked to her just yesterday. She informed me that when you were born she was constipated. The baby died and the shit lived."

"Not only that," Screwball added. "You're just a bunch of candy ass bastards!"

Helping the gangling, gawky kid out of the water, the leader shouted back, "Come on up on this bank. I'll teach you to talk about my mother." His face took on a fiendish expression. "We'll find out who's a candy ass!" He breathed in black mud from his face and coughed to clear his throat.

Hog cheered him on. "Cough up that dick, cock sucker!"

Through his white-circled eyes, the leader scowled at Hog and spit mud from his mouth. Then, he bent over and pulled up his wet pants. He

255

held them around his waist with one hand, and used the other hand to make a fist and waved it around in a small circle. "Come on out of that water, you smart mouth asshole!"

Hog waved his fist and mimicked the leader. "Come and get me, you big dumb sissy."

The gangling, gawky kid took a step toward the water. "Let's get those assholes."

The leader grabbed his arm. "Don't go in there. The current will suck you into a drop-off. You'll drown."

They didn't go in.

Breed tied the light-blue boat to the tree branch under the bridge, climbed in, and sat on the little wooden seat as if he were watching a movie.

The other flats gang kids ran up onto the catwalk. Blo swam to the small piece of land next to the center bridge support and slid his trumpet out from under a piece of driftwood.

The bright brass trumpet flashed in Breed's eyes. "Hey, Blo, put those babies on the bridge to sleep. Play 'Taps.'"

Blo stood tall and placed the trumpet to his lips. His fingers found the right keys. He took a deep breath and a bleak, Bllaatt!" bleated out. He couldn't play "Taps." His face contorted with puzzlement. He shook it off and the gangling, gawky kid leaned out over the railing and held out his hand. "Give me that thing. I'll shove it up your ass."

Blo yelled up, "Come down and take from me."

Holding onto another gang member's hand, the gangling, gawky kid tried to climb down, but the slanted cement was too steep for him. He quickly gave up.

"What's the matter?" Hog said treading water. "You little baby candy asses afraid you'll fall into the water."

"Yeah," Screwball added, "there ain't no soap in here. You ain't gonna get clean."

Blo pointed the trumpet up and blew – Bllaatt!

Between blasts he shouted profuse profanity for their exclusive benefit.

The leader made his way up the cinder path and plopped a trail of mud all the way to the catwalk. Everyone knew he wanted to jump in the river and shut Hog's mouth, but like all the flats gang bullies, he was afraid of the height and afraid of what could be in the dark water below.

He pointed directly at Blo. "Why don't you come up here? You horn blowin' freak! I'll stick that stupid horn right up your ass!"

Blo pointed the trumpet at him. Bllaatt!

The leader felt for his pack of cigarettes he had rolled up in his T-shirt sleeve. They were wet, covered with mud, and smashed. "You asshole! You made me ruin my cigarettes."

Blo held his trumpet at his side, looked up at the smashed cigarette-armed leader, and yelled loud and clear, "What's the matter? Doesn't the little baby have anything to suck on?"

Bllaatt!

Hog shouted up, "Your mother eats shit while I screw her!"

Bllaatt!

This harsh statement cut deep into the feelings of the leader's maddened brain. Shouting through his mud face, he leaned over the railing and shook his fist at Hog. "You son-of-a-bitch!" he yelled in tough, clipped tones. "You don't talk about my mother like that!"

Lying on his back, Hog kicked his feet and raised both hands out of the water. With his middle fingers pointing high, he yelled, "Ha-a-a-nt!"

Bllaatt!

With his face turning red with anger, the kid looked to Blo and then snapped his head back toward Hog. "We'll see who's afraid of what."

Hog lowered his hands and smiled a big mocking smile.

Bllaatt!

Trying to keep the blaring trumpet blast out of his head, the leader grabbed his left ear. Then he jerked his finger toward Blo. "We'll see whose boat that is."

"It's our boat," Screwball said. "And your dumb, red ass-face ain't getin' it."

"Yeah," Blo yelled and then, Bllaatt!

The leader turned, back away from Blo and the trumpet. "I want, Y*ou!*" he yelled and pointed his muddy finger at Breed. He leaned over the bridge railing, stretched his right arm straight, and pointed at everybody in the water — one at a time. "And I want, *You!*" — point! — "*You!*" — point! — "*You!*" — point! — "*You!*" — point! — "and *You!*" — point!

Blo set the trumpet on a rock below the center support of the bridge, jumped back in the water, and yelled up to the leader, "Don't forget me!"

As if he had complete control of the situation, the leader quit pointing and put his grimy hands on his black slimy hips. "And all your punk ass friends can come, too." His neck swelled, and he bobbed his head like an arrogant know-it-all trying to talk his way out something he couldn't control. "I want every goddamn one of you bastards to be down here at eight o'clock Friday night. Then we'll see who's afraid of what!"

"That's a nice thing to want, sir," Hog said back and blew bubbles into the water.

"I'm sorry we can't be afraid today." Screwball motioned with a flip of his wet hair. "Come back tomorrow. Maybe we can be afraid then."

"Ha-a-a-nt!" Hog added.

The kid's face grimaced and his forehead wrinkled. "Don't be callin' me names. I'll kick your ass right now!"

"Okay, penis breath," Screwball said. "You want us to be here Friday, on Monday, eight o'clock, at twelve."

The kid spit toward Screwball, but the spit dissipated before it hit the water. "You just go ahead and say what you want. I'll be here."

With his hands laced behind his head, Hog lay back and nonchalantly floated on top of the water. "That's because you're an idiot."

Screwball lay on his back and paddled around in a circle. "Yeah, idiot." Then he waved his hand as if he were shooing a harmless insect. "Don't start a big fight without us."

The kid turned to leave. Hog rocketed his arm out of the water and motioned to the kid in a come-here gesture. "Come in the water, Ballpeen's gonna let you suck his hammer."

The leader kept walking.

Screwball hung onto the side of the boat. "Why wait until Friday. If you're so bad, come in right now!"

The leader slowed.

"Yeah, don't be in such a hurry to go screw your girlfriend," Hog said. "She ain't that good. I should know. I just came from her house."

The leader turned and pointed at Hog. "And *You!* I'm going to kick your smart ass twice! Just show up."

As if it were a penis, Blo placed a long round piece of driftwood between his legs, pointed to it and smiled. "Come on down. I got something for you."

"Just be here Friday." The leader pointed to Blo. "It won't be so funny when I punch your horn blowing teeth out!"

Blo dropped the driftwood and held out his arms, pleading. "What are you waitin' on? I'm here."

The leader and the rest of the flats gang bullies stomped off the bridge.

And the gangling, gawky kid lagged behind.

Blo called after them with one final long wail of his trumpet. The sound of his ear-piercing blast reverberated across the green Rat River.

Flick climbed into the boat and wiggled the sides. "This is a pretty good boat but the wood's rotten."

Breed swung his leg over the side and plopped onto the bottom of the boat. The plywood bottom bent under his weight and a small leak started in the bottom seam. He put the palm of his hand over the leak. "This thing will never make it to Shell Island.

260

It's leaking already."

Flick pressed on the floor of the boat with his foot. "It don't matter. Those Flats kids will be here every day looking for it." Water oozed into the seam. "We'll never be able to keep it."

"That's true," Breed said. "I'd like to sink it right in front of them."

"Yeah, and with them in it. "Screwball pulled at the side of the boat. "It easily flexed. "This thing's water-logged, too."

Hog swam to the boat and stopped next to Ballpeen. "You still got that hammer?"

"Yeah, why?"

Hog jerked his head and wiped the water from his eyes. "You see that light bulb above my head, sir?"

"Cut that stupid little kid shit," Flick said. "What's the idea?"

"Give me that hammer. I'll pound holes in the bottom and sink it right here."

"That's a good idea." Breed said. "But how about if we take it to shore, pound holes in it, fill them with mud, and let it dry in the sun. And then hide it where the flats gang can find it."

As if he were holding his hammer, Ballpeen moved his hand. "I'll pound the holes."

With the movement of the boat, Screwball swayed in the current. "Why don't we just keep it?"

Flick sat on the floor of the boat and leaned back against the bow. "For the simple reason that all those bastards already know we have it."

"Yeah," Hog said and looked to the shore. "They'll keep looking for it until they find it. They don't know it's worse junk than Ballpeen's boat."

Ballpeen let go of the boat and blubbered into the water, "My boat's got a brand new paint job. It ain't junk." He swam toward shore.

Breed let out a long breath of air. "Looks like we ain't getin' a test run with Ballpeen's boat."

Flick nodded. "That's right. If we do a test run, they'll be down here at eight o'clock Friday to take it."

Hinting at Toney's drunken banter, Screwball drunkenly wobbled. "Yeah, but couldn't we carry it back that way again?"

"Heck no," Flick said. "It's too heavy to carry home and then back again every time we wanna use it."

Hog nudged Screwball's shoulder. "And back that way again. Hey! And back that way again. Hey!"

On shore, Ballpeen put his hammer into the waistband of his swimming suit and swam back to the boat. They guided the boat downriver and pulled it up on shore.

Hog looked beyond the shore and through an open space between the river willows. On the road above, a car drove past. He nodded in approval. "Those Flats kids will find it here."

Choo-gunk! Choo-gunk! With the hemispherical end of his hammer, Ballpeen smacked small round holes into the rotten plywood bottom of the boat. Breed followed behind and filled the holes with mud mixed with small pieces of grass.

They planted the boat in the weeds, and the hot sun hardened the yellow mud. To make the boat look as if it had been hid, Hog and Flick threw a few branches over the port side.

They all swam back to the bridge and waited.

Chapter 18

On the other side of the river, next to the big pollution-spewing culvert, Breed sat on the bridge railing and studied a waterlogged wooden skid beneath the surface of the water. A snapping turtle, the size of a bushel basket, crawled out from under the skid.

Screwball pointed to the turtle. Long leeches hung from its broken shell, and one of its legs was missing.

"That thing's in pain. Let's put it out of its misery." Flick ran to the edge of the bridge, picked up a big rock, and threw it at the turtle. He missed. Finding strength from somewhere, the lethargic turtle swam away.

Watching along the bank for it to surface, movement of the tops of tall grass caught Breed's eye. When the grass parted, two flats gang members, with girls hanging onto their elbows, walked toward the riverbank. They were heading toward the hidden boat.

Breed silently let the others know. They hid behind the cement enclosure of the culvert and watched.

The flats kids wore new shirts; and with each step, their highly polished, pointy, black shoes winked in the sun. As the tall kid with scraggy legs snaked his way along the river, a battered baseball cap covered the top of his blond-haired head. The other kid's freshly combed hair was slicked back into duck's butt DA. Primped and ready, they must have figured they were going to show the girls how cool they were. But like a rotten toothed smile, the battered baseball cap ruined their whole image.

While they cleared away the branches of the partially concealed boat, the girls giggled in anticipation. Being careful not to get mud on their new clothes; and as if they were thin-shelled eggs, the flats kids helped the girls into the boat. They responded by beaming affectionately.

The slim girl, with blond hair, wore tight white shorts that showed off her long, tanned legs. A bright, blue ribbon accented the other girl's long, brown hair that she had tied into a ponytail. Sitting in the boat, the girls looked like pretty prizes.

The flats gang kids pushed the boat into the water and jumped in. The DA kid noticed a speck of mud on the edge of his shoe. He sat on the wooden seat, bent over; awkwardly held his chest out; purposely flexed his scant arm muscles for the girls to see; and wiped the small spot with a clean white handkerchief. The tall kid ignorantly skipped the oars across the top of the water and attempted to row into the current. When he had finally rowed the boat under the bridge, it sprung the first leak. Water from the first leak primed the other holes. Within seconds, the bottom of the boat sprouted tiny water fountains, all flowing at once. While the DA kid frantically bailed water with a rusty coffee can, the tall kid rowed toward shore.

Suddenly, all efforts to keep the boat afloat ceased. It was useless. The two kids sat in a stupor and stared at each other.

Clucking like a big chicken, the sound of the tall kid's voice echoed across the water. "My wallet! My watch!"

The girl in the white shorts lifter her frail arm

and pointed toward the polluted side of the river and screeched, "Get us to shore!"

The other girl fluttered her hands next to her ears. With her ponytail flapping, and her bright, blue ribbon flashing in the sun, she opened her big mouth and let out a long piercing cry that drowned out every sound along the river. With eyes opened wide, she turned and twisted on the seat and searched for a way out of her fate. "We'll fall in a drop off," she cried. "We'll drown!"

The girl in the white shorts put her fist to her mouth. Biting on her knuckles, she looked toward the shore. Then she looked down at the water rushing into the sinking boat. She took her fist from her mouth and screamed, "We're going to drown!"

Together, their frantic, frenzied voices rebounded up and down the river.

It was like they were taking turns. The girls would scream, "We'll drown!"

Then the tall kid would slap his thin hands on his wallet and look at his watch, saying. "My wallet! My watch!"

While they were sitting and yelling, black sewer water flow out of a red tile pipe and flowed toward their sinking boat. As if mesmerized by the sewer water, they sat there until the water was up to their chests. Then they stood up. Even though the water was only waist high they let the oars float away.

Blo and Hog stepped away from the culvert and waved.

Blo hollered across the water, "Hey, what's the matter? Did you stupid showoffs get wet?"

The tall kid whirled around and looked toward

Blo and Hog. Breed and the others popped up out of the tall weeds, pointed, and laughed.

Blo yelled across the water, "Hey, I wanna tell you something."

"The tall kid jerked his head toward Hog. "What the hell do you want?"

Blo bellowed, "Ha-a-a-nt!"

The DA kid turned his back to the girls and shouted at Blo. "Shut the hell up."

"Ah come on," Hog said. "You'll have to agree, this is an unusual setting for the observation of human beings. Don't you wish you were one?"

As if he had not understood what Hog had said, the DA kid's face filled with confusion. "I don't know what you said, but when I come over there you're going to tell me."

"Perhaps we could discuss it at teatime," Hog said in a most friendly tone. "I would surely welcome your company." He lifted one finger and nodded once. "But please, my good man, check in with the butler first."

The DA kid cussed under his breath and didn't reply.

As the wet flats kids and their wet girlfriends stood in the waist deep water, fire burned in the girls' eyes, and revenge raged in the flats kids' clinched fists.

Blo flashed them the finger and articulated, "Perch and rotate! Mama boys!"

While they stepped unsteadily and made their way to shore, the girls hung onto the two flats kids for balance. The flats kids let them hang on until they were past the sewer pipe and knee-deep water. Then they left the girls standing in the dirty water and splashed up toward the bank.

As if he were running at top speed, Screwball stood in place and jerked his arms. "Run, run as fast as you kin, you can't catch us, we're the Rat Street Bridge bread min."

The two kids splashed out of the water. Screwball ran onto the bridge. Breed and the other followed. Cussing and shaking their fists, the two kids raged after them.

The girls took one step and fell forward. Mud flew up and spattered the bright, blue ribbon. It wasn't bright anymore. Screaming as if it were the end of their lives, they landed hands first onto the muddy bank. After the girls quit screaming, they got up; and with their muddy hands, they pushed their hair out of their eyes.

Screwball made it to the catwalk first and climbed onto the railing. The two flats kids turned the corner and ran onto the bridge. Breed and his friends made it to the railing. As if patiently waiting on a bus or something non-threatening, they sat on the railing.

The two flats kids came close. No one moved. The kids stopped a few feet from Flick and looked at each other.

Flick held out his hand and wiggled his finger in a come-here gesture. "Come on, little baby. Grab my hand."

Hog leaned back and held out both hands. As if he were an old time boxer, he turned his palms up and made fists. "Sir, you would do me a great honor if you would come over here and engage in fisticuffs."

The DA kid feinted toward Hog

Hog jumped.

The kid lunged for Flick's wiggling fingers.

Flick pulled his hand away, jumped off the bridge, and crashed into the water below.

The tall kid grabbed for Breed. Breed jumped and the others followed yelling, "Ha-a-a-a-a-n-n-n-n-t-t-t-t-t-t!" all the way down.

The distance from the railing to the water was higher than a three-story house. Breed knew the flats kids wouldn't jump in after them.

Looking as if he didn't know whether to cuss or cry, The DA kid yelled down. "You better come up here and fight like men."

Blo swam beneath him and talked up. "Come in and get us, you candy ass baby!"

Breed floated on his back. "I don't know what your problem is. You got your boat back."

The tall kid started to cuss, but looked at the girls and checked his speech. He stretched his head over the railing. As if he had just won some great prize, a superior expression formed on his face. He pointed to the dock. "Go down and get their clothes. We'll burn them."

The DA kid's face shone with relief and excitement. "Now we got 'em by the ass." He ran down the bank and searched for the clothes. They were up under the I beam right over his head, but he couldn't find them.

"Let's get their clothes, we'll burn them!" Flick mocked from across the water, and Blo shouted filthy insults at them.

The girls shook mud from their hair. It spattered on their clothes. The girl with the white shorts looked down. Brown mud stains and black sewer water stains had replaced the color of her white shorts.

With both hands, she pointed to her shorts. "Look what they did to me!"

The pony-tailed girl took one look at the girl's shorts and gasp. "Oh my God! We look like imbeciles."

As if she had just recovered from her astonishment, the girl in the former white shorts made a face. "We smell like a sewer."

"We'll get you for this!" the DA kid said and went to help the muddied girls.

"Did you screw those girls yet?" Hog said. "You should have. We did!"

The DA kid looked across the river and shook his clinched fist. "Just shut your filthy mouth!"

The tall kid chimed in, "That's right! Just be down here at eight o'clock Friday!"

"Why absolutely, my good man," Hog calmly said with a British accent. "We'll make it a point to be punctual and attempt to placate your ever wish. I pray we are surely not the cause of your immobility."

The DA kid stood bewildered.

Hog continued, "We didn't mean to come bursting into the privacy of an ignoramus." Assuming a superior posture, he tilted his head back lifted his chin. "Not to worry, dimwit, we'll not make preposterous and unlawful suggestions. With great enthusiasm, we'll be here at eight!"

"Yeah," Screwball added. "We like to get ate!"

The DA kid took one step toward the water, cussed again, and turned back. He helped the girls up the cinder path. The tall kid joined him and they

270

escorted the girls over the bridge and walked them back toward the flats.

The floating oars spun in the current and stopped at a partially submerged tree branch. Flick swam under water the full length of the river and surfaced directly in front of the oars. He grabbed the oars; and like trophies, he held them over his head. "Zackly what the doctor ordered."

Screwball tugged on Ballpeen's shoulder. "Zackly?" he questioned. "Hey, Ballpeen, your breath smells Zackly like your ass!"

Chapter 19

The next day, after Breed had heard on the radio that the baby on the path to the river had been found, Screwball and he hid behind the splintered wooden fence in Flick's backyard and watched through a split picket.

Ballpeen ran into Flick's yard and stopped at the backdoor. Looking around, he stepped up on the single brown wooden step and pounded on the dirty-white board that trimmed the frame.

Flick opened the door. "What are you doing here so early?"

"The paint's dry," Ballpeen excitedly said. "We can take the boat to the river."

"Close the door," Flick's mother said. "You'll let the flies in."

"Let me get my shoes on." Flick closed the green screen door.

A few seconds later, the spring on the door twanged like a low bass guitar string and the door opened. Flick appeared with his shoes on his feet. He stepped out and Breed took a step toward the house. Screwball grabbed him by the arm and pulled him back. "Something ain't right. Let's see what they do."

As if he were checking to see if someone were following him, Ballpeen glanced at the fence and looked over his shoulder. Then he fell in step with Flick and walked around the backyard-burning dump.

Breed and Screwball followed.

At the edge of Ballpeen's yard they stopped, crouched behind the apple tree, and watched.

Flick put his hands under the bottom of the green boat and lifted its end. "This thing's pretty heavy." He dropped the end. The boat thumped on the sawhorse. "We're going to need at least four guys to carry this thing to the river."

"Whether we like it or not, Hog's going," Ballpeen said. "But we'll need one more guy."

"I don't want Screwball going," Flick said. "He pissed me off with that Fudge-Sickle."

Screwball looked at Breed and pretended he was slurping on a Fudge-Sickle. Breed put his finger to his slips. "Shh."

"How about Breed?" Ballpeen said and pointed to the front of the boat. "He helped you and Hog get the paint, and he told me how to bend these boards."

In an I'm-going-and-you're-not, gesture, Breed puffed out his chest, pointed to himself, and flashed a lofty expression toward Screwball.

"Yeah he can fix things," Flick said. "But he'll tell Screwball. Maybe next time."

Screwball looked at Breed and silently mouthed the word, Hant!

Breed's lofty expression turned to a disappointed frown.

"Blo's pretty strong," Ballpeen said.

"Blo can go."

"You know Breed and Screwball think they're going." Ballpeen tapped on a protruding nail at the front of the boat. "What are we going to tell them?"

"Just don't tell them *when* we're going. If you have to, make something up, do it. They won't find out anyway, cause we're leaving at night."

"Can't we just tell them they can't go?"

273

Flick clinched his jaw. "Nope. If we tell them they can't go, they'll just say, 'Hant!' and show up anyway." Looking at the seats in the boat, he turned his head from side. "We'll be lucky if the boat holds four people. We can't overload it and expect to row upriver."

With anticipation, Ballpeen gripped the handle of his hammer. "Maybe I could build another boat."

Flick blinked like an owl and smiled. "We don't even know if this one will work."

"Yeah," I know, "Ballpeen whimpered, "but after my plane didn't fly, I really wanted everybody to see I could make something that worked."

Flick placed his hand on Ballpeen's back. "This trip will have to be kept secret."

Ballpeen managed a faint smile. "When we get back, I'll start on another boat."

Flick patted Ballpeen's back. "If this trip works out we can take more guys next time."

"Okay, I won't tell anybody," Ballpeen assured Flick; and the great conspiracy of silence was under way.

But it didn't matter. Before they left the apple tree, Breed and Screwball knew *when* they were leaving; and it didn't matter what Flick said, they would find a way to go to Shell Island. And one way could be riding on Breed's motorbike.

***

When Breed crawled under the porch and looked at the pieces of his motorbike, the parts he had managed to get back were scattered in the dry dust.

If he could get his bike back together he could ride to Shell Island. He would get there faster than

274

any junk boat could. Before Flick and Ballpeen got there, Screwball and he could haul camping supplies to the hill above Shell Island. It would be no trouble at all to carry them downhill, take them to the island, and set up camp. And, they could ride back and forth anytime they wanted.

Breed sat down in the dirt and leaned his back against the cool stone foundation of the house. He thought about what he would have to do to get his motorbike running again. He would have to pound and pull on the crinkled fenders until they were in shape. To keep anybody from seeing the bike, he would have to wait for dark, put the bent frame in the strong Y of a tree and jerk it back into alignment. If he couldn't get it straight, he would have to cut it, drill it, and bolt it until it was straight. The tires he had found in the dump under a crate of rotting lettuce were almost new, but the broken spokes would have to be taken out of the rims and then be inspected and or replaced. He would carefully balance and tightened the spokes until the wheels didn't wobble and ran true. The extra three broken Whizzer motors would have to be torn apart, cannibalized. If he were lucky, the good parts could be interchanged, and he could make one good motor.

Once that was done, he could thread the chrome exhaust pipe into the exhaust port and make a hollow-sounding straight pipe. It might even purr with that unmistakable boulevard rumble.

The chrome light that worked off the tiny generator inside the heart of the motor would probably never work again. He would rig something up. And the gas tank would have to be hammered back into shape. He could fill the low spots with putty. He didn't have a paintbrush, but he knew he could get a smooth surface if he painted the tank and fenders with a piece of sponge tied on the end of a stick.

Someday he would have his motorbike back together. And those little diamond knurled-shaped rubber handgrips that looked like black rattlesnake skin would be in the palms of his hands. He would sit on that oversized padded seat. The silver spring-damper on the front fork would give him a smooth ride. No bumps or potholes would jar him. He'd fly around that lot again. Then, anytime he wanted, he'd get Screwball and they'd ride to Shell Island.

He reached over his head and pulled the little broken speedometer off the board he had hung on a nail pounded into the floor joist. He blew the dust from the dial and turned it in his hands. If he found a glasscutter, he might be able to cut a piece of glass into a little round circle to keep dust and rain off the numbers and white needle. He loved that little speedometer. It was something other motorbikes had. It made his motorbike real.

He carefully placed the speedometer back on the nail and surveyed the scattered parts. He had made this motorbike out of junk before. He wondered if he could do it again. Even if he could, he would never get it back together in time to go to Shell Island. And he might be working on it for nothing. If he took the bike out from under the porch in daylight and One-Finger-Burke saw it, he would take it. He would say. "It's stolen property." He might even put him in jail.

"Damn him," Breed said out loud. "If I ever

get that Joe Louis book and learn how to box, I'll punch his lying teeth right out of his lying mouth. And if his thievin' son comes by without his knife, I'll kick his dumb ass, too. Damn! I would have never believed that dirty freak Henry would hide my bike. I'll have to punch him out, too. If it gets any worse, I'll have to make a list of people's asses to kick. Damn this Traptown."

Breed sat for a long minute and looked at his wooden dresser drawer toolbox. He didn't have any money, and he didn't have anything else to do. A crooked cop and a bunch of bullies weren't going to make him not do something. He wasn't screwy in the head.

"The hell with them," he said. "I'll build it anyway. If I have to, I'll fix that generator and ride to Shell Island at night."

Chapter 20

The next day, Breed checked the mailbox. As usual, the Joe Louis boxing book didn't come. He tinkered with his motorbike until the time for the boat launching and the trip to Shell Island snuck down the summer like a time ball, rolled off the calendar, and landed at his and Screwball's feet.

They dug a can of worms, gathered their camping gear, and hid it in the weeds a ways from the dock. Hugging the shoreline, they headed upriver, where they picked their way through tall itch weeds, and threaded a crooked path around fallen trees. Then, bending over and watching for poisonous copperhead snakes, they walked under a small bridge, sloshed along the side of a steep cliff, and stopped. A stream was before them.

Screwball looked into the clear water of the stream and then stared blankly at Breed. "If all rivers and streams run into the sea how come the ocean never fills up?"

It was just another one of Screwball's questions that made a person think. Breed figured it had to do with evaporation and rain, but he only shook his head and didn't answer.

Screwball held the minnow bucket — an empty tin lard can with a wire handle — and jumped in the water. He sunk to his knees. "Hey, Breed, let's wade upstream and scare all the minnows in one place."

Breed took the minnow seine — a torn piece of metal screen from a slapping screen door — from his back pocket, unrolled it, and splashed into the water. "Good idea. Maybe we can get some of those red-horned chubs."

Screwball hunched over and peered into the water. "They're hard to get. But that's the secret bait for those big muskies."

As they walked up the creek, a few minnows darted in all directions, but didn't rush into one place. Screwball held the minnow bucket and waited for Breed to scoop minnows out of the water.

In the shallow water next to the shore, Breed dipped the screen under rocks and skimmed it across the bottom of the creek. Seining for perfect for minnows, he sank the screen into deep pools. A few swam into it, but they were too small for bait.

He stood up and wiped his sweating forehead with the back of his hand.

Screwball looked into the empty minnow bucket. "Hey, Breed. We ain't doin' too hot."

Breed hunched over and dipped the screen into the water. "They gotta be in here." He lifted the screen. It was empty.

Father upstream, they stopped in front of a large pool. Water rushed from it through a small opening as big as a wheel rut.

Breed stood with his feet straddled across the little opening. "Hey, Screwball, this is the only place the minnows have to get out. I'll hold the screen here while you scare them downstream."

"Okay, I'll sneak up on 'em."

Excessively lifting his knees, Screwball comically tiptoed toward the back of the pool. When his shadow cast across the water, he raised his arms above his head and waved them around. "Hey, Breed! Watch this."

His dark monster shadow moved in the water. The minnows herded into a thick school, rushed toward the shore, and hid under the rocks and overhanging grass.

"Look, Breed," he said. "Those minnows are afraid of my own shadow."

No matter how many times Screwball scared them, a few minnows would not become part of the fleeing school. They darted away in different directions.

Blocking the minnow's escape, Breed stood at the wheel rut opening and held the screen in the water. "Hey, Screwball, which minnows are running away, the ones in the school, or the couple that run away from the school?"

Screwball placed his hands on his knees and bent over. He looked into the pool. "They're all running away. Most of them are running in the wrong direction and don't know it."

"Yeah, they think they'll be safe when they run with the big school. Just a couple are running away from the screen."

Screwball stood up straight and pushed his hair from his eyes. "Actually none of them are running. They ain't got no feet. They're all swimming."

Breed felt a smile on his face extend to his high Indian cheekbones. "Looks like what they say about safety in numbers ain't true."

Screwball nodded and flashed a big-toothed grin. "The ones that don't run with the school will live longer."

The minnows reminded Breed of the herds of workers that went to work in the mills. "I wonder if that's true for people."

280

As if he were sunk in deep thought, Screwball lowered his chin to his chest, and then raised it. "What are you talking about?"

"If you go in different directions, you'll look like you are running away, but you will live longer."

"Maybe." Screwball jumped into the creek. "Get ready. Here they come." He waved his arms; and kicking his feet, he splashed the water. Streams of yellow-brown water, teaming with minnows, rushed right into the screen Breed was holding with his bare hands. When Screwball was close to the screen, Breed lifted it. The trap worked. Hundreds of silver minnows and six red-horned chubs flipped and wiggled on the screen. Most fell off the sides and dripped back into their watery home. Screwball held the minnow bucket. Breed tipped the screen, and the bait for the Shell Island trip slid into the minnow bucket.

"Nothin' to it!" Breed arrogantly said. "Let's try it again. Maybe we can get some more red-horned chubs."

"Okay, get ready."

Screwball thrashed into the water and chased everything into the screen Breed held in his hands. "I think I got a big chub. Get ready to grab him."

Screwball stepped close, held out his hands, and waited.

Staying bent over, Breed raised the screen from the small opening. The weight of the catch tugged at his fingers. He pressed the screen to his chest to keep it from slipping out of his hands. He felt something running down his chest and leg.

Screwball jerked his hands away from the screen and jumped back.

Breed looked at him. "What's the matter?"

Screwball pointed to the screen. Breed hadn't notice what was hanging over the front and back of the screen. He felt a buzzing on his hand and on his leg. He looked down. A four-foot water moccasin slithered down the front of his chest. He yanked his hands away and jerked to a standing position. The screen fell into the water. The heavy snake splashed into the water and swam somewhere. Breed tried to jump out of the stream.

His legs froze in place.

He whined in a jerky voice, "I can't move."

Screwball leaped out of the water and landed on the bank. Then he bent over, moved his head from side to side, and searched for the snake. Looking toward Breed, he shuddered. "That moccasin was crawling right on your hand!"

Breed twitched his eyes and looked at his hand. The snake was gone. As if he had just touched a contagious disease, he beat his hands on his shaking legs. "I felt it on my leg." He violently shook his head and shuddered. "I thought it was a big chub."

Screwball pointed to Breed's crotch. "He crawled right between your legs. You're lucky it didn't bite you in the dick." He giggled. "I wasn't gonna suck no poison out."

"Damn!" Breed said and panted with relief. "This is a good way to get minnows, but not with that snake in there."

Screwball lifted his shoulders and tilted his head in a show of nonchalance. "Yeah, I know. That's why I got out."

Breed's legs unfroze and he stopped shaking. "Damn!" he said again, stepped out of the stream, and checked his hand.

Screwball bent over and checked it, too. "Did he get you?"

"There ain't no marks."

"I don't see any either. Let's try for some more. Go ahead. Put the screen back in the water. I'll scare 'em down again."

Breed glanced at the screen in the water. "Okay, but you hold the screen."

Screwball backed away. "Bull crap! That water moccasin ain't bitin' my dick!"

Breed stuck his foot in the water and touched the screen with his toe. Something in the water moved. He jerked his foot back. "That snake's under the screen. I ain't pickin' it up."

Screwball bent over and peered into the tin lard can. "Me either, but we got enough."

Breed looked upstream. It narrowed and ran under a clump of low hanging jaggers. "Let's get back to the dock." He turned and faced downstream. "Those guys might leave early."

Screwball picked up the full can of minnows, and Breed eyed the screen setting in the water. "Hey, Screwball, get the screen."

"I got the minnows. You get it."

"Maybe next time."

The snake and the screen remained in the stream.

***

When the streetlights burned bright, Breed and Screwball walked to the dock under the Rat Street Bridge and started fishing. A few cars buzzed across the bridge; and like the stutters of an old-time black and white movies, their headlights flickered

283

through the steel grating. Screwball caught a few black-backed crabs and a few small catfish before Breed had baited his hook with a red-horned chub and was finally ready to cast his dime-store casting reel.

He stepped back and let the line fly. As usual, he was rewarded with a bird nest mess. "Just what I always wanted, a ten foot cast with a nine-hundred foot backlash."

Holding his fishing pole, Screwball looked at the mess of line jumbled around the spool of the silver reel and read the name stamped on the side. "Ocean City, I'll have to remember that name so I can get one."

Breed pulled at the string and untied one knot. Three other knots formed deep in the spool. "This thing's junk. You get one knot out and end up with twenty-five more."

"Ocean City, good reel, heh?" Screwball flashed him an idiotic grin.

"Ocean Shitty, would be more like it," Breed said and the tangled mess got worse.

He eventually pulled the mess free and had a circle of line coiled in a neat pile on the corner of the dock. Something swirled in the water.

He jerked his head and looked down.

Then flinched back.

A monstrous silver head, with spooky-yellow eyes, big as quarters, chomped down on the red-horned chub that had been swimming on the end of his hook.

Screwball's jaw dropped. He pointed to the silent submerging fish. It disappeared beneath the water. "He's got it!"

284

"It figures," Breed said, "he just has to bite when I don't have enough line wound up on this junk reel to fight em'."

The huge fish didn't jump up and balance on its tail. It didn't twist or turn. It didn't fight at all. It swam away like an iron tank, cut a solid straight path across the river current.

Breed needed to set the hook. He cranked the cheap reel, but he couldn't wind up the fleeing line fast enough. The circle of line unraveled off the dock. If he were going to set the hook, he had to stop that escaping line. He tromped on it with his foot. The heavy black line stopped unraveling and went taut. It was at the breaking point. A huge tail swirled in the middle of the river. The line went limp and waved in the current.

"Ahh, man, the line broke," Breed said. "He's off."

As if he were showing Breed how big the fish was, Screwball spread his arms wide. "That was probably Big Mike!"

Breed hung his shoulders in defeat. "Either him or a big carp."

Screwball reeled in and took up the slack in his drooping line. "You know those guys from the pipe plant saw Big Mike the other day?"

Screwball's pole bent over.

Breed jerked his hand and hit Breed on the shoulder. He's back. He's on your line."

Screwball set the hook. His pole bent over. He reeled in. The outline of what he had caught wiggled in the blackness. "Get it, Breed."

Breed reached out. The ugly thing came into view. Breed filched his hand back.

"Hant!" Screwball laughed. An ugly brown waterdog wiggled on the end of the line. As if it had eaten a baby and the little human-like hands and legs were trying to crawl out of its body, its tiny legs clawed at the air.

"Ahh, man, Breed whined. "Get that stinkin' thing off."

Screwball swung the waterdog toward Breed. "Don't you want this devil dog?"

Breed held up his hand and turned away. "No way, you can't get rid of them. If you chop their tail off they just grow another one. They call it regeneration."

"That's creepy." Screwball let the water dog back down into the water. It swam underneath the dock. Screwball jerked his rod. The hook broke free. The horrible water dog was gone.

The thought of the ugly water dog made Breed shudder with disgust. But the thought of the big fish he had just missed whirled in his mind. He turned toward Screwball. "What did those guys say about Big Mike?"

"They said he was as big as a miniature submarine."

"I wouldn't doubt it." Breed tied another fishing hook on his shortened line. "I don't think anybody will ever catch that big muskie."

"That goofy guy with that crooked hat said he sees Big Mike every Christmas Eve."

Breed closed one eye and squinted at Screwball. "I think if you checked inside that goofy guy's head, you'd find out nobody's home. I never saw a muskie jump in the wintertime."

"Yeah, that's what I told him, but he said that

Big Mike has so many lures, spinners, hooks, and junk hangin' out of his mouth that when he jumps up under the bridge on Christmas Eve, he plays 'Jingle Bells.'"

Breed smiled in agreement. "That would be about what that goofy guy would say."

They continued to fish and wait for the great green boat to arrive.

Chapter 21

To keep from being seen, Ballpeen, Hog, and Flick, carried the boat into the tall grass in Toney's back yard.

With the light from a streetlight hovering at the outer fringes of the boat, Hog picked up a rock. "We don't need that light shinin' on the boat, somebody's gonna see it." He reared back to throw. As if someone had thrown a switch, the streetlight blew out before it could be broken.

Hog threw the rock up and caught it. "See, nothin' to it."

As the concealing darkness deepened, the secret Shell Island crew lit up, puffed on cigarette butts, and stood around the boat.

Hog impatiently waved his hand in the air. "What are we waitin' around for?"

In the distance, an orange spark glowed. Flick watched it. "We're waitin' for Blo to show."

The spark moved toward them.

Flick took one puff on his cigarette butt, threw it on the ground and mashed it out. "Hide those butts and shut up." He held his hand over his forehead and watched the spark. "It might be some creep from the flats gang."

They all breathed slow and easy. The spark glowed and brightened. Out of the darkness someone spoke. "Hey, you guys ready?"

Flick breathed a sigh of relief. "It's Blo." He bent over and grabbed onto the boat. "Let's go."

Blo tossed his sleeping bag. Thud! It landed in the boat amidst the other camping belongings. They hoisted the heavy boat onto their shoulders and waddled off into the first dark alleyway.

Ballpeen's foot bashed into an empty beer bottle. He stumbled like a drunken mill worker. "Why can't we carry this thing in the daylight so I can see what I'm doing?"

"That's a good idea," Hog said. "That way, the flats gang can take before we get it to the river."

As if he were straining to carry the boat, Ballpeen's voice rose. "They might not."

Hog jerked the boat.

Ballpeen stumbled again.

Hog leaned toward him. "What's the matter, candy ass? Is the boat too heavy for your skinny legs?"

"It ain't too heavy," Ballpeen lied. "I just don't like tramping on bottles and junk that I can't see in the dark."

"Well don't tramp on bottles and junk."

"How can I do that, when I can't see?"

"Can you see when you wipe your ass?"

"No, goddamn it, Hog, you're as bad as Screwball bringing up stupid stuff."

Blo jumped in on the friendly harassment. "You sure you don't use a mirror?"

"Come on you guys," Flick said. "Quit screwin' around. Shell Island's a waitin'. We gotta get this boat to the river."

At the second alleyway, with his legs buckling under the weight of the heavy boat, Ballpeen huffed and puffed. "Hey, let's take a rest."

"You ain't kiddin'," Blo said and they stopped.

Flick pointed to his right. "Lower it down and set it on that purple ash pile."

And they did.

289

Ballpeen let out a deep breath and reached toward Flick. "Give me a cigarette."

Flick took the pack of Winston cigarettes from the pocket of his shirt, ignored Ballpeen's outstretched hand, and lit up. We got to make these last." He blew smoke from his nose. "And nobody gets any if they don't inhale. I'm tired of this puffin' stuff you guys do. You just waste the cigarette."

Ballpeen shook his hand in a begging motion. "Come on, give me one. I always inhale."

Flick passed him a cigarette. Ballpeen lit up and inhaled for the first time. His eyes popped wide open. It seemed that chills went up his neck, and his hair stood on end; and he wanted to cough but held it in. His eyes uncrossed. He exhaled. "See, I told you."

Hog smiled in his direction. "You better get some sun this trip, Hammer-ass, you look a little pale.

Ballpeen coughed and almost dropped the cigarette. Between coughs, he looked up. "Blow it out your ass, Hog!"

"You'll get some sun, "Flick said. "Before you know it, we'll be layin' on clean white sand."

"Yeah, we'll get some sun." Hog looked down at the boat. "If we ever get this heavy thing to the river."

Blo held up his hands like a referee signaling time out. "Quiet! Genius at work."

As if he were welcoming a movie star who was about to come on stage, Hog turned the palm of his hand up and reached out his arm toward Blo. "Okay, turd brain, what kind-ah plan do you got?"

Blo stopped signaling time out and dropped his hands. "Let's get Pud to help."

"Yeah, he's strong enough." A spasm crossed Flick's face. "But then he'll want to go with us."

"So what!" Blo said and fingered his trumpet he had hid in the bow of the boat. "We'll tell him to wait on the dock, and we'll just row away."

"He's so dumb," Hog said with a triumphant grin. "He'll probably still be there when we come back. Even if we stay a week."

Flick looked toward Pud's house. "I don't know. He's so screwed up in the head you can't tell what he's going to do from one minute to the next."

When Ballpeen turned toward Pud's house, Hog intentionally flicked a hot orange cigarette ash in his direction.

Ballpeen jumped out of the way. "Cut that out!"

"Quit bitchin'." Hog chuckled. "You're lucky it wasn't a hawker."

Flick placed his foot on the side of the boat and talked moving his hands. "Pud can't cause very much trouble when he's carrying this boat. So let's get him."

"Yeah, what the hell." Hog shrugged. "We'll probably be sorry, but let's try it anyway."

Flick took his foot off the side of the boat. "Okay, you guys stay here and watch the boat. And make sure no one steals my old man's railroad lantern."

Flick and Blo cut across an open sewer and padded to Pud's house. Before they could knock on the door, inside, footsteps clomped across the wooden floor.

Flick whispered to Blo. "Let's hide and see who's coming."

They stepped around the banister of the porch and hid. Holding a blue-enameled pot in his hand, Pud walked out of the back door of his house. He was going to feed his father's mangy hunting dogs.

Flick and Blo walked softly around the wooden-slatted outhouse and stopped to watch.

Pud turned the pot over and banged on the bottom. Leftovers mixed with dry dog food plopped into the dirty dog bowl. The ancient Beagles stretched their legs and peed on the chicken wire cage. They whined once and trotted to the food as if they had wooden legs. They didn't wag their tails and beg submissively for a pat on the head from Pud, and Pud didn't offer to bend over and pet them. He stood with his hands on his hips and watched them lap up the scraps. When he blinked his square-pupiled eyes, he smiled; and his crooked teeth flashed in the dark. He turned from the dogs and closed the rickety dog pen gate.

Flick threw a rock at the pen. Pud turned his dented head. "Who's thar?" he asked in the phony hillbilly voice he used at home.

Flick threw another rock. It hit one of the Beagles. It let out a yelp. Pud ran toward the house. Flick jumped out from behind the outhouse and grabbed him. Blo jumped in front of him. Waving his hands over his head like a late show monster, he yelled, "Ye-e-e-ee!"

Pud jumped and jerked around as if he were peeing on an electric fence. His face whitened and those square pupils in his eyes became wide and round. He looked at Flick and Blo, shook his head;

292

and in a heap of relief, he sat on the ground. His eyes relaxed back to their cat-like shape. "Boy, oh boy! You guys sure did scare me."

"Did you crap your pants?" Blo asked.

Pud felt the back of his pants. "Why no, I didn't crap my pants."

Blo looked away in disbelief. Flick bent over and placed his arm around Pud's round shoulders. "Hey, old buddy," he said soft and friendly. "Do you want to go to Shell Island with us tonight?"

Pud looked up. His face beamed with surprise. "Why sure I do!"

"Well let's go. The other guys are waiting."

Pud lowered his head and his body bent into a sitting fetal position. "I'll have to ask my father. I just know he'll say no."

"Well then, don't ask." Flick tugged on Pud's shirt. "Let's go."

Blo walked in a circle like as if he had to go the bathroom and couldn't hold it.

"Come on, Pud." Flick motioned with his hand. "You can go. I said you could. Stand up straight and let's get going."

Pud straightened up. "Do you really think I could go?"

Blo quit pacing, stuck his hands in his blue-jeaned pockets and rocked on his heels. "Look Pud, you're going to get a beatin' for stayin' out here so long anyway, so why not get one for going to Shell Island?"

Flick stepped toward the dog pen. "Come on, Pud. Let's go, or we're leaving without you."

With a swinging motion of his arm, Pud tried to snap his fingers. They didn't snap. "By golly, you're right. Let's go. I'm goin' to get a beatin' anyway. Let's go."

Back at the boat, making sure Pud carried most of the weight, Flick, Blo, Hog, and Ballpeen picked up the boat and continued the secret trip to the river.

They traipsed through back yards, picked ways around the same old barking dogs; stumbled into dark alleyways; skirted around backyard dumps; and generated a trail of turned on porch lights and irate sleepers.

Under a streetlight, they stopped to rest. An old man in a brown house, stuck his head out of a bedroom window. "What the hell is going on out there?"

Blo lifted the trumpet to his lips; and blew like a Roman trumpeter— Tah-dat-tah-dah! — announcing a dignitary to the pharaoh. He cleared his throat and spoke in an orator's voice. "It's Noah's Ark! End of the world Tuesday!"

And thus, the clandestine way they carried the boat to the river managed to alert everyone in the neighborhood.

Chapter 22

Under the Rat Street Bridge, Breed and Screwball sat on the dock fishing and waiting. Screwball reeled his line in and set his pole on the dock. "You think they'll show up?"

"Maybe they snuck upriver when we went for minnows." Breed rolled his reel and felt the slight tug of a catfish but it stopped.

Screwball held out his hand and grabbed Breed's arm. "Listen."

Grumbling and thudding sounds filled the night.

Screwball lifted his fishingpole and flipped his empty hook back into the water. "That's them. Let's pretend we're fishing."

Up on the bridge, the camping supplies in the moving boat thumped, banged, and clanged. Breed and Screwball turned and looked up the steep cinder path. There they were: Balanced at the top, holding the teetering boat — the Keystone Cops reborn.

In the dark, everybody tried to do everything their own way. When someone pulled, someone pushed against the direction of the pull. Then, someone else stood still and gave orders. "Turn it around and take it down!"

"No! Let's take the stuff out first."

"No, let's take a rest, or we'll never make it."

"Let's stand still for a minute. I'm losing my grip!"

"It's my boat. Let's take a rest."

The jerking, the pulling, the stammering, and the bullheadedness continued. The boat seemed to have a mind of its own. It stood perfectly still. It did not move forward or backward. A hand reached in to unload supplies.

"Leave them in," Flick said. "We only got twenty feet to go. And don't break that lantern!"

"No, wait."

"Let me get a better grip."

"Don't push."

"Let me help."

"Quit tramping on my foot, Pud."

Everybody spouted advice. No one listened. The boat rocked back and forth. Under the yanking and twisting feet, the cinders on the path to the river broke free. The boat, supplies, and its porters tilted toward the steep path.

Flick's eyes widened with alarm. "Save the boat," he yelled. "Run with it."

They hung onto the boat. It pulled them down the steep path. It was out of control. If they fell, they could be trampled to death. They stumbled on their own feet. As they staggered under the shifting weight of the heavy boat, like marbles, loose cinders rolled under their shoes. They quickly shuffled over them and slid down the slippery path.

Flick tripped and let go of the boat. He took one step to catch his balance, but flew into the air and landed at the bottom of the path, where he rolled over and stopped.

Lying on the ground, he looked up. The boat was coming right at him. He held up his hand. "Stop!"

But the boat carriers couldn't stop. The boat pulled them down the muddy riverbank and headed right toward Flick. He rolled to his left. The tromping feet of the eight-legged boat pounded past his head, and then continued on down the riverbank where it splashed into the water; and the human idiot machine came to a stop. Its porters were waist deep in water.

Amazed, Flick stood up and looked at the crew. "See, I told you we could do it."

Screwball held his fishing pole in his hand and looked down at the boat and its wet-pants porters. Like someone who had just won an argument and was rubbing in his victory, Screwball's face had a smug expression. "What did you guys do, forget your bathing suits?"

Pud looked down at his wet pants. "No one told me to bring a bathing suit, but I kin go back home and get one."

Breed wanted to laugh out loud, but he still wanted to go to Shell Island. If he got Flick mad, he might not let him go. He held in his laughter and feigned nonchalance, but then he smiled and let out a mocking, "Hant!"

Screwball laughed out loud, pointed at the boat, took in a big breath, and flippantly blared out a healthy, "Ha-a-a-ant!"

Flick had an expression of someone who had just lost an argument. He shook his finger at Screwball. "We don't need any of your Fudge Sickle mouth tonight." He stepped into the water and grabbed a railroad lantern from the boat. "Let's get this junk out of the boat. I wanna check for leaks."

Pub bent over and grabbed a sleeping bag that was covered with other camping supplies and pulled. "I'll help." He pulled. The bag didn't move.

Flick nudged him. "Get out of the way, Pud. We ain't got time to fool around."

Pud kept a hold on the sleeping bag. "But I wanna help."

Flick shook his head. "Ahh." He looked toward the bottom of the bridge. "Just go up and stand on the shore, Pud."

Pud kept a tight grip on the sleeping bag. "What for?"

Hog giggled and waved Pud to shore. "Come on up here. We need you to watch out for the flats gang."

Pud let loose of the sleeping bag. "Oh." He waded to shore.

With Pud out of the way, the camping supplies were unloaded and placed on the dock

Flick stepped into the boat, sat down and reached for the oars. "Hey," he said. "Somebody get the oars."

Hog stepped on the steppingstone at the base of the bridge, reached over the I beam, pulled the oars off its edge, and handed them to Blo.

Blo took the oars to the dock and gave them to Flick. Flick placed the oars in the holders; and like some kind of mania man, he rowed in a tight circle. The boat leaked water more and more. He rowed it to the shallow water next to shore and sat in the rower's seat. Water rushed into the boat. It sank.

Standing in the sunken boat, Flick pulled out the cigarettes he had in his pocket. They were wet and fell apart at the touch. He threw them into the current and stepped out to the shore. "I was going to quit anyway."

Hog picked up a rock and threw it into the boat.

298

It plopped into the water. "I told you that thing was junk."

"Have a little faith." Blo smiled a cocky smile. "Ballpeen can fix it."

Flick pulled the boat to shore and tipped it over until the water gushed out. Ballpeen got his hammer, nailed down the leak, took a flat stick, and slapped tar over the holes.

Pud stuck his finger in the tar. "Is it dry yet?"

Flick pushed him aside. "Get out of the way, Pud."

Crossing his eyes and looking at the tar on his finger, Pud moved, and Flick pushed the boat back into the water. "See it floats."

Ballpeen stood on the edge of the dock and admired his floating boat. "We'll have to christen her before we start upriver."

"It floats," Screwball said and nudged Breed in the ribs. "But will it fly in a tornado?"

Ballpeen's smile turned to a frown. He ignored Screwball's wisecrack and pulled a bottle of orange pop out of his back pocket. With the words, "I christen you," he tried to break the thick glass bottle over the bow of the boat. It only cracked a board.

Hog stared at Ballpeen. "What are you, insane?"

As if his feelings had been hurt, Ballpeen slumped.

Hog pointed to cracked board. "What are you trying to do, bust it before it sinks?"

"Yeah," Screwball added. "It ain't no ocean liner."

"But it's bad luck if I don't christen it," Ballpeen whined.

Hog stood at the end of the dock peeing into the water. He looked back over his shoulder. "I'll piss on it. That'll christen it."

"Just drink the pop and don't worry about it," Flick said.

Hog flippantly pointed to his crotch. "Hey, Ballpeen. I drank some pop a while ago. You want some? You can drink it through my straw."

Making a face and shaking his head, Ballpeen shot back, "Blow it out your ass, Hog!"

Hog sunk down and grunted. "I can't. Maybe later."

Ballpeen didn't have an opener, and just to see how he would try to open the bottle, everybody claimed that they didn't have one.

Ballpeen decided to pop the cap off by hitting it on the corner of the dock. After a few strikes, the cap came off, and the spissing orange liquid sprayed him in the face. Standing there with the orange pop dripping off his chin, he watched Hog reach into his breast pocket and pull out an opener. "Do you need this? Hammer-ass?"

"Oh, shut up! Just for that, you guys ain't getting any."

While he was guzzling the rest of his drink, a sleek well-paid cop in a brand new cruiser, with all its expensive radio equipment, croaked onto the bridge and stopped. A hard-jawed officer stepped out. Above their heads, his metal-cleated boots clacked on the catwalk until he stopped. Then he bent over the railing and scanned the crew with the illuminating beam of his flashlight. "What are you kids doing out this late?"

If the cop wanted to write down names and

300

question them, it might take up just enough time for the flats gang to pass over the bridge and find them. Another delay was the last thing anyone wanted.

With a disgusted look on his face, Flick shook his head. Then he respectfully replied, "We're camping out, officer."

The cop didn't answer. He continued to flash his long chrome-handled flashlight. The light traveled through dark areas and then silently stopped and revealed Ballpeen's boat. A smile formed on the cop's lips. With the light fixed on the green boat, he spoke. "We had a report of a stolen boat." His voice was sharp and stern. Then he laughed and the light beam danced around the boat. "But I can see no one in their right mind would steal a boat like that."

With his shoulders shaking with held in laughter, he stood on the bridge, placed his elbows on the railing of the catwalk, and stared at the boat as if he were watching a comical movie. He shook his head, laughed again, and went away.

Flick waded into the water and grabbed the boat. "This boat ain't gonna float with all the supplies and one passenger. Nobody's gonna ride. We'll all have to take turns pushing and bailing."

He swung the boat around, lined it up with the side of the dock, and looked up. "Screwball and Breed, if you're going, you got five minutes to run home and get your gear." He tied the boat to the dock. "If we're not here when you get back, start coming upriver. We'll be up there somewhere."

Ballpeen greedily swallowed the last of his pop, wiped his lips, and looked to Screwball. "How long do you think it will take you guys to get back?"

301

Screwball played with the button on his shirt and looked unconcerned. "After you swiddled all that pop down, I don't know if we really want to go with somebody who won't share."

Breed let out a suppressed laugh.

Flick glared at Breed. "What are you guys waiting on?" He pointed to the cinder path. "Get up that goddamn hill. Get your camping junk, and get your asses back here before that cop comes back."

"What time will you be leaving?" Screwball asked just to agitate.

Flick's eyes widened in Screwball's direction. "If you guys don't get your Fudge-Sickling asses in gear, we'll leave right now." He looked toward the bottom of the bridge. "We can't be screwin' around under this bridge all night! Shell Island is a waitin'."

Ballpeen threw the empty bottle into the water. Pud stepped toward the dock. "You want me to get that bottle?"

In a halting gesture, Ballpeen held up his hand. "That' all right, Pud, we won't need it." Then, with a crying look on his face, he pleaded. "Come on, you guys, we gotta get out of here before the flats gang takes the boat."

Screwball threw his hands up. "Okay, okay, we're going to get our stuff."

Pud stepped in front of Screwball. "I'll help."

Hog dropped the tent into the boat. "You won't have to. They got their camping stuff hid in the weeds."

Flick looked up with a start. Screwball and Breed waded into the weeds, picked up their gear,

302

and placed it in the boat.

Flick's eyes swiveled suspiciously. "All right, which one of you assholes told them we were going? You know this trip was supposed to be secret."

Acting as innocent as he could, Screwball answered, "Nobody told us. We were going to sleep and fish, right here, all night. But you guys came down the path like jackasses in a China closet and scared all the fish away."

Breed shrugged. "Do you want us to go or not?"

"Don't get your ass in an uproar, Breed," Flick said.

"We better have them come along," Hog said. "We're going to need all the muscle power we can get to get this leaky boat upriver." He smiled a radiant smile. "And besides, they got some red-horned chubs in that lard can."

"Damn!" Amazed, Flick lifted his open hand toward Hog.. "You don't miss a thing."

Chapter 23

Breed stood on the riverbank under the Rat Street Bridge and waited. The green boat was loaded, but the water was a few inches from the top of the sides. It would float, but it would ride low in the water. Like kids waiting to go on a carnival thrill ride, Hog, Screwball, Blo, and Pud stood next to the dock. There was nothing for Breed to do but go to Shell Island.

Flick walked onto the dock, cocked his leg, and rested his foot on the dock post. Holding his body rigid, he thrust his arm out in a straight military fashion. As if he were a great stone statue, he pointed upriver. "Men, we're going to Shell Island."

Screwball crossed his eyes and let his mouth hang open. Like an abandoned puppet, he dropped his head. Standing on the riverbank, he held his arm in a sloppy fashion, and pointed like a half-wit who had escaped from a sideshow. "Tonight we change the world."

Flick groaned and laughed. "Screwball, quit screwin' around."

"Yeah," Hog said. "Let's get goin'". I wanna be the first man to write my name on Shell Island."

Screwball waited until Flick turned his back and then pretended he was slurping on a Fudge-Sickle.

Breed cringed. "Don't get him pissed off now," he whispered and Screwball quit.

Everyone except Pud stripped to their bathing suits and tennis shoes. They piled their ragged clothes into the already overloaded boat and stood on the dock.

Ballpeen looked into the boat. "There ain't no room for anybody to row."

"Good thing you noticed that," Screwball joked. "I was just going to jump on top."

Ballpeen slipped an oar into the boat. "I had my heart set on rowing upriver."

"Well un-set your heart," Breed said. "It's still easier than carrying all this stuff"— he pointed to the full boat — "all the way to Shell Island."

"If you don't like it," Screwball said and pointed to the shore, "you're welcome to stay right over there and wait until we get back."

Ballpeen's forehead wrinkled with irritation. "Ahh, man! Can't you wait until we get started before you start your stupid stuff?"

Flick smiled at Ballpeen and untied the overloaded craft. The current sucked it around and pulled the rope out of Flick's hands. The boat plowed a dark water path to the center of the dark river. It was drifting away.

Breed felt his heart sink. His Shell Island dream was fading in the dark night.

Flick flexed his legs to dive. "We'll have to get it before the current sucks it down to the falls."

While Pud stood on the shore, the Shell Island crew dove into the water and swam to the escaping boat. Breed grabbed it first, but couldn't stop it.

The others grabbed on. The overloaded boat and the strong flowing current resisted their every stroke. But they didn't give up. They pushed, pulled, and dragged the heavy boat to the fallen tree under the bridge.

Ballpeen wrapped the rope around the tree, and

let out a long breath. "I'm tired already."

"What are you bitchin' about?" Hog asked. "Look how far we got already."

"Yeah," Breed said. "If Shell Island was downriver, we'd be almost there."

Screwball dove under the water and surfaced. "Why don't we just go downriver?"

Everyone knew if they went downriver the boat would slip over the falls and be smashed. No one answered.

A crisp white stripe of light danced across the bow of the boat.

Desolate silence filled the air.

Screwball shook the boat. "You guys look like I just interrupted a funeral."

As if he had a headache, Hog's face grimaced. "Why don't you get a brain? That's probably the flats gang." Warily, he looked to the shore. "If we don't get out of here, we'll be going to a funeral, and it'll be ours."

Ballpeen looked to where the light had come from. Then he looked upriver. "Maybe we could go just a little way upriver and camp. It's gonna be hard to go all the way to Shell Island."

"What did you expect?" Flick said with authority. "This is going to be tough. But if we wanna get away from the flats gang and have all the comforts of home, we gotta get this stuff to the island."

"But—," Ballpeen said

"But hell!" Hog interpreted. "Don't start whining, Ballpeen. We ain't no candy ass flats gang kids. We'll make it."

Breed heard a weak voice in his head. "They

306

should quit," it said, "scrap the whole idea, write it up as experience. The trip is not possible."

This unwanted inkling of a defeatist attitude stuck in his mind. It would be easier to quit. He could swim to the dock, run back up that cinder path, go home, and jump into a nice warm bed. Then he could wake up in the morning and work on his motorbike all day.

He decided to go home. He let go of the boat and dog paddled toward the shore. Slowly stroking the water, he silently talked to himself like a coach would talk before a big game. "What are you swimming away for? Are you screwy in the head like One-Finger-Burke said? Tonight you can get away from Lard Man and that black panel truck. You can get away from the flats gang. You can get away from those baseball players. You can get away from Burkie and his knife. Shell Island is a resort. Yeah," he argued with himself, "but I can stay home and work on my motorbike." His self argued back, "You can work on your motorbike anytime. And if you get it done, One-Finger-Burke's just gonna take it again."

He felt the bottom of the river at the tips of his toes. He was in shallow water. When the dock was a few feet to his right, Flick yelled across the water, "Hey, candy ass, you gonna chickin' out?"

Screwball put his hands to his mouth and clucked like a chicken, "Baawwaacckk! buck-buck-buck!"

Breed stood up in the shallow water. He figured the trip was going to be hard, but no one else was quitting, and he wasn't no candy ass. He had made a motorbike out of junk. There was nothing mechanical about the boat. If something happen, it would be simple to fix it.

Suddenly he felt above the power of the mighty river. Now, he was pretty sure that the boat could take him to Shell Island. And besides, his clothes were in the boat. He turned his head and pretended he was looking for something on the riverbank. "I thought I left my blankets on the shore."

Screwball yelled across the water, "Ha-a-a-nt! They're in the boat."

Pud walked onto the dock and looked to Breed. "You gonna take me over to the boat?"

Breed didn't feel right leaving Pud on the dock. He wanted to tell him to come along. He wanted to teach him how to swim, but Flick and the others were waiting. He couldn't teach Pud anything in a few seconds, or for that matter, in a few years.

Pud asked again. "You gonna take me over to the boat?"

Breed didn't answer. He turned and swam back to the boat. "Pud wants to go." He held onto the boat.

Ballpeen lost his footing and slipped under the water. When he popped his head back up, water sputtered from his mouth. He flicked his hair back. "Maybe he can help push."

Hog splashed water toward Ballpeen. "What? Are you, crazy?

"We won't need him," Breed said. "If we stay in the shallow water and out of the current, the boat will be easy to push."

"I'll walk ahead and pull on the rope," Flick said. "If I fall in a drop-off, you guys can take up the slack and guide the boat around it."

308

Flick untied the boat from the tree branch, and Breed dropped down into the water. When his feet touched bottom, he bent his knees and held the back of the boat with his hands. Then he straightened his legs and pushed with his arms. The boat plowed a path upriver and glided into shallow water.

Pud stood on the dock.

Ballpeen splashed his arm out of the water and waved at him. "Thanks for the help, Pud. We'll see you later."

Pud whined like a lost puppy, "Come on you guys. Take me with you."

Flick swam to the back of the boat and checked his father's railroad lantern. "Go home, Pud." He covered the lantern with an old blanket. "Your old man won't beat you too bad."

"Come on, please! You guys. Let me go!"

Pushing the boat, Ballpeen waved to Pud. "We'll see you later, Pud. We gotta get upriver."

Up on the bridge, a straight-piped Chevy thundered to a stop. Dwayne Eddy's "Three Thirty Blues" blared from its AM car radio. One duck's-butt-haired, blond, bracelet-clad, beer drinker with a personality marked by steady dispassionate calmness and self-control, stepped across the bridge and clacked his steel cleats on the steel grating. He stopped at the railing and pointed down at Pud. "You one of Rat Boy's friends that took our boat?"

Pud strained his cat eyes and peered through the holes in the grating of the bridge. "Why no, mister." He smiled. "I didn't take no boat."

The other door swung open on the Chevy. Two black-jacketed beer drinkers swaggered out — looking to kick somebody's ass.

Pud innocently looked up at them. "Ya'll goin' fishing down here?"

"Yeah, we're going fishing," the bracelet-clad blond said and spit. "And your ass is gonna be the bait."

The three flats gang bullies tilted bottles of beer to their mouths, held them straight up, and let the beer drain down their throats. Then they threw the bottles over the catwalk railing. The bottles flew high into the night and speared into the river in three successive plops. In unison; and like mad dogs yearning to satisfy a rabid deficiency, the bullies wiped their mouth on the backs of their hands and stomped down the cinder path.

When they stopped at the end of the dock, Breed recognized one of the bullies. It was Burkie.

Hog hollered across the current, "Hey, Pud! You damn dummy! They're gonna kick your ass!"

Recalling how Burkie had chased him with the long sharp knife, Breed's breath caught in his throat. He looked to Flick. "That's asshole, Burkie. He'll cut Pud's ears off."

The drunken bracelet-clad blond stepped onto the dock and flashed a blade. Burkie placed his hand on the kid's shoulder and pulled him back. "I got something better than that." He took his black leather jacket off and handed it to the blond. "Hold this." He reached behind his back and pulled out the long sharp knife Breed had watched him sharpen behind the shed.

Pud jerked back, crept to the end of the dock, and teetered on its edge.

Flick cried across the water, "Jump, Pud, jump!"

310

"I can't swim!" Pud whined.

Flick cocked his legs on the side of the boat. As if his legs were a big spring, he pushed off and gracefully glided just under the surface of the water. Near the dock, he popped his head up and yelled at Pud. "You're gonna learn to swim and right now!"

"No I'm not." Pud turned his back to Flick. Now, he was face to face with Burkie. With a fiendish grin spread across his face, Burkie held the knife high. "I'm gonna cut your ears off."

Compared to Burkie's knife, the bracelet-clad blond's knife seemed insignificant. He folded it and placed it back into his pocket.

Burkie stepped onto the dock and swished the knife. It cut the air in front of Pud's face. Afraid, Pud lifted his hands and covered his ears.

Burkie took another step and lifted the knife. "That was just for practice. This time your ear's coming off."

Defensively holding his hands in front of himself, Pud dropped his hands and stepped back. His foot blindly searched for the edge of the dock. It wasn't there. His cat eyes widened and his arms flailed with fright. "Aahh!" He splashed into the black water. Sloshing his arms on the surface, he bobbed up and down. "Help . . . blub, blub . . . Help!"

Flick swam behind him, grabbed him around the neck and arm, and towed him across the current. Next to the boat, they touched bottom and stopped.

Burkie held the knife high and ready. "This is for you!" He grinned and threw the knife. It flipped one time and stuck into the wooden dock. Twanging like a blubbering, half-witted, shiny steel cartoon, the knife seemed out of place.

Hog yelled across the water, "Stick that knife up your ass."

"Yeah," Blo said, "maybe it will give your baby-fucking ass a boost to come in and get us."

Enraged, Burkie yanked on the front of his own shirt. It tore. The buttons flew off and plinked into the water. He ignored them, ripped his shirt off, and leaned his body over the edge of the dock. Veins popped out in his neck. His face went taut.

Aiming his voice at Blo, he spit forceful words across the water. "You think you're smart," he yelled and snot flew from his nose.

Breed pointed to the snot on Burkie's face and blared out, "Ha-a-a-nt!"

"Stupid pig," Screwball yelled. "We're smart enough not to blow snot in our own face."

"I'll cut that smart-mouth tongue right out of your mouth," Burkie threatened and wiped his snot nose on his wrist. "I'm comin' in after you goddamn reliefers."

"Yeah," Screwball said, "come on in and get the snot washed off your face."

"Don't do it, Burkie," the blond kid said. "You'll fall into one of those deep drops-offs."

Screwball cupped his hands to his mouth. Using his chicken voice, he yelled, "Buck-buck . . . Bawwwaacckk! Little girl-fucking Burkie will fall in a drop-off. Baawwaacckk! Buck-Buck-Buck! Drop-off, Baawwaacckk! Buck-Buck! Drop-off."

"I ain't afraid of no goddamn drop-off." Burkie jumped off the dock.

Bobbing to the surface, he tried to swim. To keep his head above water, he bent his neck back

312

and used those scared, jerky, sloppy, splashing, stupid, go nowhere, ass-down-in-the-water, amateur strokes. His arms flapped on top of the water, and the opened fingers on his hands flailed downward. His blue-ribbon ignorant strokes and the weight of his wet pants drew him down. He stroked faster.

"Baawwaacckk!" Screwball flapped his arms. "It's amateur time. Maybe they're giving out prizes."

Breed felt a big rock on the bottom of the river. He stepped on it, stood high out of the water, and yelled, "Hey, Burkie, what are you tryin' to do, win the amateur asshole award?"

"You're right on top of a drop-off!" Hog yelled.

Burkie thrashed wild and made the water white.

A chorus of, "Ha-a-ants!" rang across the water.

When Burkie looked up, the swift current grabbed him. It dragged him toward the dark bend of the river. His drunken strokes forced him to flounder and bob up and down. He gave up, put his head down into the water, breathed in, and choked. The prospect of death caused him to rise up with renewed effort and — Right Now! He gulped a sip of air and immediately coughed it back into the water. He coughed again. White water spewed from his mouth and sprayed toward the shore. He splashed and kept his head up long enough to grab one good breath of air. "Help!" he burbled out.

Holding Burkie's jacket, the blond kid on the bank paced back and forth and yelled at Breed and the others, "I can't swim. Save him, you assholes!"

"Talk nice," Screwball said, "and we might."

The blond kid walked to the end of the dock,

tented his fingers in a praying position, and begged soft and low, "Please save him."

No one answered.

The blond kid dropped his hands to his side and raised his voice. "Damn it! Just save him. I can't swim."

Hog knew the area where Burkie was. He yelled across the water. "Stand up! You dumb shit. You're only in four feet of water."

Screwball mockingly shrieked across the water, "Hant!"

The blond kid rushed off the dock, ran along the river and stopped across from Burkie. Jumping up and down and motioning upward with his hands and arms, he yelled,. "Stand up! Stand up! Burkie! Stand up!"

Burkie stood up, quit thrashing, and sloshed to shore like the dumb ass he was.

Flick guided Pud to the side of the boat. Pud immediately tried to climb in the already overburden craft. The boat tilted to one side. Water rushed over the side and into it. Flick grabbed Pud's leg and pulled. "Get out! You'll sink it."

Pud took his leg out of the boat and coughed. "Flick saved my life. That knife was big. Flick saved my life." He held onto the side of the boat and happily kicked his feet in the water.

Making a crazy sign, Hog waved his hand in a circle next to his ear. "I knew it."

Blo gave Hog a sideway look. "What do you mean you knew it?"

"I knew Pud would end up going with us even before you guys went to get him."

Ballpeen hung onto the side of the boat and

turned to Hog. "Just how did you know that?" .

"Simple, Hammer-ass, when Pud's around, if anything is going to get screwed up, it will."

"Yeah," Screwball said, "the only thing he can do right is fart."

Pud smiled like a little kid who had just been put on a carnival ride.

"Just like Shit Midas," Hog said, "Everything he touches turns to shit!"

"I guess you guys are right about that," Flick said and looked to shore. Let's cut the grab-ass and get away from those drunken bastards before one of them drowns and we get blamed for it."

He gave the boat a mighty shove and the great Shell Island crew was headed upriver — again.

Pud repeated, "Flick saved my live, Flick saved my life," over and over.

***

Upriver, they hit slow water. The boat pushed easier, but the walking was clumsy and their feet stumbled on the slippery algae-covered river bottom. Pud tried to get in the boat again and again. They pried him off, again and again, and continued upriver until they were below the miniature naked rocks of the backwash, where a silent cove of less polluted water built up pressure; forced its way through a skinny river passage; picked up more speed; rushed over the riverbed; raced violently into hidden boulders and sunken logs; and flew foaming into the air. Before Breed and his friends, the un-swimmable white water rapids loomed.

They fought to push the loaded boat through the rough water. It spun around and cut sideways into the moving marble water until it wouldn't

315

move upriver anymore.

Flick shouted over the roar of the rapids. "We'll have to carry it around." Like he was starring in a Tarzan movie, he clenched the anchor rope in his teeth and swam for shore. On the rocky shore, he pulled the boat in; and Pud clung tight to its side.

Breed and the others followed, thrashed to the boat, and hoisted it on their shoulders. Stumbling over sharp rocks and driftwood and cussing with each step, they carried the boat around the furious white water.

Just above where the rapids began, they lowered the front of the boat into the calm water.

Hog brushed his hands together. "It's all downhill from here."

Catching his breath, Screwball bent over and leaned on the side of the boat. "You mean it's all upriver from here."

"I don't care how you say it," Flick said. "It'll still be easier."

"It would be if Pud wouldn't hang onto the boat." Breed placed his hand on his aching back. "All he does is slow us down."

Flick coiled the rope and threw it into the boat. "If he would take those wet clothes off, it would be easier for him to walk in the water."

"I don't have a swimming suit," Pud whined. "Maybe I can find one in the boat." He skipped one foot into the water and jumped into the boat. It started to sink.

Screwball grabbed Pud by the arm. "Get the hell out of there." He pulled him out.

Breed stepped to the side of the boat and looked

316

for leaks. "We can't let him sink it now. We've come too far."

Hog jerked his head toward the road above. "Somebody should take him up on the road and hitch-hike him a ride home."

Breed glanced at the road. Dark outlines of trees and brush blocked it. "He'll get lost. And those lousy sons-a-bitichin' flats kids might find him."

As if leaden with fatigue, Pud stepped toward the boat. Blo grabbed his arm and pulled him back. "We got to do something. If we don't, he'll sink the whole damn trip."

Flick tilted his head back and looked toward the road above. "If somebody was brave enough, they would go up on the road and hitchhike to the hill above the island."

"That's a good idea," Hog said with sudden inspiration, "that way they could get to the island first, build a fire, and set up the tent poles."

"If that's such a good idea," Screwball said with a self-satisfied smile, "why don't you do it? Or are you scared?"

"I ain't scared of nothin'." Hog walked to the boat, took out his clothes, pulled them on, and grabbed Pud by the shoulders. "Come on, Pud, let's go."

As if in a daze, Pud started toward the boat. Hog turned him around, pointed him toward the road, and walked in front of him. Pud shambled after; and they smashed through the twigs, kicked the brush aside, and swished over the dead leaves.

Flick eased the boat back into the water and continued upriver. Breed followed until he was

317

waist deep, where he turned and watched Hog and Pud disappear into the dark.

Pud had always been a nervous feeling. He was like a hidden sharp corner everyone had to watch out for. If a person remembered to walk around it, no problem; but just forget about it, one time. Don't look down, and you'd get sucked into the ignorance of the moment, and everybody would wrinkle their foreheads like they had a headache and say, "Awww man!"

Breed was glad Pud was gone. Even when he couldn't see him, he knew he was always somewhere close, lurking around like a bad luck charm, ready to go into action, and at any time.

318

Chapter 24

At the side of the road, Pud stopped and blinked his cat-like eyes. Water from his wet clothes dripped on the pavement and spotted it dark-black. With his wet bathing suit soaking through his pants, Hog stood next to Pud and waited for a car.

Down the road, a low riding forty-nine Hudson Hornet sedan zigzagged and swayed along the winding river road. Inside; behind the wheel, a fellow whose very appearance suggested that he lived like he felt, smiled and laughed. When his hand, as big as a bear's paw, came off the steering wheel, he took a healthy pull from a fifth of Jack Daniel's whiskey, swallowed hard, and tucked the bottle into a hole in the raggedy seat. The bottle stayed upright. He liked it that way. It wasn't necessary to screw the cap on and off when he wanted another swig of the soothing liquid.

Hog stuck out his thumb. For some reason Pud didn't stick out his thumb. Instead, he pointed his index finger. The car zoomed past, but Hog could see inside. The driver's arms straightened on the wheel and his face tensed. He mashed the brake pedal. The wheels locked and skidded in the gravel along the side of the road. As dust and dirt rolled out from under the Hudson, it came to hulking stop. The driver pushed the clutch in and slapped the shifting stick up to reverse. The engine roared and the back tires spun gravel until they met the pavement where they squawked and smoked. The Hudson stopped beside Hog and Pud.

The driver leaned over to the passenger side

and pushed the door open. "You guys want a ride?"

"Yeah," Hog said and they hopped into the heavy Hudson. The driver hooked the transmission into low gear, popped the clutch, and drove down the road.

After he was in second gear, he asked, "How far are you going?"

Hog looked at the driver. His arms were huge. "We're going to the top of Shell Island. You going that far?"

"I'll go as far as you want. My name's Neal." He pointed to the Jack Daniel's. "Want a little nip?"

Before he could answer, Pud repositioned his wet butt on the seat and spoke up. "Flick saved my life."

Neal looked puzzled. "What?"

Hog didn't want Neal to know how Pud was; he might throw them out. He shrugged. "Sometimes a little nip can save your life."

Neal whispered in a raspy voice, "You don't mind if I have one, do you?" In the dark, he smiled and displayed a black missing tooth smile.

The driver dazzled Hog, but he didn't want to disturb the delicate balance that existed between a fresh passenger and the questionable hard-jawed ride giver. If he said something the driver didn't like, or if the driver saw Pud's wet clothes, he might stop and throw them out.

Hog talked as if he were on tiptoe. "No, go ahead. I don't want to be a moocher."

Neal stuck his head out the window for a second. His black hair billowed in the rushing wind. "Ahhh! Good air goes good with a good

320

drink." He gulped a big slug down, lifted his huge arm, and wiped his mouth with the back of his hand. Then he held the bottle toward Hog. "You sure you won't have just a little?" he said with a tinge of anger in his voice. Keeping the bottle toward Hog, Neal looked down at Hog for a brief moment, and his eyes narrowed with suspicion. "I won't think you're a moocher." He snarled and jammed the bottle into Hog's chest. "Here!"

Hog felt uncomfortable. "I'll have a little one." He pried the bottle off his chest.

Neal put his hand back on the steering wheel and smiled his missing-tooth smile. Hog noticed that his teeth were only missing on one side of his mouth. He figured it must have been a good left hook that took them out.

He took a small slug and passed the bottle back. Neal grabbed it, stiffened his elbow, and held the fifth under Pud's nose. "Here, slake your thirst!"

"Thank you." Pud took the bottle.

"Where's that little black haired, Breed kid?" Neal asked and rubbed the back of his head. "I always pick that kid up. Fixed my car one time, I didn't know what was wrong. He fixed it right off."

Hog reached out and rested his hand on the dashboard. "Yeah, Breed's good at fixin' stuff."

Squinting through the bug-spattered windshield, Neal nodded. "Yeah, I owe him one."

The car swayed and buffeted over the rough road. Pud tilted the bottle to take a small slug. The car hit an oversized pothole and jerked. The potent alcohol rushed into his mouth. He opened his cat eyes wide and looked at Neal's huge arms. As if he didn't want to spill a drop and get Neal mad, he swallowed the cheek-expanding mouthful. It rushed down to his stomach; and like a hundred game pay-off on a pinball machine, it rang his limited mind and made his whole body shudder.

As the car cut a nimble turn, Pud handed the bottle to Hog, relaxed, and acted somewhat normal. He talked freely. "My name's Pud and he's Hog."

Neal's eyebrows lifted. "Hog? What do they call you that for?"

"Because that's what I am," Hog proudly acclaimed and took a long pull from the depleting bottle.

Neal broke into a roaring laugh and banged on the steering wheel. The round metal encased plastic wheel vibrated like a tuning fork.

Hog looked down and watched the heel of Neal's dog-bitten, torn shoe rest on top of the accelerator. With each pound of his fist on the steering wheel, his foot sank down until it was all the way to the floor.

Following Hog's gaze, Neal looked at his torn shoe. "Never trust a man with a bit foot." He laughed a deep belly laugh and eased up on the accelerator.

While wind shrilled through a small crack in the wing window, short bursts of tall telephone poles zipped past. Hog tilted to the side and watched the speedometer. The skinny white needle climbed, but the distance traveled and the speed registered didn't matter. Hog knew they were going fast.

As the Hudson Hornet churned on down the highway and gobbled up the fading yellow line, under the hood, the big cast-iron engine purred effortlessly. The road got rougher and the turns got sharper. Neal's mouth was like his forty-nine Hudson. It ran nonstop. He gave the engine more fuel. The haphazard clip increased. While Pud braced himself and tried to push his foot through the floorboards, Hog pushed the air with his right foot and searched for a brake pedal that wasn't there.

Neal continued his reckless abandonment for life and limb, but his athletic body stayed loose and graceful. He didn't fight the bumps or the humps. He didn't fight the sudden snaps or sharp turns. He didn't fight the Hudson. He relaxed his bull-necked head and rode as if he were on a cheery carnival ride. As the Hudson edged closer to the side of the road, Hog watched the outside world zip past and braced himself for a wreck.

"Hey, Partner." Neal settled back into the seat. "Relax. Go with the flow, Joe. Remember" — he lifted his finger —"the main thing is . . . Don't get excited."

Hog semi-relaxed and looked out over the front of the Hudson. A clean, waxed, shiny hood met his eyes. A coat of dinged-up chalky paint covered other body parts that were dented, dirty, or scratched.

Breed turned toward Neal. "How come you only wash the hood of your car?"

Neal let out a deep belly roar. "That's all I see when I drive. The hell with the rest of the world. I ain't got nothin' to prove. I'm not going to work my ass off cleaning and waxing this car just for them to gawk at it for a little second when I drive by." As if he were throwing away the thought, Neal threw his hand toward the roof of the car. "I don't

323

have to shine it for idiots that wait around to have their futures explained. I don't have to wait around for something to happen, or wait around for someone to tell me where I should go and how I should live. I don't have to be a part of the ignorant world's tears or mental breakdowns." He smiled a big rebellious smile that broadcasted freedom. "Why should I announce I'm coming? When I get there, they'll know I have arrived."

Pud blubbered something unintelligible and said loud and clear, "Flick saved my life."

Neal turned his head sideways and wrinkled one eye. "That's nice." He put the bottle in the hole in the seat. With the outside world zipping past, he began a drunken physiological stream of speech. "Screw the bull shit, go with the shit wit. Maybe I won't get nowhere in this life, but I'm going to have a lot of fun trying."

"Yeah!" Hog said. "Thanks for picking us up. But I don't know what you're talking about."

"You don't have to know what I'm talking about at this exact moment. It ain't no use fighting." Neal waved his huge fist around in front of the windshield. "The whole world is a land fill project."

"You mean a dump!" Hog added.

Neal slapped himself in the forehead. "Yes . . . oh yes, a dump!"

He paused for a moment, let the word sink into his alcohol-altered brain, and continued. "Just like the calendar pages are ripped off every month and thrown away and taken to the dump, so are the people lied to. Tax monsters flip them off their little claimed piece of America and take them to the human dumps." He lifted one finger. "And, at great expense . . . I may add! And then they call the entire process civilization. You were made of garbage and you will return to garbage."

The Hudson slowed. Neal jammed his foot on the accelerator and slammed it clear to the floor.

Being sarcastic, Hog suggested, "Can't you give it any more gas?"

As if he were pushing it through the floorboard, Neal straightened his knee and ground his foot on top of the accelerator. "Nope, that's all there is. There ain't no more."

Up front, like anti-aircraft tracers, white lines shot under the car. But Neal kept on talking. Smoke poured out the back of the car; and when they went around the corner, both tires rolled over the sides of the road, Breed felt the tension, but Neal's voice never wavered.

Hog looked out the open window. Familiar sights above Shell Island flashed past. He interrupted Neal's raging flood of speech. "Hey! We went past the hill where we want to get out!"

Neal didn't answer. It was as if he were in a trance. He continued his banter. "E equals MC squared if foolish insolent talk . . . Yes! Yes! Yes! You see, it's just a trick! There is no matter. There is no particle in the nucleus of an atom. It just does not exist. The only things that exist are forms of energy. We are only various forms of vibrational density that appear to exist. We are all just energy, charging things here, discharging things there. We only appear to be here. It's all vulgar nonsense . . . Or better yet" — he took a drag from his cigarette — "maybe it's a Communistic plot to take over the free world."

He jabbed Hog in the ribs with his elbow. "Aaarr Matey! Do you know that everything you've ever done in your life could potentially be wrong? Do we really know what is real? Do I know? Do you know? Watch this!"

He put his finger into the side of his mouth and popped out the black wax that had made his teeth look like they were missing. He smiled a full white tooth grin in Hog's direction. "See? Just ask Neal. You never know what's real!" He threw his hand toward the roof of the car and snapped his fingers. "How about that, gentleman?" The expression on his face changed from confident to confused. As if he had forgotten what he was going to say next, he shook his head. "Yes! Yes! Yes!" He continued. "Just a bunch of rat faced people out there. And you know if you don't connect to something larger than yourself, they'll bite the balls right off your repetitious dick!"

As if he were going to sleep, Pud rolled to his side. "Ain't gonna let a rat bite my dick. Flick saved my life."

Hog raised his voice. "Neal! We rode past the hill!"

Neal flicked his cigarette butt out the window and looked at Hog. "Want a smoke?"

"Sure."

Neal took threw a cigarette at Hog. Hog caught it and put it to his lips. Neal clinched a cigarette in his teeth and lit it. He took one puff, and it fell to the floor.

He reached for it. "What did you say?" He bent over; and steering with one hand, he strained his neck until his head was below the seat and looked for the hot orange ash of the lost tobacco stick. The car weaved from side to side. Feeling the floor under the seat, he continued to blabber. "You know the faster you go, the closer you get to stopping, because if we were going the speed of light we would be stopped."

Hog put his unlit cigarette in his pocket, shook his head, and tried to digest Neal's strange logic.

Up ahead, like the back of a dead end street, a late wagon load of fresh, yellow bales of hay stretched full length across the road.

"Watch where the hell you're going!" Hog screamed.

As if it were a prize he had just won in a contest, Neal jumped up with the cigarette in his mouth. With smoke escaping from his mouth, in three small puffs, with each word, he proudly stated, "I got it!"

The sight of the wagon flashed in the windshield. "Don't get excited!" Neal advised his excited self. He stomped the brake pedal — hard. All four wheels locked. He cut the steering wheel to the right. The car spun into a one hundred and eighty degree turn.

It was a merry-go-round.

Wagon wheels rushed toward the right side windows. Then, sides of the road blurred to a wild gray and sailed toward the back window. The haze of the green and black front wheels of the tractor rolled next to the left side window. After a line of fence posts whizzed past the windshield, a big solid black telephone pole popped up like a crazy clown in a jack-in-the-box. The car shot at it. Hog braced himself for the crash. Neal lifted his foot from the brake, cut the wheel, and mashed the gas feed. The tires spun. Gravel and dirt blasted out the back. The car shot away from the pole.

As if nothing had happened, Neal kept his foot on the gas pedal and merrily drove down the road.

Hog took the bottle from the hole in the seat and downed a big gulp. He put the bottle under Pud's nose. Pud's head tilted and his eyes rolled. Hog put the bottle back in the hole. "Neal, do you know we're past the hill?"

Neal bobbed his head and snapped his fingers to an imaginary beat. "We're past the hill?" he questioned, then said, "No. Hum me a few bars. I'll catch on."

Hog squirmed in the seat. "We got to get to the Island before Breed and the other guys get there."

"Breed?" Neal asked with sentimental look in his eyes. "That little black-headed kid? No problem. I owe him, you know. We're going back now." He flicked the spent cigarette out the window. As if it were an exhibition for their benefit, he smiled a toothless grin.

Hog looked into Neal's mouth. He couldn't see the black wax he had used before. He shook his head as if he were confused.

Neal turned toward Breed and held a big smile. "Now you see." He turned back toward the road ahead. "They ain't real at all, Aaar ha! Matey." He put his false teeth back in his mouth and continued. "What's the difference in time? We all have the same amount. Time is just something they dreamed up to keep everything from happening all at once. In the end we all live until we die."

In a tone that did not invite discussion, Hog said, "And everybody's legs are the same length. They all go from their ass to the ground."

As if Neal had finally realized that he was becoming a bore, he pointed his finger toward Hog. "You got a point there."

Pud sat up and grabbed the door handle. "I'm sick. Let me out."

Neal cut the steering to the left. The heavy Hudson swerved. Pud's door flew open. He quickly overcame his sickness. With one hand on the handle of the open door and his other hand clutching the strange beat in dashboard that looked as of a former passenger pounded it while keeping time to music on a long cross country trip, he hung on.

"Oh yeah," Neal said and smiled. "I forgot to tell you about that door. It does that now and then." He swerved the car. The door slammed shut.

As if he had just realized he had almost fallen out, Pud shuddered and jerked his head in Neal's direction. "Why don't you turn around the right way?"

Neal took a drink from the emptying bottle. "You mean to tell me that you didn't like that hay wagon turn?"

Pud wagged his head around in a circle. "That made me dizzy."

"This is my day off. I don't have to do anything. Heh?" He elbowed Hog in the ribs. "And anyway, what's right? It gets the job done. You want to end up being some old coot doing the same thing every day and saying, 'Same ole', Same ole', every day until you die? Why should we let uneducated people dangle promises of riches and happiness in front of our faces and lead us around like we're some kind of jackasses running after a carrot? You know, after they use you up and make you believe you're happy, they'll only yank those promises away and keep them for themselves."

Neal's information was a little too much for Hog to take in all at once. He didn't want to believe it. "All people aren't that bad, are they?"

Neal let out a roaring laugh. Hog couldn't tell if it was from relief or amusement. But there was haunted hurt in his eyes.

"There are still a few decent people left in this world. But you have to remember, that the rich people have been what they are a lot longer than you've been what you are."

"So what?" Hog shot back. "That don't make them better than anybody else."

Neal's face took on an expression of bitterness. "They aren't better. But society tricks you into believing things that makes you think they are. The funny part is that they don't even believe it themselves. They're the last people to believe it. But make no mistake about it." He pointed to Hog. "They want you to believe it. That's how they create a world where impossibly wealthy people can do anything they want."

Hog didn't reply. He felt good. He wasn't rich, but he had always done just about anything he pleased. If Neal was right, he was halfway there. Now, all he had to do was become rich. It was as simple as that.

Up ahead, the glassy eyes of a possum sitting in the road burned in the headlight beams. Neal cut the steering wheel to the right, then to the left. The Hudson swerved with a sudden sideways pull of centrifugal force, sending Neal into Hog, Hog into Pud, and Pud into the door. The door flew open — again. The sound of the hard pavement racing under the opened door rushed into the crazy interior. Pud's hand slipped off the dashboard. His foot was an inch from hitting the speeding pavement, catching it, and sucking him under the wheels.

Neal cut the steering wheel to the right. The pull of the centrifugal force reversed the pervious string of events. Neal was back behind the steering wheel, smiling as if it was an everyday occurrence.

He glanced toward Hog. "I didn't scare you guys, did I?"

Hog smiled back. "Naw, give me another drink."

"I knew you guys weren't fossilized bastards afraid of everything different. I'll drink to that!" He tipped the bottle toward the front windshield in a toasting gesture.

Hog took another drink and the ride continued.

A ways down the road, Hog couldn't see anything familiar. In the distance, he thought he saw the glow of the morning sun rising. He looked to Neal. "Are you lost?"

Neal tilted the bottle, emptied every last drop, and answered, "You're never lost. You're always right here!"

After a few more miles, what Hog thought was the morning sun became the moon; and Neal tooted his horn at telephone poles that seemed to keep jumping onto the road.

The poles managed to stay off the road; and

after a while, Hog discovered that they weren't lost. They were right here. Here on the hill above Shell Island. Neal stopped the weaving metal chariot.

Pud and Hog staggered out.

Hog closed the door on the shiny hooded Hudson. "Thanks for the ride."

"Yeah, anytime. Now I'll fumigate my car."

Pud stood at the side of the road and waved bye-bye!

Neal raced the engine. The clutch burned and the charred smell of asbestos escaped into the night air. The mighty Hudson stalled. The starter turned with a tired moan and almost died, but the engine caught and rumbled to life. Neal stuck his head out the open window. "I don't have to do anything. It's my day off. I don't even have to start out in low gear."

His laughs echoed, loud and clear, into the quiet dark. The overworked engine groaned and putted. The car of the great night rolled forward in second gear.

Neal took the finishing pull on his second bottle of Jack Daniel's, wiped his mouth on his T-shirt, and tossed the empty bottle onto the road. It spun around. The pavement nicked the black paper label and the bottle stopped. Its neck pointed toward Pud.

Neal drove off.

Suffused in a weird blue glow, the shiny hooded Hudson disappeared into the dark.

Hog looked at the bottle and then turned toward Pud. "Wanna play spin the bottle?"

Pud smiled a goofy smile. "Yeah, I'll play."

"Good," Hog said. "When it points to you, kiss my ass."

The attempted humor didn't register in Pud's limited brain. All he said was, "You know Flick saved my life?"

Hog shook his head. "What a combination, Neal the nut and Pud."

And they walked into the darkness.

Chapter 25

The Shell Island crew stood on the rocks at the shoreline and looked at the quiet water above the rapids. High up on the hill, one of the smaller steel mills poured its first cast of the midnight turn. Like sudden rays of morning sun, the awesome light from the hot molten metal surprised into the thick dark air. The horizon ignited into an orange glow that silhouetted a wall of tall trees and sent an eerie light to hover above the river where weeping river willows with long curved branches lined the banks and bowed exquisitely, letting their long, graceful ends gently touched the deep glossy surface of the soundless river of inky water.

The crew eased into the water. Breed slid his hand along the surface and felt its velvety smoothness. Flick gave the boat a gentle shove. It plowed across the dark mirror water and gently parted its deep rich shine. Tiny waves flowed in its wake and gently rolled to the peaceful shore.

Further upriver, after the first bend, the water was flat, and for a long stretch, the current stayed tame. In these ideal river conditions, Breed, Flick, Ballpeen, Blo, and Screwball made up for the lost time Pud had caused when he had hung onto the boat and continually tried to climb into it.

In the shallows, Flick pulled on the rope, and Breed pushed until the boat plowed around the second bend. When they looked up ahead, the reflection of a dim-yellow light fanned across the wide river and illuminated the little waves that rolled from the bow of the green boat and made them glow like long lines of miniature golden ropes.

Ballpeen put the palm of his hand in front of his mouth. "What's that light?" His voice filled with fear. "You think the flats gang's waitin' on us?"

Flick peeked around the back of the boat. "Don't get excited, Ballpeen. We'll find out when we get there." He gave the boat another pull.

The light grew brighter. Ballpeen swam to the dark side of the boat and kept his head down. Breed kicked his feet and splashed the water. The resulting waves cut the water ropes and rippled over the river until they kissed a cement wall, where a lone, dirty light bulb shone on a white-haired steelworker. He sat on the top of a rust-dusted cement wall with his legs crossed and watched the river below.

Powerful pumps groaned and huge pipes sucked river water into the mill. Right across from the boat, another pipe burped from deep in its hollow cavity and barfed thick yellow brine into the water. Sickening fumes enveloped Breed and made him cough. He pushed the boat away from the gushing bile.

Drawing agitated sniffs of air, Ballpeen took a quick look around the side of the boat.

"Watch out, Ballpeen," Breed said. "Don't let that stuff get on you. It might be acid."

The skinny old steelworker looked toward them. "It ain't acid. They only let that out on Wednesdays. You'll be okay."

The yellow brine flowed next to the boat. Breed felt his skin tingle, and a dry-sulfur-toothache taste formed in his mouth. "You got your days mixed up, this stuff burns." He steered the boat further away from the brine. "How come you guys dump this stuff in here?"

As if Breed had been talking to an invisible person, the toothless man ignored him and talked to the air. "Greedy billionaires don't want to spend a few dollars to keep the river pure and the sky free of pollution." He patted his pockets as if he were looking for something and changed the subject. "You fellows sure got it made," he said in a cheery voice.

He must be deaf, Breed thought, and his feet touched bottom. He hung onto the boat and stopped.

Flick dipped an empty tomato can into the water and poured the fresh water into the lard can to oxygenate the chubs. Then he bailed a few cans of water out of the boat. "We would have it made if this boat didn't leak."

The old steelworker smiled, uncrossed his legs, and found his pipe in his pocket. "That's not what I mean. You boys are young. You don't have to go to work every day."

As if he were in pain, Screwball contorted his face and stared at Ballpeen. "You think tuggin' this heavy piece of junk upriver ain't work"?

Ballpeen didn't respond to Screwball's attempt to set up a jeering, Hant!

The steelworker struck a wooden match on the rough concrete and held it to his pipe. His lined face brightened like a dried up jack-O-lantern, and his gnarled fingers held the worn pipe to his lips. He sucked and puffed smoke. With each puff, his rubbery lips sunk into his toothless gums. "You boys just enjoy yourselves," he said through the wisps of smoke. "Don't mind me. I just wish I was

336

in there with you."

Flick waved his arm. "Well come on in. We need all the help we can get."

"I'll have to pass this time, my lunch break's over." With a flick of his wrist, he shook the match out. "But I'll give you boys some good advice."

"What's that?" Screwball chuckled. "Don't take any wooden cunts?"

The steelworker laughed but checked himself. "If you want to get rich, buy land."

"I'd rather buy a house," Ballpeen said.

"That's okay, but it's not as good as buying land. They can always make more houses, but the last time I checked, they ain't makin' any more land." And when it's almost all been sold you'll be able to sell it for a lot of money."

"What do you want land for?" Flick asked and dipped the can into the water in the boat. "You make big money in the mill."

The watchman sighed. "Yeah, that's what I used to think, but I found out working for someone is no way to get rich." He paused and a spark of pain flashed from in his old eyes. "Just don't work for someone unless you absolutely have to. And if you do, take that money and buy land. After a while you won't have to work in the mill."

Breed reached up and pushed his wet hair away from his forehead. "How you going to eat if you don't work and you ain't got no money for food?"

The steelworker sat up straight. "Sell things. People will buy crap if you put it in a nice package. Work for yourself."

Screwball popped his head around the side of the boat. "Oh yeah? How come you're not working

337

for yourself?"

The steelworker's shoulders slumped. "Cause I started too early and got used to it. By nature human beings always resist change. Once you start working for someone it becomes a way of life."

The noxious chemical smell drifted over the boat. Screwball wrinkled his nose. "What's the matter with working every day?"

"Nothin, if you're ignorant. It's like an old pair of shoes. Even though they're worn out and hurt your feet, because you're too ignorant to change, you keep wearing them."

Screwball grinned wryly. "So what?"

"Old shoes are like the mill. They trap you into feeling secure." A hurt expression filled the old man's face. "Then you can't quit."

Blo puffed out his chest. "I'd quit."

The old steelworker stood up and teetered until he caught his balance. His thin shoulders slouched over, and his back humped out like there was a growth under his flannel shirt. "You think you'll quit," he said. "I almost quit when acid ate all my teeth out, but I just kept on working day after day." As if leaden with fatigue, he let out a long breath of air. "Before I knew it, I was just too damn old to do anything but work."

Screwball shook his head in quizzical amusement. "You mean you can't even take a piece of ass anymore?"

The old steelworker chuckled. "You'll have to wait until you're as old as I am to find that out."

Like a three thousand pound bull moose echoing in a commode with the dry hangover heaves, the mill whistle blew. The hollow haunting

338

sound of the beckoning steam whistle seemed to throw a switch in the steelworker's brain. Like a Pavlovian conditioned dog, he turned and tramped up the long sad path.

Just loud enough to hear, he talked to himself. "Start your own business. Don't be a lazy dimwit. Don't stay in a goddamn silly mill and die in your own ignorance. Any money you make will disappear into debts anyway." He stumbled, threw his foot out, and continued walking. As if he were angry with himself for wasting his life, he said to himself, "Serves you right, you dumb, stupid bastard."

Mesmerized, Breed watched the acid brine oozing into the water. Hate for the mill that flushed the acid into the water burned into his mind. He watched the teetering old man. The hate turned to sorrow. Almost like Jummy was a prisoner in his yard, the old man had become a prisoner of the mill. A mother like Jummy's or bars and locks didn't keep him in there. The need to do what every other mill worker did, kept him in there; and that need was to make decent money and create a half-decent life for others.

Flick compassionately called after him, "We'll see you, old timer."

The crew trailed their good-byes. The steelworker stopped halfway up the path and put his dirty finger on one side of his nose. He took a deep breath and blew out one nostril. A rocket of snot flew out and splatted on the lifeless slag-covered ground.

Surprised, Screwball looked at Breed. "Look!" He pointed to the steelworker.

339

The steelworker put his finger to the other side of his nose and another rocket of snot flew out. As if he were going to make an important point, he lifted his hand and pointed to Screwball. "Ha-a-a-nt!"

Surprised, Screwball turned to Flick. Flick pointed to the steelworker.

As if saying, "Hant," had been too much of a chore, the old man coughed, shook his shaggy, gray-streaked head, trudged into the dirty stinking mill, and continued to grow old before his time.

Breed pushed the boat to a crawl and edged its bow into the slow current. "You know that old man wasted his whole life in that mill. He never got out of Traptown."

And he never will," Flick said. "When he dies, his epitaph will read: Worked In Traptown Mill" — he poked his finger against the side of the boat — "period."

A patch of some kind of shimmering filth snaked toward the boat. Blo pushed the boat out of its slithering path. "That old man's been in the mill so long, he didn't even know what day it was."

Breed moved to the other side of the boat and let the filth slink past. "If we end up there, we won't know nothin' either."

"So what?" Screwball said. "We'll know how to blow a snot rocket out of our nose."

"Ha-a-a-nt!," Blo said. "If you're on overtime you'll get paid time and a half for it."

"Ahh man," Breed said and the crew tugged on upriver.

340

Chapter 26

At the big bend in the river, Flick braced his feet on the sandy bottom, dug in, and gave the boat a mighty heave. It glided around the turn in the river. Breed peeked over the side of the boat. Shell Island appeared.

Headlights of passing cars zipped past on the high road above. Sprinkles of their light sparkled through shadows of weeds, bushes, and trees and continued on their way to insignificant and suggested-important destinations.

Although it was too far away to be seen, a steel mill poured a new heat of molten steel. Its orange light lit up the horizon, and cancer-causing steel ingredients and graphite sparkled into the air. Then, light brown sulfur scented vapors escaped and hid in the dark fringes of the night.

Over a mile away, like background music, diesel-powered, yard-switching engines orchestrated the night. Horns buzzed; electric traction motors whined; and heavy steel wheels clacked up and down the shiny uneven tracks. Cast-steel knuckles were bumped, couplers were cut; and various railroad cars were thrown down selected tracks and sent on their way to secret cities.

Although Shell Island was not a resort vacation site and was surrounded with minor distractions, it remained isolated, set apart, and landlocked. Situated in the center of the once Indian inhabited Rat River, Shell Island was a place away, a place immune to the bangs, bumps, and bitching of the ordinary stagnated mill of life. And it was away from Traptown.

341

Breeds knew the general public could not lower their falsely created social status and spend a few precious moments of their damnable lives on this disassociated dominion, but he knew he and his friends could. They had no social status to lower and no plans to let some rat-faced bastard drum into their minds that they couldn't do anything because they didn't have any money. There was just no time to let something that trivial interfere with a mind expanding realm of exploring the forbidden, taking the offbeat ancient Indian paths, and making things happen — just to make them happen.

Time froze. In a moment of silence, Breed and his friends just looked at the island.

Moonlight peered down through the trees. It beamed on the real meadow: A picturesque little strip of adventure — a clean vacation land that charged them with holiday energy.

On the upper part of the island, opened clamshells lined the shore and blinked baby blue lights from their reflective pearl surfaces. A rock-skip below, soft sand tapered to a snow-white point. In the background, masked raccoons softly chattered behind a black maze of trees and made plans to eat clams elsewhere. Tonight, Breed and his friends would build a roaring fire and camp on the raccoon's table.

Flick dragged the tar-pasted bow of the green boat onto the white sandy point and surveyed the island. Pud and Hog hadn't showed up. The rest of the crew waded ashore.

Flick held out his hand like a cop stopping traffic. "Be careful you guys." He pointed to an empty place on the sand. "Don't trip over that big pile of firewood Hog and Pud got."

Blo walked around an imaginary stack of firewood. "Yeah, they must've got a ride right off the bat to pile a stack that high."

Screwball and Breed looked at each other. They understood. Their task would be to get firewood.

Flick reached into the boat and took out his father's railroad lantern. "Here, Blo. Light this." A stern look formed on Flick's face. "And don't break it."

While Ballpeen and Flick unloaded the boat, Blo lit the kerosene lantern. It smoked black until he adjusted the wick. Then it burned bright yellow. He held it high. The island turned from dark to the evening gold of a prolonged sunset.

While Flick put up the tent, Breed started the fire; and it glowed orange then danced into jumping yellow curves. Blo jammed a long stick into the sand and hung the lantern on top. Screwball gathered firewood and stacked a pile high enough to last a week, and the campsite appeared. Then they all crawled into the tent. Jerking blankets and pushing each other, they tried to get their bedding set up at the same time.

"Hey! Enough of this little kid stuff!" Flick ordered. But no one listened.

Blo crawled out the tent and jerked out the tent pegs. The canvas caved in and smothered their yakking mouths.

"Hant!" Blo blurted out.

"Hant, your ass," Flick said and they grouped their way out and stood up to survey the damage. "What stupid Faulk-it-tea-hammer idiot pitched this

343

tent?"

Blo blinked. "You did, Idiot."

Flick stared into the air and rubbed his chin. "I did, didn't I?" He pulled the fallen tent off the bedding. "I'll show you guys how to put up a real tent."

Screwball pretended he was slurping on a Fudge-Sickle. Flick turned toward him.

Screwball stopped. "Like the one you just put up?"

Flick stared at him for a moment, then smiled. "Just sit on your fat asses and watch. Flip me that ax, Breed!"

Breed tossed the ax toward Flick. He caught it and trudged off into the darkness of the trees.

A thud from Flick falling to the ground came from the trees and was followed by a sickening snap.

Flick cussed in the darkness.

Screwball cupped his hands around his mouth and yelled into the trees, "Ha-a-ant!"

Flick yelled back through the trees, "Hey, Screwball, you still eaten frozen shit on a stick! Or did you quit!"

Screwball lifted his hand to his mouth to pretend he was slurping on a Fudge-Sickle; and as if what Flick said had just registered in his brain, he stopped.

Whack! Whack! Out of the darkness, heavy chopping sounds barked off the blade of Flick's sharp ax and reechoed up and down the river.

Fifty whacks later, dragging two poles good enough to be fence posts, Flick came back into the light of the fire. He thrust them into the sand, picked up a heavy rock, and drove the new and improved tent supports deep into the heart of the island.

"There" — he brushed his hands together — "solid as the lock on Fort Knox."

Screwball straightened out the tarp they used for the tent. It was an old Army-green piece of canvas left over from Breed's father's game of chance he had ran before he became trapped in the mill. It had a cow painted on it, a backdrop for 'Spill the Milk', a game where teen-agers and people who wished they were teen-agers, threw baseballs, wound with black tape, at wooden milk bottles and tried to win colorful painted canes, fragile glitter-covered plaster of Paris statues; or itchy crepe paper necklaces, dyed orange, red and green with water dye that ran onto one's clothes at the first hint of moisture.

The canvas had a fragrance of wild sawdust, cigars, and carnivals. It had been seasoned during the many hot days at the Great Stoneboro Fair and other small money making nights at lesser locations throughout the County.

Breed never had money to ride the rides or play the rigged games, but he had watched. It usually happened when the sun went down. Under the lure of colorful carnival lights, a young kid with a girl on his arm would lay down his silver coins, throw a few baseballs, and win one of those worthless necklaces; and like a badge of courage, he would wear it around his neck all night and discard it the next morning.

Breed pulled the cow canvas off the bedding. Ballpeen skinned a skinny sapling, placed it across

345

the posts to create a tent peak, and nailed it in place with his ever-pounding hammer.

Flick threw the canvas over the skeleton frame. It didn't wobble or move an inch. "It's up to stay. Pound those tent pegs in, Breed."

Ballpeen jumped in front of Breed. He waved his hammer in the air. "I'll pound them in."

Breed stepped aside and gestured to the tent. "Knock yourself out."

Screwball bowed at the waist and held his hand toward the tent. "Be our guest, cock-knocker."

Snarling, Ballpeen knelt down and knocked on the pegs.

"Soon as you get that done—" Breed looked to the woods that led to the road above. "Hog and Pud's gonna show up."

Ballpeen wiggled a peg through a grommet on the corner of the canvas and stretched it tight. "Yeah, we're almost done." He smacked the last tent peg into the sand.

Screwball placed a stick on the growing fire and wiped his sandy hands on his pants. "Those guys are probably sittin' in the weeds watchin'."

Blo aimed his voice across the river and called into the darkness. "You guys can come across now. The work's all done."

Flick poked the fire with a stick. "Quit your beefin'. They probably got lost."

Breed moved his head from side to side and searched the other side of the river. There was no movement. "Either that, or Pud pulled one of his retarded stunts and got them thrown in jail."

Screwball threw a few potatoes into the fire and waited for them to roast. Blo dabbled in the ashes

346

and Flick sang "Frankie and Johnny". He managed to sing the entire song once, but then he deliberately changed and mixed up the words.

Fishing lines were in the water, baited with those prized red horned chubs. When weak light from the lantern filtered through the tree limbs and imitated the morning rays of the sun; as if they were fooled, a few birds awoke and sporadically chirped. In the deepness of the trees, raccoons chattered hollowly; and like little amber lights, their eyes glowed in the dark.

The crew's eyes blinked. Flick's singing voice waned to weary. Hints of sleep were gestured. The last potato was eaten. Screwball rolled a good-sized log into the cricking fire and crawled into the tent.

Flick checked the fishing poles. The lines jittered from the swimming chubs but the poles were straight and still.

Flick stretched and yawned. "Let's string the fishing lines back to the tent where we can keep an eye on them." He lifted two poles.

"That's a good idea," Breed lifted two poles. "If we get a bite, we won't have to run out of tent like idiots."

Screwball stuck his head out the end of the tent. "Yeah, then you can idiot out like a tent." He contorted his face and stared at Breed.

While Flick and Breed set the poles in the Ys of sticks stuck in the sand, Breed shook his head at Screwball's contorted face. "Keep your face just like that," he said. "It's a big improvement."

"Ahh, man," Screwball said, and his face relaxed to normal.

Breed and Flick crawled into the tent, became

horizontal, and watched the orange and yellow fire curve and dance.

Flick laced his hands behind his head and looked up at the ceiling of the tent. "It's nice to be here. I was getting tired of all those ass kicking's and put downs."

"Yeah," Ballpeen said. "For no reason at all, those flats gang kids just come in and beat the livin' crap out of anyone they want, just for kicks."

"Why does it keep happening?" Breed wagged his head in a seesaw motion. "It always comes back the same way, over and over."

As if he were drunken Toney, Screwball sat up and waved on his upper body. "Hey . . . and back that way again . . . Hey!"

Blo rolled over and looked up. "You're crazy, but you know it's the same thing! It's the same days. It's the same people. It's the same town, same houses, and the same people pullin' some rotten crap on us, all the same damn time!"

Screwball tilted his head, opened his eyes wide, and smiled one of his goofy ear-to-ear smiles. "Then why don't you go in same?"

Flick sat up. "Hey wait!" His head poked into the roof of the canvas tent. "Screwball might just have something there."

"Hell yes." Breed leaned on his elbow. "It seems the whole world is rigged. If we don't behave like little puppets, some asshole steals our stuff, and we can't do nothin' about it."

"I don't have to behave like a puppet." Blo sneered through his false teeth. "I don't have to do nothin' I don't want to do. I still do what I want."

"This may be true." Flick pointed to the black

and blue mark on Blo's face. "But you always get your ass beat or end up trying to run away."

Blo rubbed the side of his beer-bottle-beaten face.

As if he were running, Screwball rolled his fist. "You gotta learn to run faster. They have to catch you before they can beat you up."

Breed felt a stirring in his chest and spoke up. "It ain't just getting beat up that I'm sick of."

"Good," Screwball said with finality in his voice, "the next time they go to beat me up, you can say, 'Hey . . . back my way again,' and take my place."

"Ahh, man," Breed moaned. "It's the other stuff that pisses me off the most."

Flick turned toward Breed. "Yeah, like Lard Man. He got on us just because we were shooting your BB gun."

Breed covered his shoulder with his thin blue blanket. "And we weren't even doing anything."

A spasm of irritation crossed Flick's face. "I wonder why stupid people always tell us what to do?"

Screwball swiveled on his upper body, waved his finger in the air, and slurred his speech. "Hey! . . . and back that way again." He pushed his hair out of his eyes and puffed out his chest. "Gentleman," he said loud and clear. "It's because the whole world is run by an Army of assholes."

Breed nodded in agreement. "And One-Finger-Burke's the General."

A whining grinding noise filled the air.

Flick tensed to fight. "What's that?"

Screwball bent forward and looked out the tent.

349

"Probably Pud and Hog trying to— Hey, Flick! That's your pole!"

The reel sung. The pole sailed out of the tent. It skied across the sand toward the water. Flick kicked his covers to his ankles. Using his hands and knees, he scrambled out of the tent. Then, he jumped up and took one step toward the pole. His feet tangled in the blankets. He stumbled and fell. The pole was at the point of the island, going into the water.

Breed yelled, "Get it, Flick!"

Flick untangled his feet. "That thing's gotta be big." He half ran, half stumbled toward the pole. Like underwear-clad idiots escaping from a crazy house, Breed and the others stampeded after Flick and rushed for the fleeing pole.

When Flick was knee deep in water, they stopped and watched. The pole was going under. Flick plunged his hand into the water and desperately grabbed. "I almost had it."

He took aim and slashed at the pole with his other hand. Water sprayed from his swishing hand

He missed.

He tried again.

This time, he snatched the pole out of the dark water, lifted it up, and yanked back.

The hook was set.

The pole bowed over to the handle. With the orange and yellow firelight flickering on the crew, they screamed and bounced up and down like disorganized cheerleaders.

The magic of the moment filled Breed's bare feet with energy. He danced and flung sand into the night air. Screwball whooped and hollered.

Ballpeen and Blo joined in. Flick had a monster of a fish on.

The handle on the reel spun wild. Flick tried to grab it. It beat his knuckles. The racing fish turned. The reel handle stopped. Flick gripped it and cranked in a few turns of line. He let go. "This reel is hot!" He frantically waved his hand in the air.

Breed stopped dancing. "Stick it in the water!"

Flick rammed the handle of the pole and the hot spinning reel into the water. It bubbled and whirred like a tiny outboard motor.

Watching the fleeing line race off the spool of the reel, Breed yelled, "Don't touch that line. It'll saw your fingers off!"

Flick lifted the pole from the water, re-grabbed the reel handle and cranked. The big fish stretched the line tight. It twanged like a bass guitar string. Breed knew it was at the breaking point. He looked at Flick's face. It relaxed.

"Don't quit now," Breed said. "Give him some line."

Flick back-pedaled the reel and let the fish run. It was tireless. He pulled on the pole and rotated the reel handle into tight little circles of blurred speed. The line coiled back onto the spool. He braced his feet in the sand. Again, the line tore off the spool. The fighting fish thrashed and noisily churned the surface of the dark water.

"I can hear him," Flick said. "But I can't see him." He pumped the pole and cranked in more line.

Breed pointed to a huge silver flash in the water. "There he is."

Flick smiled big. He pulled the pole long and

351

hard. "He's comin' in now!"

The line went limp.

Searching, Flick wagged his head from side to side. "Where'd he go?"

"He's off!" Breed gasped.

The excitement stopped.

Flick held the pole high over his head. Winding the reel, he ran toward the tent. "He's just runin' for shore." He cranked in most of the line.

Breed looked into the water. At the end of the stretched fishing line, a long dark outline appeared. He turned toward Flick. "I think it got off and you snagged a log."

"Wade in there and take it off," Flick said with excitement still in his voice. "We'll throw another chub on and try again."

Breed stepped to the line. Something splashed at the end of the dark outline. Breed jumped back.

Flick held the pole high. "Don't just stand there. See what it is!"

Breed backed up. "It's too dark. I can't see."

Ballpeen ran toward the tent. "I'll get the lantern."

He was back in a flash. Hovering behind the quiet lantern light, they all moved toward the dark outline. When they were close, a huge fish slapped its fierce tail. Water exploded and splashed into their faces. They jumped back.

"He's runin' again," Flick cried and cranked the reel.

Breed watched the line zip into the water. "That fish just don't want to be caught."

The fish twisted, jumped, and turned. The fishing line twanged and pulled straight. Gears in

Flick's reel gnashed, and the line spun off the spool.

Screwball put his hands on his knees and stared into the water. "He's makin' another run."

Flick reeled the handle into a haze of speed. "I can't turn him." He pumped the pole and cranked in a few wraps of line. The tremendous power of the resistant fish pulled it back out.

The fish weakened and came within a few feet of the shore. Flick relaxed for a second and the fish made another run. The reel handle spun against the tips of his fingers. Flick jammed it against his thigh. It stopped. He re-grabbed the handle and struck up another fighting spree. "He feels like a miniature submarine."

Breed stepped close again. "Yeah, but he's getin' tired."

After one more run, Flick dragged the gallant fish onto the muddy bottom of the shallow water next to shore.

Ballpeen held the lantern and they looked at the resting fish. Its yellow, reflecting eyes glared in every direction and signaled danger.

With eyes bulging with astonishment, everyone stepped back — mouths agape and staring.

Like a defensive weapon, Ballpeen held his hammer and studied the fish. "It's big as a car bumper!"

Flick held onto the pole with both hands. "What are you guys waitin' on? Kick it on shore."

Ballpeen stepped back. "Not me!"

Blo stepped toward the fish, took one look, and backed off. "Me neither. That big muskie ain't gonna bite my bare feet off!"

"That's right! "Breed said with awe. "Those

teeth are razor sharp."

"Talk about gargantuan chickens!" Flick bitched and handed the pole to Screwball. "Here! Take this. I'll get the goddamn thing!"

He started for the fish and stopped. "Give me that lantern."

Breed grimaced. "Watch he don't bite you. One smaller than that, took a big bite out of a little girl's leg."

Flick stopped for a second and stepped into the muddied water — slow and easy.

He held the lantern over the huge fish. Its razor-sharp-toothed mouth was wide open. In the soft yellow glow of the lantern light, its savage eyes glowed and threatened. The small hook was imbedded between its cutting teeth. It was hooked well.

Flick waded close, took a deep breath, and cocked his leg back to kick the fish to shore. When he was at the top of his punt, his other foot slipped on the slimy bottom. He dropped the lantern. Plop! It landed in the mud. Like a chrome rocket, the fish shot straight up. It splashed back down and vanished beneath the black water. A loop of line tangled around the lantern handle and burned on the hot glass. Flick backed up and searched the dark water around him. "Where is he?" He reached for the lantern.

Right in front of him, the gigantic muskie exploded to the surface. Flick jerked his hand away from the lantern and fell backwards. The fish flipped its wide tail on top of the water and lunged for the deep. Flick grabbed the reel and cranked. The burnt line on the lantern broke and the fish pulled it. Like a snake, the line crawled and knotted around the handle of the lantern. The lantern rolled into the water, and the muskie towed it into the inky river.

"Get the lantern," Breed said and watched the dark riffles from the lantern. Flick started after it. The Muskie swirled its tail next to the lantern. Flick stopped.

"I'll get it," Breed said and thought about those big teeth, the little girl, and the big bite of flesh it had taken out of her leg. He stopped.

As if mesmerized, no one went after the lantern. Towing the lantern in a straight line at an incredible speed, the fish swam into the deep. Still moving, thirty, then forty yards downriver, the hot glass sizzled and cracked. Almost out of sight, the kerosene soaked wick inside the globe fluttered a blue and orange flame until it went under and disintegrated into nothing.

Flick slapped himself on his hips and threw up his hands. "Well, there goes the lantern. I should have gone in after it."

"If your old man finds out, there goes your ass, too!" Blo reminded him.

"Yeah," Screwball said. "He'll beat your shoulders right down to your ass and then you'll have to put your hat on to shit!" He smiled in Breed's direction. "Did I say that right?"

In the tent, another reel took off whining. "Hey, that's mine," Ballpeen said.

"Grab it!" Flick said with renewed hope. "Maybe it's him again and we can get that lantern back."

Ballpeen reeled in easily. "Ahh man!" His

355

face fell into a sad frown "It's just a stinkin' carp."

"Yeah, might as well throw it back," Breed said. "They ain't no good to eat."

"But I don't want to catch it again." Ballpeen stuck a Y stick through the carp's gills, dragged the fish up the side of the shore, pushed the stick into the river bottom, and submerged the fish.

Blo, who had crawled back into the tent, looked out and pointed at Flick. "Look! Underwear!"

"Hey, look at the rich kid with underwear." Screwball pointed to Flick.

Flushing with embarrassment, Flick looked at his underwear. "Hey, what happened?"

Blo held the trumpet in his hand. "You know we can add that to our list. First there was hang-ware, that let your balls hang out. Then we had bag-ware, which Screwball has on, big enough for two asses. We have rip-wear, which Breed has on. And we can't forget what Ballpeen has on."

Ballpeen looked in his direction. "Okay, smart ass. What do I have on?"

"With those skid marks . . . crap-wear!"

"Ha-a-a-ant!" Breed chided.

"Ahh, man," Ballpeen whined. Then he turned a cold eye on Blo, paused and spoke up strong. "Blow it out your ass!"

Blo stood up, put both hands on the trumpet, and talked into the mouthpiece. "Blllaaattt! It! Ouuut! Youuur! Assss!"

Ballpeen laughed and Blo played, "When the Saints Come Marching In".

Blo swayed to the beat, and Screwball hopped around like an Indian doing a rain dance and sung, "Oh, when the hang-wear, comes hanging down.

Oh when the rip-wear, comes ripping down. We'll all want to have, underwear. Oh when the bag-wear, bags up your ass, and when the droop-wear, droops down your knees, we'll have the tight-wear, we'll have the rag-wear, but no one, will have Ballpeen's crap-wear, when the crap comes marching in!"

Ballpeen wagged his head around in a circle. "Ahh, hant on me." He jumped up and joined Screwball dancing in the circle. They all joined in, sung out of tune, and slung sand into the air.

When their feet got tired and Blo quit playing, they accused Flick of being rich because he had underwear. He tried to wiggle out of it, claiming they were tight-wear, but they all voted underwear and crawled back into the tent.

Breed looked at Blo and the trumpet. "Hey, Blo, how about playing "Taps"?"

Blo put the trumpet to his lips and blew one puff of air. Not a note came out. "I can't."

"Why not?" Breed asked. "You used to walk down the street and play 'Taps' almost every night."

Blo put the trumpet under his arm and hugged it like it was a Teddy Bear. "I don't know. Ever since One-Finger-Burke took me to reform school I haven't been able to play 'Taps'."

Breed propped his head up on one elbow. "What did they do to you? I thought it was just for a visit to scare you."

Blo stared at the bottom of the tent and scratched the side of his face. "I don't know. I don't even know what I did. I just don't know."

The river rose and fell a few inches and they were asleep.

Chapter 27

Above Shell Island, up on the hill, Hog and Pud walked under healthy trees laden with leaves. Moonlight that could have helped the late straggling travelers see through the thick brush was blocked.

In the darkness, Pud bumped into Hog. "You sure this is the way, Hog?"

"Look Pud," Hog said, trying to be nice. "Just follow me."

"Well golly," Pud whined. "How can I follow you when I can't see?" He walked on Hog's heels.

Hog stopped and turned toward Pud. "Wait a minute! You goddamn dummy!"

As if he were about to cry, Pud said, "Well, I can't see. My foot's stuck."

Hog groaned. "What do you want me to do about it? It's your foot!"

"I don't know," Pud whined. "You're not mad at me, are you?"

"No!" Hog exhaled. "I'm not mad at you. Leave your shoe here."

"But I don't want to leave my shoe here."

"Come on, Pud," Hog said, his patience growing thin. "We'll come back and get it when it's light."

"I can't see. How are we going to get to the island?"

Hog couldn't take it anymore. He walked away from Pud.

Grunting and wheezing, Pud pulled his foot from his shoe and shouted into the darkness. "Hog, where are you?"

Hog turned around, stepped to Pud, and put his

hand on his shoulder. "Look Pud." He placed the cigarette Neal had given him between his lips. "I'll light this cigarette." He lit the cigarette, took it out of his mouth, and held it in front of Pud's face.

Staring at the bright orange glow of the cigarette, Pud's square-pupiled eyes crossed. As if confused, he dipped his neck and swallowed. "Now what should I do?"

Hog shook the cigarette. "Just follow the light on the cigarette. You can see that without bumping into me. Can't you, Pud?"

"Sure!"

Hog lit another match and looked for Pud's shoe. It was nowhere near the glow of the light. He let Pud blow out the match. "Happy Birthday, Pud." He turned toward the island.

After three steps, Pud grunted and bumped into him — again.

"It figures," Hog muttered and tramped through the dark brush.

Grunting and wheezing, Pud followed right on Hog's ass. "Is it my birthday today?" – Grunt Wheeze – "Maybe they'll have a party for me when we get there."

Hog groaned inwardly. "Pud, if you don't get off my ass, we'll have an ass kicking party."

Pud tramped on the heel of his shoe, again.

Hog started to cuss, but shook his head in defeat.

He kept on walking.

After Pud managed to tramp down the heels of Hog's shoes, they made it to the riverbank where Pud tripped and fell into the water. Hog ignored him and called across the river, "Hey you guys, come and get us."

No one answered.

Pud stood ankle deep in the water, placed his hands together as if he were praying, and jerked them toward the island. "Flick!" he yelled. "Please, please, come get us, please!"

No one answered.

Hog tried again. "Hey! You lazy bastards. Get your asses out of bed!"

Flick yelled through the canvas tent. "I don't care if the President of the United States is right outside this tent. I' ain't comin' out."

Hog placed a restraining hand on Pud's shoulder. "Stay here. I'll swim across and get the boat."

Pud looked across the river and then into the darkness of where they had come from. "Hurry up. I'm scared."

Hog swam across, got the boat, and came back for Pud. Pud stepped in; and trying to row with his hands, he kicked the sides of the boat. A deep bass sound thumped across the water. The rest of the crew complained, but they weren't getting up.

Hog pulled the boat onto the sandy shore, and Pud and he dripped onto the island.

Inside the tent, using his theory that if he kept one eye open, he would only be half awake, Flick cocked open a sleepy eye. "What did you guys do? Get lost?"

"No," Hog answered and wrung out his wet clothes next to the dying fire. "We got a ride right after we left. Some crazy guy called Neal picked us up. He had a bottle and gave us a couple of sips. He was crazy. He tried to tell me the whole world was like a dump."

Flick nonchalantly tilted his head to one side and leaned back. "You guys look like you had a bottle apiece. Did you bring any back?"

"Naw, we got lost."

"I thought you just said you didn't get lost."

Hog hung his wet clothes on the tent next to the drying swimming suits. "We didn't get lost." His forehead wrinkled as if he had a headache. "We were always right where we were." He crawled in the tent and lay down.

Outside, Pud's face brightened in the light of the fire. "Let's go swimming."

"Don't forget to tie a cement block to your feet," Hog said and covered his ears.

"What?" Pud said.

"Go ahead and swim," Flick said, "but don't dive where you're standing. It's too shallow."

As if he were trying to convince himself, Pud nodded with quick jerks. "I think I can swim now." He turned his head toward Flick. "You know you saved my life?"

Flick waved his hand down in disgust. "Yeah, Pud, dive anywhere you want." He pointed to the dying fire. "And put some wood on the fire."

Pud threw a green-log on the fire. It smoked and the flames of the fire dwindled and struggled for life.

In the dying fire light, Pud flexed his knees and aimed his hands toward the water. "Watch this swan dive."

Hog peeked out from under the blanket and watched. Pud stood where Flick had told him not to dive. Flexing his knees, he bounced up and down.

Hog turned and pulled the covers over his head. "Dumb shit."

Out of the corner of his one opened eye, Flick watched Pud.

Pud dove in, headfirst. It was a half-assed frog-legged dive into two feet of water that had a black soft-mud bottom.

Ready to throw his blanket off, Hog rested his hand on its corner and faced Flick. "You gonna get that drunken half-wit?"

Flick opened both eyes. Pud's feet stuck up out of the water. And he wasn't coming up. He kicked his feet and splashed the water.

"He's drowning," Hog said and threw the blankets back.

Flick jumped to his knees. "Goddamn idiot!" He dove out of the tent, ran over to Pud, grabbed his flailing feet, and pulled him out. Black slimy mud covered his head and made it look like someone had hit him in the face with a bucket of thick chocolate pudding. Through the white ring around his mouth, he choked and gasped for breath. Flick slapped him on the back. Water flew from his lungs and sprayed out his opened mouth.

Stupefied as usual, Pud opened his cat-like eyes and looked up. "What happened?"

"I told you not to dive here!" Flick said. "Wash your face off, and while you're doing it, try not to fall in."

Pud rinsed his face and went over to the fire. It was almost out.

Flick pulled the green log out of the fire. "This green stuff won't burn, Pud." He picked up a piece of wood from the big pile and handed it to Pud.

"Use this dry stuff."

Pud held onto the dry wood and didn't throw it into the fire. "I'm sorry, real sorry. Honest. I'm sorry you had to save my life again."

Flick took a few sticks of dry firewood from the big pile and tossed them into the smoldering fire. It crackled and came back to life.

"Don't worry about it, Pud. Stay here and dry off."

While Pud stood next to the fire holding the piece of wood, Flick walked to the riverbank and searched for his father's lost lantern.

Pud threw the piece of wood onto the fire and turned. The rekindled fire grew and threw heat onto his cold back.

He smiled.

He liked it.

He wanted more.

Standing in front of the pile of firewood, he spread his legs wide, and bent over. Like a dog digging for a bone, he flung wood through his legs. It landed in the fire. Flames intensified, crawled up and around the wood, and grew tall and wide.

Heat radiated through the air and onto Flick's back. He jerked around and looked at the expanding fire. "Goddamn-it! Pud, what the hell did you do now?"

Pud didn't answer. With a happy smile on his face, he stood next the fire.

Flick rushed back to take some wood off the fire. But he was too late. The small campfire flared into a roaring bonfire. It lit up the entire Island.

The fire beamed hot light into the open flap of the tent. In the sudden heat, steam flowed from the wet swimming suits and Hog's wet clothes.

Hog sat up, kicked away the blankets with his feet, and yelled at Pud. "Hey, Shit Midas. Turn that stinkin' light out!"

Holding his hands toward the warmth of the fire, Pud turned his head toward Flick. "Are we gonna put the fire out now, Flick?"

"No, goddamn it, Pud," Flick said, agitated at his stupidity. "We ain't putin' out the fire."

"But Hog said—" Pud said and sniveled, "to turn out the light."

"Damn!" Flick said in disbelief. "Just get in the tent. You're dry now." He turned toward the tent. Pud was right behind him. He bumped into him.

Flick jerked around and shouted. "Get off the stupid shit, Pud!" He grabbed him by the arm and threw him into the tent. Pud stumbled on top of everyone and they all bitched.

Pud apologized and repeated, "Flick saved my life," until he passed out.

After everything had quieted down, in his semi-state of sleep, Screwball sung, "Pud got hit with a bucket of shit and the band played on . . . You know Flick saved my life! Ha-a-a-ant!"

Chapter 28

Above the river and up on the railroad bed, a main liner howled a sick horn. Three locomotive engines panting like big running dogs, rushed on down the line. Smashing through the summer air, lead-red boxcars, with white numbers painted on their sides, followed. Like little kids running to keep up with the bigger kids, a long line of black tank cars clacked past. At the end, a red caboose came and went. The Eastbound freight train was on its way to some magic city.

In the army-green cow tent below, Breed's sleepy eyes blinked at the sound, closed again, and he dreamed a familiar dream.

He was sandwiched in-between a mass of bubble-gummed breathed kids who had graduated from the local high school. The promise of big money fueled the pubescent air with ignorance. Enveloped in the humid bubble gum stench, it was hard to breathe. It was hard to think.

Breed tried to wiggle out of the crowd, but it drove into him like the solid steel blade on a bulldozer. He was pushed to the sounds of the steel mill.

At the entrance to the mill, the crowd parted. He walked forward, turned, and faced the crowd. Like a jury foreman, a spokesman from the crowd rose up. It was the rotten-armed cancer man who had held the dime on the Rat Street Bridge. He pointed to Breed and spoke in a voice slurred with fatigue. "Guilty of being different."

Whap! A man with a chopped off finger slammed a gavel down. "Sentenced to forty years in the mill."

The chopped off finger man and the crowd vanished, but had been replaced with the odor of sulfur-filled air mixed with sweat and alcohol-laced workers. Breed was working in the steel mill. The sour taste of stale coffee told him he was working the graveyard shift — midnight to morning with the threat of a double shift. He hated it. He regretted ever having started working in the filthy place.

When he had started, he had been just like all the other fresh-out-of-high-school kids. He had claimed he was only going to work a few years until he had enough money saved to open a business or go to college.

Step-by-step and year-by-year, Breed made excuses to stay. He put off quitting.

His dream became a movie, and it got longer each time he dreamed it. He watched older workers make the same excuses, have the same hopes for the future; and he watched the other new workers do the same thing. Twenty, thirty, and forty years later, they were in the same mill, breathing and eating the same dirt and talking the same talk. Years of observation did not show any excessive display of brilliant wit.

Intellectually Breed had become just like the others. He stayed in a rundown league of conversation that was always connected with sex or what turn someone was working. No one quit. It was the only place that paid good money. He stayed. They all stayed. Overtime pay was more than a newly graduated college person could make. After they cashed their first paycheck, Breed watched other workers buy brand new cars. They

366

had to keep working just to make the payments. They couldn't live without their new car, they might lose their girlfriends; and they might be forced to drive a used car.

Breed did not want to be in that mill. It was a nightmare. Like many before him, he had started work with his head held high. He believed he had a much better education than the ignorant immigrant workers who could hardly speak English. Even though in real life he was not even in high school, in his dream, he bragged, "I graduated from high school. See! I have a diploma."

Usually, his dream would end when he came to the part where he had sneaked under the fence, like he had done in real life and watched workers in the mill. This time, the dream would not stop. He was becoming the old, toothless steelworker they had seen by the acid pumps.

He dreamed on.

He fought the mill's drawn out process of brain atrophy. He didn't like it at first, but the mill world became a new home for him. He eventually learned that it wasn't high school, where the only thing he had to worry about was if the teacher was looking or what girl was going with whom. He never wanted to become part of the blue-collar lifestyle. He was cool and wanted to stay that way, but that cool high-school shit didn't work when a man's life was in danger. Here, pubescent ignorance would injure or kill. A dangerous unsafe worker was not tolerated or accepted. And Breed wanted to be accepted no matter where he was. But even if he were accepted, the threat of cancer still hung in his dream.

He continued to sleep.

Then, far from Shell Island, high up on the distant hill, like the irritating sound of a bad alarm clock, the steel mill's steam whistle shrieked loud and cut through the night. Breed semi-woke. He stared out the tent into the night. The low light of the fire glowed like the light that had glowed on the old, toothless steelworker when he was blowing snot-rockets. Breed thought about the old steelworker and hoped he would never end up like him. He drifted back into the continuing dream of the mill trap.

The dream placed him years into the mill with a memory of a few close calls of death. After a few drunken nights and some good laughs, he blended in with the other workers; and there was no separation of work and home; there was no cool; and there was nothing cool in the mill. All things became the same. The paper and pencil education stopped. Breed discovered that he was the one who was ignorant, not the old mill workers. He watched himself progress backwards into the limited physical world. His vocabulary increased with new cuss words, backed up with idle threats, and a learned he-man personality emerged. He tried to fight the mind-altering mill system but he couldn't. He blended in and was finally accepted. He became a part of the rude residents who felt they had to defend their workplace territories against the threat of new educated workers and new ideas that might cost them their jobs. "Don't tell them a goddamn thing! They'll learn your job and take it."

In his dream, Breed had become a permanent mill worker. A sorry stone of sadness filled his heart.

He awoke.

He kicked the flap of the tent open. A new morning met his eyes. Outside, a little stream of white smoke, from the remains of the smoldering bonfire, swirled up into the gray morning mist. The sun's first rays of the morning filtered through the trees and beamed down like cathedral light. At selected places between the leaves, little brown sparrows hopped from branch to branch and tweeted happily into the new day. Breed was on Shell Island. He was glad his dreams of being a mill worker weren't real.

He looked up. Although a damp and misty drizzle hovered over the river, above, a beautiful clear blue sunshine sky domed over the island.

As the mist rose, downriver, birds, bigger than the scrawny sparrows of Traptown, scouted over familiar water and dove for secret smiling fish that suddenly appeared. It was a perfect morning to get up early. But in the easy-going laziness of a great vacation, no one really had to get up. Breed covered his head and went back to sleep.

When he awoke again, the sun had made its way skyward and burned off the gray mist.

The other sleepy heads woke.

Flick crawled out of the tent and stood up. "Get your asses out of the tent and make breakfast."

Hog stuck his head out from under his blanket. "Blow it out your ass!"

Breed rolled over to his side and looked out the tent. Half burnt pieces of firewood slashed a circle around the smoking fire pit.

Flick bent over, picked up the ends of wood

369

and heaped them into a campfire. "All right, if you sleepy-headed bastards don't want to eat, go ahead and sleep your asses off."

The fire rekindled.

Flick wrapped his shirttail around the handle of the black iron skillet and held it over the fire. He mixed the government-surplus powdered eggs with water and sprinkled in small bits of surplus orange cheese. While the crew played grab-ass in the tent, Flick banged on the skillet and yelled, "Come get these eggs sittin' on a plate, waitin' to get ate."

Screwball imitated Flick, "I don't care if the president of the United States is right outside the tent. I ain't comin' out."

Hog rose to his knees, hooked a corner of a blanket over his arm, and stood extra erect. Imitating a waiter at a high-class restaurant, he pointed to Flick and the eggs. "Gentleman, awake! We have a litany of fabulous food on the menu."

Blo let out a low whistle. "What's litany?"

"Litany?" Screwball said with question in his eyes. Then he smiled. "Litany? Litany good farts lately."

Smiling, Hog looked at Screwball. "Gas delivery!" He grunted, but no sound was heard. He immediately left the tent.

"We ain't trying to steal paint," Breed said remembering the warehouse store incident. "But I ain't taking any chances." He immediately picked up the end of his blanket and covered his nose and mouth.

Screwball covered his head and talked from under his sleeping bag. I ain't comin out until I can see through that green cloud."

370

Pud rolled over and opened his eyes. "I don't see any green cloud." His eyes blinked and he sat up.

Breed let the blanket fall from his face, opened his eyes, and watched out the end of the tent.

Outside, Hog walked up to the fire and looked into the skillet full of yellow fluffy eggs. "They ain't on a plate."

Flick held the skillet toward Hog. "Shut up and eat. We got a lotta stuff to do today."

Ballpeen threw off his blankest and stumbled out of the tent. "Yeah, like what?"

Crawling with his hands and knees, Blo looked back at Breed. "Stay low. The Hog gas won't get you." He crawled out of the tent and looked toward the fire. "Yeah, lotta what?" he asked Flick, and dizzy Pud bumped into him.

Breed held his breath, bent over, and ran out of the tent.

Flick took a bite of egg, and waved his fork around in the air. "Well for openers, we got firewood to get." He pointed the fork at Pud. "And not that goddamn green stuff."

Pud smiled his usual sheepish grin. "Gee, I'm sorry. I can't see in the dark, you know."

"I don't see why not," Hog said. "You got square eyes like a cat."

"You can say dat," Blo said, "but can you prove dat. Pud has a hard time seeing in the daytime."

The smell of food wafted into the tent. Screwball crawled out and completed the crew. As he picked up a fork, a fish splashed in the backwash. He turned toward the sound. "I'll get your ass," he threatened and dug into the eggs in the

371

big black skillet.

The eggs disappeared, quickly.

Flick rinsed the skillet in the river and walked back to the fire. "Now that that's done." He bushed his hands together. "We can get to the important stuff."

Ballpeen stretched out on the warm sand. "Yeah, like lying in the sun."

"I'll second that." Breed lifted his arm. "I'm still cold from last night."

Pud picked up the green wood Flick had taken out of the fire and turned toward Flick. "Want me to put some more wood on the fire?"

Flick snatched the wood out of his hand. "Just leave that fire alone."

That fish jumped again. "I'm gonna get that one." Screwball grabbed his fishing pole and walked softly up the edge of the island.

"While you're up there," Hog hollered to deliberately scare the fish, "see if you can find Pud's shoe."

"Yeah," Screwball grumbled, "that's if I happened to come around that way." He paused and drunkenly weaved. "Hey! Back that way again. Hey!"

As if they were on an island of a tropical resort, Breed and the rest of the crew leaned back on their elbows and relaxed on the clean white sand.

Breed listened to the sounds of the river. Something splashed on the blind side of the island. He turned and looked. Tree branches waved but there was no wind. Screwball had not gone that way. Breed stood up. Oars splashed on top of the water. He stepped toward the boat. Two big kids were rowing the great green boat away.

He cried, "They're stealing the boat!"

Flick jumped up and started after them. "Come on you guys, they're takin' the boat!"

No one had shoes on their feet. It didn't matter. Everyone but Screwball joined the chase and ran up the side of the island. Opened clamshells lying on the shore broke under their feet and jagged into their flesh.

Breed waved his hands toward the river. "Get in the water."

They shallow dove into the water and came up stroking.

They swam fast, but the kids in the boat rowed faster.

And just like a twit who would throw grass seed into a freshly tilled garden, Pud was in the water, drowning.

Hog looked back and watched him flop around in the water. "Ahh, man! Shit Midas strikes again."

They stopped the chase, grabbed Pud, and drug him up onto the riverbank. While Pud coughed out water, Flick ran up to the railroad tracks and caught the tail end of a slow moving string of freight cars.

After Pud quit coughing and breathed easy, Hog tilted his head back and looked toward heaven. "Shit Midas, saved again!"

They renewed the chase.

Up ahead, like soft friendly foliage, light green plants stood tall. Under the heart-shaped leaves tiny crystalline needle-sharp spines pointed out. The slightest touch and they would crawl into the skin, disappear, stay there, camp out for days, infest the victim with a prickling sensation that begged to be scratched, and then rear up into red puffy rashes. Breed and the others ran around the jagged itch weed. Pud ignored the hazard and ran right on through the skin infesting plants.

Hog yelled back at him, "That's itch weed! You dumb ass."

They continued running. A fallen tree blocked their way. They jumped over it. Sharp rocks stung their bare feet.

In unison, they bitched.

Up on the railroad tracks, Breed balanced on top of the rail and ran ahead. The others lagged behind and ran on the brown creosote ties. Breed stopped and looked back. His friend's toes dragged on the rough wood of the railroad ties, and their feet tramped on cobblestones. Pain showed in their faces. Breed turned and continued running down that smooth, skinny rail.

Upriver, the train picked up speed. Flick hopped off the freight car, ran down the bank, and stepped toward the boat thieves.

Breed craned his neck to see what the thieves were doing. In the distance, they were hiding the boat under the railroad trestle.

A blond haired kid, with a purple-pimpled face, pulled on the bow of the boat, and a kid with a flat top haircut sat next to him.

Breed recognized them.

"It's those assholes from that pink Ford!" he said out loud. It was Purple and Flat Top. Fueled with hate and revenge, he ran faster.

Just above the shoreline, Flick stopped on top of a steep incline. Staring at Purple and Flat Top, he reached up and touched his lips where he had

374

been cut in the fight. "I owe you bastards." Like a bandy rooster ready to take on the world, down the bank he went.

Purple and Flat Top looked up and took notice.

"What do you want?" Purple demanded to know.

Flick clinched his fists. "Give us our boat back! You thievin' bastards!"

Purple smugly smirked. "Your boat?"

"Yeah, our boat, zit face! I'm takin' it back."

Purple dismissively waved his hand. "Go away, little man." He turned his back.

Flick took a swing. Purple jerked. The punch whipped past his head.

While Flat Top was shoving the boat into the water, Purple puffed up his chest and talked down at Flick. "How many times do I have to" — he wheeled around pushed Flick onto the muddy riverbank — "kick your ass?"

Flick slid down the slippery riverbank and looked up at Breed who was on top of the incline.

Searching for help, Breed looked back at the others. They were still stumbling down the tracks.

"Ahh man!" Breed said, and Flick quit sliding and plopped, spread-eagle, in the thick brown mud. Purple and Flat Top jumped into the boat and rowed away.

Flick jumped up and swam after them. But when he dog-paddled close, Bap! Purple whapped him in the head with the oar. He reared back for another hit. Flick dove under the water and swam to shore.

Breed slipped and fell on the riverbank. He struggled to his hands and knees and looked back over his shoulder. The others were coming. "Come on you guys," he yelled. "They ain't gonna beat all of us."

Trailing behind and tripping on the railroad ties, Pud cried, "We got them on the run."

Hog wrinkled one eye toward Pud. "Yeah, right. Don't forget to fall in again."

Standing knee deep in water, Flick held his bleeding head and breathed in deep labored breaths. Through his blood-covered eyes, he stared at a cement block setting on the bank. "If I could see, I'd drop that thing right on their heads."

Flat Top tilted his head up and hollered at Breed. "Hey, Rat Boy, thanks for the boat."

Breed stared at the boat and the two kids. He felt the pain of his kicked-in shins and the pain in his side. He touched the back of his hand. There were still scabs where Flat Top had tramped on it with his hard shoe and twisted it. Flashes of his dead dog, his broken BB gun, Blo's beer bottle beat-in face; and Flick's bloody mouth, burned in his mind. Rage filled his entire being.

He ran down the riverbank and pulled on the heavy cement block. With ease, it sucked out of the glue-like mud. He picked it up, lugged it through the mud, up the steep incline, and onto the railroad trestle.

From high on the bridge, he looked down. Pud fell down the riverbank and landed in the water next to Flick. Roaring with laughter, Purple and Flat Top pointed at Pud.

Breed took a few steps and analyzed the situation. If his friends could keep Purple and Flat Top busy, he could do it.

376

Lugging the cement block, he walked to the trestle and stopped on the steep incline.

Hog yelled to the thieves, "Come on back, you chicken shit bastards."

Breed held the block and stepped to the center of the trestle. He looked down and stopped. The longer he held the big block, the heavier it got. It hurt to hold it. He could almost hear the pain in his arms. He ignored it. He waited.

Purple sat in the boat and shouted at Flick and the others. "Come on in. We'll kick all your little asses."

"Thanks for being afraid to come back and fight," Flick yelled across the water.

Flat Top held his middle finger high. "Here, this is for your mothers."

Hog found a muddy rock, picked it up and threw it at Purple. "Catch this, crater face."

The rock plopped into the water ten feet away from the boat.

Flat Top yelled over the water, "Nice try, asshole." Then he laughed.

Flick and the others picked up rocks and threw them. The rocks all fell short but a few came close. Purple turned serious. He cussed, rowed the boat under the trestle; and with grunting effort, he tried to row upriver. But the current was too strong. It held the boat directly under the bridge. Breed was right above it. Purple made a strong pull on the oars and the boat momentarily stopped. Breed let the block fall and immediately wished he hadn't. In his mind, electric flashes and sparks flew. The switch had been pulled. He was frying in the electric chair, for murder. Lard Man was laughing.

But wait!

The flying block whooshed right between Purple and Flat Top. It smashed straight through the bottom of Ballpeen's flimsy boat. Purple's and Flat Top's eyes popped wide open. They sat in awe. The boat spun in a circle and began sinking into the depths of life ending darkness of the bottomless drop-off.

Flick and the others stood under the trestle, pointed and taunted. Purple and Flat Top jumped out of the sinking boat and swam to opposite shore, where they struggled to their feet and ran away.

The green boat disappeared below the surface, and the oars popped up from the deep bottom.

Breed had never seen a boat sink that fast. It was as if it had a mind of its own. It was as if its sole purpose in life had been to sink. It had only been waiting for a reason, any reason, to put itself out of its misery and sail into the bottomless, mysterious depths of a river drop-off. But Ballpeen had built it. That explained it all.

None of the crew would swim down into the depths of the life threatening undertows and darkness of that drop-off to find it. It was the titanic end of the great green boat.

The last swirls of water spun, and air bubbles rose to the surface. Hog turned toward Ballpeen and extended his hand. "Congratulations, Ballpeen, it looks like your boat wasn't a piece of shit after all."

A glimmer of hope shone in Ballpeen's eyes. "Thanks, Hog." Deeply touched, he wiped a tear from his eye.

Hog smiled a titanic smile. "You're welcome,

Ballpeen. But you know all shit floats and your junk boat just sunk."

Screwball tapped Ballpeen on the shoulder. Ballpeen turned. Screwball said loud and clear, "Ha-a-a-ant!"

The hope faded in Ballpeen's eyes. "Ahh, man!" He dove into the water and swam after the floating oars. He caught them, towed them to shore, and threw them in the weeds — for the future.

Flick's head stopped bleeding and all was quiet. Until, ducks quacked in the distance.

The crew swam and walked upriver and began what Flick called a "Reconnaissance Mission."

After they had traveled a respectable distance, they rounded a bend and stopped. In front of their eyes it was as if someone were holding a huge picture postcard of a vacation resort. On the right, bright-green brushes and brown stumps, just perfect for bass fishing, sat in calm water. Massive silver willows lined clean grassy banks on both sides of the river; and right in the center of this panoramic view, chained and locked to a brown wooden dock, three freshly painted boats projected out over the clean water.

Although the boats were a pleasant surprise, Breed and the crew were unaccustomed to seeing water such as this. It gave them a glimpse of what was, what should have been, and what could be.

The bright picture blackened. Up from the docks, voices echoed down from a worn path. One voice rang out loud and clear. "We'll check and make sure they didn't come up here to steal the boats."

Breed and the others dove under the water,

379

came up in the bass-hiding brush, and watched.

Eight big kids tramped down the dirt-beaten-path and unlocked the boats. Flick wanted to go right up to them and fight them for the boats right then and there. It seemed a fair exchange for all the ass kicking's and for all the boats that had been stolen from them. But Breed and the others talked him out of it. The numbers weren't in their favor; and if they had to run, there was no bridge to jump off.

They submerged their bodies in the water up to their necks and watched through the brush. While the six other kids watched, two kids unlocked a boat and rowed close enough for Breed to read the red print on the pack of cigarettes rolled up in the passenger's T-shirt sleeve. Displayed like a medal of honor, it read Winston. It was Flat Top. The other kid smiled a buck-toothed smile and playfully hit him on the shoulder. "Your old man made you feed the ducks before you could leave. What a candy ass."

Flat Top jerked sideways. "Get off my ass."

"Can't you take a joke?"

"Just row the boat."

Blo slipped and riffled the water.

As if he were trying to see through a foggy window, Buck Teeth quit rowing and gazed in the Breed's direction. "What was that?"

Flat Top stretched his white greasy neck and looked in Breed's direction. "I don't see anything. It's probably just an old carp."

Buck Teeth rowed downriver. Let's keep checking. I'm not taking any chances. Those sneaky, little cock suckers could be anywhere. I don't want them taking our boats."

You mean their boats." Flat Top chuckled. "We probably took them off them at one time or another." He punched Buck Teeth in the shoulder. "If me and Purple hadn't sunk it right in front of them, we would have had another one."

Peering downriver, Buck Teeth pulled on one oar. "I don't see anybody."

"They ain't here," Flat Top said. "Let's go. I have to help Purple steal some gas. He has to pick up your sister."

Amazed, Breed silently mouthed, Buck Teeth's sister is Purple's crooked-toothed girlfriend.

Nodding at Flat Top, Buck Teeth rowed in a circle and headed back toward the dock. "Yeah, tell Purple three guys are looking for their camp. If they find it, they'll tear it apart and kick their asses."

Flick whispered under his breath, "Why those rotten—"

Hog shook Flick's shoulder. "Quiet. Let's listen and see what they're gonna do."

And they did.

After Buck Teeth and Flat Top chained the boat to the dock and locked it, the upriver kids lollygagged around the dock, combed their hair, exchanged useless words of coolness, and decided to leave. Five went one way and three went another.

"See you guys at the Hop tonight," Buck Teeth said.

Someone said, "Sounds like a plan, Stan."

Broadcasting the limit of his intelligence, Flat Top raised his voice and uttered an old worn cliché.

381

"Yeah, don't take any wooden nickels, man!"

Watching them wigwag away and try to impress each other with overused strings of slang, Breed wondered if they would be ignorant all their lives.

Breed and the others waited for a good while to make sure Flat Top and his gang were gone. When all was calm, they swam to the bend, climbed up the soft mossy bank, walked the steel railroad rails, and headed back to Shell Island.

Close to the island and down river, they stopped and stood on the rails. A lone figure walked toward them.

Breed stared at the nearing configuration. "Maybe it's a bum!"

No one talked. They all curiously watched. The little man tramped close and made crunching sounds on the ballast between the dark-brown creosote-soaked ties.

For a lingering moment, they stood still — silent and open-mouthed. All they could do was stare. It was as if the man were an imaginary character.

With his wrinkled face beaming in the sun, he carried one of those fake paper satchels that was as old and weather-beaten as his aging face.

As he crunched before them, Flick broke the silence. "Hey pop! Where ya goin'?"

The old man didn't stop or break his quick stride. He looked over his shoulder. "Headed for Canady, going to write the great American novel." He motioned for them to follow.

No one did.

He turned his head and looked back. "Name's

Ronald K. Myers." He turned his head back. "Headed for Canady!" He kept walking with those long strides.

In a temporary stupor, Breed and his friends watched the man grow smaller. He blended into the narrowing distant tracks and became a prospective dot that disappeared.

Chapter 29

When Screwball had worked his way up the opposite side of the river, he had heard the call to get the boat; but figured it was a false wolf cry to make him walk back to the campsite for nothing. He was after that big fish. He didn't know what kind of a fish it was. It could be anything, maybe an old bushel basket-mouthed bass; and he wasn't going to take a time out for a lying trick — just so Breed and the others could say, "Hant!"

Holding his fishing pole with his arm cocked in a cast ready position, he focused on the spot where the fish had rippled the water and walked slow and quiet. The toe of his tennis shoe caught on a tree root. When he jerked his foot to catch his balance, his foot thudded on the bank and sent vibrations into the water. A Northern Pike, as big as a boat seat, scuttled out of its hiding place, headed for deep water, and stopped.

Screwball dropped the pole to his side and looked into the water. Off to his right, the wide dark outline of the fish appeared. It fanned its fins and hovered near the surface of the green water. Screwball knew the fish wouldn't stay there long.

He cast his line. The hook dropped into the water a few feet away from the fish. "Ahh, man," he whispered and reeled in for another cast. He lifted his pole and concentrated on casting his line right in front of the fish's mouth. He swished the pole in an ark. His line went out again. The hook dropped over a log. Slowly reeling in line, he tried not to snag the hook on the log. After he reeled three times, the hook sunk deep into the wood.

"Damn!" he said out loud but the fish didn't move. If he could keep quiet and get the snag out, he would have another chance.

Trying to free the hook, he twisted, turned, and jerked his pole. The line broke and he was left with no hook. As if the old fish knew he didn't have a spare hook, it swam next to shore and stopped in front of him.

"Do whatever you want," Screwball said to the fish. "I can't catch you now."

The fish bobbed toward the surface; and as if it were saying, "Hant!" it moved its gigantic tail and swam away.

Screwball sighed. "It figures."

He took off his pants and swam to the other side of the river.

Looking for Pud's shoe, he thrashed along the side of the river and into the weeds and trees. He found the disturbed path of leaves Hog and Pud had made during the night, but no shoe. He rustled through the leaves. Dead sticks snapped under his feet until he found Pud's shoe. It was stuck under a fallen tree limb. He pulled it out, and unfamiliar voices filtered through the trees. Following the sound, he walked toward the island.

Peeking around the leaves on a willow tree, he looked across the water. Three big kids dog paddled across the river and slipped onto the island.

A broad-backed kid with a funny nose was the first to speak. "Your buddy, Harpst, sure was right when he said those dumb kids would chase them when they took their boat."

"Yes-sir-ree!" A redheaded kid said, bent over, and grabbed one of the tent pegs. "They're going to

385

have a nice surprise when they come back and find their camp all tore up." He laughed a sissy tee-hee laugh and pulled up the peg.

A skeleton-armed kid picked up the small food supply. "Look at this lowlife surplus food. These assholes must be reliefers." He flung the food into the river.

The broad-backed kid grinned like a proboscis monkey. "Worthless nobody assholes!" His funny nose wiggled. He kicked the jumbled blankets and sleeping bags all over the sand; and with each kick, his long flexible nose jerked like a short, fat elephant's trunk.

Screwball held Pud's shoe and thrashed out of the brush and weeds, the trees; and leaves; and jaggers. Across the water, the skeleton-armed kid jerked on the tent posts Flick had pounded deep into the island. He couldn't pull them out. He grabbed the canvas tent and pulled. It didn't rip. He gave up, looked at Screwball's sleeping bag, ran over, picked it up, and tossed it into the water.

Screwball watched his rolled-up sleeping bag float down river. He figured something was up. Those kids weren't flats gang kids. If Flick was still mad about the Fudge-Sickle, he may have sent those guys to scare him. He decided to swim out, get his sleeping bag, and go back to the island. Then Flick would jump out and yell, "Hant."

He dove in, swam underwater, surfaced, reached out, and snagged his sleeping bag. He rolled over onto his back, placed the bag on his stomach, swam to Pud's shoe, and placed it on top of his sleeping bag, and swam to the island. When he dragged the bag and shoe up on shore, the three big kids stood abreast and blocked his way.

The broad-backed kid stepped up first. "Who in the hell said you kids could camp on our island?"

Screwball blinked the dripping water from his eyes and looked around the island. Flick and the others were nowhere to be seen. A painful feeling invaded his chest.

The broad-backed kid tightened his fist. "Did you hear me?"

Screwball dropped his wet sleeping bag and set his feet in the mud to run. "Nobody did. It's a free country. We don't have to ask anybody."

The broad-backed kid huffed up and expanded his chest. Looking for approval from his friends, he grabbed Screwball by the front of his wet T-shirt. Then he screamed directly into his face. "Says who? . . . You little cock sucker!"

Screwball knew he couldn't fight them all, but he figured he might be able to talk his way out of it.

"What?" he said out loud to give himself time to think.

"You heard me! You little cock sucker!"

"But I'm trying to quit!" Screwball whined, trying to add humor to the situation."

No one laughed.

"We don't wanna hear your smart mouth!" the broad-backed kid roared, and his cigarette and beer breath blasted into Screwball's face.

Screwball's eyes crossed. He could not keep from staring directly at the kid's funny nose. It looked like a penis. "You're the one with the dick no—" he blurted out before he could stop himself.

"What!" the broad-backed, dick-nosed kid yelled.

Screwball kept his nerve, but he couldn't help himself from staring cross-eyed at that kid's dick nose. He uncrossed his eyes. "The Government owns this island." He pointed across the river. "See that marker?"

Dick Nose loosened his grip and turned his head. Screwball dropped down to the mud and rolled into the water. He kicked, splashed and tried to escape, but in the slippery mud he couldn't get traction. His shit-footed speed was useless.

Dick Nose grabbed him and held his flailing arms. "Thought you could get away, didn't you? . . . Lying asshole!"

Screwball searched his mind for a way out. Dick Nose held him and the skeleton-armed kid punched him in the stomach. That bony fist hurt and knocked the wind from his lungs, but Screwball didn't want to give them the satisfaction of knowing it hurt. Skeleton-arms seemed puzzled. Screwball didn't even flinch. Skeleton-arms stepped back for another shot.

Screwball tensed and searched his mind. That imaginary light bulb above his head lit and shined bright. He remembered what Neal had told Breed. "You don't have to do the same thing everybody else does. There's always a way to get what you need. Sometimes people don't even know they're helping you get it."

Screwball held up his hand and lowered his head. "Wait!" he pleaded.

"What for?" Dick Nose said and grabbed Screwball by the shirt, again.

"If you guys are so tough, why don't you have a gang fight?"

388

Skeleton-arms stepped back to throw another punch. "We don't need a gang fight to kick your little ass!"

Screwball kept his stomach muscles tightened and talked with a strained voice. "Yeah, you guys act pretty tough, three against one."

Skeleton-arms punched him — Humph! — in the stomach. "Just shut up."

Screwball breathed out and relaxed his stomach. "You're chicken to take us all on."

Dick Nose loosened his grip. "I ain't no goddamn chicken!"

Skeleton-arms leaned over and talked directly into Screwball's face. "Yeah, we ain't afraid of you little assholes."

As if to say thanks, Screwball glanced toward the sky. "If you ain't afraid, then let me go. I'll tell the other guys to meet you at the Rat Street Bridge at eight o'clock, Friday."

With severe displeasure showing in his face, Skeleton-arms leaned back and stared at Screwball. "Why Friday?

The redheaded kid poked his finger at Screwball. "And why eight o'clock?"

Screwball thought he had blown it, but an answer popped into his mind that fit right into the kid's dislikeable can-opened values.

"Because we have so many guys, it will take that long to tell them about it." Screwball didn't know if they were buying it, but he kept talking. "And the Hop isn't over until eleven, in case you're not allowed out of the house after curfew."

Dick Nose grinned with sarcastic satisfaction. "That's close. We'll meet you there. Rumble time at eight o'clock, sharp, Friday. And if your guys don't show, I'm going to kick your ass every time I see you! And I'll be looking."

Dick Nose released his grip, snorted with a hollow big nosed laugh; and as if he were garbage, he pushed Screwball away.

The redheaded kid gestured with his hand for his buddies to leave. "No matter what happens, you're gonna get your ass kicked real good."

They waded into the water.

Screwball didn't say anything. He watched. In a half-assed display of their poor swimming abilities, the three kids kicked their feet and flapped their arms harder than necessary and splashed to the other shore.

Screwball figured they were just trying to show off. They had only swum a few feet. Now, they were breathing hard; and they were having a hard time pulling their sorry asses up on the riverbank.

After they were gone, Screwball picked up his pants, fishing pole, and Pud's shoe, dropped them next to the fallen tent, and tried to salvage the campsite. Picking up camping gear, he couldn't get over the sight of that kid's dick nose; and he wondered if he had escaped from some kind of a circus sideshow.

He shook his head in disbelief. "Damn! That kid was ugly."

Chapter 30

Across the river, Breed and company grab-assed down the riverbank toward the camp. Pud tripped over his own feet and stumbled into the water. Flick went after him, again. After he towed him to the island and dropped him on the sand, Pud immediately began scratching himself where the itch weed had caused a rash.

Flick shook his head and scanned the scattered campsite. The tent pegs had been pulled out of the ground. As if a slouching midget was under it, the cow canvas drooped; and blankets and bedding lay in various places on the sand. When he looked to where the muskie had taken his father's lantern, the handle of the big black skillet stuck out of the muddy part of the shore. He stooped over, pulled the skillet out of the mud, and turned toward Screwball. "What happened?"

Screwball lackadaisically flapped his arms. "Three of those big kids came and ripped the place up."

Flick took a deep breath and exhaled with a low whistle. "Why didn't you call for us?"

Screwball rocked back on his heels. "Because I knew you were too far away, and anyway" — he shrugged — "I saved most of the stuff before that big kid with a nose that looks like a dick punched me in the gut." He looked at Pud. He was still sitting in the sand, scratching.

Screwball picked up the lost shoe and offered it to Pud. "Hey, Pud, here's your shoe. You think you can stop scratching long enough to put it on?"

"Okay, I won't scratch anymore," Pud assured

him. He put his shoe on, tied the strings in knots, and continued to scratch.

As if he couldn't believe it, Flick slowly wagged his head. "You sure all they did was punch you in the stomach?"

"Yeah, they were going to let a skinny kid punch my guts out, but I got out of it."

Flick looked at him in disbelief. "Oh yeah? What bright idea did you come up with this time?"

Jerking his thumb at his own chest, Screwball talked in a deep tough-guy voice. "I just kicked their asses off the island."

"Yeah right," Flick said as if convinced. "I know damn well you didn't take on all three of their asses."

"Okay, Screwball, we give up. Blo suspiciously stared at Screwball. "What kind-a off-the-wall stunt did you pull off this time?"

Hog put his fist on his nose, stuck out his elbow to make it look like a big, long nose, and bobbed his head. "What did you do, suck that kid's dick nose?"

"Blow it out your ass, Hog!" Screwball barked back.

Hog hunched over, moved his arm like an elephant's trunk, and grunted. "Hant! Hant! Hant!"

Flick reached up and stopped Hog's swinging arm. "Let him talk."

Screwball spread his arms and lifted his palms. "I just challenged them to a gang fight."

Alarm shown in Flick's face. Searching, he looked up and down the river. "You what?"

"I told them they were chicken to fight all of us

392

and made a gang fight for eight o'clock, Friday."

Flick threw his hands up in disgust. "Oh just great!"

Hog peed in the sand and wrote his name. He turned toward Pud. "That's your spelling lesson for today."

Pud nodded and smiled.

As if "gang fight" had just registered in his mind, Hog snapped his head in Screwball's direction. "A gang fight? That's terrific, just fine and dandy, exactly what we need. Another gang down on our asses."

Flick walked around in a circle. "Yeah, it ain't bad enough we got to play shit and piss with those bastards downriver. He threw his hands into the air. Oh, hell no!" He stopped walking. "Now you got to go and start something with these guys. It ain't bad enough that we have to put up with their crap up here. Now you fixed it so they'll be coming down to the bridge." He started walking in that circle again. "Hell! With both gangs after us, we won't have a place to swim."

Like an extra jab, Blo added, "Yeah, dumb ass!"

Screwball rolled his hand as if he were cranking some kind of a machine. "Pay no attention to the man behind the curtain." He whistled into the air. "If you kids are done bitchin', I'll give you a treat!"

Flick quit pacing. His forehead wrinkled with confusion. "What's the matter with you? Ain't you tired of gettin' your ass kicked all the damn time?"

While Flick waited for an answer, Screwball shrugged, dropped down, and sat cross-legged on the ground.

Flick placed his hands on his hips and looked down at Screwball. "Well?"

Screwball picked up a handful of dry sand and let it sift through his fingers. "When you guys are done talkin' out your ass, I'll tell you the plan, man."

Flick stared at Screwball.

Screwball's expression didn't change. He just sat there.

"All right, smart guy," Flick said and took his hands off his hips. "Let's hear this great plan."

Screwball leaned back in the sand, pointed his finger, and waved it back and forth. "Do you guys remember when we got the flats gang pissed off, and they told us to meet them on the bridge Friday on Monday, eight o'clock, at twelve?"

"Yeah," Flick said. "We remember you started that Friday on Monday crap." He jerked his hand sideways. "So what! We just don't show up."

"What's the big deal?" Ballpeen folded his arms across his chest. "I don't remember the time anyway."

Screwball leaned back on the palms of his hands. "Well, children, I told this upriver gang to meet us there at eight, Friday."

Breed, who had been quiet, let out a short laugh. "That's gonna be funny."

Flick stared at Breed, and then as if something had just registered in his mind, his eyes lit up. "Hey, that's right! All we got to do is keep the flats gang pissed off and make sure they show up for the fight. They won't know the other gang isn't ours."

"No kiddin'," Screwball said. "I'll bet it took

you three days and five nights to figure that out."

"So what are you saying?" Hog asked. "That we're stupid?"

"No we ain't stupid," Flick announced like a man giving a speech. "We got to start getting our minds to work."

"Hey that's what we were talking about last night," Breed said, "just before Pud got his head stuck in the mud."

Hell yes," Hog said. "We're smarter than those dimwitted flunkies."

"When you think about it," Breed said, "It's actually our own fault that we get all these ass kicking's and put-downs." He was suddenly mad at himself for not thinking of it sooner. "What are we, ignorant or what?"

"You're what!" Blo said just to agitate and sneered through his false teeth.

Breed burst into a tension-releasing laugh. "Blow it out your ass, Blo!"

"Hant!" Blo flecked back.

Screwball continued the conversation. "All those big kids think they are so clean and white but run around with dirty assholes just like the rest of the world."

Flick paced up and down the sandy point on the island. "What the hell are we always doing?" he questioned out loud and waved his hands around to help him talk. "What is this stuff all the damn time? It's the same stuff over and over. We ain't workin' in the mill. We don't need to be doing this same stuff over and over!"

"Oh Yeah?" Screwball questioned. "We must like it. We keep doin' it."

To make a point, Breed made a fist and threw out his finger. "That's right." He gave a faint tilt to his head. "And because everybody else took it when they were growing up, everybody thinks we're supposed to take it, too." He paused. "And the more we take it, the more they dish it out."

Flick lifted an eyebrow. "Maybe it's a big game, and those are the rules we're supposed to play by."

Screwball flashed a crooked smile. "Sounds like a game where they bring an extra sack of shit and throw it right in your face."

Hog pointed his finger at Flick. "The main thing is—" He waited for Flick to look at him. "Don't get excited."

Flick's eyes narrowed. "What are you talking about?"

A maddening certainty filled Breed's chest. "That's the problem. Just like they expect us to do, we've been getting excited and fighting back." He reached down and felt his kicked-in shins. They were healing but still hurt. "If we're smarter than those dummies, then we don't have to keep on blaming them when we let them get something over on us."

Screwball crossed his eyes and wiggled his shoulders from side to side in a mocking manner. "You must like what happens to you," he said. "You ain't doin' nothin' to change it."

Breed knew Screwball was trying to be flippant, and he did look funny. Breed started to smile, but suddenly stopped. "You know that's true."

Screwball scratched his head and lifted one

shoulder. "It would be true, if I knew what I said."

"It's simple," Flick said. "Just what do they have over on us?"

Hog threw a little pebble into the water. "They ain't got nothin' over on me."

"That's right," Flick said. "We have everything over on them."

Something clicked in Breed's mind. He felt his pulse quicken. It was as if he had just found gold. He shouted. "We don't have to be in their goddamn same parade over and over."

Flick started to speak. Breed was too excited to stop. He talked over Flick's words, pressed on, spitting the words out. "We ain't in no race to see who is the dumbest. We don't have to do what their same money-eaten asses want us to do. Even if we ever got to a finish line, it wouldn't matter. They'd use their shiny new money. They'd rig it."

Flick nodded. "Don't get excited, Breed. Just tell us what you're talking about."

Breed felt ashamed and relieved at the same time. The words may not have come out like he had wanted, but it was clear in his mind what he was going to do. His pulse slowed. He continued in a calmer voice. "We don't have to dress alike, talk alike, look alike, or think alike." He paused. "For the rest of my life, I'm not gonna do the same rotten stuff over and over."

Blo's eyebrows shot up. "That's something like they told me in reform school. They told me that they were going to work the situation, and that there was no way they were going to let the son of a mill hunky work the situation."

Flick turned and slammed his fist against the

palm of his hand. "I'm sick and tired of this same crap people throw at us!"

"Then why don't you take a rest?" Screwball flippantly asked. "Then you'll only be sick!"

"Ahh, damn it, Screwball, you know what I mean. It's the same! Same! Same! Crap!" Flick bent over, picked up a handful of sand, and flung it forcefully into the water.

Ballpeen blinked in surprise and backed away. "I think you really lost it this time."

Flick's face beamed like a bright moon in a dark sky. "I ain't lost nothin'." He pointed to Breed. "He's right. They're controlling us, just like they control everybody else!"

Breed gave Flick an understanding look. "Those big kids come around and make trouble just to control us. They're just like those guys that start strikes and wars. They never get their asses kicked. They control who goes on strike and who don't go on strike, and they never fight in any wars."

"That's right." Flick jerked his arms up. "It's the same stuff alatime. It just pisses me off."

Hog butted in, "Yeah, what do you want to do? Go in same?"

Breed pointed to Hog. "You mean insane."

"Hell no!" Flick said loud. "It's not insane, he's right! We will go *in same* if we keep doing the same things." As if he were trying to get a bad taste out of his mouth, he jerked his head. "Damn! We'll be like ignorant piss ants. We'll end up working in one of those stinking mills like that old toothless steelworker, eaten' dirt, breathin' in acid fumes, and drinkin' three quarts of cheap rot gut beer every night just to bring home a paycheck and

398

raise some smart ass kids who will do the same thing over and over. Going in same is the same as going insane."

Breed held his head high. "Ya know what? I'm not takin' anymore of these ass kicking's and put downs."

Beaming a sarcastic smile, Screwball said, "Don't you wanna be like that rotten guy that tried to give us a diseased dime?"

"I think you have something there," Hog sarcastically said. "Look at all the fun we would have in some stinkin' mill, getting' cancer, drivin' a piece of shit car, and rotting away."

Blo buzzed on his trumpet, lowered it, and looked up. "Heck yeah, we could live to be twenty-three."

"That creepy guy in that three-hole Buick was in bad shape," Hog said and his face brightened. "But he had money."

As if he were shaking off a cold chill, Flick shuddered. "That guy was creepy."

Standing with his arms folded across his chest, Hog nodded. "That's true, but he still had money."

"Think about it." Flick tapped his head. "That money ain't gonna cure his cancer."

"You wanna know what I think about that?" Screwball picked a charred piece of wood out of the fire pit and drew a big black S on his chest.

Watching Screwball, Ballpeen made a sour face. "Now what?"

Screwball stood tall, waved his finger, and tapped his foot on a flat rock. "Slower than a herd of turtles, less powerful than a candy ass." He pointed up. "Look! Look up in the sky. Is it

Rotten Arm? No! Is it Mill Worker Man? No! Is it Cancer Man? No!" He stood like Super Man, chest out, hands on his hips, and his elbows out. "Is it Super Man?"

"No!" Hog butted in. "It's Stupid man."

"Close," Screwball said, smiled with approval, stared stupidly, and stuck out his stomach.

Flick raised his hands in exasperation.

Screwball ignored him, sucked in his lips like he had no teeth, dropped his chin to his chest, hunched his back, stuck out his butt, and limply stood like a simpleton.

Holding the ignorant pose, he pointed to the S on his chest and announced, "It's Same Man!"

Hog gawked in disbelief. "You gotta be out of your mind."

Imitating Screwball, Flick placed his hands on his hips and puffed out his stomach. "Same Man!" "That's who we'll be if we keep on doing the same stuff."

"Yeah!" Breed puffed out his belly. "It's like the old timer said, 'The longer you stay, the harder it is to get out.' I don't know about you guys, but I'm not going to work in a stinkin' mill. I'm not going in same."

"Yeah, let's fire that stinkin' mill." Flick relaxed his stomach. "Fire it before it kills us. If we ever work there, you know that will happen."

"You may have something there," Hog said in one of his rare agreeable moments. "But Screwball's still a halfwit."

Still holding the pose, Screwball turned his head toward Hog. "You're just saying that 'cause you can't be a hero."

"I'll hero you ass." Hog reached out to grab Screwball's foot. Screw broke the pose and dashed away.

Pud sat and scratched his rash; and although he had turned his head from one speaker to the next, Breed knew Pud hadn't understood a single thing about what was happening in front of him.

As if Blo had reached back into the far reaches of his mind, he came out with, "Eeuu can jump down the chimney of your mind, come out the fireplace and think you saw something."

Smiling, Flick looked him right in the face. "Did they let you out of the nut house too early?"

Blo turned his teeth upside down, "Euuck!"

Flick urgently peered around. "I know we have something here. Stick with me. You'll be wearing horse turds as big as diamonds."

Screwball stood up in agreement, "I ain't followin' behind nobody. I ain't no second-rate fly-back fart catcher."

Like a fairy-faced kindergarten kid, Breed said, "Let's make a pact or something to not go in same." He immediately regretted saying something so asinine that just didn't fit the moment.

"We don't need that baby crap." Hog jerked his head back. "We'll just do it!"

And all was quiet. As the new thoughts sank into their awakened minds, Ballpeen pounded slowly on a rock. "But how are we going to keep the upriver gang pissed off until the big fight?"

Blo smiled happily. "If you remember what was upriver, you would know."

Flick snapped his fingers and jumped in the sand. "That's it! We'll take those boats and let the

401

flats gang take them off us."

"It's a sure fire bet!" Hog said with triumph in his voice. "Every time we get a boat, they come right out of nowhere and take it off us."

Ballpeen quit pounding and rummaged around the scattered campsite. "Hey, Screwball, what did you do with all the food? I'm hungry."

"Oh yeah, I forgot to tell you. Those big kids threw it all in the river."

Ballpeen shot Screwball a nasty glare.

"Don't get excited, Ballpeen," Hog chided. "The catfish and carp got it now."

"Yeah!" As if he were reading a newspaper, Screwball held his hands in front of his face. "They're reading and eating by lantern light."

The thought of his father's lantern caused Flick to momentarily wince. He shrugged it off and looked to Ballpeen. "Hey, worry ass, food's no problem, but we'll have to wait until it gets dark. In the meantime, let's get some rest. It's going to be a busy night."

Chapter 31

As birds flew tweetlessly in the quiet; and a high sun began its long roll toward the lazy river's end, Breed and his friends lay around the island and tried to rest.

Splaasshh! That big fish jumped in the backwash.

It was early afternoon. The time when the fish of the river thrash and play on top of the water and just dare you to catch them, but they never bite.

As if contemplating to go after the jumping fish, Screwball stared at his fishing pole and then looked to where the noisy fish had jumped. "Hey, fish. Blow it out your ass."

Hog paced and waved his arms restlessly. "And blow this waitin' around out your ass. Nobody's restin'. Let's go get those boats."

Flick jumped up and grabbed a stick out of the stack of firewood. "We need a plan!" With the palm of his hand, he smoothed out a place in the sand. Using the pointed end of the stick, he drew a map. The crew gathered around. "This is the plan." He pointed the stick at Hog. "Can you still pick locks?"

"I can pick anything."

Ballpeen slumped toward Hog. "Why don't you go pick your ass?"

"Hey, cut the crap," Flick warned, "or you'll be pickin' your ass out of the mud."

Ballpeen straightened up. "Hant!"

"Hant, your ass." Flick continued to draw. "All right, Hog, you'll come with me and Blo. We'll swipe the boats" — he pointed to the place where he had drawn the boats in the sand — "right here."

Pud, who had been scratching all this time, squatted and farted.

Hog closed one eye, and surveyed him sideways. "What are you doin', Pud, clearin' your throat?"

"No, I'm not clearing my throat." Pud scratched again.

Hog offhandedly flipped his hand toward Pud. "It's a good thing you didn't wipe your ass with that itch weed."

Pud's lips spread into a dirty-toothed smile, and he kept scratching.

Waving Pud's stinking air away from his face, Ballpeen turned away. "That smells like a good plan."

As if he didn't want to miss an opportunity to irritate Ballpeen, Screwball whirled around and pointed to him. "You mean smelling your ass with itch weed is a good plan?"

"You know what I mean, smart ass."

"Your ass would smart if you used itch weed."

Ballpeen ignored Screwball and looked to Flick. "Hey, Flick, I'm hungry. Can't we cook that carp I caught?"

"We could, but they taste like shit."

Blo reached over and shook Pud's shoulder. "Hey, Pud, leave another fart so Ballpeen can eat something that's just as good as carp."

Ballpeen snapped his head toward Hog. "Hey! Blow it out your ass!"

Hog smiled big and applauded. "Way to go, Ballpeen." He flashed him a thumbs up. "You finally got the right answer."

Breed and the others giggled like cold car engines trying to start and settled to a serious idle. Flick continued the plan. "Did you guys hear those ducks upriver?"

"Hey, yeah." Screwball wagged his head from side to side. "We can just buy food up at the store and put it on their bills."

Flick's expression turned hard. "If you don't stop your smart mouth" — he smiled — "we're gonna improve your looks. We're gonna kick your ass up to your face."

Blo bared his false front teeth and sneered, "Eeeuuu!"

Hog squinted one eye toward Blo and looked to Flick. "Those ducks are wild. We'll never catch them."

Flick lifted the stick and pointed at Hog. "They ain't wild."

"How do you know that?"

Flick slouched over and puddle ducked in the sand with the stick. "If you could remember from one minute to the next, you'd rememember that we saw Flat Top in the boat razzing that kid with the buck teeth because he had to feed the ducks before his old man would let him out of the yard."

Screwball sat up and looked downriver. "And there ain't no wild ducks in this river. The muskies ate them all."

As if he had just woken up, Ballpeen's eyes shot wide open. "You're crazy. There ain't no muskie gonna eat a duck."

"The heck there ain't." Screwball shook his head in serious protest. "Didn't I ever tell you

405

about the time I saw one do it?"

"No."

"I was fishing below the rapids one day when I looked out the corner of my eye and saw two ducks. They kept walking along the shore like they were afraid to come in the water."

Breed cocked his head and studied Screwball's face. A small grin began to form.

Screwball continued. "Then, almost in the middle of the river, I saw a piece of corn on a rock. I knew that duck wanted that piece of corn. But it wouldn't come and get it because I was too close to the rock."

As if he were casting a fishing rod, Ballpeen threw his arm sideways. "Why didn't you snag one of them with your fishing hook?"

"I didn't want to snag a duck. I only wanted to see if it would swim out and get that corn. After I waded away from the rock, that duck swam up to that rock and bit that corn right off it."

Ballpeen leaned his head toward Screwball. "So then what happened?"

"That duck started to swim away. But before it got to shore, a big muskie jumped up and grabbed it, pulled it right under the water."

Ballpeen nodded. "I could believe that." He looked to Flick. "That muskie he had on last night had a mouth big enough to eat a duck."

Giggling inside, Screwball shouldered next to Breed. "Yeah, but I think it wanted to eat that other duck."

Astonished, Ballpeen turned to Screwball. "Just how would you know what a muskie would want?"

406

Screwball half closed his eyes in blissful enjoyment. "Because that muskie came up out of the water and put another piece of corn on that rock."

Everybody except Ballpeen broke out in triumphant laughter.

Agog with befuddlement, a moan of dismay flowed from Ballpeen's lips.

Hog jumped up and waved his hands in front of Ballpeen's face. "Hant!"

With his face contorting as if he had just bit into a lemon, Ballpeen turned his head toward Screwball. "Hant, your ass."

Suddenly the day darkened. Everyone looked up. A cloud's moving shadow fled down the river and the day brightened. Flick looked back to the plan in the sand. "Okay, just to make sure none of those big kids are hangin' around; at dusk we'll scout the area around the boats."

"They won't be around," Breed assured him. "Didn't you hear them talking about going to the record hop?"

"Yeah," Screwball said. "They'll be there trying to pick up ugly girls to match their ugly faces."

Flick stood up and brushed the sand off his legs. "You're probably right, but I don't feel like getting my ass kicked again. So we'll check it out anyway."

Pud lowered his head and whimpered.

Flick kneeled next to him. "Now what's the matter with you?"

Pud blinked his square cat-like eyes. "You guys are going to go upriver tonight and leave me here, and those big kids are going to cut my ears off."

Flick put his hand on Pud's shoulder. "Pud, old buddy, you don't have to worry about Burkie. He's down river, but if it'll make you feel better, you can go with Ballpeen and those guys to get the ducks."

Screwball snarled. "Yeah, if you don't mess things up."

With a blank look on his face, Pud smiled.

Ballpeen raised his hand like the star pupil of the fourth grade. "Everyone in favor of the plan raise their hand."

Shaking it furiously, Hog raised his hand. "I'm in favor of Ballpeen suckin' my dick." He smiled a big mocking smile. "Hant!"

"What? I didn't hear you." Hammer smiled back.

His voice laden with vehement determination, Flick said, "The hell with that candy ass shit. We're doing it."

"Owl!" Ballpeen stubbed his toe on a rock buried in the sand. He dropped to his knees, cleared the sand off the rock, and pounded on it with his hammer. The dull toneless sound throbbed into the air and created a churning cadence.

As if he had a headache, Flick's forehead wrinkled. "Why don't you go someplace and vomit?"

"Yeah, Ballpeen," Blo added. "You could make your life interesting."

Ballpeen pretended he didn't hear him. Flick persisted and sang, "Oh, Ballpeen wrapped his mouth around my balls, da-da-dat-da-da!"

Ballpeen quit pounding and stretched out on the

warm sand. "What? I didn't hear you!"

"Let's get some rest for tonight," Flick said, lay down, and laced his hands behind his head.

Breed sat next to him and scrunched over. "Nobody's sleepy."

Flick sat up and waved his arms like an orchestra conductor. "Hey, Blo, play 'Taps' and put us to sleep."

Grimly nodding, Blo lifted the trumpet to his lips; and without a flaw, he blew three lines of "Taps".

Breed reach over and patted Blo on the back. "Hey, way to go."

Flick's eyes brightened with confusion. "That was really good. How come you haven't been able to play 'Taps', lately?"

Blo slumped to the sand.

Breed bent over and looked into his face. A tear fell from the corner of Blow's eye.

"You okay, Blo?"

Blo's face twisted in anguish. He looked as if he were going to cry.

Flick knelt on one knee and leaned toward Blo. "What's the matter?"

Blo talked slow and low. "I couldn't remember it before. It just came to me when I played 'Taps.'"

"What?" Breed asked.

Blo held back the tears and whimpered, "One-Finger-Burke."

With an alligator grin on his face, Hog stepped close. "Well you don't have to bawl about it."

"Yeah," Ballpeen said with authority. "You don't have to be a candy ass."

Breed knew if he showed compassion for Blo,

409

the others would gang up on him, call him a candy ass or a crybaby. He sucked in his feelings, turned his palm up, and slowly shook his head. "Yeah, we know Burke's a crocked cop."

"It ain't that." Blo raised his voice. "I watched him kill old lady Vanko's husband." He slumped into a heap of relief.

"What?" Flick questioned.

Everyone turned toward Blo, watching, waiting, and listening.

Blo's eyes cleared. He straightened up; and with renewed confidence, he talked louder. "One-Finger-Burke and his cop buddy, Hank, killed him. I was going to walk down the street and play 'Taps' just like I always did. A car came and I thought it was the cops, so I jumped in the bushes by Vanko's house — stayed there till the car passed.

Hog impatiently waved his hand. "Was it the cops?"

"Heck no, the cops were at Vanko's. One-Finger-Burke and his buddy dragged her husband out and took turns digging a big hole in the garden."

Breed shuttered and remembered the day old lady Vanko had accused him of taking that worm-eaten turnip Pud was eating. He was glad he never took anything from that garden.

Hog leaned forward, his voice urgent. "Did they see you?"

"They might have seen the bushes move. I think that's why One-Finger Burke took me to reform school, questioned me all day. I wouldn't talk. I thought they would kill me if I did. I held it in so they wouldn't find out I knew." He turned his false teeth upside-down but didn't sneer. "I guess I

410

held it in too good. I just remembered it now, when I played 'Taps.'"

"Are you sure it was him?" Flick asked and clinched his fists.

"Can't be anybody else. Her husband must not have been dead, cause when they went to shove him in the hole, he jumped up and grabbed One-Finger-Burke. Only thing is, Burke didn't have a missing finger then. He tried to choke Vanko's husband, but he wiggled his head around and bit down on Burke's finger, bit it right off. That's when Burke's buddy kicked him in the ribs and hit him in the head with the shovel. Vanko's husband went right into the hole like a bag of dead cats. Didn't even move after that. One-Finger-Burke and his buddy used a flashlight and looked for his finger." His voice dropped. "I can still see that flashlight shining on Burke's white handkerchief. When he wrapped it around his bleeding finger stump, it turned red." With hope, he looked up. "They never did find his finger."

"Why didn't you tell somebody the next day?" Breed asked.

"I wanted to tell you guys that same night, but I was so scared that I left my trumpet at the side of the road and ran all the way home." He shuddered, but jerked his head and shook the feeling off. "I threw up right after it happened. I was going to tell you guys the next day, but One-Finger-Burke showed up with my trumpet the next morning and took me to reform school."

Breed tapped the side of his head. "They must've brainwashed you."

"Naw, they just wanted to find out if I saw

411

them kill him or if I just dropped my trumpet."

Breed wanted to do something about it. "One-Finger-Burke's a cop, but he ain't gonna arrest himself."

Blo slowly turned his head and stared at the river. It ran smooth and true. "I know that, but I feel pretty good right now."

Screwball smiled. "Kind'a like you just took a good crap."

"Well." Hog exhaled loudly. "There's only one thing I got to say about that."

Blo looked up with a serious look on his face. "What?"

Hog lifted his leg and farted. "That's what."

A little smile formed on Blo's face.

"Oh, and one more thing," Hog said and paused.

"What?" Blo impatiently asked.

Hog bent over and blasted a taunting, "Hant!" right in Blo's face.

Blo broke into a big laugh of relief. "That's stupid, but I feel like I just took a good healthy dump out of my chest."

"How can we tell the police?" Breed wanted to know.

"Maybe you can make an anonymous phone call," Hog suggested.

Blo shrugged. "Maybe we could call the governor or something when we get back, but right now I don't feel like sitting around." He stood up. "I gotta do something."

"Maybe you could sit on a most kissable lips contest paper." Screwball looked to Hog.

The memory of Pud eating the rotten turnip he

had taken from Vanko's garden where her dead husband had been buried nagged at Breed's sub consciousness and sent death chills down his back. He shook them off. "Buried in the garden?" He shook his head. "That gives me the willies. I feel cold. Pud burned up all the little sticks we had to start the fire." He shrugged. "I'll go find some."

"You won't have to." Flick jerked his head toward the other side of the river. "We can go up to the railroad yard and get some monkey shit."

"Hey that's a good idea," Hog said. "That stuff will start a fire in a few seconds."

Flick bent down and tied his shoelace. "And while we're there we can play with the railroad phones."

Ballpeen jerked his head sideways. "What phones?"

Flick acted as if he didn't hear Ballpeen. He lay back on the sand, put his hands behind his head, and stared at the sky. "We were down by the bridge swimming, and I was lying under the checkered crosswalk."

Joining in the taunting of Ballpeen, like a festival figure in a parade, and pointing at Ballpeen, Screwball marched across the sand and pretended to be silently laughing.

Ballpeen ignored him. "What about the railroad phones?"

Screwball continued marching and pointing.

"What! I didn't hear you," Flick said and continued. "I was lying under the checkered crosswalk, in my checkered bathing suit, trying to get a checkered suntan through the checkered grating."

413

"All right! Quit!" Ballpeen said, agitated. "What about the railroad phones? I suppose they were checkered, too."

"No, but your checkered head must have been checkered when you built that checkered boat that fell apart when that little piece of cement block hit it."

Screwball quit marching and laughed out loud.

Ballpeen's ears reddened.

Hog smiled and pointed two fingers at Ballpeen. "Hant!"

Ballpeen ignored him and looked to Flick. "You're lucky you don't end up in the mud like Pud."

"Keep it up and you'll be in there," Flick playfully warned.

"You and what Army?"

"Me and my checkered Army." Flick dove for Ballpeen's leg.

Ballpeen jerked his leg back. "Oh no you don't."

Flick lunged again. This time, Ballpeen's agile move didn't work. Flick snagged his ankle. Ballpeen tripped backwards and flipped into the water. Flick dove in after him. Ballpeen turned and dove away from him. Flick swam under water, came up behind him, and lifted him into the air. Ballpeen sissored his feet and they both crashed into the water. Like a fake wrestling match, they took turns throwing each other into the water. Their rugged bodies radiated the strength that the environment of the river and the hardships of the slum neighborhood had forged. They didn't tire.

After they tried to dunk each other, they finally

414

began to breathe hard. When they stopped, they helped each other to shore, and sat down.

Catching his breath, Ballpeen watched Flick. "Are you going to tell me about the railroad phone, or do I have to push you in the water again?"

Flick exhaled. "All right, tough guy. Up over the bank and down river, close to the switching yard, there is a railroad phone." He stared at him with an enormous smile on his face.

"Come on, Flick," Ballpeen said in a begging tone. "What's so great about a railroad phone?"

Lifting his arms, Screwball shrugged. "It's better than playing leapfrog with unicorns."

Flick gazed around the island and directed his voice at the others. "Hey, you guys, want to go up and get that old coot pissed off?"

"Heck yeah!" Blo said. "I'll take my trumpet."

Flick glanced at Pud. "We'll get there faster than a turd of hurdles."

Pud scratched his itch weed rash, again. Flick bent over and looked directly in his face. "Did I say that right?"

Pud didn't answer. With his jaw open, he continued to scratch.

"Hey, there's jaggers and junk along the railroad path," Hog said. "We'll have to put our clothes on to keep from getting all scratched up."

"I don't feel like runnin' around in wet clothes. It will slow us down," Screwball said. "How are we going to get them across the river without getting them wet? We don't have Ballpeen's junk boat anymore."

Breed gestured toward Ballpeen's hammer. "All we have to do is nail some driftwood together,

415

put the clothes on it and push them across."

Screwball lifted one hand into the air. "Yeah, all we need is nails." He pointed to the river. "Those big kids threw them in the water. All we have to do is dive down and find them."

Ballpeen lifted his hammer and let it drop. "Never thought of that."

"No problem, Flick said. "We'll hold the driftwood together long enough to get across."

Breed and Screwball ran along the side of the island, came back with three pieces of driftwood and placed them into the shallow water. After everyone except Pud, piled their clothes on the makeshift raft, Flick placed his pilot hat on top.

"Just like a cherry on top of an ice cream Sunday." He pushed the raft into the water.

Fully clothed, Pud hung on. They towed him and the raft across the river.

Chapter 32

On the other side of the river, everyone except Pud, whose clothes were soaking wet, pulled their pants over their swimming suits, stepped into their tennis shoes, and threw their shirts on. As they trudged up the riverbank, Pud sloshed behind.

At the top of the riverbank they hopped over the main railroad lines, then tromped through the stag horn sumac.

On the other side, a panorama of green gondola railroad cars blocked their view.

They walked around the gondolas and stopped. There, shiny steel railroad tracks ran north and south and were intersected with cross tracks that had little switch stands with red and green flat-metal arrows pointing in different directions. In the distance, maroon, green, and brown boxcars sat like little children waiting to be taken on a trip.

Beyond that, lines of shiny black tank cars were interlaced with a few maroon flatcars that had tall, gray transformers on top. Further away, alongside a string of flat-black hopper cars, filled with coke, a long gray dusty road ran toward the shingled roof of a railroad yard office that looked like a dark-green triangle on the horizon.

Breed and the others walked over a few railroad tracks and stopped next to a brown wooden box that had been bolted to an aging concrete post. Inside, a black dusty phone waited to be used. The lock on the little door had long ago been ripped off or rotted away. Its splintering wood and crumbling concrete fit right in with the surroundings of the worn-out brake shoes and railroad car scrap that littered the dirty ballast that tapered off into creosote treated tramp paths that were lined with strange and nameless weeds that struggled in the toxic dirt and shed strange odors that blended with the lifeless creosote smell that created that unmistakable atmosphere called a railroad yard.

Moving his finger, Flick pointed along the old railroad branch line, and stopped. "Hey, it's that pink Ford."

Everyone froze and waited for something to happen.

Nothing did.

The sight of the pink Ford renewed that rotten feeling Breed had when Flick had gotten beaten up. "If nobody's in it" — he breathed with excitement — "let's flatten the tires."

Flick paused and thoughtfully stared at the Ford. "We could, but if we do, they might not wait until the big fight on Friday. We gotta do something else."

Hog grinned with delight. "I'll pick the lock."

Flick winked approvingly and nodded one time. "Hog and Breed, come with me." He looked at the others. "If you see somebody coming, whistle."

The others spread out and watched the yard. Breed, Hog, and Flick sauntered up to the Ford. Breed looked at the roof of the Ford. The dent, where his BB gun had been smashed into it, stood out like a wanted poster in a post office.

In an arrogant manner, Hog lifted his chin. "Excuse me, gentleman."

Everyone stepped back.

Hog tipped an imaginary hat. "Thank you, kind sirs." As if he were the owner, he stepped to the

418

Ford, unlocked the door, and opened it. "Let's see what we can take."

Flick reached into the glove box. "No, wait!" He pulled out five packs of rubbers.

Hog sat behind the steering wheel and leaned back. "Now what?"

Flick pulled the big brass safety pin from his World War II pilot hat and held it in his hand. "Watch!"

One by one, he removed the rubbers from the unsealed cardboard package and poked a pinhole in each one. Then he put the perforated rubbers back in the glove box, smiled, and closed the door. "Looks like Miss Crooked Teeth and Purple are gonna have to get married."

Hog slid out from behind the steering wheel, walked to the front of the Ford, and sprang the hood open. Flick and Breed peered into the engine compartment. Hog reached in and pulled the spark plug wires off the distributor.

Breed felt a sense of satisfaction. "They'll never get it started."

Hog counted the timing order on the engine block and held the spark plug wires in his hand. He selected wires and switched them around in his hand until they were in a complicated order. "Yes they will." He replaced the wires on the distributor.

Breed didn't want Purple to be able to start the car. "What did you put them back on for?"

Hog gently and quietly closed the hood. "Don't be stupid, Breed. It'll start but it won't run worth a shit."

Breed remembered how erratic his motorbike ran when he didn't adjust the timing. "I got it now."

He nodded in approval.

"Those dummies don't know nothin' about timing," Flick said. "This thing will spit, sputter and backfire. As long as it runs, they'll never figure it out."

Hog opened the side door, flipped the front seat back, reached into the back, and picked up the floor mat. "We can use this to carry back the monkey shit."

As if he were a waiter carrying a try of food; with one hand, Hog held his head high; crooked his elbow; held the floor mat slightly over his head; and walked down the tracks.

Breed and Flick followed and stopped at the railroad phone.

Blo stepped in front of Pud and Screwball. "What did you guys do?"

Hog's eyes brightened. "We messed up the timing."

"We poked—" Flick started to say and looked to Hog.

"Holes in their rubbers," Hog finished.

Breed felt a hint of mischievous revenge for his broken BB gun, the pain in his side, and his kicked in shins. "Hant!" He smiled inwardly.

Blo swept his hand toward the phone. "Let's try and get the cops up here to pick up that Ford. No one's allowed on railroad property."

Flick lips widened in a knowing grin. He blew the dust off the black phone, picked it up, but placed it back into the brown wooden box. "Let's get the monkey shit first."

Breed and Hog walked to a dirty-black gondola setting on the tracks. Breed lifted the journal box

420

cover on the side of the wheel and pointed to a piece of wood next to the tracks. "Get that broken board over there. We'll scoop it out."

Hog picked up the skinny board, put it into the wheel journal box and dug out the monkey shit — blue, yellow, and green strands of thick yarn soaked with heavy oil that lubricated the wheels like a wick — and piled it onto the floor mat.

After they hid the monkey shit into the bushes, they returned to the phone.

Flick picked the phone up off its holder and held it so everyone could hear. Screwball turned the rusty crank. A dull ringing chattered somewhere at the other end of the line. A gruff whisky voice answered. "East end. Hello!"

"Hi there!" Flick said as if he had known the guy all his life.

"East end, hello! Who is this?"

Flick held the phone at the end of Blo's trumpet.

Blatt! Blo blew into the receiver. Flick turned the crank in the guy's ear. "Hello, you old, dried-up coot!"

"What the hell is that?" The voice said on the other end. "This phone is for business only!"

Flick turned the crank again. Raaaggtt! "Get the hell off this," — Raattt! — the guy said between the provoking cranking.

Flick yelled into the receiver, "Blow it out your ass." He stretched the phone cord and held the phone under Blo's trumpet. Bllaattt! Blasted into the receiver and traveled on down the line and into the guy's ear.

Flick held the phone out for everyone to hear.

421

"Son-a-bitch!" the guy said and there was silence over the line.

Blo held his trumpet in the ready position. "Maybe he gave up."

Another voice cut in. "Bill, I got some wise ass kids playing with the phone. Are those detectives finished investigating that engine that went on the ground?"

"I heard them. The deceives are coming up the road now!"

"Good! They'll teach those little bastards to play with railroad property."

Flick turned the crank once and talked. "Come on up and try. You'll never catch our Ford!"

Breed looked toward the yard office. The railroad detectives' car was barreling up the road. Rushing along the long line of hopper cars, its tires kicked up small stones, and a cloud of light-gray dust billowed behind. When the car stopped next to the Ford, the cloud of dust caught up to it like it had been in a race and had just lost, but was thankful it had finished.

The little red flasher on the dashboard of the car blinked through the haze, and its back bumper barely touched a big strong oak tree. Waving dust from their faces, two railroad detectives stepped out of the car. With their chrome badges flashing in the sun, they walked toward the Ford.

Breed pulled on Flick's arm. "Come on. Let's get out of here."

Flick whispered, "When they get close, then run to the Ford and pretend you're trying to open the doors."

The detectives turned and looked at Flick

standing next to the phone box. Breed and the others backed away, ready to run.

The detective with the Dick Tracy hat motioned with his hand as if he were a friend. "Hey, you kids, come here. We just want to talk to you."

Screwball pulled his head back and stared at the detective. "You think we're gonna believe that?"

The detective's face tensed, but he extended his hand. "Come on, pal, we just want to talk."

Screwball's lips spread into a toothy grin. "You wanna talk to something that looks just like your face? Bend over and talk to your dumb ass."

A ripple of laughter rippled erupted from Breed and the others.

With an expression of disbelief, the detective stared at Screwball. "You think that's funny?"

"Yes sir," Hog politely replied. "Yes, we do."

With his eyes glaring with disapproval, the other detective took a step forward. "It won't be so funny when you're smart asses are sitting jail for trespassing and interfering with railroad property."

Flick stretched out his hand and wiggled his fingers in a come-here gesture. "Come here and arrest us."

The detectives started after him.

Everyone except Flick ran to the Ford. He kept talking into the phone. "And blow your phony railroad dicks out your ass, too." He turned the crank. Rraatt! "And shove this rattlin' junk-ass phone you salvaged from the seventeenth century right up your ass. And it will probably fit, too!"

When the detectives were a few feet away from him, Flick gave the phone one last crank, ran to the Ford, and stopped.

Breed and Hog held their hands on the door handles of the locked Ford. Turning his head from side to side, as if he were scared, and loud enough for the detectives to hear, Hog excitedly yelled to Flick. "It's locked. Do you have the keys?"

Flick slapped his pockets. "No! I think I left them in the car."

With Flick trailing behind, they all took off running.

Screwball ran up the tramp path, looked back, and tripped over a rusty log chain. "Ahh, man!"

Flick came up behind, grabbed Screwball by the shoulders, lifted him to his feet; and as if he had remembered something, he stopped. Screwball jerked on Flick's arm. They ran into the cover of the weeds.

The detectives ran a few feet up the tramp path and stopped. Huffing for breath, the detective in the Dick Tracy hat shrugged with defeat. "We're not going to catch them." He smiled big. "But we got their car."

With looks of satisfied satisfaction, they both walked back to the Ford.

Flick put his hand over his mouth and broke into a muffled maniacal cackle.

"What's so funny?" Breed asked.

"Do you see where they're parked — by that tree?"

"Yeah."

"What do you think would happen if we got that chain and tied it around the rear axle and then got them to take off in a hurry?"

"Oh man!" Breed said. "We couldn't do that."

Blo's eyes lit up. "Hey! Why not?"

424

Shaking his head, Breed held up his hand and waved it back and forth. "That would cause a lot of damage to an official car. We could go to jail."

"No, we won't," Flick said. "They'll think Purple and his asshole buddies did it."

As if his brain just kicked into high gear, Hog looked across the yard. "How do we get that chain hooked on without them seeing us?"

Flick pointed to the railroad yard. "You guys go across the tracks and get them to chase you. I'll get it."

Before anyone could say yes or no, Blo yelled, "Let's go!" He ran across the tracks. Breed and the others swarmed after him.

The railroad detectives renewed the chase and Flick went for the chain.

During it all, Pud crouched in the weeds.

Flick picked up the chain and snuck around to the oak tree next to the car. He watched the detectives chasing the crew, and when it was clear to go under the car. . .

Pud jumped out of the weeds yelling. "They're going to steal boats and ducks and break your car." He jerked his hands into the air. "Please don't shoot officers!"

As if he were a prisoner, Pud kept his hands stretched high over his head; and with his mouth running like a broken faucet gushing words, he walked toward the detectives.

In alarm, Flick whipped around, dropped the chain, and ran for concealment.

The others danced over the rails and sprinted into the cover of the brush and watched.

With his eyes bulging with astonishment, Blo

425

puffed hard but managed to say, "That goddamn idiot! He must think he'll get a reward for squealing on us."

"When he gets home," Breed said, breathing with labored gasps, "his old man will give him a reward."

Hog calmly sat in the weeds and talked like a great mister know-it-all. "See, I told you guys he'd do something retarded."

Flick rustled through the brush. "I almost had that chain on!"

Screwball shrugged. "It figures."

"What did you expect?" Hog said with a wave of his hand. "Did you ever see Pud do anything right?"

"What the heck?" Breed let out a breath of despair. "He's retarded, you know."

Flick brushed his hands together and dusted off the chain rust. "It looks like he's doing something right now!"

Hog leaned back in the tall grass and put his hands behind his head. "He'll screw up his great squeal. Just wait and see." Waiting and watching, he chewed on the tender end of the piece of grass.

As Pud's blabbermouth flap in a torrent of uninterrupted speech, the detectives listened to him until the detective with the Dick Tracy hat noticed his eyes.

"Hey," he said. "What are you . . . on dope or something?"

"No I ain't on dope or something!" Pud rolled his square eyes. "Honest officer. I'm just trying to tell you what they're going to do."

Infuriated, the other detective held his square

426

jaw firm. "This kid's a goddamn dope addict."

The detectives took him by the arms and escorted him into the car. They drove away and the chain lay beside the tree.

"Well, that'll teach him," Breed said. "They'll take him back to the nut house after they find out he isn't on dope."

Hog took the grass he was chewing out of his mouth, held it for a moment, and threw it on the ground. "Oh well." He picked up the floor mat with the monkey shit on it. "They won't take him anywhere before they call his old man and he kicks the livin' crap out of him for taking off with us."

"Yeah, we won't see him for a while," Flick said and they started back to the campsite.

"He'll probably stay in longer than the time he cut his finger, "Breed said.

"What did he do that time?" Blo asked.

Breed walked through the tall weeds and moved his hands. "That was the first time I saw the squared-eyed dummy. As usual, he had snuck out of the yard to see what we were doing. I ran over to see what he had in his hand. It was his old man's straight razor. And you know what that stupid bastard did?"

Blo talked into his trumpet. "Whhaattt!"

"He opened the razor and said, 'Gee, I wonder if it's sharp!' And ran his finger down the sharp edge — dam near cut his finger off. I told him to get his ass home and get it fixed. He started to cry, ran home with that finger sticking out in front of him and watched it bleed all the way home. Then I heard his old man beat his ass."

"Dumbbb asss!" Blo buzzed.

427

As they walked single file along the river path, up ahead, Flick held onto a branch and walked a few steps. The branch loaded up with a spring action. Flick let it fly back. Screwball tried to block the stinging branch. He was too late. Swwaatt! Stiinngg! The branch swatted right into his face.

Screwball grabbed his face. "Hey! Cut that out!"

"Ain't gonna catch my Fly Backs!" Flick announced and kept on walking through the brush and weed-covered path. "Yes, pay attention. Watch for those fly back shit-flinging branches, don't even try to stop them, they will only flick their stupid shit on you!" He stopped and pretended he was fighting an imaginary bull. "Step aside! Ol'e, asshole! Yes, step aside and let the shit slide by. Just don't get any on you. It's contagious. Let them hog it all for themselves. They will eat it all with their ignorant-brain-controlled mouths. You don't have to stop any fly backs in life. You do not have to eat shit forever."

"What in the hell are you talkin' about?" Ballpeen wanted to know.

"Pay attention!" Screwball let a branch fly back. It flapped into Ballpeen's face.

Breed let out an appropriate, "Hant!"

Ballpeen grabbed the branch, broke it off, slammed it on the ground, and looked at it for a second. He rubbed his face, dropped down on one knee, and pounded the stick with his hammer. "Goddamn fly back son-of-a-bitch!" he cussed with each stroke of the beating hammer. The branch broke into splinters and water came out of the ground. He stopped pounding. "Hey, Flick! Is this water good to drink? I'm thirsty."

Flick turned around and looked. "If it's coming out of the ground it usually is, but this is Rat River."

"I wouldn't drink it." Hog backed away.

Ballpeen dropped to his knees and hands. "It looks clean to me." He put his thirsty mouth to the water and sucked in a big swallow. Then he wiped his mouth on his arm and watched something moving in the ground where he had just drunk. Then it started to squeak there.

"What's that?" Flick asked and they watched the moving squeaking ground. A big stinking brown turd popped up out of the ground. A gigantic sewer rat was right behind it.

As the rat ran into the weeds, Flick said, "Those rotten bastards."

Breed thought about the stinking sewers ditches in front of his house. He believed he had gotten away from the stink and the filth of Traptown, but it was right at his feet. "Damn! Some asshole from the railroad connected their sewer right into that spring."

Screwball pointed toward the turd. "Ballpeen just ate shit."

Hog tapped Ballpeen on the shoulder. "Excuse me, sir."

Ballpeen turned.

Like a waiter at a high-class restaurant, Hog held the floor mat piled with monkey shit in front of Ballpeen. "Would you enjoy a bit of monkey shit to go with that?"

"Hant!" Screwball added.

Overreacting, Ballpeen choked and tried to

429

throw up the freshly ingested turd water, but only turned light blue in the process. He kept trying to rid his stomach of the dirty water, but he needed help.

"Hey Ballpeen." Screwball grinned. "If you're still hungry throw up, then you can have a hot meal."

That did it!

Ballpeen looked up at Screwball and groaned in pain, "You rotten bastard!" He turned his face toward the ground and coughed up the turd-flavored liquid.

They continued down the path, and Ballpeen spit every few feet to get the turd taste from his mouth.

Tramping down the bank toward the camp, Flick said, "Well, Ballpeen, one thing's for sure, when you say something tastes like shit, you'll have first mouth experience."

"Yeah, shit mouth!" Hog added.

At the campsite preparations were made for the boat and duck heist. Flick checked the blade on his Boy Scout ax and slid it under his belt. "If we can't pick those locks, I'll chop them off!"

And they waited for dark.

Chapter 33

Breed stood at the tip of Shell Island and looked across the evening panorama of the river. Like life-giving shafts of spiritual power, peaceful beams of silver sun slanted onto the calm surface. As if it were related to Screwball, a mischievous gust of wind rushed down the river, chopped the top of the water into a thousand chrome triangles, and hurried away.

After the water smoothed again, a raccoon chattered. Breed turned toward the sound and looked into the darkened green background beyond the trees. That big fish jumped. He snapped his head back toward the river. Small circles spread across the calm water and fanned out until they were at his feet. In the distance, a slow train clacked past on the tracks. The silver rays of the sun faded, and the sky mellowed to a magenta masterpiece.

Flick walked up and stood next to Breed. "Ain't no artist in the world can paint like the great artist in the sky."

"I'm glad we don't have to pay to see it."

"Yeah," Flick said and exhaled. "Some day some asshole will figure out a way to make everybody pay to see it."

They tilted their heads upward and gazed. The late sun show winked shut, and the magenta masterpiece faded to almost black. It was time to go.

The crew piled their clothes and shoes on the driftwood raft and crossed the river.

Hog splashed up onto shore and pulled the raft

up the riverbank. "It's a whole lot easier, now that we don't have to stop and pull Pud out of the water every five minutes."

"Yeah," Breed said. "It'll be easier up on the railroad bed, too. We'll have our shoes on this time."

Up on the railroad tracks, Breed and the others walked with ease. Behind them, a slow moving freight buzzed its air horn. They jumped off the tracks. The moving train clacked close. They stood and watched. From the engine's cab window, the engineer smiled and wave a friendly hello. At the trains end, a conductor was hanging out over the steps of the red caboose and urinating off the steps.

"Hant!" Hog yelled at him and laughed.

Surprised, the conductor jerked back and peed on his hands and pants.

In unison, Breed and the others yelled, "Hant!"

As a spasm of irritation crossed the surprised conductor's face, he lifted his pee-covered hand and thumbed his nose at them. When he realized he had placed his peed on hand next to his face, he shook his fist and cussed at them until he was out of sight.

Hog took his hand from his pocket, waved it around, and talked. "That guy really looked stupid."

"About as stupid as that scout master that said we could be Boy Scouts," Ballpeen said.

"What was so stupid about him?" Screwball asked.

Breed knew Ballpeen sensed a setup and didn't want Screwball to trick him into saying something stupid. "Oh, you know," Ballpeen said and looked away.

432

Screwball tugged at Ballpeen's shirt. "No, I don't know. Hammer-ass junk maker."

Ballpeen jerked his head toward Screwball. "Shut up, Shit Foot. You're just trying to start something. If you were there, you would'a got lost just like he did. And I would'a had to show you how to get out of the woods, too."

"Hey, would'a," Hog said, "the only thing you could find your way out of would be a junk yard, but you wouldn't want to leave anyway."

Flick placed his hand on his Boy Scout ax and continued to walk. "I think that dummy really told everybody he was an asshole when he tried to tell us that the sound from the sawmill was a mountain lion."

Breed walked on top of the shiny steel railroad rail like a tightrope walker. "That guy sure changed his mind about making us Boy Scouts after he found out we didn't have any money to pay dues."

Screwball talked as if he were thinking out loud. "He wasn't bad. He wasn't too bad. He was too bad. It was too bad he didn't want to mind you little children."

No one said a word. If anyone said anything, they would become part of attempted humor that had failed. It wasn't important. They kept walking in a screwed up silence caused by a joke that wasn't funny.

When the boats were right around the bend in the river, Breed felt like a rotten thief. To ease his conscience, he told himself that they weren't actually going to steal the boats. They rightfully belonged to them. If they hadn't swam out and got them when they had drifted down the river, they would have plunged over the falls and broke into a million pieces. But it didn't matter what he told himself. That uncontrollable fight or flight, built in survival mechanism deep in all mankind, surfaced anyway. Danger was right around the bend. His heart raced in his chest and made him wondered if anyone else was scared, but he couldn't ask. He couldn't show one tiny bit of fear. He wasn't a whiny candy ass.

"All right you guys," Flick said, "it's time to get serious."

"Yeah," Screwball said with a slight waver in his voice and then spoke up loud and clear. "But not asshole serious."

Breed smiled and felt his heart slow a few beats. "Yeah, okay. Let's spread out and check the area."

"And pay attention," Flick said sharply. "We don't need any leftover surprises."

They separated, tramped through dry leaves, and searched for signs of the upriver gang.

There were none.

They regrouped at the railroad tracks and huddled around Flick.

With his butt almost touching the shinning chrome-like rail, Flick squatted by the tracks. "Look here, you guys. Those upriver gang kids might sneak back, then we'll have to fight. Let's stick together until after we get the boats. Then we'll go after the ducks."

As if he were about to cry, Ballpeen's face crumpled. "How can we take the boats on an empty stomach?"

"What are you worried about food for?"

Screwball asked, turned toward Ballpeen, and blinked quizzically. "All you're gonna do is eat it."

"If I ever get enough wood," Ballpeen said and clutched his hammer. "I'll going to build a nut house for you guys. You'll be right at home."

Blo put his trumpet to his lips and buzzed a respectable, "Hantttt!"

Breed smiled and then turned serious. "How about posting lookouts? That's a lot of boats to take all at once."

"We won't need lookouts," Flick said. "There are so many twigs and old leaves around here that we'll hear anybody coming a mile away."

Hog stuck his arms out and balanced on the rail. "And those candy asses never go into the dark without a light."

***

Around the river bend and beyond the dock, dark weeds jerked in the slow current. Breed scanned between their movements for signs of life. "Hey, Screwball," he whispered. "Those weeds look like they are signaling for us to go ahead."

"Yeah," Screwball said, "go ahead, back up!"

"Yeah, okay," Breed said and they crept to the boats.

At the dock, Hog lifted a chain from the first boat. He had a lock in his hand and reached for his lock pick when: Bam! Boom! Sputter! Wheeze! A backfiring engine interrupted the secret night. Above their heads, car lights flickered through the treetops.

"Ahh man!" Flick moaned and the lights went out. "You guys stay here with the boats and hide. Come on, Blo, we'll check it out."

435

While Breed and the others crouched next to the wooden dock, in the silent dark, a scary feeling crept up Breed's back. Something tugged at his arm. He jerked around. It was Ballpeen. Breed breathed a sigh of relief. "What?"

Catching his breath, Ballpeen pointed into the dark. "What's that?"

Blo tramped out of the dark and walked to the dock.

Breathing easier, Ballpeen looked to Blo. "What did you find out?"

"There's only one of them. He's parking with some girl."

Ballpeen shifted his weight for one foot to the other. "Where's Flick?"

Flick slipped around a big black tree and snuck behind Ballpeen. "Right here!" he said right in Ballpeen's ear.

Ballpeen jolted, reached for his hammer, and backed onto the dock. He was ready to fight back. He looked at Flick. "Cut that out." He dropped his hand from the hammer.

"Hey, Breed. "Flick smiled. "It's that pink Ford."

Breed thought about doing something to the Ford but didn't say anything.

"I knew it was that Ford," Hog said with a casual lack of concern. "When I crossed those wires, I told you it would run like a piece of junk."

Trying to imitate a misfiring motor, Screwball jerked his shoulders and dipped his neck. "Sounds pretty good."

With a flick of his hand, Flick motioned downriver. "We're going down and get that chain."

436

Breed remembered how Flick had broken his BB gun on the Ford. He glanced at his own hand. Where Flat Top had stepped on it, it still hurt. That Ford was like a weapon of the enemy. It needed to be destroyed. He stepped forward. "I'll help!"

Flick held up his hand. "Not this time, Breed. Stay here. These guys will need your brain if something complicated comes up.

A glimmer of mischief beamed from Screwball's eyes. "Yeah." He looked at Hog, "I might have to pee and you'll have to show me how to spell my name."

"Come on, Screwball," Breed said, "Quit foolin' around. We got to work together if we want this thing to work."

"It'll work," Flick assured him.

"Yeah it will," Hog said with a look of cunning expectation. "Pud ain't here."

"That's right," Flick agreed. "You guys take the boats and get the ducks. And don't take any if they're like those dirty shit-eatin' chickens of old lady Vanko's."

Breed shuddered at the thought of eating one of Vanko's diseased chickens that ate food from a garden where a dead man was buried. "I don't think any duck could be as bad as those chickens."

"That ain't no lie," Screwball said. "They look like she buried them for a few days and then dug 'em back up."

Flick took an oar from under the dock and handed it to Ballpeen. "It's a long way down and back. You guys should have those ducks by the time we get back with the chain."

Click! A lock snapped open. A skinny chain

437

clinked on the floor of a boat. "There's one," Hog said. "Too bad these chains are too weak for that Ford."

"Yeah, it would save us a trip," Flick said and scanned the shadows of a line of black trees. "Keep your eyes peeled for those upriver kids." He turned. "Let's go, Blo."

Blo followed and they disappeared into the darkness.

Hog picked up a boat chain and inserted his lock pick into a lock. "Let's get this show on the road." Snap! Another lock swung open. Clink! Another chain fell.

Screwball jumped into the first boat. "You mean get the otter on the water."

Breed hopped into the second boat, but he stepped on something. When he looked down, something round had coiled around his foot. Snake! Flashed in his mind. He jerked his foot away and jumped on the dock.

Hog looked into the boat. "What are you doing, Breed?" He waved his hand around in a circle. "It's just a rope."

Screwball pointed at Breed. "Hant!"

Breed stepped back into the boat and picked up the rope. "Too bad we couldn't use this rope to hang Purple."

"We probably could," Hog said, "but he's so rotten the devil probably won't let him into hell."

"If we hang him," Screwball said, "we won't have to give him some Gallo wine. He's already Purple."

Ballpeen cringed and looked from side to side.

438

"If we did hang him, do you think he'd come back and haunt us?"

Screwball shook his head. "Naw, he's too lazy to do something like that."

Breed picked up the strong rope and jerked it between his hands. "Maybe we could hang him for just a little bit."

"Yeah," Ballpeen said and tilted his head as if he were hanging from a rope, "just enough to scare him."

"I'd try it," Breed said, "but Flick's so mad at Purple, he might let him hang for real."

Screwball reached into the boat and wrapped the end of the rope around his neck. "Hang me!"

Hog's eyes grew wide. "What?"

Breed felt devilish and smiled. "I know what he means. His old man really beat his ass that time." He lowered his head in remorse. "I guess he shouldn't have done it. His grandma really got scared."

"Scared ain't the word for it," Hog said. "He scared the goddamn shit right out of her."

Screwball freed the third boat. "Are we going to talk about it all night?"

Ballpeen jumped into the boat and pushed it away from the dock. It plowed into the current. Breed and the others pushed their boats away from the dock and chased Screwball downriver.

Around the bend, the faint quack of ducks drifted over the dark water. Breed and the others stopped the boats and chained them to a sunken log.

Ballpeen looked to his right. Thick black trees lined the riverbank. "I don't hear any ducks. How are we going to find them? It's dark as night."

439

Screwball closed one eye and squinted in Ballpeen's direction. "That's why it's dark. It is night, you know."

"Hey, let's go up on the road," Hog suggested.

"That's right, those ducks are probably on a farm," Breed said. "And a farm has to have a road leading to it."

Ballpeen turned back toward the boats. "Let's untie the boats and drift to the bridge."

"That's a splendid idea," Hog said. "Then Purple's buddies can see them when they drive past . . . Pud."

"Oh, that's right," Ballpeen said with a dumfounded look, and they waded to the bridge.

When they slipped into a stretch of thick mud, Breed stopped and Ballpeen bumped into him. "Hey, I thought Pud left."

"You're the Pud for stopping in the dark." Ballpeen pushed on Breed's back. "Get out of the way."

"No, wait." Breed bent over and scooped up a handful of the thick mud."

"Now what?" Hog asked.

Breed smeared the thick mud over his face and hands. "If we put this mud on, it will be harder for anybody to see us."

"That's a good idea." Ballpeen smeared mud onto his face.

Screwball and Hog did the same, and they all tracked up onto the bridge and dripped along the road.

Down the road a stretch, and beyond the crickets that sang along an open field, a lone light on a tall wooden pole lighted a small lane that led to

440

a farmhouse.

Under the light, Hog looked to Breed. "Way to go, Pud brain. That was a great idea to put mud on our faces."

"Hant!" Screwball rubbed off some of the light colored mud from the side of his face.

Hog held out his hands toward Screwball and Ballpeen. "We stand out like a bunch of zombies."

Breed shrugged. "We don't have time to go back down to the river and wash it off."

"It don't matter." Screwball looked at his shadow on the ground. "We can wrap our shadows around ourselves and be invisible."

Hog wrinkled one eye toward Screwball. "If you can pick up your shadow, I'll wear it."

"I would," Screwball said, "but it would disappear when we got out of the light."

"Come on you guys," Breed said, "quit messin' around. We got to get those ducks before Flick and Blo get back."

"The mud's still a good idea," Ballpeen said. "This way even if they see us, they won't be able to recognize us."

Hog stood under the darkness of an apple tree that was next to the light pole and threw a rock. "We'll see if those ducks are there."

The rock hit the brown duck pen and let out a faint clunk. A few muffled quacks and some cackling sounds came from the old building.

Screwball gracefully bowed and gestured as if he were introducing an act about to come on stage. "There they are!"

Hog pointed up. "And —" He paused. "Up there on that pole we have a light."

441

Ballpeen stiffened. "What good's that?"

Hog smiled a big mocking smile. "That's so we can see what we're doing."

Breed grinned but shook his head. "If the cops cruise by they will, too."

Screwball threw a rock up about a foot and caught it again and again.

Nodding his head, Breed watched the rock. "Now what?"

As if he were the major stockholder of the world's time supply and wanted to drive the prices up by using as much as he could, Screwball flipped the rock over and over. Finally, he said, "If you kids are good I'll give you a treat!"

Like he was watching a happy drunk, Ballpeen stared at Screwball. "Come on, I ain't gonna wait all night for you to do something."

"Don't get excited." Screwball threw the rock higher and higher until it nicked the light. "That'll do it!"

The light smoked, ever so slightly, then more. It flashed a blue ark into the night and went out.

"Well, so much for that," Ballpeen said with his voice shaking. "Now let's get those ducks."

Breed knew by the sound of Ballpeen's voice that he was scared. "How about a plan?" he said as a last minute gesture to relieve his own nervousness.

"I'll stay here and watch for the cops," Ballpeen said and exhaled in a torrent of relief.

A stray mosquito buzzed in Hog's ear. He swatted at it. "What's the matter, Hammer-ass, you think the bogeyman is gardin' those ducks?"

"Hey, blow it out your ass!" Ballpeen snapped back. "I'll go in myself, and you guys can watch."

Screwball picked up another rock and held it in his hand. "Okay, we're watchin'."

Ballpeen took one step back. "No, I mean you guys can watch over there, closer to the fence."

Breed and the others walked down the purple ash lane and posted themselves at the chicken-wire fence. Ballpeen stepped toward the gate. Screwball threw the rock into the weeds beside the duck pen. Ballpeen jerked back and jumped — about two feet into the air.

Holding his hand and over his mouth, Screwball let out a muffled laugh.

Ballpeen's heart raced. He forced it back down his throat and whispered, "Hey, quit that!"

Screwball leaned forward and looked directly into Ballpeen's face. "Where's the ducks?"

"I'm getting' them. Just wait a minute." Ballpeen stepped toward the pen and touched the wooden turn-block on the door. The ducks quacked and a few chickens cackled.

Ballpeen froze.

The chickens stopped cackling.

More time passed.

Ballpeen didn't move.

"What are you waitin' on, Ballpeen?" Hog half whispered.

"They make too much noise. Let's forget it," he pleaded and gutted his whole show of courage.

Now Breed knew why Flick wanted him to go with them. "Just run in there and grab one, and we'll get the hell out of here."

"Yeah," Screwball said. "If you keep screwin' around, those people in the house will be out here with shotguns."

Ballpeen cringed and opened the gate.

"Quack!" A duck quacked and a rooster crowed.

Ballpeen put one foot in the pen and stopped, again.

"If we don't get them now," Breed said, agitated, "we ain't getin' them, and we don't eat."

Hog threw his hand down in disgust. "Ahh man! Screw this chicken shit!" He turned toward Breed. "Stay here and watch that guy don't stick a gun out the window." He jerked his head toward the pen. "Let's get 'em Screwball."

Breed jerked his eyes from side to side and watched the farmhouse and the area around it. As he searched for movement and a gun, Hog shoved Ballpeen out of the way.

Ballpeen ran down the lane, stopped, and watched from a safe distance.

Inside the pen, white ducks quacked, gray geese flapped, and red chickens clucked like shredded flat tires slapping on fresh black top. Hog ripped the lock from the door of the pen and went in. He grabbed anything that moved. Screwball was right behind him.

In the farmhouse, a dark silhouette moved across the yellow-lighted window.

"Somebody's coming!" Breed loudly whispered, and Hog stepped out of the coup with a duck in each hand.

"Here catch one," Hog whispered and threw a duck over the chicken wire. Breed ran, jumped on the clipped-wing, beating duck, grabbed it around the neck, and kept it quiet. He looked toward the duck pen. Screwball was still in there trying to catch one.

"Let's take them all," Breed said and raised his voice in anger. "That flat top asshole kid still owes me for my BB gun." He held the duck with one hand and started into the pen for another one.

Hog reached out and grabbed him by the arm. "Hey, get out! Somebody's coming with a gun!"

The light on the farmhouse porch threw a white stripe of light into the pen. Screwball bolted out the coup through a flurry of white feathers and flapping chickens, and raced down the purple lane.

Ballpeen ran down the lane after him and stopped.

Boom! The sound of a shotgun blasted into the night.

Breed realized he didn't make them take the ducks fast enough. Now they were going to get shot. He shouldn't have gone after another duck. He was a dumb ass.

He took off and ran faster. He didn't turn to look back. There was no time. Screwball, Hog, and Ballpeen were already out of sight. He ran past the lone light pole, leaped over the road, cut across the open field, and blazed a trail through the tall grass. The duck flapped at his knees. He looked ahead. Screwball stood at the edge of the bridge, and Ballpeen lay on his side holding his rear end. He ran to Ballpeen and stopped.

Ballpeen looked up. "They shot me."

"Ahh man," Breed moaned and bent over. Move your hand so I can see how bad it is."

Ballpeen's face contorted in agony. "Call an ambulance," he whined. "I don't want to die."

"Okay, okay," Breed said and handed the duck

445

to Screwball.

Ballpeen breathed in quick breaths and held his hand tight to his rear. "Run down" — huff — "to the farmhouse" — huff — "and call an ambulance."

Breed knelt down and placed his hand on Ballpeen's. "Just let me check it first. I might have to stop the bleeding. Move your hand. Ballpeen's knees trembled and Breed gently pulled back his hand. "There ain't nothin' here."

Hog looked down. "I don't see a damn thing."

"Hey, Ballpeen," Screwball said. "You sure a mosquito didn't bite you in the ass?"

"It burns," Ballpeen cried. "Call me an ambulance."

Hog bent over and pulled Ballpeen's pants down to see the wound. "You candy ass. It's just a little piece of rock salt, didn't even go in, just under the skin."

"Hey, Ballpeen," Screwball said. "You're an ambulance."

Ballpeen squinted and looked at Screwball. Then he put his hand on his forehead and moaned.

Breed picked the piece of rock salt out with his fingernail. "Okay, Ballpeen, quit being a crybaby. We gotta get out of here before that guy shoots you for real."

Ballpeen pulled his pants up and limped a few steps. The lights of a car flashed down the road. He quit limping and sprinted away.

Screwball and Hog clutched at their quacking dinner and hightailed toward the river. Breed and Ballpeen skidded down the riverbank behind them. At the bottom, they all lay down and panted under the bridge.

Chapter 34

Close to the dark water of the river, Breed, Screwball, Hog, and Ballpeen sat and listened for that guy with the shotgun. Above their heads, dim-yellow lights beamed into the night, but were interrupted by a black pickup truck with a broken muffler blatting across the cement bridge. Teenagers on their way to or from a party sat on the end of the tailgate of the truck. With their legs hanging down, they locked arms, weaved back and forth, and sang, "Ninety-nine bottles of beer on the shelf."

That song had the same lines, over and over. Breed hated it. He figured with enough repetition, even a dumb monkey could be taught to sing a song like that; and anyone who sang a no-where-same-song was dumber than a monkey. They were idiots.

He was glad the teenagers and their sweet, sickening bubble-gum-stinking breaths had traveled on down the road.

He turned his ear to the bridge and listened. The warm night air hushed to silence.

The duck Hog was holding quacked. He got up from the muddy riverbank he was sitting on and stepped into the river. He held his quacking duck under the water. It quit quacking.

A voice beamed down from high up on the bridge. "Hey, is that you guys?"

Breed stood up in the mud, ready to run. He breathed quiet and slow. He didn't answer. "Hey, is that you guys?" the voice asked again.

Breed squinted up at the dark figure on the bridge. "It's Flick."

Hog yelled upward. "Yeah!".

Flick and Blo ran off the bridge and squished down the muddy bank.

"Where were you guys?" Flick asked. "I thought those big kids got a hold of your asses."

Blo stared and moved his head back and forth. "What's that mud on your faces for?"

Ballpeen smiled. His white teeth flashed in the dark. "Night fighters."

The side of Flick's face curled with confusion. "Yeah, okay," he said dismissively and looked at the ducks. "Hey, way to go!"

Hog picked his duck up out of the water. "No sweat."

"Yeah, Ballpeen did it all!" Screwball said like an unemployed liar auditioning for work.

"Hey, blow it out your ass!" Ballpeen blasted back. "I was the one that got shot."

Hog gave Ballpeen a hostile look. "Shot, my ass!"

Screwball pointed at Ballpeen's butt. "No, shot *in* his ass."

Flick placed his hand on Ballpeen's shoulder. "Are you okay?"

Ballpeen lowered his head and put his hand where the rock salt had gone thought his pants. "I think so."

"One little piece of rock salt," Hog said airily, "hardly broke the skin."

"I picked it out," Breed said. "It wasn't nothin'."

Flick clutched at his Boy Scout ax. "We got the chain and that kid's still there. So let's chop these duck's heads off and get back upriver."

Breed jerked his thumb toward Screwball. "He wants to hang himself."

Flick turned toward Breed. "What?"

"Yeah," Screwball said, "I'll put more of this light mud on my face and hands and hang myself with a harness."

Blo studied Screwball's face. "You'll look like you're already dead."

Breed reached down and grabbed a handful of mud. "We can all look like we're dead."

"Not me." Flick leaned back. "When I stand in front of Purple and pull out trees by the roots, that rotten bastard's gonna remember who I am."

Breed giggled at the thought. About this time last year, Flick and he had dug out eight-foot high Maple trees, placed them back into the holes, and covered them with dirt and leaves. When two unsuspecting flats gang kids came walking past, Flick jumped up, grabbed both trees with his bare hands; and in what seemed to be an incredible show of strength, he pulled both trees out by the roots. Amazed and scared, both kids ran away.

Blo peered into the darkness. "If I didn't know how you did it, I'd be so scared I'd have to jump in the river to wash my pants out."

Flick whacked the duck's heads off with his ax. They flapped and bled into the shallow water next to the riverbank.

Breed, Hog, and Screwball caked more mud on their faces and bodies. Flick and Blo picked up the ducks and waded toward the orange boat. Like Mark Twain characters come back to life for a secret river mission, Breed and the others followed.

Upriver, while Hog made a cowboy-hanging

noose, Flick and Breed rigged up the harness to hang Screwball; and Blo found a flat rock to dig out the trees.

Flick retrieved the heavy chain out of the weeds, and they all took turns dragging it to the Ford.

When they got there, Screwball put his mud-covered finger to his mud-covered lips and whispered. "If Purple asks what I'm doing, tell him I'm just hangin' around."

Breed smiled. Pieces of dried mud flaked from his mouth. Loud music blared inside the Ford and filtered into the surrounding trees. Breed stepped close and looked inside.

Purple was in the back seat with the crooked-toothed girl, making time.

Hog stepped back from the Ford, held up his hands, and whispered, "Let's wait until he starts to do something."

"We could be here all night and he still might not do anything," Flick whispered. "I got a score to settle with that pimple-faced bastard." He gestured to two Maple trees. The trees set off to the side but were in the line of sight of the Ford. "Let's get those trees dug out."

While Flick used his ax and chopped the dirt from around the tree roots, and the loud radio mask their actions, the others took turns scoping out the dirt. In a few minutes they had the trees out by the roots. While Flick held the trees, one in each hand, the others covered the roots with dirt and topped it off with a layer of concealing leaves. The trees were ready.

Ballpeen whisked his hands together. "That

450

was hard work. I'm ready for roast duck."

"Don't talk so loud," Flick whispered. "He'll hear us."

Inside the Ford, Purple didn't look up.

"That radio's too loud, Breed said. "He can't hear anything."

Screwball cocked his head to one side. "I think he can hear that radio.

Breed shook his head in quizzical disbelief.

Like an Army sergeant, Flick stood tall and straight. "You guys keep an eye on Purple. I'll tie the chain around the axle."

Blo bent over and picked up the end of the chain. "I'll tie the other end around that rotten tree he's parked under."

"Okay," Breed said. "But leave as much slack as you can. I'll put some big rocks under his tire. When he takes off, he'll get a good jerk.

"He's already a jerk." Screwball hunched over; and moving his head, he pecked the air like a chicken.

On the ground, behind the Ford, Flick wiggled and stretched, but he couldn't get under the low rear end of the car. "Screw it! I'll hook it onto the bumper." he whispered under his breath. In frantic exasperation, he got up and walked to the tree. Blo wrapped the chain around the tree trunk, and Flick pulled the chain toward the Ford; but it was too short. He couldn't hook it onto the bumper. Blo and he crept back to the crew.

Hog asked, "Did you get it on?"

"No, it's too short."

"Are we going back to the island now?" Ballpeen asked and felt his empty stomach.

No way, Pud," Hog said referring to Pud's ignorance that seemed to have rubbed off on Ballpeen. "We're hanging around for the hanging."

Breed looked up at the dead tree. "Throw the rope over that branch. We can lower Screwball right in front of the car."

"Not too close," Screwball said. "I don't want that asshole runin' over me."

"He won't," Breed assured him. "We'll let you hang just high enough so that he'll go right under you. When Purple turns on his headlights they'll shine right on you."

Blo flicked his finger sideways. "If we get him mad enough to peal out, he might rip the bottom of his car out on those rocks under his wheel."

With the music blaring from the radio inside the car, Breed threw the rope over the branch. Screwball put the noose around his neck and tilted his head to one side. He looked like his neck had been broken. Hog and Ballpeen pulled him up. He swung out just above the front of the car and high enough to be out of view of Purple.

Breed wrapped the end of the rope around the trunk of a small tree and looked up at Screwball. "He looks dead."

"Now, let's get the asshole pissed off." Flick walked to the Ford.

Blo followed close behind.

Breed and Ballpeen stood back and watched. Purple lay in the back seat on top of the girl. Flick banged on the back side window with a heavy rock. The window cracked. Purple jerked his face away from the girl's mouth. Arching his back and bending his neck, he tried to look through the

452

cracked lines of the window. His eyes bulged white. Trying to see what was outside his cracked window, he wagged his head from side to side.

"Hey! Zit face!" Flick shouted through the semi steamed-up window. "We're takin' your boats. What are you going to do about it?"

The girl pulled her dress down and jerked away. Purple sat up, pushed the back of the seat over, reached over, and opened the door. The radio blared louder. The inside car light clicked on.

"I kicked your ass before," Purple said matter of factly.

Infuriated, he opened the door and bolted out from the back seat of the car. Standing with his legs apart and his fists clinched, he spat out the words, "I'll kick your ass again."

Flick ran to the trees.

Blo stepped close to Purple. "Don't let your elephant mouth overload your canary ass." He pointed to where Flick stood.

With his arms outstretched, Flick held both of trunks of the Maple trees.

"What?" Purple lifted his hands in a questioning gesture. "You think I'm scared?" With both fists clenched, he advanced toward Flick. "I'll just go over *there* and kick his ass."

Flick let out a mighty roar. It thundered loud enough to rattle the loose bark on the tree limb above. He ripped the trees from the ground. With dirt and leaves avalanching off the roots, he held the trees in the air, and stomped toward Purple.

As if in shock, Purple stopped.

Blazing with fury and screaming like a banshee, Flick ran toward him.

Paralyzed with fear, Purple just stood there. When Flick was three feet from him, Purple turned and ran toward the Ford. Blo stepped aside; and like a graceful toreador, he stuck out his foot. Purple stumbled and fell toward the ground, but broke his fall with his hands and jumped up.

Smiling her crooked-tooth smile; and as if she were going to enjoy watching her boyfriend beat somebody up, the girl stepped out of the Ford. She looked past Blo. Holding the trees over his head, Flick was in her line of sight. She turned and jumped into the front seat.

Purple jumped up. "No body trips me." He started toward Blo, but when he saw Flick shaking the tree roots above the mud-caked faces of Breed and Ballpeen, he instantly whirled around, jumped back into the car, slammed the door, and locked it. The loud sound of the radio deadened. The little yellow dome light stayed on. The girl reached up over the seat. Her bright-red fingernails flashed in the light. She lifted her pale-white fist and pounded her door lock down.

Breed and Ballpeen stepped to the passenger-side window and banged the palms of their mud-caked hands on the glass.

Ballpeen walked up to the window. "This will work better." Choo, gunk! He whapped the window with his hammer. The round end of the ballpeen hammer popped through the window and created a small round hole. The window cracked and formed spider web lines but didn't break.

Flick dropped the trees. He and Blo took hold of the sides of the car and rocked it. With her head jerking her head from right to left, the girl inside

454

looked out the cracked window. Her eyes grew wide with fright. The light inside the car made the outside look more dark, graveyard dark. Breed and Ballpeen stared into the window as if they were crazed zombies. Flick and Blo bounced the car as hard as they could.

Inside, Purple and the girl rocked and jerked like they were on a nightmarish carnival ride that wouldn't end. Purple reached over to turn the ignition key. The car bounced. His hand jerked away. He reached again, grabbed the key, and turned it. The radio quit. The engine started. Like sporadic thunder, the car's loud glass-packed mufflers racked off and cracked in the night. The girl screamed. The radio played again. The engine misfired and stuttered. Purple hooked the transmission into second gear.

Jerking on his arm, the girl wailed in his ear, "Take me home."

Purple clinched his jaw and jammed the gas pedal to the floor. Black smoke and orange fire flew out the tail pipes. He popped the clutch. The tires went against the stone in front of the wheel. He turned on the headlights. The engine stalled. The radio quit.

As if amazed that the kid was too ignorant to fix something as simple as the messed up the firing order on his own car, Hog yelled through the window, "Dumb shit!"

The radio started again.

The girl balled her hands into fists and pounded on Purple's shoulder, screaming, "Take me home. Take me home."

Purple turned away from her and looked out the

passenger's side window. He stretched his neck until his purple-pimpled face was right next to Breed's face, and yelled thought the glass, "I know who you are."

"Good!" Breed screamed and felt the blast of his voice in his own ears. But deep in his chest he felt like he had just punched Purple right in the mouth.

With the screaming girl pounding on his arm and the radio blaring, Purple jerked his head forward and looked out the windshield. Now in sight, Screwball was there, hanging, right above the car.

With her hand shaking and pointing to Screwball, the girl gasped. "They hung him!" She vigorously shook her head and screamed louder.

Breed lifted his stiff mud caked arm and pointed to Screwball. "You're next!"

The girl breathed in short bursts.

Screwball waved his death hand and motioned to them.

The girl covered her face with her hands. Purple started the engine. The radio quit and started again. The engine rattled and jerked. He shifted into reverse, raced the engine, and let out the clutch. Tires rolled against the stone behind the wheel, and smoke from the burning asbestos clutch rolled out from under the car.

The pink Ford hopped over the stone, lurched backward, immediately picked up speed, and the back of the car crashed into the dead tree. The tree shook. The branch cracked. Screwball dropped three feet, but stayed in the air, hanging.

With his feet flailing in midair, he tugged at the

456

rope around his neck, and yelled, "Get me off this thing!"

Purple shifted into low and revved the engine. The car rolled forward and leaped over the stone. The front of the car bounced one time, and the misfiring engine broke into a rough race. The white-walled tires spun with awesome power. Dirt, grass, and stones shot out the back, and dust blasted into the night air.

Breed ran over and unwrapped the rope from the trunk of the small tree. Hog and Blo lowered Screwball down — and fast. He landed on the roof of the Ford.

"Jump!" Breed cried.

Purple shifted into reverse and backed up — more. Screwball stumbled over the rope, slid down the windshield, and flopped on the hood of the car.

The engine stalled.

The radio quit.

With the rope still around his neck, Screwball rolled off the front fender and jumped clear. Flick ran over and pushed the rock under the back tire. Purple turned the starter, again. The radio quit. The engine started, died, backfired once, and started. The radio played. Purple pumped the gas pedal, and the engine raced like a stuttering wild animal. Black smoke sprayed out the exhaust. The wheel jumped over the rock, and the car shot backward like a stone out of a slingshot. The right half of the bumper caught the trunk of the dead tree and screeched like someone had stepped on a giant cat's tail. Then it bent away from the frame. The car backfired with loud bangs, jerked, and skidded sideways. Purple and his girlfriend slid across the seat and slammed against the locked door.

The engine moaned, shuttered and stalled.

The radio quit.

Crack! The branch above the car broke and tumbled down. It hit the ground and sent out a dull-bass thud that pushed through the night air and imbed deep into Breed's chest.

Then, like a delayed reaction of a Judo flip, the upper part of the Y limb rolled into the rear window, smashed it, and then crashed into the body of the car. Rough bark spun off the rolling limb, flew up into the dark, and the limb thudded onto the ground.

Breed looked at the Ford. The fallen limb had put a huge round dent into the metal trunk. Purple sat inside — motionless, lethargic. He stared out the cracked side window. His purple-pimpled face had turned white. It was as if he were in a trance.

Staring a frigid stare straight toward Purple, Flick stood next to the rolled-up cracked window. Exaggerating each word, he yelled, "I told you! I didn't shoot nothin' at your goddamn car!"

The crooked toothed girl beat Purple's chest with her frail fists and screamed, "You dumb stupid bastard! You dumb stupid bastard!"

And that radio started blaring.

Headlights flickered down the road.

"Those backfires sounded like gun shots, "Flick said in haste. "Maybe it's the cops. Let's get out of here!"

"Maybe, my ass!" Screwball threw the coiled rope over his shoulder. "It is the cops!"

The siren bawled. Emergency lights from the top of the cruiser crashed through the black treetops and split into long red lines. Breed and his friends scattered into the brush, ran down the riverbank, eased into the water, and dog-paddled to the boats.

Flick breathed deep and freed a boat. "Did you see Purple's face?"

Ballpeen freed another boat. Screwball stepped in. "Yeah, he looked like a man with his dick locked in a vice and someone just handed him a sharp knife and set the garage on fire."

"Blew out his brain because he had to think." Hog freed another boat.

Breed jumped in.

Flick stepped into the third boat and Blo hopped in.

While Hog shoved the boat into the current, Breed pulled on the oars. He wasn't too keen on the prospect of getting caught and going to a Traptown jail. He needed to get away. He rowed faster — leading the pack.

The others rowed behind and swung into the current. Breed, Screwball, and Ballpeen dipped their hands into the river, scooped up water, and rinsed the mud from their faces.

Once they caught the current, they all sat back and drifted down river.

About an hour later, the current carried them around the bend. The upriver concrete bridge was before them.

Up top, Purple and Flat Top milled around a police car. Their voices drifted across the top of the slow moving water.

Breed's boat drifted toward the bridge. He whispered, "Listen to those ass-kissers."

"Yeah," Screwball whispered, "now they want

to be the good guys."

Hulking over the bridge railing, Flat Top craned his neck and squinted into the darkness. "They should have come downriver by now."

"We know where they are, officer." Purple arrogantly leaned against the side of his Ford and reached into his pocket for a pack of cigarettes.

Wiping the glass on his spotlight with a rag and staring at Purple, the cop seemed to be annoyed. "Why don't you go and get them?"

"Not at night" Purple whined. "They hung a dead body right in front of us." He pointed to the hood of his car. "Look there's the mud where it fell."

The cop smiled at the Purple. "Are you sure you weren't drinking. We didn't find anything up there except a little bit of mud and a rope harness."

Taken aback, Purple replied, "There was a dead body. Maybe they put it in the boats and threw it in the river."

"I find that hard to believe."

Stepping toward the back of the Ford, Purple pointed at the dent and the broken back window. "See what they did?"

Flat Top turned and looked back over his shoulder. "And we don't know how many of them there are."

"We can wait until—" Purple said but stopped. He started again. "We can wait until you catch them."

"We know they'll come out this way," the cop said. "We saw their tracks on the other bridge."

Purple opened his mouth to talk, but the cop turned away from him and opened the door on the police car. He sat down on the edge of the front seat and let his legs hang over the rocker panel. He reached up and turned on the chrome spotlight that was mounted on the doorpost. Then, as if he were operating a complicated piece of equipment, he twisted his wrist and directed the strong beam downriver.

Watching for the light to hit the boats on both sides of his boat, Breed slowly twisted his head from side to side. Flick was hunched down. Hog had his head held high, watching. As if he were relaxing in a lawn chair, Screwball had his back against the back of the boat and his feet propped up on the seat. Curled into an almost fetal position, Ballpeen lay on the floor of the boat shaking. Blo held on to the sides of the boat like he was ready to jump in. They all looked like stone statues.

A cover of clouds covered the slim moon and blocked the starry sky, but the boats floated under the bridge and drifted toward the white light that was dancing back and forth across the water, searching.

They floated closer. Ballpeen lifted his arm to paddle to shore. Flick held up his hand and signaled for him to stop. He did.

Breed knew they could not make a single sound. He held his mouth shut. He didn't move.

Everything flashed in Breed's mind all at once. Mind pecking newspaper headlines: 'Thieves Caught On River'. 'Sent to Reform School'.

Breed figured the cop on the bridge was as crooked as One-Finger-Burke. He was the one that held the end of that legal rug that would trip them up. Being in the light, the cop probably didn't have

461

his night vision, but the second that bright light cut through the shield of darkness he'd jerk that rug right out from under them. They would tumble and land in jail.

When they were almost out from under the bridge, Breed watched the light, and felt his heart pound in his chest. Wait! he thought. Maybe that light will miss us. He tried to swallow, but his throat was dry. He continued his thought process. That darting light can't miss. Lard Man will be right. When the cop shines that strong light on the duck in my hand, he'll see it. He'll say, "That duck's stolen property." I'll go to jail. Before they see it, I could let it float away. They'll never go down river to get it, no evidence.

He eased the duck over the side of the boat and held it under the water. No use hanging my ass twice.

The bright spotlight was only a few feet from the tip of his boat. Breed held the duck tight, shifted his eyes toward Screwball, and then looked up at the bridge. They were about to drift out from under it and be bathed in light. He prayed the cop wouldn't shoot. Now Screwball's ignorance came to mind. He wished he could wrap himself in his shadow.

Chapter 35

A lone mosquito landed on Breed's arm. He wanted to slap it off, but any movement would reveal his position. He clinched his jaw, let the mosquito have its fill, and helplessly watched the actions on up on the bridge.

The cop took his hand off the spotlight and looked toward Purple. "Maybe they're upriver."

Purple pointed downriver. "I think I saw something. Try again."

Breed's boat drifted out from under of the darkness of the bridge. The cop placed his hand back on the handle of the spotlight. Its beam nicked the bow of Breed's boat. Breed loosened his grip on the duck. It slipped from his hand and floated on the water. He couldn't let it float. They would see it.

The light went out.

The cop grunted. "There ain't nothin there."

Breed slowly re-grabbed the duck.

The door on the cruiser slammed shut and the engine started. Its headlights lights flicked on and bathed half of the top of the dark bridge in fresh light. It would kill the cop's night vision for sure.

Breed watched the light from the headlights travel a few yards down the road and stop. Then, it traveled parallel to the trees alongside the road for a few seconds and beamed back over the bridge. The cruiser had turned around. It was back on the bridge. Now the spotlight searched upriver, but the new search would be in vain. The last boat drifted under the bridge and out of the light's range.

Breed exhaled with relief, and slipped the duck

463

back into the boat. The voices up on the bridge grew faint, and the crew floated to safety. The last thing Breed could make out was Purple wanting to know what he could do about his car.

For all I care," Hog whispered, "he can stuff it up his ass."

Breed tilted his head back and looked toward the sky. The clouds danced away, and the slim moon returned in a star-studded sky. "If there's such a thing as the phantom of fate," he whispered, "I think it just tapped us on the shoulder."

"Yeah, pretty lucky," Screwball said, "and we don't even have a rabbit's foot."

As they drifted farther away, the occasional dancing spotlight appeared on the bridge.

While they drifted toward the island, Screwball and Breed pulled feathers from the ducks.

"The island is right where we left it," Screwball said, trying to be flippant, but fatigue had dulled everyone's brains. No one laughed.

With mosquitoes buzzing around their heads, they pulled the boats onto the sandy point of Shell Island.

Waving the mosquitoes from his face, Flick pointed to the fire pit. "Get that fire going. It'll get rid of these mosquitoes."

They went to work.

Ballpeen tied up the boats, pulled out his hammer, and for no reason, he tapped the ends of the boats. Hog snapped off a green branch, took Flick's ax, and fashioned a wooden spit. Breed and Screwball finished cleaning the ducks. Flick and Blo piled the monkey shit — that they had gotten from the railroad car's journal boxes — under a pile

464

of sticks and lit it. Blue and yellow flames licked up and thick black smoked rolled into the air.

Nostril-flaring fumes from the fire spewed into Screwball's face. He waved his hand in front of his mouth. "That stuff really burns, but it stinks."

Flick waved a mosquito from his face. "And it'll keep the skeeters away."

Ballpeen shook his head. "It should keep everything away. It smells like shit."

Blo threw the car floor mat and the remaining monkey shit onto the fire. "Why do you think they call it monkey shit?"

Watching the floor mat burn, Screwball let out a low whistle. "I don't know, but what do they call a kid with no legs and no arms lying on the doorstep?"

Blo looked at him with guarded curiosity. "I don't know and I don't care."

The fire crawled up the mat and sent more stinking smoke into the air.

Screwball poked a stick at the burning car mat. "Matt."

Blo turned his back to the fire and shook his head. Screwball couldn't see it, but Breed watched a smile form on Blo's lips.

The monkey shit and the floor mat burned off. The wood caught and bloomed into a great yellow-white fire.

After Hog speared the wooden spit through the ducks and placed them next to the flowing flames, they all sat in the sand and watched the ducks. Fat juices dripped and sizzled in the embers. The ducks roasted slowly and the crew waited.

A few minutes later, Ballpeen rubbed his

stomach. "Are they done yet? I'm hungry."

"Well don't feel special," Screwball said and sucked in his stomach. "I'm so hungry my stomach's touching my backbone."

Breed remembered the saying, a watched pot never boils. "Don't watch them," he said. "They'll never get done." But he continued to watch.

Minutes passed.

Ballpeen reached for the spit. "Are they done yet?"

"No, Pud," Hog said, "they still ain't done."

"But they looked good enough to eat. "Ballpeen lifted the spit, and grabbed a duck. It burnt his fingers. He jerked his hand back.

"Hey, Ballpeen." Screwball stared at him.

Ballpeen waved his fingers in the air. "What?"

"Hant!"

"Hant your ass." Ballpeen wiped his hands on his pants, and carefully touched the duck again. It was cool. He pulled it off the spit. There, smart ass." He held the duck like it was a trophy. "Blow it out your ass."

Returning the other ducks to the flame, Hog looked at Ballpeen. "Test it first Ballpeen. See if it tastes like shit."

"Ballpeen's our official shit tester," Screwball said, referring to the sewer water Ballpeen had drunk.

Ballpeen was too hungry to reply. He ripped a sliver of meat from the breast and chomped down. He swallowed a mouthful, bit for another, but stopped. "Ahh man!" he whined. "It tastes like a sponge." He spit the second bite into the water.

Hog grabbed Ballpeen by the shoulder and

shook him. "Hey, Hammer-ass, don't throw that away. The goddamn thing ain't done yet. Put it back on the fire."

Ballpeen's face looked like a little kid's face who hadn't gotten anything for Christmas. "It should be done by now."

Flick took the duck from Ballpeen and jammed it back on the spit. "If it was done, it wouldn't taste like a sponge."

The flames danced around the ducks and turned the skin dry and dark brown. Hog watched them and complained. "That dick-nosed kid just had to throw the butter in the river."

Flick held the end of the spit and flipped the ducks over. "That would sure soften them up."

"They'll be okay," Breed said. "Ducks are greasy anyway." He looked at the freshly painted boats. "Too bad we can't find a way to keep those boats."

Blo looked at the boats and nodded. "After those two gangs fight for them, it'll be worth losing them."

"That is," Breed said and ticked a finger, "if we can pull it off."

Flick's eyes crinkled with amusement. "I think we got Purple pretty pissed off."

Hog turned the ducks. "We can't stay here long." He looked nervously around. "Those upriver kids will be down here just as soon as the sun comes up."

Screwball staggered in the sand. "If they get drunk enough" — he tilted an imaginary bottle of beer to his lips — "they might try to come downriver tonight."

Flick crouched next to the fire, held the handle of his Boy Scout ax, and pushed the end of a stick into the fire. "They might. But without their boats, we'll hear them coming." He stood up. "Test those ducks again."

Hog stuck a sharp stick into a duck leg and pulled it back out. "They ain't done yet."

"Instead of sitting around," Breed said, "let's get what's left of this camp tore down and loaded into the boats."

"Might as well." Flick walked toward the boats. "The ducks might be done by then."

They dismantled the campsite and loaded the boats.

Hog tested the ducks again and announced that they were done. Ballpeen was the first to step up. Hog handed him a wing. "Don't be spittin' this in the river. Someone might shoot you in the ass."

Ballpeen smiled faintly and bit into the wing. "Hey, this is okay."

The others stepped up, gulped down the hot meat like starving wolves, and got sick of it.

After Flick scanned the area to make sure they had loaded everything, he placed one foot on the bow of his boat and looked at the island one last time. "I guess it's good night, sweetheart."

Blo dipped a rusty coffee can into the river and walked toward the fire.

"Don't put it out," Breed said, "those upriver kids might still come after us. If they see the fire, they'll think we're still here."

"That fire ain't gonna go anywhere," Screwball said. "It can't burn the island down."

"Yeah, let it burn," Flick said and waved his

468

hand down. "It'll slow them down."

Ballpeen walked to the carp he had stuck in the mud with a stick. He pulled the stick out. As if had never been caught, the fish swam free. "Don't carp ever die?"

"Not hardly," Flick said. "But we might die if those upriver kids come downriver. Let's get out of here."

Screwball walked to the shore and looked into the water. "Does anybody want this railroad lantern?"

Excited with sudden expectation, Flick ran over to him and stopped. "Where is it?"

The lantern wasn't there.

Screwball turned toward Flick. "Hant!"

"Hant on your Fudge-Sickle ass," Flick growled. "If I don't get that lantern back, it'll be my ass."

"So that's where your lantern went," Screwball said. "Just like magic, it turned into your ass."

Breed looked away to hide his grin, and Flick stepped into a boat. "Let's go!"

They shoved the boats off the sandy white point, jumped in, and glided out into the current.

Now the campsite was abandoned.

Breed cast a long lingering look back at the island. Except for the halo of yellow light, created by the dying fire, it returned to its original state. As they slowly rowed away, Blo sat back in his boat and played perfect "Taps" on his trumpet.

Shell Island faded. The raccoons chattered and stared out of the dark. Their eyes flashed sporadically and then glowed yellow. They would reclaim their dining table. They would come closer to shore and dig for clams nuzzling in the sand. They would pry those clams open, lick the shells shinny clean, and new diamond-like winks would glitter on the neck of Shell Island.

Breed and the others caught the current, sat back in the boats, and drifted down the river. A lone muskrat swam toward the shore and disappeared into a hole in the riverbank.

Across from the steel mill, where the old steelworker had been, acid wasn't gushing from the pipe. Water flowed calm and lazy. Breed and the others sat up and manned the oars. A few strong healthy pulls brought them to the calm water above the rapids.

Breed glanced at the start of the rapids. A tree branch curved out over the water. He pulled on the oars and rowed toward shore. They would be carrying the boats around the rapids.

Flick pointed to the branch. "Look! There's my old man's railroad lantern."

Breed looked back at the branch. Almost by magic, Flick's fishing string had somehow gotten tangled around the branch. On the other end of the string, the lantern lay on its side with water rushing beneath it."

Screwball placed his hand on the side of the boat and leaned forward for a closer look. "It looks like it's water skiing."

"So what?" Ballpeen's body straightened to a rigid position. "That water's too fast. We can't get it."

"I don't think it's that fast." Breed said with feigned confidence. "There might be air in the empty bottom of the lantern making it float like

470

that."

Flick looked toward Breed. Hope shown in his eyes. "I don't need another ass kicking from my old man. Let's get out there and get that lantern."

Staring at the lantern, Ballpeen's gaze intensified. "Are you crazy? We'll get caught in the rapids and die."

"No we won't." Breed reached for the rope on the bottom of the boat. "We can tie the boats together and make a floating bridge like they do in the Army."

Ballpeen's face froze. "You're crazy!"

"Ahh man!" Flick scowled. "Don't be a candy ass." He pointed to the shore. "We'll tie the last boat to that tree over there. I'll get the lantern, and we'll pull ourselves back into the calm water."

"Sounds like it'll work," Breed said staring at the lantern. "But we'll still have to carry the boats around the rapids and they're heavy."

"We'll all carry each boat one at a time," Flick said. "That won't be so bad."

Ballpeen rowed his boat to the tree on the bank and tied it secure with a rope on the port side. The others connected the other boats end-to-end in a long line. Flick took the lead and rowed his boat, which was at the end of the string of boats, toward the branch, the lantern, and the raging water that roared like rocket exhaust.

Ballpeen yelled over the roar, "The water's too strong. Forget that lantern. Let's just carry the boats around."

Flick waved his hand down toward Ballpeen. "No way!" he yelled back. "I'm getin' that lantern."

471

Every few seconds, the connecting chains and ropes between the string of boats went slack and jerked taut. The boats bumped and rocked. Like the hand of a powerful devil, the river pulled and forced the boats into the strong water above the rapids. The heavy draw jerked the boats to a stop and pulled them out straight. The rope around the tree pulled tight. The mighty water flowed under the string of boats, and gracefully waved Flick's boat next to and then away from the lantern on that branch.

On a second wave, Flick reached out over the side and grabbed for the lantern. The boat swung back the other way. He missed.

When the boat swayed close to the branch again, Flick grabbed. He missed, again. The boat swayed into the branch. The lantern banged against the boat. Flick swooped his hand into the water and snagged the handle of the lantern, but the fishing string was tangled around the branch. He bent over the side and slipped it up over the end. His boat yanked back and threw him to the other side of the seat. But he held onto that lantern. Regaining his footing, he motioned for Ballpeen to pull the boats back.

Ballpeen grabbed the rope tied to the tree and pulled. The string of boats didn't move. He looked back toward Flick. Flick motioned for him to pull again. Ballpeen and Screwball grabbed the rope. They both tried to pull the boats.

"The current's too strong," Ballpeen whined. "We can't stay here for the rest of our life." He looked to Screwball.

Making a slashing motion, Screwball said, "Cut

the rope."

Ballpeen's eyelids flew wide open. "No!" he yelled in instant panic. "I'm not going over those rapids. Let me out."

"What are you afraid of?" Screwball asked. "You got shot and lived through it. A little fast water ain't gonna hurt you."

Ballpeen stood at the side of the boat and flexed his knees to jump to shore. Before he could jump, Screwball opened his pocketknife, reached down, and sliced the rope.

Twang! The rope jerked free.

"Too late, salt rock ass!"

"Blow it out your ass, you crazy bastard!" Ballpeen shot back, sat back in the boat, and hung on.

Blo looked back over his shoulder and yelled, "Hey, Ballpeen . . . Hant!"

Ballpeen yelled something back, but his voice was lost in the noise of the rushing water.

Like cars in a funeral headed for the graveyard, the boats floated toward the rapids. Breed and Hog untied the rope ends connected to their boat.

"Now we won't have to carry the boats around," Screwball said and the boats quickly spread apart.

Breed pulled on the oars to row to shore. But the mighty current had them. It was too late. The water roared like death. It pulled them down — faster, faster — into the dark unknown.

Breed quit rowing, placed the oars in the boat, and shouted, "Keep in the current." No one answered.

Flick and Blo shot over first. Hog and Breed

473

were sucked in after and bounced over a sunken log. In a blind panic, Ballpeen rowed faster and faster. His boat twisted around and rushed into the white water, sideways.

Breed's boat jerked and the hardwood seat pounded on his rear end like a jackhammer. He hoped he could hang on, but figured he'd be lucky if he lived through it. The boat tipped to one side. The sudden movement jerked his hands out from under the edge of the wooden lip of the seat. He reached back down and re-gripped.

The water roared. Screwball and Ballpeen spun past. They hit a small rushing drop off. One end of their boat jerked up like a seesaw. Screwball and his camping gear flew into the air. His rolled-up sleeping bag tipped into the water and spun in the swirling current. He crawled to the back of the boat and held on for the next whipping spin around.

Breed and Hog hit a drop off, bow first. They went over without a tilt. But a strong swirl switched them around, and Breed lost his sense of direction.

Screwball and Ballpeen followed behind. They missed every obstacle. As if they were riding a gigantic, dime store mechanical horse, they rocked and buffeted.

The bow of Breed's and Hog's boat rose up and splashed down. Water gushed over the sides. The bow lifted. The water stopped coming over the sides, and the boat took one last turn around in the thrashing water. When Breed looked up, they were all out of the rapids.

Screwball fished his wet sleeping bag out of the water and threw it into the boat. "The thrill ride's over." He pointed upriver toward the rapids. "Go to the back of the line."

Exhausted, Ballpeen leaned sideways and looked at Screwball in quizzical disbelief. "Go to the back of the line, and blow it out your ass."

Screwball gave the appropriate response, "Hant!"

As the current carried them downriver, they lay back, rested, floated past the stream where the red-horned chubs swam and the water snake lived. Diesel horns from the roofs of locomotives rolling along the Erie Railroad that ran alongside of the river, buzzed into the dark air. Breed took one long pull on the oars. The boat glided toward the right side of the river.

The Rat Street Bridge was before them.

When the boat drifted under the mighty brown steel structure, he looked up. An outline of the bridge silhouetted flat-black against the sky, and its dark shadow crawled over him like a dark phantom. He felt small and insignificant. He pulled on the oars and plowed toward the dock.

Screwball held up his hand. "Listen!"

Voices came from the dock.

Ballpeen gasp. "Maybe it's the cops waiting for us."

"Don't get excited, Hammer-ass," Hog said. "It's not them. The cops would have a light."

"Yeah," Screwball said, "don't you know they're afraid of the dark?"

They rowed the boats closer. On the riverbank, two dark figures moved.

As three cars passed overhead on the bridge above, light from their headlights fluttered through the steel grating and illuminated the two figures. A wide at the waist kid, with dirty-brown hair matted to his sweating forehead, reached up and wiped his sweating gray face. Through eyes set far apart on a hard face, the other kid ran his hand through his thinning hair, and directed his stare at the dock.

"It's the flats gang kids," Flick whispered. "But there's only two of them."

Breed noticed that the sweaty faced kid did not have a powerful upper body and his hands seemed frail. As if the kid had never had to lift anything heavier than the beer can, he held in his hand, he seemed to be a filthy, unprincipled pig, devoid of morals.

The hard-faced kid seemed to be a typical flats gang kid: Motivated by pathological brutality and what he could take from others, his stratum of society would never rise to any useful cultural or economic status. And he seemed to be intoxicated.

"We should be okay." Breed rowed toward the dock. "They're probably drunk on their ass."

Blo let his boat bump into the dock. "I'm too tired to care." He grabbed the chain, and tied it on a dock post.

The hard faced kid threw a beer can into the water, walked to the dock, and pointed at the boats. "Look what the little turd faces brought us."

Using the church key — a metal pointed can opener — the sweaty faced kid wore around his neck tied to a dirty string, Pop, spizz! He opened another can of beer. "Thanks you little cocksuckers!"

Hog lofted his nose in the air and talked in his British accent. "No problem, my good man. Just another attempt to add beauty and sophistication to

476

your domain."

As if he hadn't heard a word Hog had said, Sweaty Face just sat there.

Flick jumped up on the dock, and Ballpeen tied up the boat. "If you guys want these boats you're going to have to fight for them."

Sweaty Face sat in the sand with his elbows on his knees, gulped his freshly opened beer, and spit on the ground. "Fight? Who? You little pee-wees?"

"Fight?" Hard Face staggered toward Flick. "I'm ready. Come on, *man!*"

The rest of the crew hopped up on the dock.

Lifting his hands in defense, Hard Face backed away. "Hey, man, I ain't fightin' all you guys!" He staggered and fell on his ass, but was careful not to spill his beer.

Screwball looked at Breed and grinned.

Blo turned his back to Hard Face, unloaded his camping gear, and whispered, "Dumb ass."

Making no effort to hide it, Flick laughed at Hard Face's drunken stupor. Hard Face jumped up. His hard face drew tighter. He reached into his pocket and filched a knife. Then, as if he were dying of thirst, he gulped down the rest of his beer and threw the empty can. It bounced off the dock and splashed into the water.

The drink gave him strength. He stood tall. "Look here, you little cocksucker." He shook the shining blade. "You laugh at me again, I'll cut your little nuts off."

Flick cringed as if he were afraid. "I'm sorry. I didn't mean it. But those guys told us to do it."

Hard Face lowered the knife and took a

staggering step forward. "What are you talkin' about?"

Sweaty Face calmly sat in a drunken stupor and drank his beer. As if what Flick had just said had finally registered in his brain, he jumped up and clinched his frail fists. "Yeah, what guys?"

Flick lowered his head and answered like a candy ass begging for mercy. "The older guys in our gang told us that they were taking over this dock."

"So what's that got to do with these boats?" Hard Face wanted to know.

"How many people do I have to tell?" As if exhausted, Flick let out a long breath of air. "They said that they would be here at eight o'clock tomorrow night, and they'll beat anybody's ass that says these boats and this dock ain't theirs."

Blo tucked his trumpet under his arm. "They said you guys wouldn't bother us because you were chicken to fight them, and that you guys wouldn't even show up."

"We ain't afraid of nothin'," Sweaty Face shot back. "We'll be here at eight, but we're takin' those boats right now!"

Hard Face snapped the blade on his knife shut, opened it again, and waved it around in a threatening motion. "Get your sorry-ass-relief junk out of those boats, and get the hell out of here before I slice your asses up!"

Making sure he had his father's railroad lantern, Flick threw all his gear on one shoulder; and with his free hand, he cupped his fingers over his mouth and silently let big hawkers drop into them. Walking past Hard Face, he flicked the hand

478

full of hawkers onto the back of his shirt.

Breed braced for a fight, but Hard Face didn't feel the hawkers. Breed breathed a sigh of relief.

The crew held in their laughter; and like whipped bitches, they lumbered up the cinder path in single file.

Sweaty Face laughed an exaggerated laugh and jerked his thin finger at Breed. "If you guys want your asses kicked, just be here tomorrow night." Pop, spizz! He opened another beer, and the hawkers slid down Hard Face's back.

Chapter 36

Night aged toward dawn. Breed woke up and looked at the end of his gray-striped pillow. The Joe Louis boxing book had finally come in the mail. It was turned upside down and opened to the last page he had read. The book wasn't as thick as he had expected.

After coming home from Shell Island, he had been dog-tired; but before he went to sleep, he had started reading the boxing book anyway. He had read how to stand just like the Brown Bomber, and this stance would be effective for awesome punching power. He had lain on the bed, moved his right foot with a twist, threw his shoulder, and practiced the right cross. Now, he knew how to throw a power punch that had been used in a championship knock out. He had been amazed at how much knowledge came from the little book. And then it dawned in his tired mind. He could get A's in school without Flick and his friends calling him a teacher's suck ass, or an 'A' Student; and treating him like he was a candy ass. All he had to do was say he had lost his report card. He would keep the old one and get a new one from the teacher. Then, on report card day he would fill in the expected Fs, Ds and Cs and show that card to Flick and the gang. He smiled at his new plan and drifted off to sleep.

Now that he was awake, he wanted to know more about boxing. Maybe on the next page was a left hook. He picked up the book, and his stomach growled with hunger. When he read the next page, the exhaustion from the trip to Shell Island caught up with him. The words didn't register in his tired mind. His eyes drooped. The opened book fell and covered his sun-browned face. He continued to sleep into the day.

In his dreams, he heard a trumpet. Someone was playing "Reveille". Maybe it was Blo. He popped up like a cork released from the bottom of the river. The Joe Louis book fell off the bed and onto the worn linoleum floor. Blinking his eyes until they were clear and steady, he looked out the window. Blo was nowhere to be seen.

But, across the road almost hidden in the tall grass, Burkie sat on a little girl. Leering at her, he began unbuttoning his shirt, but he didn't have his knife. Breed glanced at the Joe Louis boxing book. Maybe he could use what he had learned and save that little girl from getting raped.

He jumped into his clothes and looked at his wet tennis shoes. The black electricians tape still held the dog-bitten toe together. He forced the wet shoes over his bare feet. Being in a hurry, he made it to the bottom of the stairs in three leaps. Outside, he sprinted across the road and into the tall weeds. Burkie and the girl lay next to a shoe box. Its lid was off. Inside, human ears, some mummified, almost filled the box. Burkie had the girl siccored between his legs. Her hands were tied behind her back, and Burkie had gagged her mouth with cloth from her torn dress. He held his knife over the side of her head. He was going to cut her ears off.

"Get off her!" Breed thundered.

Burkie jerked his head toward Breed. A look of puzzlement filled his pale face. "What the hell do you want?"

481

The exhaustion from the trip to Shell Island vanished. The emotions Breed had kept bottled up since Burkie had first threatened to cut his ears off, raged in his chest, gave him strength. Knife or no knife, he was no longer afraid of Burkie.

"I'm gonna beat your sick ass."

Burkie unsissored his legs.

The girl fell free.

With the knife still in his hands, Burkie jumped up, lifted his foot to stomp on the girl's head.

With strength from his anger-filled body, Breed pushed Burkie. Before he could stomp on the girl's head, he fell to the ground.

Half running, half crawling, and with her hands still tied behind her back, the girl rose to her feet and ran off into the tall grass.

Burkie jumped up. "You let her get away." He lifted his long sharp knife. "Now you'll pay."

Breed jerked to back away. His foot caught on a hidden stone. Falling to his back, his foot, with the tape on the tennis shoe, flew up and hit the knife. The knife flew from Brukie's hand. Burkie looked toward the knife. Breed sprang to his feet, blocked Burkie's path to the knife.

Burkie arrogantly lifted his chin. "I won't need a knife for a candy ass like you."

Breed assumed the correct boxing stance — left foot out, left arm out to jab, right arm cocked, ready for that one-two, followed by a powerful right cross. He was ready to beat Burkie's brains out. Without hesitation, he threw a left jab and followed up with a right cross. Stunned but still on his feet, Burkie staggered and went for the knife. Giving him no time to get the knife, Breed charged into him. With barrages to the head, stomach, and anywhere his fist could land, Breed pummeled him backwards. Raising his hands in protection rather than trying to fight back, Burkie tried to block the blows. Breed never realized how weak Burkie was. Just because he was older, it didn't mean he was stronger or smarter. As Burkie teetered, Breed let loose with a powerful right cross. It sent Brukie to the ground. He was out.

Breed looked at the knife. If he picked it up, Burkie wouldn't have a knife anymore, but Breed's fingerprints would be on it. If the little girl told her parents and real cops came, he would be blamed for raping little girls; and using the influence of his crooked cop father, Burkie would go free.

Breed stared at the grotesque box of human ears. He couldn't pick that up either. Hoping the little girl would return with real cops and find Burkie and the box of ears, he let Burkie and the ears lay in the weeds.

As he looked across the field of grass, he felt he had been dreaming. He walked back to his house, lay down, and watched for the cops to come.

But they never came. Burkie got up grabbed his knife, tucked the shoebox under his arm, and limped away.

Sitting on the end of the bed, Breed looked at his tennis shoe. Where he had wrapped the black electrician's tape was a slit. The tape had protected his toes from being sliced open with Burkie's knife. Sometimes being poor had advantages.

A while later, after Breed's heart had settled down, Blo stood in the middle of the street and blasted his trumpet. Flick and the others sat along

483

the road, waiting.

Breed yelled down at them. "What time is it?"

"Past five," Flick yelled back. "What did you do, Breed, sleep all day?"

Until he could figure out what to do about his fight with Burkie, Breed didn't want them to know about it. And he didn't want them to know how long he had slept. They might think he needed to sleep long hours like the weak kids in the neighborhood.

"Naw, I was just lyin' here waitin' for you guys," he lied.

Flick motioned with his arm. "Well, come on down."

Breed's stomach growled and he felt lightheaded. He went downstairs and looked in the kitchen for something he could eat — quick. No one else was home. The bread was gone. The greasy taste of duck coated his mouth. The crew waited outside. He wouldn't have time to cook anything. An empty bean can was tipped over in the sink. It had a few beans in it. He grabbed it, held it under the faucet, and turned the brass valve. The pipes groaned in the cellar, and water streamed into the can. Shutting the water off with one hand and with the other, he swished the beans and water around until it diluted into a weak cold soup.

Outside, Blo played the trumpet.

They were getting impatient.

Breed put the can to his lips and felt something at his feet. He looked down. The gray cat brushed against his leg. He gulped the soup down and left a mouthful in the can. The taste in his mouth changed from greasy duck to cold uncooked beans.

484

He dumped the mouthful of bean water into the cat's dish. The cat ran to it, sniffed the brown liquid, looked up at Breed like a disappointed beggar, and walked away. Breed wiped his mouth on his arm and went outside.

Stepping over the open sewer where his broken BB gun lay rusting, out of the corner of his eye, he glanced at it. If he got back alive, he would try to fix it. He turned toward Flick. "Why are we going so early? Those guys ain't supposed to be there till eight?"

Flick reached down and pulled up his drooping sock. He stood upright and re-pinned his ripped shirt with a safety pin. "We want to put up those 'Road Closed' signs. That way the cars won't go over the bridge and give them an excuse not to fight."

Hog looked at a rock that was setting on the side of the road. "And we gotta get hid before they send out their scouts and see us."

Breed held his thumb up as if he were hitchhiking. "What scouts?"

Flick let out a disgusted breath of air. "I just got done telling Ballpeen that they send out a couple of little guys to look around and watch for the other gang."

Breed opened his hand in a questioning gesture. "What for?"

Flick's voice gained a businesslike edge. "So both gangs can show up at the same time." He looked down the street. "They think it makes them look stupid when they wait around."

Screwball crossed his eyes and waved his head around. His haystack hair flared out and made him

485

look dimwitted. "They look stupid whether they wait or not."

Blo buzzed into the trumpet, "Duuummmbbb shittt!!"

"Blow that thing when the fight starts," Flick said. "It'll make them think it's our gang."

"Okkaayy!" Blo buzzed.

Staying in the center of the road, Breed and his friends trooped down the hill. Little Jummy was out of his jail yard. He stood at the very edge of the road with the toes of his shining shoes almost touching the pavement.

Breed smiled inwardly. He knew Jummy had worked up enough courage to sneak out of his yard, but he wasn't going to take a chance of getting caught on the road.

Breed and his friends walked passed Jummy. He waved.

Somewhere behind Breed's back, a powerful engine roared. Lard Man's guttural voice boomed over the roar of the engine. "I'll run over all you low life sons-a-bitches!"

Flick reached in his pocket. "I was waiting for this." He pulled out a handful of one-inch galvanized roofing nails, threw them on the road, and jumped over the ditch at the side of the road.

Breed and the others followed. Now they weren't targets for Lard Man. Breed watched the Buick. With a big ugly smile on his monkey-ass face, Lard Man zipped past. All four of his tires picked up the nails.

Flick grinned with satisfaction. "He wanted to run over something. He did."

Screwball clapped his hands once in approval.

486

"He got nailed."

Blo held his brass trumpet to his lips and blew. Blllaaannttt!!! Sounded into the blue summer air.

Lard Man slowed and watched them through his rear view mirror.

Hog flashed the proper gesture and yelled, "Hant!"

Lard Man drove out of sight. Breed and his friends sauntered to the middle of the road and continued toward the big fight.

Ballpeen turned his head from side to side and searched up and down the street. "Where did Lard Man go? If he calls the cops, they won't fight."

"Don't sweat it, Ballpeen," Screwball said. "That elephant ass went home to continue his diet. He only eats food you know."

Hog picked up a nice throwing sized rock. He threw it up in the air and caught it in his hand. "If that lard ass comes back and tries to hit us again" — he tossed the rock into the air and caught it — "this goes right through his windshield."

Breed noticed that Blo looked like a man who had just been discharged from the Army — unburdened and happy. He didn't know if it was the right time, but he couldn't wait to ask. "Did you do anything about One-Finger-Burke?"

Blo smiled extra big and re-gripped the brown paper bag in his hand. "Nothin' much, just made a phone call."

"Those Traptown cops won't do nothin'," Hog said and edged off the center of the road.

"I know that," Blo said. "That's why I called the State boys."

An empty beer bottle sat on the side of the road.

"That just might work," Hog said and kicked the brown bottle into the sewer. "Those State cops don't take no crap."

Breed pointed to the bag Blo was carrying. "What's in the bag Blo?" he asked and looked back to see if little Jummy was still in his yard waving.

Blo lifted the bag. "Just a possum,"

Breed turned his head to look at the rounded sack. Before he could look, off to his left, dull black flashed in his eye. "Watch out!"

It was the black panel truck that had run over Screwball's bike. Its tires rolled onto the side of the road. Gravel flew out of the deep tread. The truck spun out of the loose gravel. The backside swung around and slammed into Jummy. Jummy flew into his jail yard and landed on his back. He didn't cry. He didn't move.

The truck came right at Hog. Hog held the rock he had been throwing up and down. He drew back and let it fly. It rocketed straight into the dirty windshield. The glass cracked into a white-lined spider web that blocked the driver's view. The truck veered off the road, slid in the gravel, hopped up on two wheels, glided into the air, came down, and slanted sideways in the sewage ditch. The back tires spun and stinking smoke rolled into a dirty-blue circle. Digging up black, sewage-saturated mud, the tires on the truck plowed to a stop.

Breed looked at Jummy.

He wasn't moving.

Breed wondered why anyone would kill a helpless little kid, but anyone who would molest a little girl wouldn't hesitate to kill a little kid. It had to be Burkie and Henry. Maybe they had molested

488

Jummy, too. Maybe they killed him to keep him from talking. Breed's mind jumped into a rage of revenge. He clinched his fist. If he had to, he was going to throw a million right crosses. He was going to knock out Henry and Burkie.

Letting out pent up furry, he stated, "They ain't getin' out of this."

The driver's side door of the panel truck flew open. With his heart racing in anticipatation, Breed took the proper boxer's stance. Waiting for Burkie and Henry to get out, his body tensed to stone-like state. He was ready for action.

But it wasn't Burkie or Henry.

From inside the darkness of the dirty-windowed truck, a sallow-faced lady dressed in a chicken-manure-spattered black dress rumbled out.

It was Vanko.

With her babushka falling from her head, she hurried to the back of the panel truck, opened the door, and grabbed her pitchfork.

"Greek! Dirty Greek!" she shrieked and raised the pitchfork in Jummy's direction.

Breed was afraid of her pitchfork. But he felt he had to protect little Jummy. That Joe Louis boxing book was his ace in the hole. He didn't want to hit an old lady, but if he had to, he could knock her out with a right cross.

He ran up behind her. "Oh no you don't," he yelled at the back of her head, reached up, and yanked the fork out of her hand.

She lifted her fist and turned toward Breed.

Flick stepped in front of her. "Stay right there!"

Defenseless, and gasping for breath, she turned

toward Flick. For a moment, as if confused, she stood. Then she adjusted the babushka so that it covered her gray hair.

While Breed and his friends kept a wary eye on Vanko, Jummy's mother raced out the front door. She ran to Jummy, bent over, and held him in her arms. She looked at Breed and the others. "It's all your fault. You filthy kids always walk past and coax him out onto the road."

Like a herd of high-and-mighty noses looking for something to smell, the neighbors came out.

"They did it again," someone said.

"They'll never learn," another one said; and as if they were convicted criminals, the gathered crowd threw words at Breed and his friends.

"They should all be in jail."

"There ought to be a law."

"Jummy didn't have a chance."

"Probably intentionally threw him in front of that truck."

"They'll pay now. The cops are here."

One-Finger-Burke, pulled up to the scene. He stepped out of his grime-covered police car. With an air of cocky superiority, he waltzed toward Vanko. "I'll take care of her."

Vanko's feet stuttered on the hard pavement and she ran straight at him. Her arthritic fists pounded through the air. One-Finger-Burke reached for her bony fists. He missed. She grabbed him by the throat. A restricted strangling noise came from deep in his chest. Her other dirty finger-nailed-hand clawed at his face. Blood oozed.

Another police car pulled up and stopped. The perfect lettering on the side doors and its clean, solid surface seemed to demand respect.

"Careful," Flick warned. "State boys."

Breed peered into the State Patrol car. Wearing, clean freshly-pressed uniforms, two State Troopers sat inside, checking their sidearms. Breed's mouth dropped open and his eyebrows shot up. "What's going on?"

Vanko gripped One-Finger-Burke's throat — harder. "Greek! Dirty Greek!" she screamed and clawed, more. "You kill my husband and take my son, little Burkie, for your girlfriend, you Dirty Greek, Dirty Greek!"

As the Troopers bolted from the patrol car, their spit-shined boots flashed in the sun.

While one State Trooper grabbed Vanko around the neck and tore her from One-Finger-Burke, the other Trooper wrapped his arms around Burk's arms and chest and held him secure.

One-Finger-Burke struggled to get at Vanko, but he was no match against the superior trained Pennsylvania State Trooper. Giving up, One-Finger-Burke placed his hand with the missing finger over his bloody face and shouted at Vanko through his fingers "I should've killed you, too."

Vanko stood back and jerked her finger at One-Finger-Burke with such force and hate that her babushka fell to the side of her head. "Dats-ah, him. Dats-ah, him."

As if he were innocent, Hank, the other Traptown cop, wrinkled his forehead and looked to One-Finger-Burke. "Why, you rotten bastard."

With panic in his eyes, Burke turned toward Hank. "No, Hank, you got it all wrong,"

In one swift motion, the State Trooper swung

One-Finger-Burke's arms around his back and clicked the handcuffs onto his wrists. "At first we thought it was a prank call from some young kid. Dogs got sniffin' around and we dug him up this morning. We found a finger in his mouth."

The ladies, who had gathered around, collectively gasped and stared at One-Finger-Burke's hand with the missing finger.

One lady spoke up, "Did he do it?"

"We obtained a search warrant." The other Trooper professionally replied. "When we went to Officer Burke's home, his son, Burkie, ran inside the shed in the back yard and locked the door. After we broke it open, we found girls' clothing, a very sharp knife" — he made a face — "and a box full of human ears."

The women placed their hands on their mouths and gasp, again.

The lady spoke again. "He's the one that raped all those little girls."

"Oh my God!" another lady cried. "He cut their ears off, too."

Hank stepped back as if he were innocent, but he kept his face averted. "I wasn't involved in any of this."

Standing extra erect and with total authority, the other State Trooper gave Hank a cold stare. "You may have led us down the wrong path before, but we got it right this time. We have orders to take you both in."

Blo blew a soft note on his trumpet and talked low. "Does it all make sense now?"

Recognition dawned in Flick's face. "Little Burkie's Vanko's kid. No wonder she's crazy."

492

Hog made a sour face. "One-Finger-Burke made a faggot out of Burkie." He shook his head as if he were trying to get a bad taste out of his mouth. "He ain't even his son."

"Yeah," Breed added. "Not only did he train his son to be a faggot, he showed him how to rape little girls."

As if what had just happened entered his mind, a look of panic flashed in Ballpeen's face. "That crooked cop killed her husband."

Blo shrugged and looked to Ballpeen. "We already know that, Pud."

Holding back a grin, Breed nodded. "That's true, but it takes longer for things to sink in Ballpeen's thick hammer head."

"Hey, Ballpeen," Screwball said. Why don't you get in the gang fight? You could block punches with your thick head. You'd never get hurt."

Ballpeen didn't respond. Instead, he acted as if he had a ghost crawling on his skin, He trembled. "Vanko's husband was buried in her back yard all this time."

Nodding his head, Breed said, "When we stood by the telephone pole, One-Finger-Burke would always stop and give us a hard time. She didn't want him near. That's why she always chased us away."

The ambulance pulled up.

While the stretcher was rolled out, the driver stepped to the one of the State Troopers, and pointed to One-Finger-Burke. "We needed him. What happened?"

Peering from under the brim of his Smokey-

493

the-Bear hat, the State Trooper gave the driver a stern look. "Officer Burke is under arrest."

A look of astonishment filled the driver's healthy face. "I'll be danged. We wondered where he was. We just got back from the gas station. Henry, the owner's son hung himself." The driver looked confused. "But his ears were cut off."

The State trooper gestured toward Jummy. "You better do what you came here to do."

Jolting to action, the driver turned and hurried toward Jummy. When he gently placed little Jummy's lifeless body on the stretcher, it was as if the stretcher had miracle curative powers. Jummy opened his eyes and sat up.

The driver looked to Jummy's mother. "I think he'll be okay. Looks like it just grazed him."

Tears of concern filled her eyes. "Are you sure?"

"I think so, but we'll take him to the hospital to be sure."

With puppy dog eyes, Jummy turned his head toward the ambulance driver. "Can I sit up front?"

The driver felt Jummy's arms and legs for breaks. He looked to Jummy's mother. "There's nothing broken."

Jummy pointed to the front of the ambulance. "Can I sit up there and run the siren?"

The driver looked at Jummy's mother for approval.

She nodded.

"Sure." The drive smiled. "Sit up there with your mother."

As the driver carried Jummy toward the front of the ambulance, the other ambulance attendant rolled the stretcher into the back. Jummy looked back, raised his hand, and waved to Breed and the others.

They all smiled and waved. Jummy's mother shot them an angry look. The attendant crawled into the back and slammed the door. The driver set Jummy on the front seat, and his mother sat beside him. The driver ran around the front of the ambulance, jumped behind the wheel, and closed the door.

Breed turned to Flick. "At least he'll be out of his jail yard for a while."

With its siren bawling and lights flashing, the extra excitement of the ambulance went away.

Screwball looked alongside the road. A weather-beaten wooden ruler lay in the gravel. He picked it up and held it in his hand.

Another State Patrol car pulled up. Old lady Vanko was put in the back seat. One-Finger-Burke and his Traptown buddy were shoved into the other State Patrol car.

As if he were going to go home, Breed turned his head and looked up the hill.

Ballpeen stepped toward home, stopped, and looked to Flick. "We still goin' to the fight?"

Screwball tapped Ballpeen on the shoulder with the ruler. "You ain't going to let a little excitement scare you away, are you?"

Flick pulled on Ballpeen's shirtsleeve. "Don't be a candy ass."

Ballpeen turned away from Flick's hand. "I ain't no candy ass."

Breed looked down the hill toward the river. The State Patrol car cruised past his right shoulder. He looked at One-Finger-Burke and shouted through the glass. Who's screwy in the head, now?"

Burke ignored Breed, but looked out at Screwball. Screwball cocked his head sideways, and waved the end of the ruler around in a circle next to the side of his ear in a crazy sign. One-Finger-Burke tried to raise his fist in anger, but the handcuffs stopped him.

The State Patrol car picked up speed and the bubble gum machine light on top blinked away.

Breed and his friends turned and continued toward the big fight.

With a hint of nervousness in his voice, Flick said, "There's still a good chance both gangs might find out we tricked them."

Hog dropped his hands to his sides in a helpless gesture. "If they do" — he smiled —"they'll both beat the hell out of us, might even kill us."

"So what," Screwball said. "At least we'll be out of Traptown."

Now that Jummy was okay, like a dog trying to jerk a rag from a master's hand, the thought of what had just happened tugged at Breed's mind. He felt uneasy. This new way of fighting didn't feel right. Compared to what he had done to Burkie, this upcoming gang fight was going to required very little physical effort on his part; and it was strange. In the end, One-Finger-Burke had gotten his. A wrong had been righted with a simple phone call. Breed didn't have a bloody mouth or bruises trying to right it, and he didn't have to kick a knife with his taped foot. This new way of fighting was new and uncertain, and the fight they were going to was even more uncertain. If both gangs found out they had been tricked, there would be hell to pay. This fight could mean death.

Breed longed for the old comfort of the familiar past when he knew what would happen. Thinking about how easy it had been to knock Burkie out, he convinced himself that he could fight and not get hurt. He might even be the hero of the fight. He could use the secret boxing knowledge he had learned from that Joe Louis book.

"I don't really care," he blurted out.

Screwball looked at him with a puzzled look on his face. "What are you talking about, Breed?"

Breed punched his open hand with his fist. "The fight, the fight."

"We're going," Hog said. "Don't get excited and start beating yourself up before we get there."

"I'm not excited," Breed said. "If I have to fight, I'll fight."

Screwball pulled back his chin stuck out his stomach. "Breed, you fight those dummies when you don't have to" — he lifted the ruler and pointed at him — "you'll keep turning into Same Man."

Breed talked with his hands. "It ain't that. I'm just sick of it. A little kid can't even stand by the road without someone blaming it on us. I'll get my ass beat, or I'll beat someone's ass. It's always the same in this Traptown, over and over."

Screwball staggered on the road like drunken Toney. "Hey! . . . Back that way again. . . . Hey!"

As if he had just remembered that they had agreed not to go insame, Flick flashed Breed a discouraged wounded look

"Yeah, back that way again," Breed said and Hog looked into the air.

They walked around the corner. The gas station-grocery store was in sight. A 'CLOSED' sign hung over the glass of the door where Henry had said it was all Burkie's fault.

As they kept walking, Breed's confidence waned and pre-fight fear crept into his stomach. It was like butterflies, flying, flapping, flipping, fluttering, flailing, around his insides; and they intensified with each step. He wanted to stop, turn around, and just go home. But no one else stopped or hesitated. He had just said he was going to fight. He couldn't be a crybaby now. He wasn't no candy ass.

Breed's friends pushed forward. Breed followed, close-mouthed, past the gas pumps, past the coal pile, through the dense brush, over twigs, around broken glass, down the narrow path, and into the secluded weeds where they could watch the bridge and the imminent blood bath. Here in their secretive vantage point, they wouldn't be seen. Here they would be safe.

A scout waited on the near side of the bridge. A ways from the scout, a Ford coupe painted with dull-red primer paint had pulled off to the side of the road.

Flick made a helpless gesture. "They didn't see us, but we ain't gonna get those signs up."

Breed was still tired from the Shell Island trip. "They're too heavy anyway." He stood in the weeds with the others and their un-played trump. They didn't know what time it was.

They waited.

The scout turned, walked off the bridge, and hopped into the primered Ford.

The door bambed shut.

Thundering exhaust pipes racked off in the distance.

"They're on the way." Breed crouched down into the weeds.

Hopped-up cars roared toward the bridge. Skidding in the gravel at the side of the road, they created clouds of dust.

The '56 pink Ford with the caved-in trunk, broken back window, bent out bumper, and crossed sparkplug wires, lagged behind. Purple and the upriver gang were on their way.

Chapter 37

Just beyond the Rat Street Bridge, Breed and his friends crouched in the cover of the tall weeds.

Skeek! Echoed above a stutter of drunken laughter. It was the tires of that pink '56 Ford. It sputtered to the side of the road, wheezed once, backfired, and stopped behind the primered Ford.

Carloads of the upriver gang pulled around the Fords and skidded to a stop. Car doors sprang open and jerked back against doorpost hinges.

Fight seekers, with heads like hen's butts, stepped out, gathered into a group, punched each other in the arms, and acted like it didn't hurt. They smiled crooked smiles, and slicked back their butt hair-dos until they gleamed greasy.

On their feet, with each step, spit-shined shoes transmitted tiny glows of blue-black light. On the backs of their necks, turned up collars called attention to their unzipped James Dean jackets; and they had their thumbs hooked into side pockets. Heavy metal rings on their fingers that could cut deep into soft flesh, threatened danger.

From the concealment of the tall weeds, Hog threw a rock. It sailed in front of the catwalk and plopped into the river water below.

The upriver gang turned toward the sound. Their fiendish faces flashed anger, and long white cigarettes dangled from their mean arrogant lips. While they stood around and waited, they looked like they had pilfered tough-guy personalities from Brando movies, but didn't know how to use them.

Breed looked toward the far side of the bridge. Right on cue, up out of the flats, looking like some giant had threw up on them, ate them, and threw them up again, came the flats gang.

Many wore scuffed, black-leather jackets, with the backs crudely painted — broadcasting, advertising — like walking billboards — like bad commercials shouting out at the world —begging to be switched off and cut out of the continuous movie of life.

Other gang members transmitted "Hey look at me!" images from broken minds with a need to self-project ego inducing nondescript badges of unearned phony courage thought up in the basement of a beer can, and carried upstairs with all the glamour of a dud firecracker — "Sorry man, no bang!"

They were like all the wanna-be tough guys. They had the hidden fears, fears that they would not be in, that they wouldn't be accepted, that they wouldn't be wanted, that they wouldn't be needed, that they would not be admired for what they think they wanted to be, and for what they believed they were, but were not.

More flats gang members walked to the edge of the bridge and joined the show. Their bodies, decorated with little shiny chains, stars, and chrome buttons, all flashed in the sun.

Behind them, more gang members came: T-shirted, swinging heavy rusty chains. One big fat guy carried a broken ball bat; and dime-store-shirted guys held their black-handled switchblades, ready to spring open at the last moment.

Both gangs moved onto the bridge as a unit. In anticipation, faces and neck muscles drew tight. Fear showed throughout.

The two gangs spread out and started toward each other. They claimed the entire bridge structure, used the steel grating as an arena, and ignored any cars that might want to pass. None did.

Thick with hostile tension, the air on the bridge begged to be released.

Like disciplined soldiers, both gangs machined toward each other, seven abreast, followed by lesser pawns that clicked their metal cleats — hard — on the large-holed steel grating of the bridge.

For a better look, Breed and his friends stood up and peered over the tall grass. Blo held the paper-bagged-possum in his hand and whispered, "I'll bet they'll just talk and walk away."

Flick adjusted the pilot hat on his head. "I doubt it. The flats gang has twenty-seven and the other guys only got eighteen."

Hog picked up a rock and held it. "That's the way they like it."

Screwball held the ruler and smacked the palm of his hand.

Breed felt the tension and anticipated a bloody battle. "I wonder if we should have set them up."

"Don't feel sorry for them now, Breed," Flick said. "We can't be friends with people who want to kick our ass and take everything we have."

Breed slowly moved his head up and down and watched. "You're right. But this seems too easy."

"No it ain't." Hog waved his hand in disagreement. "Don't be stupid. Just remember how easy it is the next time one of those guys beats your ass. And anyway, they'll stop and chicken out when they reach each other."

Screwball lifted the ruler and pointed toward

the bridge. "No they ain't."

***

The two leaders rear back and swing.

Whap! The flats gang lands the first punch. The jacketed upriver leader jabs back. "You mother—" Smack! He is cut short with a clean shot to the jaw.

Blo lifts his trumpet to his lips and blasts a cavalry charge toward the fight.

Purple and Flat Top run to the front of the pink Ford. Then, they turn back, jump in, and close the doors.

"Those chicken bastards," Blo says, and with the bagged possum in his hand, he runs to the Ford, stops, and looks into the closed window. Screwball runs and stops next to him.

Inside the Ford, Purple rolls down the window, holds his hand on the doorpost, and looks out.

"Get the hell away from us," Flat Top says.

Screwball lifts up the ruler and smacks the back of Purple's hand. "Behave!"

Purple jerks his hand away and looks up. A confused dumbfounded look covers his face.

Screwball yells, "Hant!"

Flat Top yells at Screwball. "I'm comin' out there and kick your little ass."

Blo lifts the possum-filled bag and grabs it by the bottom. As if he were shoveling coal, he swings his arms back. "Here!" he says. "Kick this, you yellow bastards." He slings the dirty-gray sleeping possum out of the bag. In midair, it jars awake. Its scared, blood-shot eyes open wide. With its front legs spread, its rabid mouth hisses open. Its dull-pink tongue flaps out of white foam around its

503

bared, yellow teeth; and its dirty claws spread open looking for a place to land.

Wide-eyed, Purple jerks away from the flying possum and cries, "It's a big rat!"

Flat Top kicks the door open and jumps out. Purple is right behind him. They run back toward the bridge. The possum scrambles to the top of the front seat, stops for a moment, jumps onto the back seat, and curls into a gray ball. Blo reaches into the Ford, gently lifts the possum by the scruff of the neck, and puts it back in the paper bag.

Purple and Flat Top stand on the side of the bridge, outside the fight.

A member of upriver gang yells toward them. "We're outnumbered. Where the hell were you?"

A flats gang guy, with an ape-like stride that matches his build, starts for them. They flex to run. To their right, a rusted chain clanks over a kid's head. Blood flows. The kid staggers and tries to seek support against the air. Purple dodges the next swing of the chain and jumps into the fight, and Flat Top is pulled in after.

A Traptown police cruiser pulls up and stops a hundred yards from the bridge. Breed points in its direction. "Look!"

"It's all over now," Ballpeen says.

Flick turns his head and looks toward the cruiser. "They ain't gettin' out."

"I don't believe it," Hog says. "They're just gonna watch."

Flick jerks his head downward in disbelief. "They're gonna let them fight it out."

A kid, lean as a picket, runs down the cinder path and hides next to the bridge foundation.

"Hey," Blo says. "That's the creep that hit me with that beer bottle." He runs to the top of the foundation, stops on top of the black square rock, and looks down. The lean kid is watching the fight through the steel grating in the bridge. Blo unzips his fly and urinates.

Like yellow sparkling water, the hot urine sprinkles down on the kid's head. The kid turns, looks up, and yells through his pee-soaked face. "Hey! You filthy pig! I'll cut that dick right off your stinkin' body!"

Blo grabs the bottom of the bag with the possum inside. "Here, cut this!" He flings the possum down at him. The kid jerks away, but he trips and lands on his hands. The possum lands on his back. The kid rises to all fours and tries to shake the claws of the possum out of his back. A water snake rises up out of a crack in the stone and wiggles its tongue in his face. The kid shakes the urine from his eyes and the possum jumps off. The kid jerks away from the snake, jumps up, runs into the itch weed, and then zips right past Breed and his friends.

"Don't go," Blo yells. "You don't have to leave just cause you're pissy-faced."

The pee-faced kid doesn't see the Road Closed sign lying in front of him. He runs, full speed, onto the ice-like metal. His feet fly out from under him. Bang! He lands, butt first, on the tin.

Breed's friend's heads snap sideways toward the sound. The kid struggles to his feet, holds his busted butt, and trots away.

On the bridge, inherent barbarism erupts. Hair, teeth, and skin fly. Almost at will, the nimble

505

cotton-jacketed flats gang leader jumps in and out of the fight, bashing faces with his steel rings.

A fat guy tries to get a hold of him but can't. His slow moving swings only torment the air. The unruffled flats gang leader, circles, reverses, and dances in and out. He lands a few solid jabs in the fat guy's face. The fat guy gives up, looks through his swollen eye, and tries to catch someone else and douse their living flame of life.

Fierce fighting continues until only a few upriver members are standing. It looks like it's all over.

But like an emergency parachute on a falling man, more car loads of upriver gang members churn down the road, slam on the brakes, screech off the pavement, and stop in the gravel.

The late ace-up-the-sleeve has arrived.

Blo puts the trumpet to his lips and blasts another Calvary charge. All heads turn toward the sound. Breed's friends duck down but Breed stands tall.

"I'm goin' in," he states and runs to the bridge.

"Get back here," Flick says, "those big bastards will kill your little ass."

Blo buzzes in his trumpet. "Saammee-Maaannn."

Two more cars pull onto the scene. Breed runs past the shiny hood of a Hudson Hornet. Now just as he had done against Burkie, he has a chance to use that secret boxing knowledge.

Behind him loads of big heavy-muscled upriver gang-members leap out of cars. They hold thick brown beer bottles in their vice-like hands.

All fighting stops.

The flats gang fighters study the new arrivals. The expressions on their faces change. They look like they are trapped in the commode and the big pimpled ass has just sat down.

But the panting brutes of the flats gang refuse to scatter. Breed runs right for them, alone. He stops in front of the sweaty-faced kid that had been under the bridge.

Sweaty Face laughs. "What do you think you're going to do?"

Breed assumes the correct boxing stance. He turns his foot to deliver a powerful right cross. His toe slips through the cut tape in his tennis shoe, throws him off balance. He stumbles against the bridge support but manages to stay upright.

"Box this!" Sweaty Face flashes a blade and swishes it at him.

Never bring a knife to a gunfight, flashes in Breed's mind. He realizes that he has ignorantly brought fists to a knife fight. He drops his bare fists, flinches back, and catches a glimpse of a big upriver brute that is right behind him. A hand, as big as a bear's paw, starts to break a beer bottle on the steel bridge grating. But the hand stops.

"Won't even need this!" the voice of the hand says, and the hand throws the bottle off the bridge.

Sweaty Face slashes toward Breed. The knife misses. The big upriver brute, with the bear paw hands, reaches in front of Breed. As if Sweaty Face were a flopping rag on the end of a stick, the big upriver brute jerks him flying into the air. Cla lump! He lands bone-breaking and hard on the steel catwalk. The blade falls through the steel grating and plops into the river water below.

Breed turns. That big brute is right in front of him. Again, Breed assumes the correct boxing stance — left foot out, left arm out to jab, right arm cocked, ready for that one-two, followed by a powerful right cross. To counter an uppercut, he lowers his chin and peeks up at his opponent through the haze of his lowered eyebrows.

But the big brute doesn't move. He just looks at Breed and smiles.

Breed lifts his head. He had been so focussed on getting into the fight that the shiny hooded Hudson had not registered in his mind. But he recognizes that big arm. "Neal?"

Neal reaches down with one hand, grabs Breed by the ass of his pants and says, "People who start wars don't fight them." He lifts Breed into the air. "Don't let them lower you to their intellectual level. Get your little ass the hell out of here!"

Breed's pants jam up his butt, and his belt slips up around his chest. His arms and legs flail like he is trying to fly. Neal runs with him and carries him off the bridge.

"I owe you one," he says and flings Breed into the air.

Like a possum out of a bag, Breed flies, spread eagle, mouth open, and eyes wide. He lands in the gentle weeds, stands up, and turns around. Digging his pants out of his butt, he nods a look of thanks toward Neal.

Neal waltzes back into the fight. He turns for a second to check on Breed, and another knife user swishes his blade and cuts into Neal's Easter ham arm. This awakens Neal's fury. He turns and deftly lifts the knife-wielding kid up by the arm and cracks

508

it against the catwalk railing. The sound of his bone breaking and the instant never-felt-before pain overwhelms the inexperienced knife user. He wilts to one knee, bends over, and throws up through the steel grating.

The flats gang leader's nimbleness wanes. He rests for a second and then charges a newcomer. He is tossed back and forth, and rewarded with a generous poke in the stomach. A punch that seems to have come from out of the universe follows. Then, sounds of tearing tissue from a well-placed stone fist, splat in the air. The leader's head jerks back, and he is forced to harvest another punch in the stomach. He oozes back against the steel bridge support.

A gangling big nosed, heavy-jawed flats guy, with an idiotic grin, swings a chrome chain, and creeps into the pile of fight. The upriver leader sees him but it's too late. The chain smacks him in the ribs. Air is immediately forced from his lungs. In agony, he stumbles forward, grabs for something to hold on to; but there is nothing to catch. He falls to the grating and coughs up fresh blood. Neal looks down at his fallen friend, turns, and as if it were made of rubber, he walks right into the swinging chain. With one powerful arm, he holds the chain swinger; and with his other arm, he wraps the chain around the chain swinger's body. Then he lifts the wrapped chain swinger above his shaggy buffalo head and throws him into the multitude of hectic swarming combatants.

A few spurts of whipped up courage continue, but the physical power is quickly expended. The turmoil dies down. Most of the flats gang members run or just stop fighting. A defeated kid holds his bloody mouth and looks in the gravel for a lost tooth. Another kid hangs on an open car door and tries to get his equilibrium back.

As a parting gesture, to indicate that they had not been beaten, a hardheaded flats gang guy, with a body like an enormous egg, shouts through his red face, "It's just an intermission. So you guys can get ready."

"Take care of my light work," Neal says to the upriver leader next to him, "Humpty Dumpty needs to fall off another wall."

The upriver leader dances in and punches Humpty Dumpty in the stomach. His eyes bulge. He grabs his fat stomach and belches beer foam. Neal steps to the belching round man, reaches down, grabs his T-shirt and pulls it up over his head. Humpty Dumpty can't see. He windmills his chubby arms around in the air and wobbles away.

Neal turns and walks to his shiny-hooded Hudson, opens the door, and points to Breed. "See you on the road. You owe me one." He smiles, slides behind the wheel, and drives away — in first gear.

All fighting has stopped. Like badgers, the defiant upriver gang stands across the bridge. The leader slicks back his hair and smiles wryly. Looking around, he returns his comb to his back pocket and defiantly asks, "Anybody else?"

Another kid steps up and lights up the total range over which his thought process extends — a cigarette — and, talking through his clenched teeth, he blows a long stream of smoke. "Yeah, anybody else need their ass kicked around this bridge?"

The deranged dick-nosed kid stands, legs apart, and combs his hair. He forms a turd curl in the middle or his forehead. Then snorts through his long nose and fiercely states, "Of course we'll just naturally kick the hell out of whoever comes near us."

But he seems out of place. The threatening statement comes out like a joke. He projects the zany image of a jester who substituted a dick nose and a turd hair-do for a pointed cap and bells. A buffoon on leave from the king's court come here to make people laugh, but got caught up in the situation and couldn't remember the words.

No one on the bridge laughs. They are accustomed to this old joke.

For the first time in his life Breed knows the kid and all his temporary glory has been deceived by the system. That kid is standing on the bridge waiting for some kind of award. He went "in-same" and doesn't even know it, and he doesn't have enough brains to realize that his great gang victory has just won him nothing.

The flats gang hobbles, runs, and crawls away. The upriver victors advance in groups of four, walk down the cinder path, get their boats, carry them to the roofs of their cars, and tie them on. They triumphantly tilt bottles of beer to their mouths and jump in their cars. With beer bottles flying out the car's windows, engines rev, clutches pop, and the tires let out stupid skeeks; and the "winners of nothing" race down the road.

A lone cop cruiser pulls onto the bridge and stops. The trouble they didn't want to stop is over.

They drive away.

511

In awe, Breed and his friends stood in the weeds.

Flick smiled a humble smile. "I don't believe we did it."

Breed unbuckled his belt and adjusted his pants from around his chest. "You know we don't have to fight anymore."

"You ain't gonna fight anyway." Screwball lifted the ruler and pointed to Breed's butt. "If you do, Neal will just jam your pants up your ass and throw you out again."

"You're probably right," Breed said, "but what do we do now?"

Flick grinned with satisfaction. "Whatever we want."

With an air of superiority, Blo tilted his head back. "You know this is power."

"This is something like the union leaders do," Breed said with realization, "they never fight."

"That's right," Flick said and locked eyes with Breed, "they just arrange things and then they just sit back and watch."

"Yep, that's just what we did today," Hog said with victorious merriment. Then, a faint glimmer of mischief shone on his face. "And" — he lifted on finger and pointed to Breed. "Except for Breed trying to fly, we didn't get a scratch."

Breed squirmed uncomfortably, but recovered. "It's about time we started using our brains." He rubbed his sore butt.

Screwball held the ruler in one hand, and with his other hand, he wiggled his fingers as if they had strings and were attached to the ruler. As he jerked the ruler he said, "Those guys were just like puppets."

Breed smiled at Screwball's imitation of a ruler puppet. "We might even get them to be nice."

"If we work it right," Flick said with a triumphant smile, "they won't even know we're pulling their strings."

Screwball turned his back to Flick. As if he were cranking some kind of machine, he rolled the ruler in a circle. "Don't pay any attention to the man behind the curtain."

Breed and his friends, lay down on the grass, kicked back, and basked in a mental stupor.

Flick turned on his side and leaned on his elbow. Through the weeds and down the narrow path, a small figure lurked behind him. A stone was fired from a small overhand pitching arm. It found its mark and landed with a dull thud in the center of Flick's back.

Hog jumped up. "Hey!" he yelled and pointed into the weeds. "That little cocksucker's throwing rocks at us!"

Another rock zinged past Flick's head.

In pain, Flick rose to his knees. He screamed, "Get that little bastard!" He reached around, rubbed his back where the stone had hit, swallowed hard, and jumped up with his feet running. He was after the fleeing rock thrower.

The kid ran right down the path where Screwball and Breed had dug those miniature pit holes for Burkie and Henry to fall into. In spite of the time that had passed, the grass concealed them. The fleeing kid managed to miss every hole.

Flick raced behind. He tripped into the first

hole, tried to catch his balance, then immediately stepped into the second hole. He stumbled. "Gott-damm-fault-it-tea-mammer!" he stuttered and landed on top of the rock throwing kid. The kid crumpled to the ground. Flick grabbed him by the throat, sat on his chest, clinched his fist, and drew back. He was ready to do some serious damage.

"Punch his stinkin' teeth out!" Hog advised matter of factly.

"Yeah, bust his goddamn snot-gobblin' nose!" Screwball chimed in.

Flick relaxed his fist. He gently let go of the bulging-eyed, scared kid's throat. "Iss muss be your lucky day, kid. If I let you up are you going to get out of here before I change my mind and mess you up?"

The kid nodded.

"What'a ya lettin' him go for?" Ballpeen wanted to know.

Still sitting on the kid, Flick looked embarrassed at his sudden change. "I'm not going in-same any more!" He glanced in Breed's direction.

Breed unconsciously nodded his head and understood.

"He's not going to do nothin' to that kid!" Ballpeen whispered to Breed.

"Yeah, I know," Breed said with an I-know-that tone of voice. "But if you could remember from one day to the next, you'd remember we said we weren't going to do the same stupid things anymore."

"Why should I beat his ass?" Flick asked. "Just because I got mine beat? If I do, this dead end habit

514

of doing everything over and over will never end." He got off the kid's chest and stood up.

The kid jumped up and ran down the path.

"I don't know about you guys." Flick brushed the dirt from the front of his shirt. "But I'd like to get out of this trap town someday."

"Yeah but," Ballpeen said with disappointment in his voice. "You still could-a hit him just one time."

Screwball held out the ruler. "Here, Ballpeen, go catch him again, you can smack his hand with this ruler."

Ballpeen, shook his head, lowered his shoulders, and walked toward the bridge.

Breed and the others followed. Breed caught up to Ballpeen. Walking shoulder to shoulder with him, as if he wanted to make an important point, Breed held up his finger. "Ballpeen, I just don't think you get it."

Hog formed a blank look on his face and tilted his head toward Ballpeen. "Just call him, Pud."

Ballpeen clutched at the hammer in his belt and turned his head toward Hog. "Just blow it out your ass, Hog!"

Hog bowed to Ballpeen in mock appreciation at the remark and said, "Why thank you, sir!"

Breed laughed and continued. "If you want to get it, Ballpeen, all you have to do is look at Lard Man."

"How can you miss?" Screwball took a deep breath and puffed out his stomach. "He's fat as a quart of beer."

"That's right." Breed moved his hands while he talked. "He looks like a fat beer bottle because

515

he lives with one. When you do the same things over and over long enough, you turn into the thing you're doing, even if you hate it."

Hog nodded in agreement. "Like that kid with the dick nose. He's been a dick head for so long, he's turning into a dick."

"Yeah," Screwball added. "Pretty soon he'll be nothin' but a big prick."

Flick stepped onto the blood-spattered catwalk of the bridge and stopped. "We don't have to be in their fights the way they want us to." He put his elbows on the railing. "If we do, we'll be just like them. We'll be assholes."

Breed turned his back to the railing and leaned back. He thought about what Neal had told him. "You don't have to do the same thing everybody else does. There's always a way to get what you need. Sometimes people don't even know they're helping you to get it." He sighed with satisfaction. Now he knew what Neal had been trying to tell him.

He turned the palms of his scraped hands up. "We actually fought them today, but it was our way, and they still don't know what we did."

"That's right." Flick waved his hand in the air. "And anyway, why would you want to follow behind somebody and do the same things all the time."

"Yeah." Screwball cocked his head. "They're probably fartin' anyway."

"That's right," Hog said with a determined air, "who wants to be a fly back branch catcher?"

Sinking down as if dumbfounded, Ballpeen scratched his head. "You mean that because we did the same thing over and over is the reason we got

516

our ass beat all the time?"

"No," Screwball said and smiled. "You got your ass beat cause you're a second rate fart catcher." He bent over and flashed a big ear-to-ear smile right in Ballpeen's face.

Ballpeen took the hammer out of his belt and shook it at Screwball. "Hey, blow it out your ass." He whacked the steel hand railing on the catwalk.

As if his feelings had been hurt, for a moment, Screwball turned away. He turned back. "Hant! See, you still do the same thing, every time."

Heat thunder talked across the sky. Breed looked up and thought about how nice it would be to ride his motorbike. Although he would still have to dodge an occasional flying beer bottle, he wouldn't have to hide his motorbike from crooked cops, and he wouldn't have to be afraid of Burkie cutting his ears off.

Breed and his friends shuffled off the now tranquil bridge.

Blo walked on the gravel next to the road and looked down. An empty red and white Lucky Strike cigarette pack lay right next to his foot. He tromped on the red circle, "Lucky Strike!" He punched Breed in the arm.

"Hey!" Breed yelled. "Cut that out!" He rubbed his arm. "There's some in there."

Flick picked up the pack of flat cigarettes and passed them around. Breed and his friends lit up and blew smoke into a new lilac evening. They walked off into the neighborhood and listened to Ballpeen's plans to build a cabin in the big woods.

Breed and his friends would sleep well. The dogs would sleep all through the night. That

517

mongrel dog would crawl under the shingle-bitten roof of his doghouse, smile, and dream about biting the ass right out of Breed's pants. Lard Man's garbage cans would be upright in the morning, but Breed and his friends would be awake again, tomorrow.

Epilogue

It was a new day and a new way to live. A new way to think jumped up and took control. Ignorance in the name of tradition fell in line and no longer led Breed and his friends down a worn out path. They learned that they didn't have to kick some lesser kid's ass just because they got theirs kicked when they were that age.

The bullies grew older. Some went into the service and a few went to jail. Most of them took jobs in one of the cancer causing mills. Others continued their dishonest ways and cheated their way through college. The same pecking order started again.

Cars changed. Hairstyles changed. Dialect and fads changed, but underneath all the hype and newness of it all, it was still all the same.

The big rich kids could not escape from Traptown. The degenerate rebellious gangs could not escape from Traptown. And it didn't matter how far away they traveled or moved away they would never escape. They all had gone "In Same." They followed tradition, ate from the foul end of the stick, jiggled on its controlling end, and never knew any different. Being ignorant of the trickery and fraud that controlled them, they let their minds hobble through life and run on an unnecessary broken crutch; and they believed they were happy. What else could they do? They stayed on the end of that stick. More fat, curtain-ass executives were created, and that bully on Shell Island still had a nose that looked like a dick.

After that day of change, Breed recruited

younger kids to join him and his friends and live a new way. Of course there was still an occasional constructive ass kicking. It was hard to break tradition.

And in the midst of it all, a few miss-fitted shakers of the neat orderly society dodged those pitchforks of stupidity, ran through the beckoning alleyways of ignorance, jumped over the controlling sewers of life, swam under that mind-blinding shit shield, and somehow emerged out the other side. They did not only see, they pulled unannounced visits and shouted, "HANT!" right into the surprised face of the bewildered man behind the curtain.

A few, just a few, did not become a part of the school of trained minnows. A few threw off the restraining shackles created from nothing and changed the world for the better. A few closed the bridge to ignorance. They did not "go in same." A few held that stick, sailed up the powerful river of life, and escaped from Traptown.

Hant!

Breed

Somewhere out there, a lone goose flies. All its friends have gone south. It is out there without the security of the flying Vee. It is separate from the flock. Is it lost or what? The cold north winds are already blowing. The lone goose no longer fits in with the accepted order of things. Like the kids from Traptown, it must be crazy.

THE END